Where thou art,
That is home.
EMILY DICKINSON

A Liverpool Secret

GERALDINE O'NEILL

ORION

First published in Great Britain in 2018 by Orion Books
This paperback edition published in 2019 by Orion Books,
an imprint of The Orion Publishing Group Ltd
Carmelite House, 50 Victoria Embankment,
London EC4Y 0DZ

An Hachette UK company

1 3 5 7 9 10 8 6 4 2

A CIP catalogue record for this book is
available from the British Library.

ISBN 978 1 4091 6673 3

Typeset at The Spartan Press Ltd,
Lymington, Hants

Printed and bound by CPI Group (UK) Ltd,
Croydon, CRO 4YY

www.orionbooks.co.uk

A LIVERPOOL SECRET

is dedicated to our precious boy,
Edward Michael Feely

Chapter One

The black-clad, middle-aged nun looked around the classroom of girls, her eyes narrowed. She pointed to a tall, serious-looking girl with long dark hair.

'Lillian Taylor,' she said. Then her eyes scoured the room and she pointed to the smallest, thinnest girl in the room. 'Molly Power. Both of you stay behind and wipe the boards, sweep the floor and leave everything tidy.'

She pursed her lips in a tight line. 'Sister Agnes is in here first thing in the morning, and I don't want to give her any cause for complaint.'

The two girls looked at her. 'Yes, Sister Dominic,' they said simultaneously.

Sister Dominic gestured with an upward motion of her hands, and everyone stood up. She made an elaborate sign of the cross with her right hand, the girls following suit. She started off the closing prayer, 'Angel of God', and they all chimed in, '*my Guardian dear, to whom God's love commits me here. Ever this day, be at my side to light and guard, to rule and guide. Amen.*'

She led the class in blessing themselves again, then stood silently, her gaze roving around the room. All eyes were cast downwards.

'It will be a hard day's work for any guardian angel who has to rule and guide you lot.' Her lip curled. 'The apple does

1

not fall far from the tree, and there are few amongst you who knew mothers, far less your fathers. God forbid that we might have the odd legitimate one. And it's left to the poor nuns here in Gethsemane House to try to make decent human beings of you all.'

Suddenly, a girl in the middle of the classroom gave a half-muffled sneeze, then covered her nose and mouth with her hands. 'I'm sorry, Sister... I couldn't help...'

Sister Dominic snatched a long ruler from her desk, then delved quickly between the desks to land several blows on the girl's shoulder and back. 'You dirty amadán! Get out – out!'

The girl, crying now, staggered to her feet and half ran towards the door.

'Get out and wash those germ-ridden hands!' the nun shrieked. 'Isn't it enough to endure being stuck in here with a class of guttersnipes, without being surrounded by all your dirty, filthy germs?'

The others kept their heads bowed, knowing what would happen if she caught a hint of sympathy in anyone's eyes. She pointed the ruler towards the door. 'Out!' she hissed, 'and not a word between you or you will feel the wrong end of this ruler on the back of your heads.'

Row by row they made their way in single file out of the classroom and into the Victorian, wood-panelled corridor. The two girls remained behind as instructed. Sister Dominic turned when she got to the door.

'Now Miss Taylor and Miss Power, make sure this place is spotless. If I hear a single complaint from Sister Agnes, you will know all about it. When you're finished, get upstairs to the dormitory and get changed into your clothes for working in the laundry.' She went out, banging the door behind her.

They stood in silence until the nun's footsteps grew fainter as she walked down the corridor, then the small girl turned towards the other and said, 'Old bitch!'

'Shhhh...' Lillian Taylor said. 'We'll be murdered if she hears you.' Unlike most of the other girls, Lillian was well spoken and had a quiet dignity about her.

'It's the truth, she's a cruel bitch,' Molly said in a wheezy voice. 'Her and Sister Agnes are the worst.'

'I don't want to get into trouble,' Lillian whispered. She moved towards the teacher's desk. 'I'll clean the board,' she said, 'I can reach the top of it easier. You better get started before someone comes in or we'll both be in trouble.'

'Stop worrying, there's nobody around.' Molly grinned at her. 'They don't care about us as much now. They get more pleasure frightening the younger girls.' She lifted a brush and started sweeping up.

They worked away in silence, then, after Lillian had wiped the teacher's desk, she stopped to examine a map of the world on the wall behind. She pressed her right forefinger onto Liverpool, then traced her way across the Irish Sea and over the Atlantic Ocean. She went halfway across Canada, then stopped.

'That,' she whispered to Molly who had come to sweep by the desk, 'is where Alice and her brother were taken to last year. A place called Ontario. I was supposed to go too, but only a few days before, the nuns told the priest who organises things that I had a bad cough, and he wouldn't take me in case I spread it.'

Molly moved closer to examine the map. 'They never even put me on the list because of me bad chest,' she said. 'They don't take anybody that's not in the whole of their health because they wouldn't be fit for the journey.'

She was used to Lillian talking about Canada and the other girls who had gone. Molly was rake-thin and tiny, more like a girl of ten or eleven than a fifteen-year-old. The only redeeming feature in her pinched face was her big, blue eyes. She had been one of identical triplets, born to an unmarried mother. One triplet had died at birth and the other little girl wasn't right, physically or mentally, and had been in a home for disabled children since she was a baby. Molly also had a fourteen-year-old brother, Daniel, who was in the boys' orphanage, and who she was allowed to see for a short while on Saturday afternoons.

Daniel Power, a quiet, brooding sort of boy, also stood out from the other children. Unlike Molly, it wasn't his size that made him different – he was above average height for his age – it was his dark skin.

Lillian knew that Molly had something wrong with her. Some nights, when she had been coughing for ages, the small girl would be taken out of the dormitory and brought down to sick bay by one of the nuns. Lillian had also heard one of the elderly nuns telling Maggie, the local woman who worked in the laundry, that Molly was 'neither use nor ornament', and that women like her mother were a scourge for bringing sickly children into the world.

'It might not have been because of your health they didn't take you to Canada,' Lillian said now, trying to be kind. 'It might be because they can't send you abroad when your mother is still alive...'

'Me ma might as well be dead, for all the good she is. She's never been any use to me or Daniel. When me granny was alive, she was in and out of the mental hospital or gone off with some fella. I haven't a clue where she went after me granny died, but she's never bothered to come back and get me or our kid.'

Lillian looked back at the map. 'Imagine if we'd gone to Canada. Maybe some rich family would have fostered us.'

'Norra chance,' Molly said. 'Maggie down in the laundry said that the nuns were only sending boys and girls to work out there to make money for the church. When they were old enough some of them were sent to work for farmers out in the country, miles from anywhere. That's as bad as being here, if not worse.' Maggie, who supervised the girls with washing and ironing, was kinder to the girls than the nuns were, but she could be moody.

'I was a bit frightened of the boat journey over, but sometimes I think it might have been worth it to get away from here...'

'What if yer had been put in the same place as Delia Sweeney?'

Lillian felt her chest tighten at the mention of the bully, a hefty girl with long, curly blonde hair. 'Sister Ignatius had said we would be kept apart. They were sending her to somewhere

4

called Quebec, and I was to go to Ontario with Alice.' There was a silence as Lillian thought of her best friend, whom she guessed she would never see again. 'It doesn't matter now,' she sighed.

'Well, I'm glad yer didn't go. I don't know how I would stick this place if it wasn't for yer. I'd rather be dead.'

'Ah, don't say that...' Lillian turned to put her arms around her sparrow-like friend. 'You don't need to worry, I'm not going anywhere. You're my best friend now, and we'll look out for each other until we get out of this place.'

The small girl nestled into her as a young child would to its mother, seeking reassurance and comfort. 'It's not as bad here now Delia's gone... is it?'

'No, it's not,' Lillian smiled at her friend, then pulled away. 'We need to be careful. If any of them thought we were friends, they'd separate us. Even Sister Ignatius. Me and Alice were moved into different dormitories a few years ago when they thought we were friends.'

'That was Delia Sweeney's fault. She was always telling tales.'

'We won't give them anything to say,' Lillian told her. When she first saw Molly, she had thought her a crabby, wizened little thing. Although they were in the same class, she had little to do with her, as she and Alice were always together. But she had never been unkind to Molly or mocked her because of her size or made any reference to Daniel's dark skin, like some of the other girls or the nastier nuns did.

Then an incident occurred that showed Molly in a different light. One morning Lillian had climbed the dark wooden staircase to clean the toilets in the corridor where the girls' sleeping quarters were. As she passed the dormitory, she glimpsed a white-faced Molly sitting on the edge of the bed.

'What are you doing here?' Lillian asked in a heated whisper. 'Sister Agnes is on her rounds, and she'll be up soon to check the dormitories and toilets. You'll be in trouble if she catches you up here.'

Molly had looked at Lillian with anguished eyes. 'I don't know what to do...' Her head drooped. 'I've wet me bed, and

Sister Agnes said if I did it again, she would wrap the sheet around me and make me walk around the yard so everybody can see it. She did it to me before.'

'Oh God...' Lillian said.

'I don't do it often,' Molly said, 'it's only when I have a pain in me kidneys, and me back's been sore for days. She won't believe me, she never does...'

Lillian's eyes narrowed. 'Pull the sheet off and give it to me. I'll hide it with all the dirty towels and take it down to the laundry, and hopefully they won't notice.'

Molly pulled back the thin, frayed old blankets and then stripped the patched sheet from the bed and deftly folded it into a square. 'Just make the bed up to look as though it's fine, then get downstairs quick before you're seen.'

Both girls suddenly froze as they heard Sister Agnes's voice screeching in the corridor below.

'Quick!' Lillian whispered, lifting her cleaning stuff. 'Tidy the bed and get down the stairs.' Holding the wet sheet she went rushing out into the corridor and along to the toilets.

A minute later Molly came to hover by the toilet door.

'What are you waiting for?' Lillian hissed.

'I wanted...' Molly hesitated. 'I just wanted... to say ta for helping me. Ta for being nice to me.'

Lillian stared at her in surprise, then her face softened in pity. Something told her that Molly had led a darker and more painful life than most of the other girls in Gethsemane House. Everyone in the orphanage had a sorry tale, but she instinctively felt that Molly's story was worse than anyone could imagine.

'We all need to help each other when we can.'

'The others don't care, and they'll always get yer into trouble to save themselves. But I don't forget them that have done me down, and the few that have been good.'

Later, Lillian was glad she hadn't done Molly down. When Delia Sweeney had tried to pick on her – ridiculing her for being small and calling Molly's mother a prostitute – Lillian discovered that Molly's size didn't hold her back but belied her strength and determination. When Delia had grabbed Molly and swung her around as you would a toddler, Lillian saw the bully's shins being kicked so hard that they bled, and later they turned black and blue. When she dropped Molly to the ground, Delia was then yanked so hard by her long, curly hair that she fell over, dizzy and crying, while her tiny opponent triumphantly held up a handful of her hair.

The mortified Delia had given Molly a wide berth after that, telling everyone that she was a 'little lunatic' who had inherited the same mental illness as her mother. To divert attention from her humiliation at the hands of Molly Power, Delia quickly moved on to the quiet and reserved Lillian Taylor. Lillian, she told everyone, was a snob with a posh voice, who sucked up to the nuns, carrying tales to Sister Ignatius.

When two girls were beaten for scorching a pillow case with an iron, Delia reported that she had seen Lillian talking to Sister Ignatius shortly afterwards. Later in the dining hall, a note was slipped under the table and passed along to Lillian, saying that the two girls would 'get her' in the dormitory after lights out.

Lillian's stomach had churned when she read the note, and although she wanted to rush to the toilet to hide, she had to sit and finish her greasy soup. Life was bad enough with the nuns without having to battle with the other girls.

Molly must have seen Lillian lagging behind in the line-up after lunch, with tears in her eyes, and guessed something was going on. Later, in the geography class – taken by the elderly and hard-of-hearing Sister Martha – she confronted the pair and warned them not to lay a finger on her, and they told her Delia had set it all up.

'Well, yer can tell Delia Sweeney that I'll tear every hair out of her head if anyone lays a finger on Lillian Taylor. And yer can tell Lillian the note was a mistake.'

When Lillian heard what happened, she was amazed that Molly had taken such a bold stance on her part. She remembered the bed-wetting incident, but had not expected anything in return. When she got Molly on her own, she had quietly thanked her.

'Yer were a friend to me and I hate that Delia Sweeney,' Molly told her.

Lillian had felt a little uneasy at being described as Molly's friend as they had little in common and she was wary of the smaller girl's temper, and afterwards she kept the same distance between them. Then things had changed after Alice and the other girls departed for Canada. There were only a few of the older ones left and she and Molly were put working together more often. Molly seemed more settled since Delia had gone, and not quite so defensive all the time.

Now they worked on in companionable silence. Lillian felt any time away from the nuns was a good day, and was grateful for small mercies. They were just finishing off the classroom when footsteps sounded along the corridor. They both froze. The door was thrown open and Sister Dominic came in.

The nun stared around the classroom. 'I hope you haven't missed anything.'

'We were just checking the floor again in case there was anything the brush didn't catch.'

The nun turned towards Molly. 'You're very quiet, Miss Power. Have you checked everything is all right?'

Lillian glanced at her, terrified that if Molly didn't answer quickly or respectfully enough, it would trigger one of the nun's rages.

'Yes, Sister,' Molly said, 'I think the floor and everything is clean.'

'Well, we all know what your thinking is like, don't we? Your brain is like the rest of you – far too small to be of any use. And we know how easy it is for you to make mistakes, don't we?'

Lillian's stomach churned. Why did the nun have to be so cruel? She seemed to get pleasure out of making the girls suffer by saying the most horrible things, like sticking a knife in and then slowly twisting it around.

Molly's shoulders drooped. 'Yes, Sister,' Molly said quietly. 'I've done me best.'

'Good,' Sister Dominic said, 'because you're going to have to do your best from now on. There's no hope of you going home now, wherever home was, to that useless mother of yours. This is the only place you have left, and you'd better make the best of it.'

Molly's brow wrinkled in confusion.

'We received a message from Father Sutcliffe to say your mother has been found dead.'

Lillian's hand flew to her mouth. She turned and could see that Molly's blue eyes were wide open, and her face as white as the chalk dust she had rubbed from the board. She watched as Molly's right eyelid came down like the top of a heavy box, while the other eye remained as normal. It stayed like that for a few seconds, before Molly managed to blink it open again, but it wasn't as wide as her left eye.

'Come on,' Sister Dominic commanded, pointing towards the door, 'the priest is on his way to speak to you. Arrangements will have to be made for a funeral.'

'I don't want to go!' Molly suddenly screeched, and stumbled across the desks to Lillian, to grasp her tightly around the waist. 'Don't let her take me...' Then she buried her face in her friend's pinafore, sobbing loudly.

Lillian's heart was racing, as she worked out what to do for the best for Molly. There was not an ounce of compassion in the nun, and she was likely to lash out with her hands or a ruler to try and silence the girl, rather than comfort her. 'Will I bring her, Sister? Would it help you?'

Sister Dominic gave a loud sigh. 'I can't waste any more time on this nonsense – I have another class to attend to. Finish what you have to do here, and then get her along to Mother Superior's office.'

When the nun left, Lillian tightened her arms around Molly. 'I know what's happened to your mother is terrible, but you're going to have to be brave...'

*

Later that evening when Molly was returned to the dormitory, Lillian took the first chance she could to check she was all right.

'The priest was nice,' Molly said, in a dull voice, her eyes downcast. 'He took me over to the boys' orphanage to get our Daniel, and then he took us out for fish and chips. He said he'll come back in a few days to take us to the funeral.'

'I'm really sorry,' Lillian said. 'It must have been a terrible shock for you both.'

'It was,' Molly said, 'but it doesn't matter. When I was crying earlier, it was because I didn't want to go on me own with Sister Dominic, not because of me mam. Like I told yer before, she wasn't much of a ma to us.'

When she looked up, Lillian noticed the eyelid fluttering shut every so often as it had done earlier in the day. She hoped it was just a temporary thing because when it came to looks, the only thing that poor Molly had going for her was her lovely eyes.

Chapter Two

On Friday – the morning of Molly's mother's funeral – Lillian also received news she could never have imagined. With a pounding heart, she accompanied the quiet Sister Ignatius along the corridor from the laundry to see Mother Superior, who informed her that she would have her first-ever visitor on Sunday afternoon.

'It's a relative, an aunt, who has come forward and said she would like to meet you.'

'An *aunt?*' Lillian echoed.

The elderly nun had raised her grey eyebrows and nodded slowly. 'Yes, it seems she has been living away from Liverpool, and has only just discovered where you are. Apparently she knows one of our benefactors, who had someone search you out. She seems a woman of decent background, and she says she would like to come and meet you.'

Lillian knew to ask no further questions of Mother Superior, but as she walked back to the laundry, she whispered to Sister Ignatius, 'Do you know anything about my aunt?'

'Nothing,' Sister Ignatius whispered back. 'I don't get to hear much. From the way she talked about your aunt, Mother Superior seemed to approve of her.' She gave a little smile. 'It will be nice for you to have a visitor, won't it?'

There was a pause, then Lillian said, 'I don't know…' After all the years of envying other girls whispering excitedly about visitors, now it came to it, she wasn't sure how she felt about a complete stranger visiting her out of the blue.

Saturday dawned cold, but with a bright blue sky. Lillian was put to work in the garden with some of the other older girls. Molly's chest had been bad the night after the funeral, so she was assigned indoor work, washing the marble stairs and polishing the mahogany banisters. As she passed her friend on the way downstairs, Lillian stopped to whisper her news about her forthcoming visit.

'I hope yer aunty is nice,' Molly said. 'Maybe she'll take yer out for the day. She might take yer to the zoo or someplace exciting like that.'

Lillian shook her head. 'It's just for tea in the visitors' room.'

Molly's eyes widened. 'They give you a biscuit with the tea.' She halted. 'The priest and Sister Ignatius took me and our Daniel to a hotel after the funeral. We got soup and sandwiches.'

Lillian wondered how Molly could think about biscuits so soon after losing her mother. Although it was ten years since Lillian's own mother had died, she could remember not wanting to eat at all when she came to Gethsemane House. At times now she couldn't even remember what her mother's face looked like. She knew she had been older than the other mothers in the street, but she always dressed nicely, smelled of soap and wore her dark hair in a tidy bun. She wished she could remember her mother's face as clearly as Mother Superior's face the day she strode into the dining hall, not long after five-year-old Lillian had arrived in the orphanage, and marched over to her table.

The head nun had grabbed her by the hair, pulling her backwards in her chair so Lillian was looking up into her blazing eyes. 'No more of this crying and not eating nonsense!' she had said in a low hiss. 'Your mother is dead and gone and you'll have no special treatment here because of it. Why do you think the other girls are here? If they had worthwhile mothers, they would all be at home.'

She had stood over her while she finished a bowl of horrible, cold stew. After Mother Superior had left, Lillian had sat in shock for ten minutes, then silently vomited all of it back up. She had been lucky that Sister Ignatius was the nun in charge of the dining hall that afternoon. Lillian would later discover that the young nun had arrived at the convent only a few days before Lillian, and was feeling homesick for her family in Newcastle, and in many ways, was as disorientated as the girls now in her care. She quietly got two of the older girls to help clean up Lillian and the floor.

She had bent down and put her hand on Lillian's shoulder. 'Lillian, you must eat or Mother Superior will get very angry with you. And you must eat for your own sake or you will become very sick.' She had squeezed Lillian's hand. 'Do you remember in class that we were talking about how we had to give plants water, and give animals food, or they would die? People are the same. We need food and water or we will get very sick and die. Do you understand?'

There was a few moments' silence, then the little girl nodded. Lillian was beginning to understand that her life had changed forever. Her quiet mother, who had loved and protected her, and dressed her nicely and taught her to always speak properly, was gone. She had no other relatives, her father having died before she was old enough to remember him, and she was now in a place where she had to learn to survive on her own. And surviving meant eating and not drawing attention to herself.

And so gradually, over the weeks and months, Lillian changed and adapted to the harsh environment that was now her new home. The years in between had dimmed most of the memories about her mother, but she had never forgotten the kindness of Sister Ignatius.

As Lillian swept up the piles of brown and yellow leaves, she felt a sense of peace descending over her. Every so often she paused to look up into the clear blue sky, enjoying the feel of the autumn sun on her face. She loved the freedom of working outdoors, even when it was cold and damp. She gave no hint of it to the nuns, as she had learned that it was a sure way for something good to be stopped. She moved around quickly to keep warm, pulling out small clumps of grass or stray weeds on the stony path.

At one point she paused to look towards the high stone wall that ran all the way around the garden. The wall blocked any view into the world outside, apart from two large wrought-iron gates, through which the girls could catch glimpses of the street on which Gethsemane House stood. Glimpses of the real world, where horses and carts and the occasional car went by, and where ordinary people walked freely. But those glimpses were rare, and the girls knew that it was a cardinal sin if they were caught too close to the gates. The girls were rarely allowed outside the walls, as the nuns told them everything they needed was within the orphanage. They didn't even have to go outside for Mass, as the priests brought the Holy Sacrament to them.

She thought again about this aunt who was coming to visit her. One half of her felt frightened, but the other half wondered if things worked out, her aunt might someday take her on a tram into Liverpool city, as she had heard that occasionally other girls had been taken out by relatives.

Lillian slept little that night, going over all the things her aunt might say, and trying to think of all the things she might say herself. She felt she had barely closed her eyes and drifted off when Sister Dominic was in the dormitory, shouting and hitting the bottom of each bed with a pointer as she marched along.

She stopped in the middle of the room and waited until each girl had their bare feet on the cold wooden floor and their hands joined together. She went along the beds again, checking for wet nightdresses, then, satisfied, she blessed herself and called out the Morning Offering, with the half-awake girls joining in. Prayers over, there was the usual military line-up for the toilet and the washrooms.

Lillian was sent to work in the kitchen after breakfast. Bleary-eyed, she went around collecting the piles of plates, which were wiped cleaner than usual. Every morsel of the toast – barely smeared with jam in honour of it being a Sunday – was devoured.

Afterwards, she joined three other girls, including Molly, and went to a room beside the laundry to clean and polish the nun's shoes. They worked in silence as Sister Agnes was prowling around, in a particularly bad mood. When Lillian got a chance to look over at her friend, she noticed her eye was still closing again.

'Is your eye okay?' she asked. 'One of them keeps closing...'

Molly shrugged. 'I dunno, it just started doing it by itself.'

She pressed her finger on the eyelid for a few seconds, and then she looked up at Lillian. 'Mother Superior noticed it too.' She pulled a face. 'She told me to keep it open as it made me look more stupid than usual. Does it look dead funny?'

Lillian shook her head. 'It's probably just a little nerve in your eye, and will stop as quick as it started.'

When they finished they were sent to the kitchen to peel potatoes and carrots, which would accompany a scrap of meat, followed by a spoonful of rice pudding for the Sunday lunch. After they had eaten, Lillian felt the afternoon crawling along as she washed and dried more dishes, and went for the usual after-lunch walk around the gardens saying the Rosary.

Later, the girls were split into two groups, the larger of which went off to the hall for craft classes where they unravelled old knitted jumpers and cardigans and then wound the crinkled wool into perfect balls. Later, they would re-knit them into squares for blankets. They also had piles of socks which had to be darned. Afterwards, the smaller group went back to the cold dormitory to get changed into their Sunday clothes for the visitors.

Lillian's stomach churned as she washed her face and brushed her long dark hair out before tying it up again in a ponytail.

The girls were led by Sister Agnes into the dining hall where the usual scrubbed wooden tables were now covered with plain white tablecloths. There was a flowery jug and matching sugar bowl on each table. It was no surprise to her as Lillian had often helped to set the places with some of the other older girls. Even so, the difference made by those small adornments was startling, and made the place they ate three times a day strangely unfamiliar. The children stood in silence while the nun

15

read their names from a list and then pointed to the table they were to sit at.

When her name was called, Lillian felt her long, thin legs suddenly shaky as she walked across the tiled floor to a table by the tall, sashed window. She sat down, her hands folded in her lap. When all the children were seated, Mother Superior came in to stand in the middle of the room, her gaze sweeping across all the tables.

'I will remind you all again – you are to be on your best behaviour. If you are asked by your visitors how you are treated here, make sure you tell them you are very well looked after. You have clean, warm beds, three good meals a day, and you are being well educated in school. I don't want any complaints about food or the small chores you are asked to do. Girls who complain will be dealt with severely. *Very* severely.' She paused, her eyes narrowing. 'Is that understood?'

'Yes, Mother Superior,' the girls replied.

'I said,' she repeated in a louder voice, 'Is... that... understood?'

Every eye turned towards her now and they all chimed in clear voices, 'Yes, Mother Superior.'

As she sat waiting, Lillian suddenly shivered, feeling a cutting draft from the window behind her. She glanced outside and could see large leaves falling from an old chestnut tree and she wished she was outside brushing them up, instead of waiting in silence for a stranger. A stranger whom Mother Superior approved of. She didn't approve of many people, and for some reason that thought made Lillian feel even more anxious.

The sound of the heavy, wooden door creaking open startled her, and she sat bolt upright as a group of adults came in. The sound of voices began to fill the dining hall and, since the nuns were engaged showing the visitors to tables, Lillian felt it was safe to discreetly glance at the tables around her. Most of the visitors were lone women, but there was the occasional couple that she thought looked like a mother and father, or an older woman who might be grandmother. They all looked pinched, grey-faced, undernourished and poor – too poor to look after their own children.

She saw Sister Dominic closing the door and it dawned on her that everyone was sitting down at a table. Her aunt hadn't come!

A wave of alarm washed over her. What would she do now? Would she just sit on her own and wait until visiting had finished, or would the nuns come and march her out of the hall? A hot feeling started in her chest and she could feel it rising up her neck and face. She recognised it, and knew that it would make her all blotchy and red. Everyone in the hall would notice. The thought of it all made her feel quite sick.

And then the door creaked open again, and a woman came in: a tall, well-dressed, elegant lady who looked nothing like the other women. She spoke to Sister Dominic and then came along the row of tables towards where Lillian was sitting. Lillian's heart was racing and she dipped her head, waiting until the woman came to stand at her table. She did not dare to look up at the lady's face, but she could see she was wearing a matching coat and navy dress, with white gloves and three strands of pearls.

'Lillian Taylor?' she said, putting her hand on the back of the chair.

Lillian finally looked at her. She was a very pretty-looking woman, with dark hair smoothed back in a bun.

'Yes ... I'm Lillian.'

The woman sat down, then put her navy and white bag on the table and removed her white gloves. 'Mother Superior has told you who I am, hasn't she?'

Lillian swallowed hard and then said in a funny crackly voice. 'She said you were my aunt ...'

'I am your Aunt Anna.'

'I never knew I had any aunts ...' Lillian's voice was a whisper, but there was a determination in it to know more about herself. 'The nuns never mentioned you before.' Lillian stared at her now, and she noticed her aunt's hands were trembling. She was surprised to think an adult might be nervous meeting someone her age. 'I don't remember you.'

'That's not surprising because you were very little. But I remember you.' Anna smiled, and there was a softness in her eyes. 'Your face looks exactly as I remember you... although you are so much older, of course.'

'Where do you live now?'

'In Liverpool, just off the city centre.'

'Is it near where I lived with my mother and father?'

Her aunt's eyes moved downwards. 'No...'

There was a little silence, then Lillian said, 'Is there anyone else? Any more aunts or uncles? Do I have any cousins?'

Anna's brow creased. 'No. There is only me.'

'Have you any children of your own?'

'There is only me,' she repeated.

Lillian thought of all the questions that had gone through her mind. 'Did you know Mother had died? Did you look for me or did you forget about me?'

'No, no... I never forgot about you. Not for a minute. I spent a long time looking for you.'

'When you couldn't find me, did you think I had died?'

'No, no... I always knew I would find you.' Lillian noticed the determination in her voice.

Then, before Lillian could say any more, two older girls came towards their table, each carrying a cup of tea.

'This is very nice,' her aunt said, seeming relieved to find a break from Lillian's questions, and lifting the milk jug. 'Shall I pour it for you?'

'Yes, please.' Lillian lifted her teaspoon. 'I can do my own sugar though.' She then proceeded to spoon two heaped spoonfuls of sugar into her cup. It was a rare sweet treat as the girls usually had watery tea, mixed with a drop of milk and poured from a large kettle. She was stirring her tea vigorously when one of the girls came back with a small plate with three digestive biscuits.

'Thank you,' Anna said, smiling at the girls. After they'd

18

walked away, she pushed the plate over to her niece saying, 'You have one if you like, I'm not over-fond of cakes and sweet things.'

Lillian reached out for a biscuit. She went to take a bite from it, but then paused for a moment. 'My mother used to bake apple tarts and fruit cakes. Do you remember her baking?'

'Yes,' Anna said, lifting her teacup and taking a sip. 'She was a wonderful cook.'

Lillian took a bite of her biscuit. 'Do you remember other things about her? I find it hard to remember...'

'We can talk about that another time.' She paused. 'I have something important to tell you. I've told Mother Superior that I want to take you out of this place...'

Lillian felt the piece of biscuit was suddenly too big for her mouth and she tried to swallow. Was it possible that her dream of getting a day outside the walls of the orphanage might actually become real? Would her aunt take her to a tearoom or maybe a café? Would she buy her fish and chips?

'I want you to come and live with me.'

Lillian felt her heart begin to race. Never for a minute had she thought that she might leave the orphanage and the nuns forever. She had heard of some of the younger girls being taken to live with relatives and others who had been adopted, but she had never considered it for herself. She had been there too long. It would be like hoping for a miracle. She had never imagined what it would be like to live in a real house again or to be free to walk about the streets of Liverpool amongst ordinary people. Now that it seemed like a possibility, she knew she should be happy, ecstatic even, but instead, she suddenly felt a sense of alarm and confusion. She knew nothing about this woman sitting in front of her. She took a deep breath to calm herself, but some of the crumbs from the biscuit got caught in her throat. She started to cough.

Anna leaned forward. 'Take a drink of your tea...'

Lillian took a quick gulp of the hot liquid. The coughing continued, then she started to splutter and choke. She could see the other girls and their visitors turning to look at her now. She lowered her head but out of the side of her eyes she could see a black-dressed figure moving towards her and her heart sank further. It was probably Sister Dominic coming to take her into the corridor, where she would give her a hard slap for coughing. Tears filled her eyes now and started to spill down her cheeks.

'Are you okay?' Her aunt got to her feet. 'I'll get you a drink of water . . .' As she turned, she almost collided with Sister Dominic. 'We need to get her a drink.'

'Come along with me, Lillian,' Sister Dominic said.

Lillian, still coughing and choking, stood up. Her aunt put her arm around her shoulder. 'Are you all right?' she asked, anxiously.

'She will be fine,' Sister Dominic said. 'Hurry up now, Lillian.' The nun turned and started to march briskly towards the door and they both followed her out.

As she moved past the other tables, Lillian knew everyone was looking at her. Sister Dominic stood holding the door open. She turned back to Anna. 'There's no need for you to come. I'll sort her out.'

'I want to come,' Anna said firmly. She put her hand on the door and then guided Lillian through.

Sister Ignatius appeared with a cup of cold water and Lillian took it from her.

'Go back into the dining hall and check the others are behaving,' the older nun said, and Sister Ignatius quickly did as she was told.

Lillian took a little sip from the cup and then another. The cough started to build up again, and as she tried to stifle it, she suddenly felt sick and made a retching sound.

'Don't you dare!' Sister Dominic hissed. 'Get upstairs to the toilets if you're going to be sick.'

Anna was appalled at the nun's manner. 'The child can't help it!' she snapped. 'She almost choked earlier on.'

Lillian closed her eyes, beads of hot sweat coming out on her forehead with the effort not to cough.

Sister Dominic, unused to being challenged, seemed to freeze and her eyes bulged in suppressed anger. 'She will be fine.'

Lillian took a few deep breaths and the coughing and the sick feeling started to subside. There was a silence, during which she was aware of the tension between her aunt and the nun. 'I think I'm okay now,' she whispered.

'Take another sip of water,' Anna said, in a kind voice. 'And then when you are ready, we will go back inside.'

'I think we should leave the visit for today,' Sister Dominic said. 'It looks like it's all been too much for the girl. That coughing business is just a reaction to all the attention she's got having a visitor.'

'Really?'

'She's one of the girls who have been here for years, and anything different from their normal routine upsets them.'

'I want to take her home with me today,' Anna said, in a calm, low voice.

Sister Dominic's brow wrinkled. '*Today*?'

'Yes, today.'

As she listened in amazement, Lillian's throat started to close over and she fought back the urge to start coughing again.

'Ah, that's impossible,' Sister Dominic said. There was a smile on her face now, as though she thought Anna was mad. 'You certainly won't be allowed to take her today. There are official papers to be sorted and signed before anything like that can happen. '

Anna smiled back. 'I shall speak to Mother Superior and have it organised immediately.'

'As I said, it's impossible.'

Anna looked the nun straight in the eye. 'It is entirely possible when I have the authority over one of your main benefactor's estates. Mother Superior would not want to lose that annual donation.' She waited a few moments until what she had said registered. 'I have made up my mind. I am taking my niece home with me today.'

Sister Dominic turned on her heel and strode down the corridor towards Mother Superior's office.

Anna watched her go, then she turned to Lillian. 'Are you okay?'

'Yes...' Lillian said. She gave a few short coughs, not as violent as before.

'Sister Dominic seems to be a lady who is used to getting her own way. I suspect many of the nuns are like that. They were the same in Ireland, where I grew up. Has she been very hard on you and the other girls?'

Lillian was surprised to hear her aunt had grown up in Ireland, as her accent sounded more English. She wondered if she was related on her mother's side of the family or her father's. She knew her mother had come from an ordinary Irish family from near Dublin with only a small farm. She remembered her talking to a neighbour about how the family had to leave to go to England and Scotland for work because the eldest son would inherit the farm. Her father she didn't remember at all. She knew he was also Irish, and had a small ironmonger's business in the centre of Liverpool.

She bit her lip now, terrified to say anything in case this new aunt was only pretending she cared. Sister Agnes sometimes pretended to be nice, asking questions about the other girls or even the younger nuns. She would smile and put her arm around them, then ask a string of questions, digging around to find something. But Lillian learned long ago to say nothing. She had seen girls used as evidence against others. When they had finished telling her whatever she wanted to hear, they would then be dragged along the corridor to repeat the tale in front of the person.

Anna bent down and put a hand on her shoulder. 'You needn't be afraid to tell me anything. Have the nuns been very harsh to you?'

Lillian looked up and saw the genuine concern in her eyes. 'Sometimes...' she said.

'Well, it's all finished now. You're coming to live with me, and that's that.' She reached to stroke Lillian's cheek. 'I'm going to make up for all that you have gone through here, and give you the life you should have had.' She smiled and waved her gloved hand in the air. 'You're going to forget about all this.'

As Lillian smiled back at her aunt, she felt that in minutes, everything had changed. Her aunt had just saved her from a beating by Sister Dominic. The only other person who had protected her had been Molly. Sister Ignatius had been kind, but could only do so much.

Anna took Lillian's hand. 'We'll go back into the hall for my coat and things, and then we'll go and see Mother Superior.'

Lillian looked up at her and realised that life as an orphan had ended. Whether she was actually allowed to go today didn't matter. She knew that she would leave here very soon. The thought filled her with a hope she had never felt before in her life.

It was as if some kind of miracle had happened to her.

Chapter Three

Lillian sat on a chair outside the main office while her aunt knocked on the door and went inside. Within a minute or so, Sister Dominic came rushing out, without glancing at her. As Lillian watched her long black skirt swishing down the corridor, she prayed she would never see her or the other cruel nuns again.

Ten, then fifteen minutes passed, then the door opened and Aunt Anna came out, followed by Mother Superior. Lillian's heart started to race again. She could not imagine anyone telling this nun what to do. No matter what her aunt wanted, she feared she wouldn't be allowed to leave the orphanage today.

'Everything is organised, Lillian,' her aunt said. 'Mother Superior has kindly agreed to let you come home with me. Is anything you would like to bring with you?'

'If you will excuse me,' the nun interrupted, in a tense tone, 'I have more important business to attend to.' She went back into her office, banging the door shut.

Lillian felt weak with relief.

'Hurry now,' Anna said, 'go and get your things.'

She looked up, bewildered. 'What sort of things?'

'Clothes... you don't need to bring much, just enough until we buy you new ones tomorrow. And maybe your personal possessions? Any little things you might like to bring with you?'

'I only have my mother's rosary beads,' she said, feeling in her gymslip pocket.

Anna's face darkened. 'Where is your coat?'

'Upstairs in the dormitory. And I'll get my nightdress and dressing gown.'

'Well, go quickly. I'll have a hackney cab waiting to take us home.'

Lillian trembled as she went back along the corridor and up the stairs, hoping she wouldn't meet any of the nuns. *Home, home, home. A hackney cab to take us home.* The words kept circling around in Lillian's mind. Could this really be happening, she wondered.

Luck was on her side – when she reached the corridor at the top of the stairs, there was no one around. She went to her bedside locker and lifted things out. She quickly rolled her slippers and a pair of knickers inside her nightdress and dressing gown, then put her coat on and went back downstairs. To see her aunt waiting for her at the bottom gave her a wonderful feeling. A feeling she didn't recognise. Something she had never known in all the years in the orphanage. It was a mixture of hope and anticipation.

Anna held a brown paper bag out to her. 'Put your things in this,' she said. 'It will have to do. I never thought to bring a proper bag for you to use.'

Lillian did as she was told. She hoped she could make it out of the building before anyone else came along. She didn't want to see anyone – any of the girls or any of the nuns. And then her eyes widened and her hand flew to her mouth. How could she have forgotten? 'I have to say goodbye to Molly.'

'Who is Molly?'

'My friend. I can't go without seeing her. The nuns won't tell her ...'

'It would be best if we go now. You can write to her.'

'But she might not get the letters ... nobody ever gets letters.'

'I'll arrange it ...'

'Molly's mother just died this week, and she'll be all upset and worried if I just disappear without telling her.'

Her aunt halted. 'Her mother died this week?'

Lillian nodded. 'The funeral was on Friday. Her brother is in the boys' orphanage ...'

'Dear God.' She turned and looked back at Mother Superior's office.

Then footsteps sounded and when Lillian looked around, she saw Sister Ignatius coming along the corridor towards them. 'Ask her if I can see Molly, please... She's the nicest of all the nuns.'

Her aunt moved quickly down the corridor and spoke to the young nun for a few minutes. Then, she beckoned to Lillian.

Sister Ignatius was smiling. 'I've just heard your news, Lillian, and I'm so pleased for you. Won't it be wonderful to have a new home with your family?'

'Thank you, Sister Ignatius.' She was grateful to get the chance to say goodbye to the only adult who had been kind to her. 'Can I please see Molly before I go?'

The nun's eyes flickered over to Anna, then back to the serious-faced young girl. 'Molly was taken to the sick room just after lunch. Her chest and back are paining her. She might have caught a chill in her kidneys when she was at the funeral.' She looked at Anna and raised her eyebrows. 'It was such a cold day, and she is such a small, delicate girl. She has been given something to help her sleep until the doctor comes to see her later this afternoon.'

Lillian slowly nodded. A doctor coming to the orphanage happened rarely, and she understood the circumstances would make it impossible to see Molly. 'Can you please tell her what happened to me and that I tried to see her? I don't want her to think I just went away and forgot all about her.'

'Yes,' Sister Ignatius said, 'when I get the chance.'

A door opened somewhere down the corridor, and Sister Agnes's stern voice could be clearly heard.

Sister Ignatius took a step backwards. 'Goodbye Lillian, I wish you happiness in your new life with your aunt. You're a lucky girl – so many of us would love to be in your position.'

Lillian thought she saw tears glistening in Sister Ignatius's eyes, but told herself she must have imagined it. Nuns would never cry because they were so close to God.

Sister Agnes's voice came again and the nun suddenly turned on her heel and hurried off down the corridor.

'We need to hurry now,' her aunt said, 'the man will be waiting with the taxi.'

Lillian walked out of the orphanage door with her aunt as though she was in a dream. They crossed the street together and walked down to where the black hackney cab was waiting. Anna spoke to the driver and then came back to the passenger side. She seemed calm and assured, as though she had done this many times. Lillian's heart quickened as she wondered what it would be like to ride in a vehicle.

As soon as they were settled, the driver turned the key and the engine roared into life, startling her. She gave a gasp and her hand flew to her chest.

'You're okay,' Anna said, smiling reassuringly. 'I suppose you're not used to cars, are you? They are noisy things, but they're very useful. I intend to get one in the near future, and when you are older, you will learn to drive your own car.'

Lillian caught her breath. The thought of women driving cars was something she had never considered. The car started to move and she sat back, gripping the brown paper bag. As they went along one street after another, Lillian looked out of the window at the houses and the shops, and observed the people who were walking about freely. At times she felt excited and at other times she felt frightened when she saw how poor and shabbily dressed some people were.

As they passed by the back of large, drab-looking buildings, she caught sight of young children, some barefoot, playing tag amongst bins and rubbish, and running between lines of grey washing, seemingly without the control of any adults. She had presumed all children had to be kept under strict control, as she had been for years. From what she could remember, her mother had also been strict about how she spoke and ate, but she had never been cruel.

The taxi stopped in a queue of traffic now, and she watched boys around her own age playing football on an area which had once had grass, but was now hardened mud with the odd clump of green which had miraculously survived. Along the edges was a collection of rubbish which had blown in from the street or the backs of the old buildings.

When the boys turned and came running after the ball in the direction of the taxi, she noticed that their hair and faces were dirty and their clothes – little better than rags – were even dirtier. It suddenly made her think that her own orphanage clothes were far superior. She had never imagined that she would feel better off than any other children. Orphans, she supposed, were the poorest of the poor – and yet, she could see quite clearly now, this was not the case.

Something happened or something was said that made the group of boys laugh out loud. They were laughing so hard they were falling against each other, and one boy sank to his knees on the ground and then rolled over – laughing all the while.

Lillian stared at them in shock. She couldn't remember ever hearing anyone laugh as heartily as that. They were happy. How, she wondered, could they possibly be happy living in such appalling conditions?

The taxi moved along a few yards and on the other side of the road she saw a group of men outside a pub, all shabby, wearing cloth caps. One of them made to move away, but he only staggered a few feet and then he fell on the ground. No one seemed particularly concerned. He tried to get back on his feet, with the help of another man, but within a few moments, the exact same thing happened. He staggered and fell down again.

He was drunk, Lillian thought, suddenly curious. She had never seen a person drunk before. Molly had often told her about her mother getting drunk on whiskey or beer, staggering around and bringing drunken men home to the house.

A screeching voice caused her to look up at a window in one of the taller buildings, and she saw a woman hanging out of it, her long dark hair covering her face. When she pushed it back,

Lillian was startled to realise she was naked on her top half. The boys and the drunks all looked up, and then some started shouting at her. The woman screamed back, gesticulating wildly and uttering words that Lillian knew must be curses. The woman withdrew back inside and then the window was banged down.

Lillian thought this must be the terrible life that Molly had been used to.

As the taxi moved nearer the city, where the buildings were cleaner and smarter, she began to see a different kind of life where well-dressed people like her aunt were walking around. She saw nice couples strolling along, the women taking the men's arms. She saw families out walking together, mothers and fathers holding toddlers by the hand and pushing babies in prams. There were poor people walking around the city too, and she was shocked when she saw numerous people with dark skin – much darker than Molly's brother, Daniel.

A strange feeling came over her, a frightening feeling of being lost in this big, new world outside the orphanage walls. It was so strong she almost wanted to jump out of her seat and ask the driver to turn his taxi around and take her back to the nuns – where she knew what to expect and what to do. She felt acutely aware that she knew not a single person in Liverpool city apart from her aunt. And when she looked at her aunt, she realised she did not know her either.

Anna glanced at the anxious-looking, dark-haired girl beside her. They had only been together for little over an hour, but they had made massive strides. Lillian was out of that godforsaken place and on the road to the life she should have had all along. They had started to bridge some of the missing years.

She knew they had to take time to get to know each other, and for Lillian to get used to her new surroundings. From what she had already established, the girl had far more about her than she could have hoped for. She had a truly beautiful face with high cheekbones, thick dark hair, and she was tall with an elegant bearing. She even spoke well, pronouncing her words clearly and properly. Most importantly, she was willing to take instruction. One of the benefits of living with those horrendous creatures in the convent.

There had been the awkward issue about her friend, which, Anna supposed, was only to be expected. Especially since the other child had just lost her mother, and it was only natural that Lillian would empathise with her. It was as well that Lillian didn't get the chance to see her, as it might have caused her distress. Although she had sympathy for the poor child losing her mother, it was better that Lillian make a clean break from her past.

There was a lot to do, and certain things that would have to be sorted out immediately. With it being a Sunday, new clothes would have to wait until tomorrow. They would be organised first thing in the morning. She couldn't wait to have the poor-looking coat, pinafore and spit-through blouse at the bottom of her bin. Her navy knitted cardigan was the only thing that looked halfway decent, but it would also go nonetheless.

There would be nothing to remind either of them about the orphanage. Everything would be done to ensure Lillian settled into her new surroundings without drawing too much curiosity. Inevitably, there would be some. No matter how she explained it and brushed aside questions, there would be certain people – both inside and outside her house – who would want to know where this long-lost niece had come from.

Anna gave a little sigh. She was under no illusions that it would be easy, but she would deal with things as they arose, and evade everything else in her usual way. The main thing was to get Lillian away from the nuns and back where she belonged.

Chapter Four

By the time the taxi had driven down past Lime Street Station and up Renshaw Street, past the Adelphi Hotel and grand shops, Lillian was in a daze. She was overwhelmed by all the big buildings, the noise of the traffic and all the people walking around, and she hadn't given any thought to what sort of house she might be coming to. She had only vague memories of the semi-detached house she grew up in with her mother; her only other home had been the large, old rambling buildings of the orphanage.

The taxi turned down Rodney Street and stopped outside number 77: a large, imposing house at the end of the terrace. They both got out, then Anna paid the driver and led Lillian over to the steps.

Anna stopped outside the door and turned to her niece. 'When we go inside, we are going straight upstairs to our private living quarters. If anyone speaks to you, I will deal with them. You just keep going as though you have not heard them. Do you understand?'

'Yes,' Lillian said in a low voice.

'You have no need to worry.' Her aunt's voice was kinder now. 'The people who lodge here are nice enough, but they don't need to know anything about you, apart from the fact that you're my niece. And whatever you are asked, don't tell anyone that you have come from an orphanage.'

Lillian suddenly felt bewildered. Was her aunt asking her to tell lies? She had been warned by the nuns that liars went to hell. Was it still a lie, she wondered, if her aunt told her to say something? And who were these people who were going to ask all these questions. 'What will I say?' she whispered. 'I'm afraid to tell lies.'

'Well, it's not really lying as such. We don't have to explain ourselves to anyone. People are entitled to keep their own business to themselves, especially when we are the owners of the house.'

Lillian looked blankly at her.

'The other people in the house are paying guests.' She must have realised that Lillian had no idea what she was talking about. She had lived in a convent since she was five – what would she know about the outside world and how real people lived?

'The others rent rooms from me, so I make the decisions about who comes into my house and what goes on in it. You are my niece and that will mean something to them. Even though you are young, just remember that they will look up to you.' She put her hand on Lillian's shoulder and smiled. 'Are you ready now?'

Lillian nodded and followed her aunt inside. She found herself in a large tiled hallway with a gold-painted table with a white marble top, which held a vase of colourful fresh flowers. Above her head hung a glittering, glass chandelier. Her aunt put a finger to her lips, then beckoned her to follow as she moved quickly across the floor and up the polished wooden staircase. There was a red patterned runner with gold edging which went all the way up, silencing their footsteps.

Anna waited for her at the top of the stairs, and then she turned to the left, where there were doors to three rooms. There were more rooms on the right-hand side, and a smaller staircase which led to another floor. Her aunt walked quickly to the first room nearer the staircase, then halted at the door to take the key out of her handbag. Just as she put it in the door, they heard another door opening, and her aunt ushered her inside and closed the door.

'Did you see anyone?' Anna checked.

'No ...'

'Good.' She took her hat off and smoothed her hair down. 'This is *our* own private sitting room for our own use.'

Lillian looked around the room. Plump pale green velvet sofas with tapestry cushions, gold curtains with tasselled pelmets. Glittering crystal lights hung in the middle of the room, and there were smaller, identical lights on either side of the white marble fireplace, which had a coal fire burning in it. The marble hearth looked spotless, as did the shining brass companion set with tongs and small fancy brushes. Someone, Lillian thought, must have been tending to it while her aunt was out at the orphanage. She knew from years of cleaning fireplaces in the nun's convent – to which the orphanage was attached – that only hard work kept a fireplace so clean and tidy. Mother Superior only allowed certain girls to look after the fire in her office, and the job often fell to her and Molly, although Molly struggled to carry the pails of coal.

A tight feeling came into Lillian's chest as she thought about her friend. She really wished she had had time to say goodbye properly to her. To distract herself, Lillian did what she often did in the orphanage: she clenched her hands tightly until her nails dug into her palms. Then she made herself concentrate on the wall opposite, lined with a dark wooden bookcase which had glass-panelled doors and shelves of serious-looking books. She looked around the room, taking in the various tables of different sizes, some displaying lamps and ornaments. Two matching plant stands stood either side of the window, holding tall plants with wide palm-shaped leaves. On another wall was a sideboard which had flowers painted on the doors and held a display of silver items.

'We currently have four guests, and they use the main drawing room downstairs where they can sit at the fire,' Anna said. 'They have a dining table for eating at or working on. They all work in the city, and one of the current guests, Mr Guthrie, is an accountant so he often brings work home from the offices.

There's also a library across from the drawing room, where the men often go after their meals to smoke or have a brandy. It's rare that people come up here; it's really only just in emergencies.' She paused to wave her hand around the room. 'Do you like it? Do you think you will like living here?'

Lillian hesitated. 'Yes,' she eventually said. 'It's very nice... thank you.'

She noticed her aunt's shoulders slump and she could tell that she was disappointed that her answer wasn't enthusiastic enough. She felt her aunt's gaze upon her, and she suddenly became conscious of her drab clothes. She knew she looked at odds with the palatial surroundings. A sense of shame crept over her. She wasn't good enough to be in a place like this, and anyone in the house who saw her would know that immediately.

Her aunt walked towards the door. 'I'll show you the bedroom where you will sleep, which isn't far from mine. We just have to go out into the hallway again, and they are just a few yards along.' She put her finger to her lips. 'Just remember what I said earlier. Speak to no one until I tell you it is all right.'

Lillian followed her along the hallway, stopping to have a brief look into her aunt's room, which was equally as well furnished as the sitting-room: polished dark wooden wardrobe, matching dressing table and bedside tables with marble tops and lamps with figurine bases and flower-shaped glass shades. They then moved on to a door that opened up into a beautiful bathroom, with a roll-top white bath with gold claw feet and a sink and toilet both decorated with blue and white flowers.

'Your room is at the bottom of the corridor,' her aunt said, leading her along and down three steps.

Everything she had seen so far had been on a grander scale than she could ever have imagined, and having just seen a toilet cistern which was fancier than any vases she had seen in the convent, she now felt more out of her depth than ever.

'I hope you like pink,' Anna said, smiling as she opened the door. 'The lady in the department store helped me choose everything. She said it was the sort of style that would suit a girl who would soon grow into a young woman.'

Lillian stepped into the bedroom and stood in silence as she gazed around at the three-quarter-size canopied bed with the matching pink satin eiderdown and pillow-case, the pink flowered tieback curtains and the pastel oriental fringed rug. Her gaze focused on a bookcase which was filled with both books and magazines. Over by the window which looked down into the street, there was a green leather-topped desk, and a chair which had a floral cushion on it. There was a box on top with a selection of pens and pencils and a wooden ruler.

'What do you think? Will it suit?'

Lillian heard the anxious note in her aunt's voice as she repeated the question she had asked earlier. Her coming to live in this house was going to be a big change for them both. 'It's all lovely ... everything is lovely.' She drew her cardigan around herself, not knowing what else to say.

Her aunt crouched down a little, so she could look straight into Lillian's eyes. 'I know it's a different world to the orphanage, but you will get used to it. This is your home now, Lillian. This is your *entitlement*. Do you understand?'

Lillian nodded and whispered, 'Yes,' although she did not understand exactly what was meant by her 'entitlement', she knew by the grave look on her aunt's face that it was something serious.

Her aunt left her in her room while she went downstairs to sort an evening meal for them. 'We have our meals cooked for us in the morning and evening,' she had explained, 'but Mrs Larking only works until three o'clock on a Sunday, so I asked her to leave some of the meat and potatoes for us. I'll go down to the kitchen to see what else there is.' She gestured towards the bookcase. 'You might find something there that interests you.'

When she reached the door she looked back. 'Do not,' she warned Lillian again, 'open the door to anyone. When I come back I'll give two quiet knocks to let you know that it's me.'

When the door was closed, Lillian gave a deep sigh, as though she had been holding her breath for a long time. She went over to sit down on the soft, luxurious bed. Her bed. She stayed there for a few minutes staring down at the oriental rug, then lifted her eyes and looked around the room. A sense of panic filled her again and she made herself go over to the bookcase to look through the books.

She looked at the books and bent down to the bottom shelf where the magazines were neatly stacked. These were something entirely new to her. The only magazines she had ever seen were religious. She lifted out one called *Good Housekeeping*. She took it over to her desk and leafed through it. She was surprised at the contents, especially the advertisements for things she had never heard of. All sorts of things like perfumes and skin creams and make-up, things she had only heard whispered about in the orphanage. She saw pictures of happy, well-dressed children around a breakfast table eating something called cornflakes, and recipes for sweet cakes and puddings she didn't know existed. There were pages of women modelling coats and dresses, which the title said were for the 'fashionable lady'. All the ladies in the magazine, Lillian thought, looked like Aunt Anna, and the clothes were the sort of things that she imagined her aunt would wear.

She was startled when she turned a page and found herself looking at women who were modelling brassieres and girdles. She had never seen anyone in such a state of undress, nor had she imagined that knickers existed that weren't large cotton ones in navy or grey. These were quite beautiful, and she felt intrigued as she stared with great fascination at the lace-trimmed garments. She flicked through the pages and stopped when she came to a page headed *Dear Mary*, which published letters from readers outlining their problems in all areas of life. She read a letter from a young woman requesting advice about spots on her skin, and was lost in another from a 28-year-old spinster, desperate to know where was the likeliest place to meet an eligible husband, when a noise outside the room startled her.

She quickly closed the magazine and placed it back in the

bookcase. She waited a few moments, and when there was no further sound, she went through the top shelf of books. Her eyes lit up as she picked up a copy of *Little Women*, a book that Sister Ignatius had read to the girls in their English class. She had only got halfway through it, as Sister Agnes had come into the classroom one afternoon when the girls were all sitting in silence, enraptured with the story. She had whipped the book out of the younger nun's hands and told her that she was wasting valuable time reading American rubbish to girls who wouldn't understand a word of it.

The feeling washed over her again – something akin to homesickness for that miserable, grey building and cold-hearted nuns. How could she miss it? She knew the other girls would give anything for this miraculous chance, but Lillian felt so lost and alone that given the choice, she might wish to go back to the orphanage, to everything that was familiar and predictable.

Tears suddenly rushed into her eyes. She blinked furiously, then clutching the copy of *Little Women*, she went back to sit on the bed to refresh her memory of the story she had loved. By the time the two taps came on the door, Lillian was deeply engrossed in the first chapter. She went quickly across the floor and could hear the low voice saying, 'It's only me.'

Her aunt came in carrying a wooden tray with two plates which held sliced beef in gravy, mashed potatoes and a mixture of vegetables, and two glasses of milk. The portions were double, if not three times the size that Lillian was used to at the orphanage.

'I had to warm them up in the oven,' her aunt explained, going over to the desk, 'so be careful as the plates will be very hot.' She put the tray down and then went over to the bookcase and lifted two magazines. 'We might as well eat in here at the desk.'

Apart from the odd comment her aunt made, they ate in silence, both gazing down into the street. There was little movement, just the occasional car or resident going in or out of one of the houses across the way. Lillian saw a family with three little girls with lovely hats and coats coming out of a house. Later, she noticed a fair-haired boy around her own age, going into another house with an elderly man, who she imagined might be his grandfather. All the people she saw were very well dressed, which made her conscious of her own poor attire.

As though thinking similar thoughts, her aunt said, 'I have a nice navy skirt and a matching navy and white jumper, which I think I can alter to fit you. I've also got a short swing-coat which you can wear to the shops tomorrow.'

'Thank you,' Lillian said, still worrying with every word that she would say the wrong thing and her aunt would decide bringing her here had been a mistake.

'We don't want to draw attention to ourselves in the shop,' Anna said, 'with you dressed in...' her eyes flickered over Lillian's cardigan and then down to her boots, '...in a school uniform.'

Lillian looked down at her plate, which still had almost half the food left on it. She tried another small forkful, but could not manage anything more.

'Have you had enough?' her aunt asked.

Lillian glanced up at her and nodded. 'I'm sorry...'

Anna smiled. 'There's nothing to be sorry about. Next time I'll ask Mrs Larking to give you a little less.'

Lillian felt a wave of relief that her aunt was not at all angry with her for leaving the lovely food. She was surprised herself that she could not eat it all as she was so used to feeling hungry in the orphanage.

Chapter Five

It took Lillian a long time to get to sleep. It felt strange to be in a room all on her own after years of sleeping in a dormitory. Every noise she heard filled her with a sense of panic. She heard footsteps coming up the stairs and she wondered if someone might walk into her room as there was no lock on the door. She heard noises out in the street, voices and the sound of cars rattling past on the cobbled streets, and other sounds she didn't recognise. In the orphanage she knew every noise – the coughs, the rattling old pipes, the sound of the door creaking when a nun came into the dormitory. There, she knew exactly what to expect. Here, she was surrounded by strangers and had no idea what might happen next.

She wondered about Molly and whether she was sleeping in the sick room tonight or back in the dormitory. It was strange, she thought, that they might both be sleeping in strange beds on the same night. When she thought of poor Molly and her crackly chest, her eyes filled with tears. Lillian forced them back and buried her face in the soft feather pillow.

She heard a clock in the distance chiming midnight, and sometime later her eyelids began to flutter and eventually closed. She woke several times in the night, and each time felt a sense of alarm, realising where she was. She reached for her bedside lamp and put it on and lay back with her heart beating rapidly. On one occasion she sat up to read two chapters of *Little Women*, which relaxed her and half an hour later she lay back and drifted off to sleep again.

She woke for the final time when the weak autumn sun crept through the crack in the curtains. She lay, staring up at the ceiling, alternately worrying about what would occur on her first full day in this house, and then going over in her mind the events of the day before. She felt she would soon need the toilet, and was wondering if she was allowed to leave the room when she heard the tap on her door. Her aunt came in with a tray with tea and a boiled egg and two slices of toast. Lillian asked if she could use the bathroom first.

Anna nodded. 'I'll leave the tray on your desk,' she whispered, 'and I'll go and get the skirt and jumper I fixed for you last night.'

Lillian went quickly along to the bathroom, and as she came out, she caught sight of a man coming up the stairs, so she stepped back inside and waited for another minute before quickly scurrying to her bedroom.

The navy skirt and jumper, trimmed with navy buttons and pockets, both looked and felt strange on her. Not only were they still big – wide in the shoulders and long in the sleeves – but they looked like something an older, fashionable woman would wear.

'They look fine,' her aunt said. She paused, thinking. 'They were bought in Lewis's, and that's where we're going shopping this morning. Anyone who sees you dressed in these clothes will know we have the money to shop there.' She looked down at Lillian's boots. 'There's nothing we can do about the footwear, as I'm a few sizes bigger than you.' She gave a faint smile. 'I imagine you're not used to wearing heels anyway?'

Lillian, serious-faced, shook her head.

'You don't need to worry, dear. I'll take care of everything when we are shopping. I'll make a little joke of it before anyone has a chance to pass any remarks. I will say we didn't know you were staying the night and you had to borrow my clothes.'

Lillian did not understand the point her aunt was making, but it didn't matter. Her aunt would make all the decisions, and all she had to do was keep quiet and do as she was told. Just as she had done with the nuns.

'And we are lucky having money to shop,' her aunt said, 'because there are many poor people living in Liverpool who have no jobs and who haven't enough to feed their families. I'm sure the nuns were strict and hard on you at times, but at least you had decent food and a bed to sleep in each night, and that's better than a lot of unfortunate children have, isn't it?'

'Yes,' Lillian agreed.

'Have your breakfast, and I'll go and run you a nice hot bath. You don't need to wash your hair because we're going to go to the hairdresser's after we've organised your clothes.' She studied her for a few moments, and then she smiled. 'You're blessed with good thick hair, but it needs a good cut to straighten the ends of it. Some of the hairdressers should be able to fit you in since it's a quiet Monday morning.'

They came downstairs as silently as they had come in the day before, Lillian feeling strange in her aunt's outfit and the pair of beige stockings and garters her aunt had found.

'When we are trying on shoes, you will need stockings. You're too old for socks now.'

When they stepped outside, Lillian had to shield her eyes against the startlingly bright sunshine. It was cold, but somehow the sun seemed to lift her spirits.

Her aunt paused for a few moments, then gave a great sigh as though she had been holding her breath. She checked her hat was straight, then squeezed Lillian's shoulder in a reassuring manner.

'Off we go,' she said, in a high, almost excited voice. 'Lewis's will be opening now, and we'll soon have you looking like a very different girl, like all the other girls in Rodney Street.'

Lillian walked alongside her aunt, already feeling different. After a poor appetite yesterday, she had enjoyed everything this morning. She had also drunk two cups of the nicest-tasting tea she had ever had. Whether it was the food or the sun, or just the freedom of being outside, she definitely felt better.

As they crossed the street, Lillian glanced back at the tall regal house that she would learn to call home. Her aunt's Georgian townhouse looked as impressive as all the rest, the pristine grey-painted door with the white surround, the lace panels on each window sitting perfectly. As she turned away, something caught her eye, and she looked back again to make sure. The lace on one of the bottom windows – the window of the paying guests' sitting room – was pushed aside, and a man was staring out at them.

Lillian suddenly felt self-conscious. She turned away, her cheeks burning. She wondered if she should have mentioned him to her aunt, but something held her back. She had learned at the orphanage that at times it was better to say nothing. Just then, she was distracted when a car came around the corner and they had to move quickly out of the way.

'That corner is getting busier,' Anna said. 'More people seem to be buying cars, so make sure you always look twice before crossing the road.'

Her aunt pointed out the names of the streets as they went along. 'Our house is a quiet part of Liverpool city centre called the Georgian Quarter. When we are all sorted and have time to spare, I'll take you for a walk around the other nice streets in our area. We might have a look at the cathedral which is just behind our house.' She looked at Lillian now and smiled. 'It's a beautiful building, but it's Church of England, so not many Catholics would admit anything beautiful about it, especially the Irish Catholics who tend to think theirs is the only religion.'

Lillian's heart lurched at the suggestion of them going to visit a Protestant cathedral, and was shocked her aunt had mentioned it in such a casual manner. She was also taken aback at her aunt's criticism of Catholics and Ireland, where she said she'd been raised. What the nuns would have to say if they heard she had been near a Protestant cathedral she couldn't begin to imagine. She and her aunt would probably be condemned to the pits of hell.

Her aunt kept up the running commentary on the street names and pointed out places as they went along. 'I suppose this big city must all seem very strange to you after living in one place for so long?'

Lillian thought for a few moments. 'I didn't know what to expect, but I suppose I never realised it was so very big and busy. I read about it in books and I often looked at the city map in one of the classrooms, but it is hard to imagine what it is like in real life. I didn't think how noisy it would be when there are so many cars and lorries.' She saw the dismayed look on Anna's face and then added, 'But I'm sure I'll get to like Liverpool very much...'

Her aunt turned to look at her now, a warm smile on her face. 'Oh, I'm so glad to hear that.' A few moments later she caught Lillian's arm. 'We'll cross the street here, there's someone I know coming up the street, and we haven't time to stand and chat.'

'Hello Anna!' a slim woman with blonde hair cut in a bob, called out. She was around the same age as her aunt, and attractive. Like her aunt, she was dressed well in a red coat and hat, but Lillian thought she was a little more showy.

'How are you? I haven't seen you around for a while?'

Lillian noticed the woman's Irish accent, as it was similar to one of the nun's in the convent. She thought it might be a Dublin accent, but she wasn't sure.

'It's got cold, hasn't it?' The woman slowed to a halt, as though she might cross over to have a chat.

'It is indeed.' Her aunt's voice was bright and cheery but she kept moving, Lillian walking quickly to keep up with her.

'I hope you're keeping well?' the woman called.

'Yes... very well thanks. I'm sorry, but we're in a bit of a rush.'

Her aunt moved her gloved hand upwards in a gesture of farewell. 'She's a nice woman,' she told Lillian, 'but it's the wrong time.'

As they continued down into the city centre, Lillian felt she was on constant watch all the time for something that might catch her unawares. When they approached the shopping area, she was taken aback to see a girl a little younger than herself wheeling a baby in a ramshackle old pram with a broken hood. The girl was dressed in dirty, ragged clothes, and had bare legs – blue with cold – in broken plimsolls and matted, greasy-looking hair. As she passed them by, Lillian noticed there were two children in the pram, which Lillian presumed were her younger siblings: a baby, crudely wrapped in an old, worn blanket, and a boy of maybe two or three, wearing a grubby knitted hat that came down over his ears. He was covered by a man's tweed jacket, the sleeves doubled around him and knotted at the front.

'Oh, God love them,' her aunt muttered in a low voice. 'What life do children like that have? Their families are obviously in dire straits since the Depression or else have useless, drunken sorts that don't look after them.'

Lillian instantly thought of Molly, and the stories she had told about her and her brother, Daniel, when they were under the care of their feckless mother. She turned to look at the be-draggled girl again, who had pulled the ancient pram to a stop at the kerb, in order to cross the road. She was surprised to see the girl smile, and she realised that under normal circumstances she would have been pretty. She watched her as she reached into the pram to tenderly stroke the older boy's face. The girl's affectionate gesture made Lillian suddenly feel like crying. They looked like they had absolutely nothing, but the smile and the touch displayed a genuine love – an emotion Lillian had never felt from anyone since she had entered the orphanage.

'I don't know if you read any news when you were with the nuns,' her aunt whispered, 'but the big financial crash in America affected places like Liverpool very badly. Unemployment has shot up since, and it has affected lots of families like the ones you see around. Some of them were struggling before, so things must be unbearable now.'

The girl rumbled off with the rickety pram, while Lillian was guided by Anna across the road. 'The slump hit everyone,' Anna explained, 'but I was very lucky as I was with employers who were well off. I do my best to donate money to charities that give food to families, and help whenever I can.'

When they reached the department store, her aunt marched directly to the ladies' shoe department, saying they needed the correct footwear before trying on clothes.

'Always remember, Lillian,' she said confidentially, 'that good shoes are the mark of a lady or a gentleman.'

Lillian tried not to look down at her feet, more self-conscious than ever.

Fifteen minutes later, Lillian had tried on over a dozen pairs of boots and shoes, and was now wearing a lovely pair of mid-length, black leather, fur-lined boots with a row of tiny leather buttons going up the side. They had a small heel, which she had imagined would be hard to walk in, but she had never felt anything so comfortable on her feet. Her aunt had also picked out a fancier pair of black patent boots, which she said would be suitable for special occasions. The heels were a little higher, and the assistant suggested that Lillian take her time walking up and down the floor to get used to them. Then her aunt disappeared with the helpful young lady to look at some shelves on the other side of the department, while Lillian went over to a low mirror to check how they looked. A short while later Anna and the assistant came back with half a dozen pairs of slippers for her to try on.

'You will need something comfortable to wear at night or in the morning around the house,' her aunt whispered, guessing that Lillian hadn't worn anything like that before.

A pair of blue velvet slippers was chosen, then her aunt paid for the shoes, and asked the lady to get rid of Lillian's old boots as she would be wearing her new boots home. They left the bags with the patent boots and slippers to be collected at the desk on the way out. As they moved to the ladies' fashion department, Lillian kept glancing down at the beautiful fur-lined boots, thinking that her feet looked so elegant that they looked as though they belonged to someone else. Her aunt found a young sales assistant tidying up a display of sweaters, and had a quiet word with her and then indicated towards Lillian. 'This is my niece, and I want several nice day outfits of skirts and blouses and cardigans, and a good suit. We will also need two coats and hats to compliment them.'

Lillian almost gasped aloud at the list of items her aunt was planning to buy her. It all sounded very expensive, but she had no way of knowing if this was normal or not.

The first few outfits were big on her, but seeing that Anna was prepared to pay for the best, the assistant was determined to find something. 'She is between the children and adult sizes,' the assistant told Anna, 'but I think we might have something in the petite range which would suit.'

She came back with a wine-coloured knitted skirt and a heavy matching wine- and cream-coloured cardigan with pockets. Lillian tried it on in the changing room, and when she looked in the mirror, an elegant young lady whom she hardly recognised looked back at her.

'Perfect,' her aunt said, when she came out. 'We can turn the cuffs back this year, and next winter they will be just right when you have filled out a bit more with Mrs Larking's lovely cooking. Go back in now, like a good girl, and try on the blue woollen dress.'

Lillian felt a little glow at being called 'a good girl'. It was years since she remembered being called that – certainly before the orphanage. The good feeling was brief as her mind was suddenly clouded with the memories. She concentrated on unbuttoning the outfit she was taking off, and then buttoning up the next one. The double-breasted dress fitted her nicely, as did the following outfit – a navy and pink bouclé wool suit with a short jacket trimmed with navy, and a box-pleated skirt. Another dress with a drooping bow at the neck was taken to the pay-desk along with a deep blue dress and matching jacket, followed by a black winter coat with a velvet collar.

As the assistant was wrapping things up, her aunt lifted a cream, tartan-lined Burberry raincoat from a rack and told

Lillian to try it on. It was long in the sleeves, a little wide at the shoulders and came down to her calves.

'It's better to have it slightly big as you will have outgrown the smaller size by next year,' her aunt said. She picked up a tan, canvas hat. 'A good waterproof hat will never go wrong in Liverpool, and will save ruining your felt hats.' She walked quickly over to a stand full of silk scarves and came back holding a square Burberry headscarf, with a cream, beige and light red check printed on it, and told Lillian to try it on.

Lillian felt strange as she placed the hat on her head, as she had never worn one before. She remembered wearing knitted hats and straw bonnets with ribbons as a child, but had never worn a hat or a scarf like the one her aunt handed her. She put the silk square around her neck and then just stood, looking and feeling awkward.

Her aunt stepped forward. 'Let's just see...' She took the scarf and quickly folded it on the diagonal until it was a long, thinner shape, and then she put it around Lillian's neck, checking that both ends hung evenly. She tied the ends together and then stood back, and then she came close again to fiddle around with it until it was tied in a double-knot.

She took a few steps backwards and stood appraisingly, with her arms folded and her eyes narrowed in thought. After a few moments she smiled. 'Perfect! The coat is fine on you and the hat and scarf really lift it.' She moved forward to squeeze her niece's arm. 'You look lovely.'

'Do I?' Lillian said, her voice uncertain. She looked down at the coat and the beautiful boots and felt even more uncertain.

'Come over to the mirror,' her aunt said, guiding her towards a corner where she could clearly see herself without anyone else viewing them. They both walked over and then Anna put her hands on Lillian's shoulders and moved her in front of the full-length mirror.

'Just look at yourself,' she said in a low, excited voice. 'You're like a different girl altogether. No one from the convent school would know you at all.' She paused, her face crumpling as

47

though she might cry. 'And more importantly, looking at you now, no one would know you had ever been in such a . . . in such a place.'

Lillian looked at her reflection, and thought she looked like a younger version of her aunt.

'Turn around,' Anna instructed. 'Let me see how it looks from the back and the front.'

Lillian did as she was told, the movement making her feel dizzy. Then, as she came back to stare at herself in the mirror again, a strange feeling washed over her. She didn't look like herself, nor did she feel like herself inside. It was as though she had lost all sense of who she was and where her place in the world now was.

Her aunt went back over to give the coat and things to the sales assistant. 'I'll be back in a few minutes to pay for these things; we're just going to the lingerie department to pick up a few items.'

However awkward she had felt putting on the outer clothes, Lillian was excruciatingly embarrassed when she was inside a changing room with a curtain, with a lady measuring her chest with a tape.

'So you have never worn a brassiere before?' the lady said, when she saw Lillian's grey vest.

'No . . .' Lillian said.

'You're a well-developed girl,' the assistant said, 'and quite a few of the modern young ladies in Liverpool are beginning to wear them now.'

Lillian had never worn a brassiere before, nor had she even seen one apart from in her aunt's magazines. The assistant went off to find her size and she stood there, her arms crossed over her bare chest, blinking back tears.

A few minutes later her aunt came to the curtain. 'I have some nice items you might like to try on. Do you need any help to check they are the right size?'

'No . . . no,' Lillian said quickly. Covering herself with the curtain, she stretched an arm out and took four brassieres from her aunt – two white and two in a pale peach colour.

'Choose two that are comfortable,' her aunt said. 'That will do you for the time being.'

Lillian set them down on the table, and then lifted one up to study it and work out how she might put it on. It was plain white cotton edged with lace. It was, she thought, quite delicate and lovely. She put one arm through the straps then the other, and after fiddling around for a while, she managed to get the hooks in the correct place. Two of the brassieres were quite loose in the cups, so she picked a white and a peach which seemed a reasonable fit to her.

By the time she was dressed and back out on the shop floor, her aunt informed her that she had picked several other necessary items: two pairs of jersey pyjamas, a long pale blue nightdress with a short matching bed-jacket, six pairs of lace-edged knickers and four pairs of stockings. Lillian was almost lost for words. 'It must be very expensive...' she ventured.

Anna glanced around her to make sure no one was listening. 'You need to have all the right things,' she said, smiling warmly at her. 'You're a growing girl with a woman's figure, so there's no point in buying you children's things.'

As Lillian watched her aunt talking to the saleswoman and arranging for the parcels to be delivered to the house in the afternoon, she saw a glimmer of excitement in her aunt's eyes, as though she seemed happier and elevated by all the shopping. She had enjoyed buying everything, and didn't look like someone who was concerned by the price of things. Money seemed to be no object to her, and it made Lillian wonder where it had come from.

Her mother, from what she could remember, was not very poor and they had always had food. Her mother had always been fussy about things like speaking properly and keeping clean in both the home and in personal appearance, but she couldn't have imagined her mother having the money to shop so freely in a shop like Lewis's.

As she waited, she saw her aunt pick up the Burberry raincoat, a dress and the scarf and hat. 'Lillian will change into these now,' she said, smiling at the assistant. She beckoned Lillian and told her to go into the changing room and put them on. When she came out, her aunt was waiting nearby and she took the other clothes from her.

She looked Lillian up and down. 'Don't you look lovely now?' she said approvingly. She checked her watch. 'Time for the hairdressing salon now.'

The salon was quiet as Anna had anticipated, and they only had to wait ten minutes until one of the ladies was free. While they waited, Anna picked up magazines for them to look through. She held out one to Lillian which was filled with pictures of hairstyles.

'What do you think?' her aunt asked. 'Would you like a completely new style or are you happy with the way your hair is now?'

'I don't know… whatever you think.'

'We might let the hairdresser decide,' Anna said.

Half an hour later Lillian came out with her long hair shining, and three inches shorter. The hairdresser said she had good, thick hair but wondered what kind of shampoo she had been using, as it was dull and tangled underneath. Lillian had just shrugged, as she didn't want to admit that she had never used shampoo and was lucky if she had found a sliver of soap to use on it in the orphanage. Occasionally, if Molly was working in the laundry, she would steal the ends of the bars of soap and put them inside her boot to share with Lillian later.

'She is a lucky girl to have such pretty looks, and good strong, healthy hair,' the hairdresser told Anna, 'so I just took a few inches off the end to even it off.'

Lillian blushed, unused to being the focus of attention. She noticed that when her aunt paid the lady and then received her change, that she gave her an extra coin as a tip. She wondered if the hairdresser said nice things to all the customers, and thought it must be worthwhile if everyone gave her a little extra for it.

By the time they got up to the tearoom it was getting busy. Lillian felt more relaxed now, as she didn't look so very different from her aunt any more. The clothes were already making her feel like a different person.

Her aunt studied the menu. 'I think we will just have soup and a sandwich, as we have a cooked meal in the evening. Is that okay with you?'

Lillian said it sounded lovely, amazed at being consulted over what she ate.

A short while later, a waitress, in a black dress with a white frilly apron and cap, arrived at their table to open out the large linen napkins and place them in their laps. She went away and a few minutes later arrived with their food on a tray. The soup was thick with chicken, potatoes, carrots and onions, and bore no resemblance to the thin, barely coloured liquid with the odd vegetable floating around that she was used to.

It was served with a large, crusty bread roll filled with cheese, tomatoes and lettuce. When she started eating, Lillian found she was much hungrier than she had thought. The food was delicious and she had to keep telling herself to slow down; she was gulping it quickly, as though afraid someone might come and snatch it away from her.

When they came out into the cold but bright afternoon, Lillian could see herself and her aunt reflected in the glass, moving along with all the other people around them: the businessmen, the women shopping, the older girls linking arms and chattering and laughing. People leading vibrant and purposeful lives – and she didn't look different to them any more.

'We'll walk home a different way,' Anna said, 'through the city centre, to let you see the shops.' As they crossed over to Duke Street, they passed a music shop and Lillian could hear a piano being played. The music was lively and cheery – unlike the serious hymns that Sister Agnes played on the piano in the convent. The sound suddenly made her smile, lifting her spirits yet further, and made her think that there were some very good things about living in the middle of a city.

Just last night she had lain in bed wishing she was back within the familiarity of the orphanage walls. Today, out and about in this big new world, she found she wasn't so nostalgic for the place she had left behind. Lillian could now see what she had been missing all those years, cooped up with the cruel and unfeeling nuns.

The unfamiliar sound of a ship's horn blowing loudly as it entered the docks suddenly startled her. She looked anxiously at her aunt, and said, 'What's that noise?'

'Oh, you will get used to that,' Anna said, smiling at her. 'It's just a ferry coming into the port. We might take a walk down there on the next fine day.' She squeezed Lillian's arm. 'I'm going to enjoy showing you all the lovely, interesting places in Liverpool.'

They walked on a little further until her aunt came to a halt outside a baker's shop. The left-hand side of the window was filled with an array of pies: pork pies, meat and potato pies, beef and onion pies, and various others. The right-hand side was filled with bread and rolls, and the middle was filled with pastries and cakes.

'I think it would be nice,' her aunt said, 'if we had some cakes tonight for both the paying guests and the staff in the house. Something a little special to mark your arrival.'

Lillian gave a little smile. Although she was nervous about meeting people, she would do whatever her aunt wanted.

Chapter Six

As they walked towards the house, both carrying large cake boxes, Anna turned towards her. 'When we go inside, I am going to take you into the guests' drawing room and introduce you. I'll tell them that you are my niece, who has come to live with me, as we have recently lost your mother who was my older sister. I'll say we are too upset to talk about it. This means that you won't have to explain anything about the convent or where you were.'

Lillian slowly nodded her head, noticing that her aunt was now referring to the orphanage as a convent all the time.

'Sometimes people ask very personal questions that they wouldn't be prepared to answer if they were asked the very same things,' Anna explained. 'You are entitled to your privacy ... and so am I. Just remember, Lillian, you are to give no information about yourself or your background. Do not mention anything about your mother or me coming from Ireland, either. It grieves me to say, Irish people do not always have the best reputation in Liverpool. I have done my best to fit in – I had lessons in English grammar and pronunciation so my Irish accent isn't very noticeable. I've always had very high standards, and I intend to keep things that way. Do you understand?'

'Yes,' she said. Her aunt had been very clear.

As they mounted the steps, Lillian felt the apprehension of the previous day descend on her again. She followed her aunt through the door.

'We'll take the cakes down to the kitchen,' her aunt said over her shoulder, her voice now lighter, 'and we can introduce you to Mr and Mrs Larking. Nan does most of the cooking in the house and Michael looks after the house and gardens. We also have a young maid called Lucy, and an older woman called Miss Magill who comes in several times a week to do laundry and change the beds.'

Lillian followed her, thinking how strange it was that she now lived in a place where staff did the sort of menial cleaning work that she herself had done in the orphanage.

As they passed by the open door of the guests' living room, a man in a dark suit came quickly out. Lillian immediately recognised him as the man who had been watching them from the window as they left this morning. She had a feeling that he might have been watching for their return.

'Ah, Mrs Ainsley,' he said, smiling at Anna. 'I was looking for you earlier...' He turned towards Lillian, his smile broader now, showing his teeth. 'Oh, I see you have company. I apologise for interrupting you. Maybe I could have a few words with you later, when you are free?'

'Of course,' Anna said, smiling back at him. 'This is my niece, Lillian, who will be staying here with me for a while. I was planning to bring her into the guests' sitting room in a few minutes to introduce her to anyone who is here.'

'Oh, your niece... indeed.' He took a small step back as though to get a better view of her, then he stretched his hand out. 'Such a pleasure to meet you, Lillian.'

'This is Mr Guthrie,' her aunt said.

Lillian carefully transferred the cakebox to her left hand, and then moved her right hand slowly towards him. She couldn't remember anyone shaking her hand before, and was conscious of her aunt watching them, and she hoped she was doing the right thing. When he took her hand in his, she felt his tight grip, almost crushing her fingers. She allowed him to shake it for a few moments, then pulled her hand back.

'If you don't mind, we must get on now,' her aunt said briskly, 'I need to have a word with Mrs Larking about dinner this evening.' She quickly turned on her heel and moved down the hallway.

Lillian followed her aunt, aware that Mr Guthrie was still standing, watching them, and she felt relieved when they were out of his sight. They went down some stairs and along another corridor. As she went along, Lillian could smell something sweet and lovely baking.

'The kitchen is in the basement,' her aunt said as they went down a further set of plain stone steps. 'And our maid, Lucy, has her room down here too. The Larkings have their own house on the other side of the city. They already know about you coming, so there's no need for us to explain anything to them.'

Lillian walked into the cinnamon-scented kitchen behind her aunt, feeling very self-conscious. When the small, stocky, soft-featured woman working over by the sink turned towards them, Lillian felt her spirits lift. The woman had a welcoming smile on her face and a warmth in her eyes.

'Mrs Larking,' Anna said, 'this is Lillian.'

'Oh, lovely to meet you, my dear!' Mrs Larking said, in a strong, Liverpool accent.

'Hello, Mrs Larking,' Lillian said, putting the cake box down on the big scrubbed pine table. She stood for a few moments, uncertain what to do.

The cook quickly dried her hands on a rough towel, then came over to greet her. 'I've heard all about you, and I've been looking forward to meeting you.' She gave a big smile and shook her head. 'What a pretty girl you are! And that lovely long hair!'

She took one of Lillian's hands in both of hers, and Lillian thought they felt like two warm little cushions.

'Oh, you're cold!' Mrs Larking exclaimed, taking her other hand as well. 'Can I get you a nice hot cup of tea?'

'Tea would be lovely,' Anna said. 'We bought some cakes for you and Michael and Lucy, and another box for the guests upstairs. Would you mind putting them on plates and bringing them upstairs for us when you have time?'

It occurred to Lillian that food wasn't scarce here, as it was in the orphanage where the girls felt hungry every single day. She was reluctant to leave the warm, fragrant kitchen and the friendly cook, and felt apprehensive about meeting the guests upstairs.

As they turned to go out, the back door opened and a girl not much older than Lillian came in carrying a box of vegetables. She was wearing a plain black coat and a knitted hat pulled down over her ears. Anna introduced her as Lucy, the house-maid, and although she seemed shy and a little awkward, Lillian immediately liked her.

Anna asked Lucy if the greengrocer's shop had been busy, and Lucy answered in a strong Liverpool accent, her curious eyes flitting back to Lillian ever so often.

'Now, Lillian,' her aunt said, as they went back upstairs. 'I have a short letter to write, and then we'll come back down for tea.'

When she was alone in her bedroom, Lillian took off her new hat and coat and hung them up in the wardrobe, and as she closed the door, she checked herself in the mirror. The blue dress and the boots were lovelier than she remembered from the shop, and she found herself smiling at her much-improved reflection.

She took the brush from the silver set on her dressing table and smoothed down her glossy, wind-blown hair. She wandered to the window to look down on the street again. The afternoon sky had dulled to a dark grey, and she noticed lights appearing in some of the houses. She stood for a few minutes, wondering about the people living behind the other doors. As she stared down, her mind flitted back to the orphanage and she wondered what the other girls were doing. Chores before the scanty even-ing meal: washing, scrubbing, polishing, dusting, ironing. She wondered what Molly was doing and how she was managing without her, and her eyes misted over. Then she noticed a move-ment down in one of the houses opposite, and saw a boy staring straight up at her window, smiling and waving. She remembered seeing him the day before, when she had just arrived.

Lillian caught her breath, and stepped to the side of the

window, using the curtain to shield her. Had she imagined it . . . or had he really been waving at *her*?

After a while, she leaned forward to discreetly look out again, and there he was, still standing and still looking up at the window. She heard a noise out in the hallway and she quickly moved to sit down at her desk. A few seconds later her aunt tapped on the door for them to go downstairs.

As they went, Anna said, 'You have no need to feel nervous about meeting the guests. When you are introduced, if they say, "How do you do?" you just smile and say, "How do you do?" back to them.'

'What if they don't say anything?' Lillian asked. The nuns and visitors at the orphanage often treated her and the other girls as though they were invisible.

'They are nice people and will make some gesture of being polite to you. I am the landlady and you are my niece, and they are staying under our roof.' She reached for Lillian's hand and gave it a little squeeze. 'You look like a fine young lady in your new outfit,' she whispered, 'and will be treated as such. Just remember first impressions are lasting impressions.'

Lillian looked down at her new boots without saying anything.

'If you are not sure about how to eat the cake, just watch and copy me.' She lowered her voice. 'And keep in mind that *you* are every bit as important as any of the people you are going to meet. So, shoulders back, and smile, smile, smile.'

Lillian felt her head whirling from all the advice. She wondered how she could be in any way important compared to an adult. She might be wearing an expensive dress and boots, and her hair might look the best it ever had, but underneath it all, she was still an orphan, and the same as all the other girls like Molly, who were still stuck behind the high walls of the orphanage.

A tight feeling came into her chest and moved upwards to her throat. She put her hand up to the neck of her dress, and tried to ease it out a little to let her breathe more easily. She felt hot and suddenly thought that she needed fresh air. She looked down the hallway towards the front door, imagining herself breaking free from her aunt and running towards it to escape. But where would she escape to? Back to the nuns? The thought of the orphanage made her feel equally claustrophobic. She closed her eyes as they walked along, then, as they reached the drawing room, she took a long, deep breath to calm her racing heart.

Anna looked back and smiled at her. 'Okay?' she mouthed.

Lillian nodded, then remembered what her aunt had said earlier. She pushed her shoulders back and followed her inside.

Chapter Seven

The guests' drawing room was large, with three tall windows dressed with green velvet curtains and pelmets decorated with gold cord and tassels. It was as big as some of the rooms the nuns used in the convent, but this looked and felt warm and inviting. To the left was a long, dark, polished table with eight chairs around it, and a tall silver candelabra in the middle of it. There was a long black sideboard, the doors inlaid with oval panels of delicately painted birds and branches. On its marble top stood a deep silver dish filled with a variety of fruit.

On the opposite wall hung an oil painting depicting a hunting scene. To the right of the room was the sitting area where the guests gathered around the open fire in armchairs or sofas. Chandeliers, similar to the ones upstairs, hung over both the sitting and dining areas.

The guests all looked up when Anna and Lillian entered. There were two women – one thin and serious-looking, with curly fair hair in a bun, and the other one, younger, pleasant-faced and curvier, with dark hair loosely tied back. Lillian noticed that the fair lady, wearing spectacles low down on her nose, was reading a book, whilst the younger lady was engaged with a piece of embroidery.

Opposite them were two smartly dressed men both reading newspapers. And Lillian was dismayed to note that the older one was the man she had met earlier – Mr Guthrie. They were all sitting around the white marble fireplace, which had a cheery coal fire burning. The ladies perched in high-backed, tapestry-covered armchairs, whilst the men were at either side of a large, leather Chesterfield sofa on which were placed green velvet cushions, trimmed with the same gold cord as the curtains. In front of the fire there was a long coffee table which had a neat display of periodicals, a silver box holding playing cards, and a dictionary for crosswords.

'Good afternoon,' Anna said, smiling at them. 'I hope you don't mind me interrupting, but I thought it might be a good time to introduce a new member of the household.' She turned to bring Lillian forward so everyone could see her, placing a protective arm around the girl's shoulders.

'Ladies, I would like you to meet my niece, Lillian Taylor.' She indicated towards the lady who had been reading the book. 'Lillian, this is Miss Jane Dixon, and the lady next to her is Miss Rose Moran.' The two women laid aside the reading material and the sewing, and both smiled and said, 'How do you do, Lillian.'

Her aunt looked at her expectantly and Lillian suddenly remembered what she had been told. She gave the biggest smile she could muster, and replied, 'How do you do?'

Anna then approached the men, saying, 'Mr Guthrie, you were of course introduced to Lillian earlier this afternoon.'

'Indeed I was,' he said, nodding and raising his eyebrows. 'And it was a great pleasure to meet her.'

Lillian could feel his eyes on her, and she directed her gaze down to the beautifully decorated Persian rug at her feet.

Anna turned her attention to the other, younger man. 'Mr Collins, I would like you to meet my niece, Lillian Taylor.'

Mr Collins stood up and gave a little bow and said, 'How do you do, my dear?' His warm sincere smile made Lillian feel more relaxed, and she found herself smiling back easily at him as she returned his greeting.

'I have arranged a late afternoon treat of cakes, as a little welcome for her,' Anna told the guests. 'And Mrs Larking will bring tea up to us soon.' She turned to her niece. 'Lillian, would you mind going down to the kitchen to let her know that we are ready?'

When Lillian had gone, Anna went over to close the door and returned to the middle of the room. She clasped her hands together. 'I think it would help everyone if I gave you some brief details about my niece's situation.' She paused for a few moments. 'Lillian lost her widowed mother recently – my sister – and was living some distance away under the care of a family guardian who organised her education in a convent boarding school. On a recent visit, I discovered she wasn't happy in the school, and after giving it some thought, I decided she was mature enough to leave school, and I have brought her home to live with me.'

'The poor girl,' Mr Collins said. 'You did the right thing.'

The two ladies nodded and made similar comments.

Mr Guthrie chimed in, 'That is very commendable of you, and you must have been upset to know that she was unhappy and her guardian didn't get in touch with you before.'

Anna stiffened up. 'It was rather complicated, Mr Guthrie. Everyone did what we thought was best.' She lowered her voice. 'I think I have said enough about Lillian, and I know you will all respect my wishes.'

'Of course, of course...' Miss Moran said. 'We wouldn't dream of saying anything out of place.' Mr Guthrie inclined his head. 'Have you thought about continuing her education?'

Anna glanced towards the door. 'She has had enough of school, Mr Guthrie, and I think it would be best for her to be at home with family.' She held a hand up. 'But I do intend to organise some private tuition for her in certain subjects.'

There was a tap on the door and when Anna quickly went across to open it, Lillian was standing there holding a silver tray with the cakes on it. A red-faced Mrs Larking was just behind her.

'I didn't ask her to carry the cakes,' Mrs Larking said, all flustered. 'She insisted and was away with them before I could stop her.'

'I was coming back up to the drawing room,' Lillian said, 'and it saves Mrs Larking making another trip.'

Anna looked from one to the other. 'Well, it's very kind of you to help, Lillian,' she said. 'Put the cakes down in the middle of the table, please, and Mrs Larking will organise the china for serving tea.'

The two female guests moved to their usual seats at the dining table, and helped Mrs Larking and Lillian to set each place with the necessary china and cake forks. When the table was complete the men moved to join them.

Mr Collins surveyed the table with the long silver plate holding the selection of fresh cream puffs, chocolate eclairs, custard slices and meringues. 'Well, isn't this a lovely unexpected treat?'

Mrs Larking offered Lillian her choice of cake first. Her face and neck flushed as she looked at all the beautiful pastries, unable to decide. Eventually, she chose a pink concoction with cream and strawberry sauce and slivers of fresh fruit.

'Could I have the pink one please?' Her voice sounded crackly and nervous.

'The meringue?' Anna checked.

Lillian hesitated, having never heard the name before. She bit her lip as she scanned the plate. There were only two pink ones – both identical. 'Yes, please,' she whispered.

Mrs Larking slid the meringue onto her plate.

'You have a pastry fork there with your dessert spoon, don't you?' her aunt asked, and when Lillian looked down at the small fork alongside a matching spoon she realised that was what it was. 'Yes,' she said quickly, 'I do...'

Anna smiled and gave a little conspiratorial wink. When everyone was settled with their chosen cake and a cup of tea, the atmosphere suddenly seemed to relax and a murmur of conversation took over.

Lillian lifted her fork, unsure how to start eating. Through lowered eyelids, she glanced at the others and saw that they were using their forks. She gave a quick dart over at her aunt, and noticed that Anna had the other meringue on her plate.

She guessed she had deliberately chosen it to help her out, and watched how she used her fork to cut the hard crispy shell and then use it to push the dessert onto the spoon. She carefully copied her aunt's movements.

When she put the first spoonful of meringue into her mouth, Lillian thought it was the most delicious thing she had ever eaten. She savoured it, and then after a few moments she took another spoonful. Already, she had eaten more food today than she usually ate in two or three days. She wondered if she would ever get used to it.

Anna smiled over at Miss Moran. 'Rose, I see you're reading the new Agatha Christie novel,' she said. 'It's called *The Secret Chimneys* or something like that, isn't it?'

'You're very close – it's *The Secret of Chimneys*.'

'I must remember that. Is it as good as her others?'

Miss Moran nodded enthusiastically. 'It's excellent. Her books just seem to get better. When it was first published, we had to order in six copies as we had a huge waiting list for it.'

Anna turned to Lillian. 'Miss Moran works in the main city library. I thought when we get time, we might take a walk down and enrol you as a member.' She looked back at the librarian. 'I'm sure Lillian would find it very interesting.'

'Do you enjoy reading, Lillian?'

'Yes,' she said. 'I love books...'

'And what would be your preference?'

There was a silence, during which Lillian looked very serious. As Anna watched her, she wondered exactly what sort of an education Lillian had received during her years in the orphanage. She realised that she had not asked her anything about her time there. It was something she couldn't even bear to think about, and she preferred to view it as a convent boarding school.

'I liked *Little Women* and the books which followed the sisters when they grew up,' she said, 'and I very much enjoyed Charles Dickens's books, such as *Oliver Twist* and *Little Dorrit*, and I want to read more.'

'Excellent choices,' Miss Moran said. 'We have a whole section of Dickens's books.'

Mr Guthrie straightened up in his chair. 'Don't you think they are a little radical for an impressionable young girl?'

'Not at all,' Miss Moran said. 'They are both entertaining and educational.'

Lillian's first impression of the librarian had been right, she decided. She was cheery and interesting, and not afraid to voice her opinions.

'I'm not so sure,' Mr Guthrie replied. 'I think some of his writing gives rise to all sorts of ideas. Literature can be used as a vehicle for subversive ideas.'

Although she didn't understand all that Mr Guthrie was saying, and although he smiled a lot, Lillian thought he had similar ideas to some of the nuns.

'In my opinion,' the librarian said, 'Mr Dickens sheds a light on aspects of life that are not usually written about because they make people feel uncomfortable. He presents the good and bad in people from all walks of life. I particularly like the fact that his female characters are often strong and capable, unlike some of the other writers who show them as simpering and less worthy than men. I think Charles Dickens has an admirable social conscience.' She looked across the table at Lillian and smiled.

Mr Guthrie slowly nodded his head, then gave a sidelong smile. 'Well ... not everyone shares your political stance, Miss Moran. And it has been rumoured that he didn't always treat the women in his life too well.'

Mr Collins suddenly cut in. 'If you don't mind me joining in with the conversation, I would have to agree with Miss Moran. Politics and personal life aside, Charles Dickens is a fine writer, with a great talent for description.'

Anna moved her chair back, quite taken aback by Lillian's confident answers and impressed by the books she had mentioned.

'If you will excuse me, I must go as I heard a delivery van

outside.' She had heard enough of the discussion now to satisfy her that her niece was a bright young girl, and that going to the library would be a good pastime for her. She went towards the door, then she stopped and looked back at Lillian. 'When you have finished, dear, come up to my room.'

Anna went off, pleased that Lillian had done so well. Nervous though she was, she had managed the messy meringue and had done better than Mr Guthrie, who had dropped a piece of his custard slice down his tie.

There was a small silence after the house owner left the room, then Mr Guthrie looked over at the librarian again. 'In my younger days,' he said, 'it wasn't quite the thing to borrow books from a public library. There was the fear of catching germs and diseases from the books.'

'I've never heard such a thing,' Miss Moran said.

'If you say so,' Mr Guthrie said, raising his eyebrows.

Miss Dixon, who had remained silent during the discussion, suddenly stood up. 'If you will excuse me, I have a letter to write.' She turned to Lillian. 'Lovely to meet you, my dear, and I look forward to a discussion with you about *Little Women* – it was one of my favourite books when I was your age.'

Lillian smiled and thanked her.

'That was a lovely treat,' Miss Moran said, putting her spoon down on her plate. We are lucky to have such a nice landlady.'

'I suppose you get what you pay for,' Mr Guthrie said, 'and we are in one of the best streets in Liverpool.' He craned his neck to look out of the window, and pushed his chair back. 'If you will excuse me ...' he said, wandering over to stand at the window.

Lillian finished the last mouthful of meringue. She touched the napkin to her lips as she had watched the other women do. She excused herself to the nice Miss Moran and Mr Collins and then she went out into the hallway.

As she went along, she was conscious of footsteps coming behind her. She looked over her shoulder and saw Mr Guthrie.

'I see your aunt did a lot of shopping in Lewis's earlier today,' he said, catching up with her. 'Did she treat you to anything nice?'

Lillian felt flustered and not sure what to say. 'Sorry, but I am in a rush,' she said. 'My aunt will be waiting for me upstairs.'

He touched her arm, drawing her to a halt. 'Before you go... could you just confirm something for me? It's been niggling away since this morning.' He leaned in closely to her and whispered something in her ear.

Lillian's face paled, and she drew away sharply from him. 'My aunt is waiting for me.'

'I hope I haven't offended you, my dear?' he said. 'I was simply curious...' The sound of heels tapping down the stairs stopped Mr Guthrie in his tracks.

They both looked up to see Anna coming towards them. 'Lillian?' she said, a note of concern in her voice.

'I'm coming now,' Lillian said, going quickly towards her aunt.

Mr Guthrie turned away and headed back towards the drawing room.

'Are you okay?' Anna said. 'You look a bit pale.'

'I'm fine.'

A frown appeared between her dark, well-shaped eyebrows. 'What did Mr Guthrie say to you?' She moved closer and put her arm around her niece, guiding her back down the hallway.

'Did he say something personal to you – or ask you an improper question?' She said in a heated whisper. 'If you don't tell me, Lillian, I shall have to go and ask him myself, which will be much more awkward.'

Lillian's shoulders drooped and she looked down at the floor. 'He asked me... he asked me if I was the same girl he saw coming into the house yesterday evening and going out of the house early with you this morning...'

Her aunt waited.

'He said he was curious because I'm dressed so elegantly now, and yet he was sure he saw me wearing...' she stopped, shaking now, 'he saw me wearing strange-looking, clumpy boots and very different clothes to the ones I came back in.' She took a deep breath. 'He said that I was a lucky girl coming to live with you because he saw the delivery man coming in. He said you must have bought half of Lewis's, and he was sure some of them must be for me.'

Anna closed her eyes and shook her head. 'That bloody man . . .'

Lillian was shocked at her swearing.

'Did you tell him anything?'

'No. I thought it was best to say nothing.' Her face crumpled. 'I know it was a kind of lie . . . a sin of omission, but . . .' She shrugged and tears suddenly filled her eyes.

'Come on now, we will go up to my room.'

They walked up the stairs and down towards Anna's bedroom. When she opened the door, Anna saw the huge pile of boxes and bags that Mr Guthrie had referred to.

Her aunt turned to her now, and said in a soft tone. 'You have committed no sins whatsoever, Lillian. *You* are the one who has been sinned against by various people. Nothing that has happened is your fault.'

Lillian was confused by her aunt saying that many people had sinned against her, and she wondered whom she was referring to.

Her aunt walked over to stand by the window. 'I'll speak to Mr Guthrie later, and I'll make sure nothing like this happens again. If he says another wrong word to you, he can find new lodgings.'

Lillian felt her stomach churn at the thought of the accountant being turned out of the house. From what had been said, he was unlikely to find a place as good. 'I wouldn't like to think it was my fault, that he lost his home because of me . . .'

Her aunt suddenly whirled around. 'For God's sake, Lillian! Will you stop saying things are your fault! The blasted man has crossed me on a number of occasions, and he needs putting in his place.'

Lillian took a step back, her head drooping.

'Oh, I'm sorry for being so cross,' Anna said. She put her arm around Lillian. 'Don't worry, we will sort this, and hopefully without me throwing Mr Guthrie's bags out into the street.'

'The others were all very nice,' Lillian said, 'especially Miss Moran and Mr Collins.'

'Yes, they are both very sociable and polite. Miss Dixon is more reserved, but she is a nice woman, and a clever one. Do you know what she does for a living? She works in a watch-maker's business in town. She is the person who checks the quality and standard of workmanship of the finished watches. Isn't that an interesting and unusual occupation for a woman?'

Lillian agreed it was, but she admitted she knew little about watches.

'I would be lost without mine,' Anna said, smiling now. 'Who knows, you might get one as a special Christmas gift.'

Lillian smiled back, although she didn't feel she deserved anything more, and couldn't imagine owning or wanting such an expensive item as a wristwatch.

'Okay!' her aunt said now. 'Let's get all these boxes and bags opened and we'll have a little fashion show. I want to see how beautiful you look in your new clothes.'

Half an hour later, after hanging all her lovely clothes in the wardrobe, and putting the smaller items in her chest of drawers, Lillian suddenly felt very tired, and was glad to be on her own in her bedroom. It was just after five o'clock, and her aunt said she would call her at around half past six, to join her for dinner in their private sitting room.

Lillian took her boots off and lay down on top of the bed, drawing only the counterpane over her. As she lay in the silence of her room gazing up at the decorative ceiling, she went over the day's events in her mind. When she remembered the poor, grubby-looking girl with the pram, a sadness washed over her.

Her thoughts turned to Molly again. Memories of her friend were clear, but there was already now a greater distance between herself and Gethsemane House than just the few miles that separated them. When she tried to picture the building and the dormitories, it was now as though she was looking back at it through a fog. In only a day, the house here in Rodney Street seemed more familiar to her.

She drifted off into a sleep, during which she dreamed her mother had turned up at the door of her new house. Lillian had come downstairs, overwhelmed with happiness at seeing her mother again, but her mother hardly seemed to notice her. 'Will I get Aunt Anna?' Lillian had asked. For the first time in years, she could see her mother's face quite clearly. She looked lovely but older than she had thought.

'No,' her mother had said. 'Anna should never have brought you here. This house is no place for a daughter of mine.'

Mr Guthrie had intervened. 'Are you taking the girl back to the orphanage? If you are, she will require the boots and clothes that she came in. The girl must leave as she arrived. First impressions are lasting impressions.'

'I am taking her back to where she belongs.'

'And where exactly does she belong?' Mr Guthrie had wanted to know.

'Who are you to ask?' her mother had said quietly. 'Where do you belong? Where does everyone in this house belong?'

Her mother had then reached out for Lillian's hand. As Lillian moved forward to take it, her mother suddenly started to fade away, back into the mist.

'Wait for me,' Lillian called. 'Take me home with you...'

It was then that she had wakened and looked around her.

'Lillian?' her aunt's voice called from outside. 'If you are ready, Mrs Larking has brought our meal up.'

It was obvious to Anna that there was something wrong when they sat down to eat. She left it for a while, but when she saw Lillian was only picking at the cottage pie, she put her cutlery down on the plate and asked. 'Is everything all right?'

Lillian put her knife and fork down too, and looked across at her aunt. 'I must have fallen asleep for a little while, and I had a strange dream about my mother...'

'Oh,' Anna said, looking surprised by the statement. 'I suppose dreams can be very disconcerting...'

'I haven't dreamt about her for years. I had forgotten what she looked like. In the dream, I could see her face clearly. I don't think you look like her.'

Anna bit her lip for a few moments. 'I have never really thought about it. There was such a big age gap between us...' She went to lift her knife and fork again.

'Were you close to her?'

'In all honesty, no. She moved over to Liverpool when I was young, and I only saw her once or twice when she came back to Ireland. That happens to many families.'

'When did you move from Ireland to Liverpool?' Lillian asked. 'The way you speak doesn't sound like the way my mother did.'

'I left Ireland a long time ago, and I lived in London for years. All my – our – family in Ireland are gone, either dead like your mother or emigrated to America. There are only distant cousins whom I hardly knew, so there is no one there to go back to. I think of England as my home, and it has made me the person I am now.' She halted. 'I don't like to discuss my personal life, as at times I find it hurtful going over the past. But there is something I wanted you to know, and I was going to tell you soon... I was married for some years, but sadly my husband died early last year.'

Lillian looked at her. 'I'm sorry...' she said, 'I didn't know.'

'Well, how could you? But I am conscious that some of the guests or even the staff are likely to mention it, and that's why I am telling you.' She indicated around the room with her hand. 'This was his house, and where we lived. I inherited it after he died. As you can see, it's a big house to run, and expensive, so that's why I take in paying guests.'

'What was his name?' Lillian asked.

'Edward... Edward Ainsley.'

A look crossed Lillian's face and Anna anticipated her next

question. 'As I explained, I lived most of my adult life in London – this house in Liverpool was quite a recent idea of Edward's – and no one had my address when your mother died. That's why I didn't know what had happened to you.'

Lillian fell silent.

'I know all these changes must be hard for you, Lillian, but looking back will only make things harder. It's best to leave the past behind.'

'I was thinking about my friend, Molly,' Lillian said. 'You said I might be able to visit her.'

'The girl in the convent?'

Lillian nodded.

'I'm not sure the nuns would be happy for you to visit yet. It's a bit soon after your leaving, and I had to really put pressure on Mother Superior to let you come with me. I don't think she would be inclined to do any favours for us so soon... Maybe if we leave it for a while.'

'Some of the girls have relatives who collect them and take them out on a Saturday or Sunday,' Lillian ventured. 'If the nuns don't want us to visit, could we bring Molly here?' In truth, she only knew of two girls it had happened to, but it showed it was possible.

'Here?' Anna repeated. 'Bring her here to the house?' Anna was silent then as she weighed up the situation. She knew things weren't going to be plain sailing having Lillian to live with her in Rodney Street. She had thought that a clean break from the orphanage was the only way, but maybe she had been naive. Not everyone adapted to new surroundings as easily as she herself had done when she was younger. Maybe one visit might make all the difference between her settling or not. The idea of getting in touch with the nuns again wasn't one that Anna relished. She only hoped that Molly was reasonably presentable so that if they took her out, she wouldn't draw too much attention to them. 'Let me think about it...'

The shocked look on her aunt's face was evident, and Lillian instantly realised a visit to the house wouldn't work. Molly would feel uncomfortable in this big, grand house. But where else could they go? The weather was a bit chilly and drizzly this week for walking around a park or around the city streets. Lillian felt that if Molly's visit was left until some vague time in the future, that it would never happen. Molly was the only link she had left to her old life, and if she wasn't allowed to see her again, it would be as though a door had been shut on most of her life. That had happened when Alice left for Canada, and she had never heard from her since. The thought of losing another friend made Lillian's throat tighten. Then she remembered. 'Molly was allowed out for the day for her mother's funeral, and she said the priest took her and her brother to a café afterwards. Do you think we could go somewhere like that?'

'It may not be up to me,' Anna told her. 'But I'll think about it and see if anything can be done.'

'Thank you,' Lillian said. 'I would be very grateful. It would be great if I could see her to explain what had happened. She must have felt very hurt when she heard I had gone without saying a word.'

As they ate Mrs Larking's lovely cottage pie, Lillian felt more relaxed in her surroundings. She liked their private sitting room, and thought it a more comfortable size than the guests' large drawing room. She could not wait to tell Molly all about the house and her experiences so far. Some of the other girls would have been jealous, but Molly had never been like that. She would be happy for her, and would want to know everything about the house and all the people in it.

The more she thought about meeting with Molly again, the happier she felt. As she ate her meal and drank lemonade out of the heavy, cut-glass tumbler, she imagined all the things they would talk about and what they might do. Molly would have new stories to tell her about the orphanage, although it was unlikely that any of them would be happy tales.

There was a tap at the door, and Lucy came in with a tray to collect the empty plates. She hesitated at the door, then said in a low voice, 'Excuse me, Ma'am, but Mrs Larking said to ask if you would like apple pie and custard for dessert.'

'Just a small piece of apple pie for me, please,' Anna said. She looked at Lillian. 'Would you like both the pie and the custard?'

'Yes, please,' Lillian said, smiling hesitantly at Lucy.

Lucy caught her eye and gave a little smile back, then turned towards the door, concentrating on the tray.

'Be careful going down the stairs,' Anna said. 'Take your time.'

'Yes, Ma'am,' Lucy said.

When the door was closed behind her, Anna explained. 'The poor girl tripped up the stairs with a tray last week.'

'Did it make a terrible mess?' Lillian ventured.

'Yes, but it was easily cleaned. It would have been a lot worse if she had been scalded. The poor girl was shaking from head to toe.'

Lillian felt glad that her aunt had been concerned about Lucy. If it had been one of the orphanage girls, the nuns would have been enraged, and the culprit punished and made an example of in front of the other girls.

Anna went over to a cabinet where she had left a notepad and a pen. She brought them back to the table. 'Now, Lillian, we have to go over our plans for the next few days. I have organised various things for you, so that you can continue your learning from home. There are certain skills that a young lady needs when out and about in Liverpool or any of the big cities.'

'What kind of skills?' Lillian asked.

'Social skills. To know what to say and do when meeting people who could help you in the future.' She smiled. 'Maybe, in a few years' time, even introduce you to your future husband.'

Lillian's mouth opened in shock.

Anna laughed. 'Don't seem so surprised,' she said. 'Surely you want to get married at some stage?'

'But I'm not even sixteen...'

'And that's good,' her aunt said. 'It gives us time to have you accomplished in all the areas that matter.' She smiled. 'I have lots of exciting ideas for you, outings we can take together to art galleries, and the theatre and the ballet, and after a while we can go for weekends away to places like London and Manchester. You will learn so much, and I am so looking forward to introducing you to all these lovely things.'

Lillian suddenly felt fearful. She had only just arrived at her new home and didn't know her way anywhere, and now she was being told that she would be soon going to London.

Her aunt looked down at her notepad. 'In the meantime, I've sorted out private tuition for you in elocution, piano and ballroom dancing lessons. Next year, we might enrol you in French evening classes, in case we ever find ourselves in Paris. Who knows?' She shrugged and gave a little laugh. 'Lots of young ladies travel there in the summer. Have you learned any French in school – or any other languages?'

French? She saw the expectant look in Anna's eyes. 'No,' she whispered, 'I haven't learned any languages at all apart from a bit of Latin that we learned so we would understand hymns and parts of the Mass.'

'Next spring, when the weather is better,' her aunt went on, 'we will enrol you in the local tennis club. I'm sure you would enjoy that, and you will get the chance to make new friends who have similar interests. What do you think?'

'I don't know, I don't know if I would be any good at them...'

'Nonsense,' Anna said, 'You're a clever girl, and you'll pick things up easily. I'm not sure what your favourite subjects were in school? What did you enjoy most? English? Arithmetic?'

'Reading... I always loved reading.' Lillian thought back to the sessions with Sister Ignatius, when the girls all listened as she read out to them. 'We did a little history and geography as well,' she added, remembering how she studied the globe of the world to see where Alice had gone to. 'I enjoyed learning about different countries.'

Her aunt pondered the information. 'I've just remembered something!' Anna exclaimed. She went over to a long walnut cabinet and opened a drawer. 'Here it is!' she said delightedly.

She brought out a sewing box, and a package wrapped in brown paper. 'I have an embroidery set for you. I saw it in Blackler's haberdashery department the other day and thought you would like it.' She held the package out, then an anxious look crossed her face. 'You do know how to sew, don't you?'

'Yes,' Lillian confirmed. She thought of all the socks she had darned, and the countless pillow cases and sheets she had mended over the last few years.

Lillian opened the package to reveal a folded piece of linen fabric with a picture of a house in the centre with trees and flowers surrounding it, and an elaborately written alphabet above it, and numbers below. There were several small packages inside wrapped in tissue paper which held a variety of coloured embroidery threads, a card with four gold-plated needles, and a sheet of instructions.

'Oh, it's beautiful!' Her eyes scanned the print, and she lifted the pastel-coloured silk embroidery threads to examine them.

'It is much too easy... or much too hard? I wasn't sure. I did sewing at school and I had an old aunt who used to help me...' She saw the curious look on her niece's face, and she waved her hand and said, 'But that was a long time ago.'

'It's perfect. I've never seen anything like this before, but I should be able to work it out.' She looked up at her aunt. 'Thank you, that was very kind of you.'

'I thought it was something that would keep you busy in the long winter evenings, or any day you have time on your hands.' She looked at her watch. 'I thought after we have our pudding, we might walk down to the library this evening? I checked with Rose Moran, and she told me that it's open until nine o'clock tonight.'

Lillian's eyes widened. 'Is it safe being out at night?' Sister Agnes had often warned them about the evils of the city at night.

'Well, it's not a good idea to be out very late,' her aunt said, 'especially around the dark side streets or the docks. But it's early now, just quarter to seven, and we'll keep to the main areas.' She halted. 'Are you anxious about going out in the dark?'

'The nuns always said that decent girls should never be out after dark. They said there are men out wandering around, looking for young girls on their own.'

'Not at this hour of the night,' Anna said. 'Lots of decent people are out and about in the centre of the city, going to the theatre or concerts or to the cinema. They were probably trying to frighten you, to make sure you didn't sneak out of the convent or anything like that.' She lowered her voice. 'Did anyone ever try getting out?'

'I don't really know,' Lillian said. 'One of the older girls did disappear two years ago. She had been in a bit of trouble with one of the nuns and was upset...' A picture of the girl flashed into Lillian's mind. She had been discovered in the nuns' private pantry with two biscuits concealed in her underwear. Sister Agnes had beaten her on the spot with a wooden spoon. She was taken to Mother Superior, who got a cardboard sign saying 'I am a thief' and hung it around her neck. She was then marched round all the classes by Sister Agnes and, sobbing and crying, she was made to tell each one what she had done. Lillian had heard later that the girl had been beaten again with a garden cane, which had left weals on her legs and arms.

'We got up in the morning,' Lillian continued, 'and her bed was empty. I remember it clearly, because I thought it was strange that the nuns didn't ask us if we knew where she had gone. We never heard any more about it, and she never came back.'

The door was tapped again and Lucy came in with the slices of apple pie, which they ate and then got ready to walk down to the library. On their way out, as they passed the guest drawing room, Anna glanced in and saw Mr Guthrie alone in the room. He was sitting comfortably at the table with his newspaper and dictionary, working on his daily crossword. She whispered to Lillian to go on to the front door, and then she quickly went into the drawing room, closing the door behind her.

A few minutes later, she came back out, pulling the door shut smartly behind her. Lillian noticed that her face looked flushed, and felt a stab of anxiety as she waited to hear what had happened.

They were out in the cold night air and halfway down Rodney Street when Anna said, 'We won't have any more trouble from Mr Guthrie. He tried to wriggle his way out of the situation, but I was having none of it. He eventually said he had made some kind of comment to you, which he could not recall. He had meant to be light-hearted, but he said he possibly got it wrong, and if so, he apologised profusely – and he offered to apologise to you in person.'

Lillian's gloved hands came up to her face. 'I don't want to talk to him.'

'You needn't worry. I told him I didn't want you upset any further, and he gave me his assurance that there would be no further personal remarks. I told him that if there were any more incidents, then I would have to consider his position. I think he got the message loud and clear.'

'Was he angry with me?' Lillian asked.

'More so with me, although he didn't let it show,' her aunt said, smiling. 'Men like Mr Guthrie don't care for women who are strong enough to stand up to them. He also doesn't care for the fact that he is dependent on me for an address in Rodney Street. But he knew I had the upper hand since I can decide whom I have under my roof.'

As they walked along, their path lit up by pools of light from the street lamps, Lillian realised how lucky she was getting out of the orphanage without anything really bad happening to her. She had heard that once they reached sixteen, some of the girls were sent out to big houses to work as domestic servants, while others were cast out on their own to find work in factories or to survive in any way they could.

As they stopped to cross the road, she glanced at her elegantly dressed aunt. She noticed the proud tilt of her head, and the bright, alert eyes, and it struck her that she was an unusually strong and determined woman. There were still questions she wanted answers to, and she still couldn't help wondering why her aunt had lost touch and taken her so long to find her, but that could all wait until everything had settled down. For now, she knew her aunt was a woman who had demonstrated she was on her side, and would look after her. A woman, Lillian realised, who would not let anything bad happen to her while she was living in her house.

Chapter Eight

The following Wednesday morning, Lillian was in her room working on her embroidery when her aunt came to her.

'You look very nice, dear.' She smiled approvingly at Lillian's mid-length skirt and fine wool sweater.

Lillian was also wearing a short string of pearls which her aunt had given her, as Anna had said she needed something to finish her outfit off. In less than a week, Lillian was almost used to wearing her new, beautiful clothes. As her aunt had advised, she now chose what she would wear the night before, so she was up, bathed and dressed before Lucy brought breakfast to their sitting room.

Whilst she had got used to certain things, Lillian was still self-conscious around the servants and most of the paying guests. The guest she found herself most relaxed with was Miss Moran, the librarian. She had asked Lillian about her trip to the library, and had suggested other titles she might like.

'Have you read *Pride and Prejudice* or *Jane Eyre*?' she had asked, and clapped her hands together in delight when Lillian said she hadn't.

'You must, they are just wonderful. Next time you are in the library, you must find them. I suggest *Pride and Prejudice* first. You will laugh and possibly cry, but I guarantee that at the end you will feel happy. The characters are so real and the situations very believable.' She had rolled her eyes. 'Sadly, some of the values, about women having to marry for money and status, are still upheld by certain people today, but Jane Austen was truly ahead of her time.' After the days when she felt every minute going slowly by, Lillian now read or sewed when she had time on her hands, and discovered the hours flew by.

When she went down to the kitchen, she always stopped to talk to Mrs Larking and her friendly husband, Michael. They told her that they lived in Anfield, a few miles outside the city centre. They had two sons who'd left for America, and a daughter who was married and lived in Ireland, but they still had their youngest son, eighteen-year-old Paul, living at home. Lillian thought Mr Larking seemed very proud when he told her that their son was training to be a tailor in Lewis's department store. 'Wears a smart suit, shirt and tie to work every day,' he told her. 'No two ways, our Paul is determined to go up in the world.'

Lucy, Mrs Larking told her in a hushed voice, lived in the court dwellings near Scotland Road. 'She's a good girl,' the cook said, 'considering what she comes from. They have no running water or anything in the Courts, so she was grateful to get the place here with her own little room.' She paused. 'And the poor girl appreciates it, her comin' from nothin', she's as spotless as you'll find.'

Lillian wondered what Mrs Larking would think if she knew the life she had just come from. Lillian found she still wanted to rush across the room to help Mrs Larking or Lucy when she saw them carrying heavy things, but she had been told by both her aunt and the cook that it wasn't her place to help.

She still helped Lucy with little things like gathering up the dirty plates or rushing to open the door for her. There were times when Lillian would have liked to ask the girl about her life outside the house, but she knew it wasn't the thing to do.

Later, her aunt came up with a cream envelope with her name written in a copperplate hand. 'Lillian, I've had a message from Mr Whyte, the music teacher who lives across the street. I enquired about piano lessons for you and he said he would let me know. Apparently he has a cancellation this morning, and has asked if you would like to go over.'

'Will it matter that I've never played the piano before? Will he think I am a bit old to start playing now? Reading music looks very complicated.'

'Well, we'll see. Mr Whyte is regarded as the best music teacher locally.' Her aunt halted, and a small shadow crossed her face. 'He was also a good friend of my late husband. We often spent evenings at the theatre or dining out with him and his lovely wife.' She sighed. 'Sadly he has lost his wife too now.'

Lillian bit her lip. In some ways her aunt was more open with her than she had expected, but in other ways she was still extremely private. There was so much about her that remained a mystery. It was like trying to build a jigsaw puzzle when you only had half of the pieces. Sometimes Lillian wanted to ask her if she could explain everything about her life, starting from her early days in Ireland through to where she was now, but the right moment never seemed to come.

At twelve o'clock, Anna came to collect her. 'I'll come over to Mr Whyte with you,' she said, 'to introduce you, and then I'll leave you to get on with things.'

Lillian wasn't as nervous as she had been earlier in the week, as she had already been for an elocution lesson to a Miss Churchill who lived a ten-minute walk away in Falkner Street. Knowing that she was apprehensive, her aunt had prepared her on the way to the teacher's house.

'I have explained to you that how you look and dress is very important, Lillian,' Anna said, as they had walked along, 'and how people will judge you on that. I learned that from personal experience. Well, the same goes for how you speak and how you pronounce words. You said you remember your mother always telling you to speak properly, and she'd be pleased to see you continue that. At times it wasn't easy for me to mix with people from a more privileged background, I was conscious of my Irish accent and very ordinary background. I didn't want people to judge me on how I sounded, rather than what I said, and I found that elocution lessons really helped.'

There was a silence, then Lillian said hesitantly, 'But... you seem *very* confident.'

Anna had given a wry smile. 'Long and hard experience has taught me confidence. It wasn't easy, but things I learned about people along the way have helped me, and I, in turn, want to help you.' She put her arm around Lillian and gave her shoulder a little squeeze. 'People from wealthy, upper-class families learn all these things from the cradle. They are surrounded by people who teach them the correct manners and the right thing to say – and *how* to say it. Their parents, families, and nannies and governesses all make sure that children follow the rules that will make them part of what is deemed to be 'polite society'. It's a small world, and it's all chance that they are part of it – no one has a choice about the circumstances they are born into.' She sighed. 'It's also unfair to the many people outside that nice little world. All the poor children who are born into poverty with parents who struggle day in, day out, to feed them. We should never look down on those poor people, and we always have to be willing to mix with them too. Most decent and intelligent people will judge on character and not on background, *but*, it just makes life easier for people like us, if we know how the system works. Anyway, I'm taking you to Miss Churchill, to help smooth things for you in the future.' They came to a halt to let some cars and vans past. 'Before you go in to see Miss Churchill, I want you to know something. She is, in many ways, a nice lady, but she has a problem with alcohol.'

Lillian's head jerked up at this news.

'I believe she has lost a number of her pupils recently because of her drinking habit and she is struggling to make ends meet. But she's always had a reputation as a good teacher, and it's not for us to judge her until we have a good reason. When I called to enquire, she seemed absolutely fine, and she told me she had space for a new pupil immediately. I'll come with you each time you go for a lesson, so I can see how Miss Churchill is. If we have any problems, naturally you won't have to go back.'

*

Miss Churchill had been on top form, with no sign of inebriation. She was a small, thin woman in her fifties, with an angular face and dark, bobbed hair. Lillian thought she looked very exotic with her brightly embroidered velvet jacket, but as they moved inside the house she had to hide her shock when she saw she was wearing wide-legged trousers. She welcomed them both profusely, and Anna introduced Lillian, explaining that she had been convent-educated, and could speak perfectly well, but that she thought there might be some areas in her speech that Miss Churchill could fine-tune.

'Of course,' Miss Churchill had said. She had looked Lillian up and down, from the tip of her brown felt hat to her fur-trimmed boots. 'I'd be delighted to work with such a lovely girl.'

Anna had then asked to speak privately to Miss Churchill out in the hallway, and had quickly told her the same, truncated story of Lillian's background that she had told her paying guests. 'I know I can be assured of your discretion, Miss Churchill?'

'Of course,' the teacher agreed. 'I'm sure we will get on very well.'

'If you have time, it might also be useful to go over the basic rules of etiquette with Lillian as well. As you can imagine, the nuns put more emphasis on prayers, hymns and Latin than the everyday niceties of life. It would help her settle in her new life.'

'I can assure you there won't be a young lady in Liverpool who will have better diction and enunciation when I have finished with her.'

Lillian found Miss Churchill to be both skilled and very entertaining. She gave her a sheet with a list of funny tongue-twisters, and then read them out in an exaggerated, theatrical way which made Lillian laugh. The lesson passed very quickly and before she knew it, her aunt was at the door to collect her and discreetly handed over an envelope to the teacher.

As they crossed the road and walked towards Mr Whyte's house, the black door opened and the fair-haired boy Lillian had seen from the window came rushing out and down the stairs. He halted abruptly at the bottom when he saw Lillian and her aunt. 'My apologies, ladies,' he said, lifting his hat, and stood aside to let them pass.

'Thank you,' Anna said, smiling graciously at him.

This was obviously Mr Whyte's grandson, Lillian realised. She noticed him staring straight at her, and her face flushed.

The door opened and a serious-looking maid ushered them inside, saying in a broad Liverpool accent, 'Mr Whyte is in the music room, waitin' for you.'

As they followed behind, Lillian could hear the sound of a piano being played. The maid stopped outside a room next to the drawing room and tapped on the door. Immediately, the music stopped and the maid held the door open to allow Anna and Lillian into a grandly furnished room with mahogany, glass-fronted bookcases and two French-style sofas facing each other in the middle of the room.

Lillian then had a clear view of Mr Whyte, an elderly man with a thick head of silver hair and a silver beard and moustache. He was dressed in a dark suit and wore a striped bow-tie.

'Ah, Anna,' he said, smiling and bowing towards her aunt. 'How are you, my dear? You are looking very well as always.'

'Thank you,' her aunt replied, smiling back at him.

He raised his eyebrows in question, as he looked at Lillian. 'And this young lady must be your niece?'

'Yes, this is Lillian.'

He bowed and smiled and said, 'How do you do, my dear?'

'I'm very well, thank you, Sir,' Lillian replied as she had been told to do.

'So,' Mr Whyte said, smiling, 'we have a complete novice here?'

'She is,' Anna said. 'Sadly, the nuns who educated her didn't place much emphasis on music.'

'Ah, we will endeavour to remedy that,' he said, smiling broadly. 'It's never too late to learn a new skill, and we are in no rush, are we?' He turned to Lillian. 'You can take your hat and coat off, my dear, you will play more comfortably without them.'

The maid came forward to take them from her and then disappeared out into the hallway.

Mr Whyte indicated the tapestry-covered piano stool. 'You can sit there, my dear, and acquaint yourself with the different sounds the keys make, while I escort your aunt to the door.' He made a little piano-playing gesture with his hands. 'Just tinkle about with them, listening to the different sounds that each key makes.'

As they went out into the hallway, Lillian heard the music teacher say, 'It's lovely to see you, Anna. We're just across the street from each other, but it seems a long time since we met up.'

'Everything has changed, Oliver, with Edward and Florence both gone.'

Lillian could hear the sadness in her aunt's voice. 'Neither of us could have envisaged this happening, could we?'

'Never – and both gone within months of each other.'

They walked towards the door, and Lillian heard no more.

So many things had happened since Lillian's arrival in Rodney Street that she had not given her aunt's loss much thought. From the snippet of conversation, it sounded as though her aunt and Mr Whyte were both still struggling to get used to what had happened.

It felt like loss had always been part of her life. She remembered little about her father's death, apart from the house being very quiet and vague memories of watching out of the window, waiting for him to reappear. Waiting for things to go back to normal.

It had been very different when her mother died, because she was older. She was initially looked after by neighbours, and she remembered priests, teachers and social workers coming to see her. She clearly remembered being in a black car with the priest, going out to the nuns. Everyday life in the orphanage, with its strict rules and routines, had taken over and given her little time to think about the devastating events which had occurred. Days passed, then weeks and then months, and she eventually stopped looking back.

It seemed to her now, that her aunt and Mr Whyte were still looking back.

She looked at the keys on the piano now, and then gently touched them with her fingers. She knew that they went from light tinkly notes to very deep ones. She played around for a while, enjoying the sounds, and then she suddenly halted when she heard footsteps. She sat up straight, her hands joined in her lap, looking down at the piano keys.

The door opened and Lillian turned to discover it wasn't Mr Whyte, but the boy she had seen earlier. He came into the room and laid his folded arms down on top of the ebony piano.

'Hello,' he said, grinning at her. 'I recognise you. You live across the street. You're the girl I saw at the window, aren't you?'

Lillian suddenly felt a hot flush coming up her chest to her neck. She had never been so near to a boy and didn't know what to say. She twisted her hands together in her lap.

'I'm glad I caught you on your own.' His face suddenly grew serious. 'I made a mistake and I wanted to apologise. I'm a total idiot, I thought I was waving at Miss Moran, and it was only afterwards I realised it wasn't her.'

Lillian's forehead creased in confusion.

'I saw you at the window, it was the dark hair, and I thought it was her.' He started laughing. 'I was an utter fool. I don't know what you must have thought of me.'

'I didn't really think anything...' Something about his open face made her relax, and she found herself smiling back at him. 'I suppose it's easy to make a mistake, it is quite a distance away.'

'So you forgive me?'

'Forgive you for what?' Mr Whyte's surprised and slightly stern voice came from the door. 'What on earth have you said or done now, Andrew?'

'Nothing, Grandfather,' he said, moving to his feet. 'It was a small misunderstanding, I waved to...' he halted, realising he didn't know her name. 'I thought I was waving at Miss Moran, the librarian and instead it was...' He looked at Lillian. 'I'm so sorry, I didn't ask your name.'

'I despair of you, boy...' Mr Whyte shook his head, but there was humour in his tone. 'You've been talking to this young lady, and you haven't even introduced yourself or asked her name.' He turned to Lillian. 'Miss Taylor, may I introduce my very socially inept grandson, Andrew Whyte?' He turned to the sheepish-looking boy. 'Andrew, may I introduce Miss Lillian Taylor?'

Andrew put his hand out to shake Lillian's. 'How do you do, Miss Taylor?'

Lillian, for some reason, suddenly felt like laughing. The formality of the situation seemed farcical after the way the boy had been lounging across his grandfather's piano. She smiled and said, 'I'm very well, thank you.'

'Thank you, Andrew,' Mr Whyte said, going towards the door and opening it wide, 'you may go now. You have plenty of books to keep you busy, and you've kept us back from Lillian's lesson long enough.'

He closed the door and came back to Lillian, shaking his head and smiling. 'He's a rascal,' he said, 'but he means no harm. Where are his manners?' Mr Whyte rolled his eyes in mock horror. 'I shall have to speak to him again later. He should be paying more attention to his books and studying, instead of acting the fool. He's at a boys' school in London. He has come here for a week, some sort of study break from school, to swot for examinations, but most days he's out gallivanting to the shops or to the cinema.'

Lillian was surprised she felt disappointed that Andrew didn't live full time in Liverpool. They had only spoken a few words, but she instinctively liked him. Even more surprising, she felt herself warming to his grandfather. She had imagined him to be more stiff and formal than Miss Churchill, but she could see he had an easier, more humorous nature.

Mr Whyte went over to the window and lifted a small tapestry armchair and brought it over to the piano to sit beside

Lillian. He talked her through all the keys and got her to listen to the sounds. He then showed her the notes that matched the keys, and after practising pairing them up, he got her to try reading randomly mixed notes. By the end of the lesson, she had progressed to playing different combinations of three or four notes, which, she was amazed at. She had not imagined that she could have made any sense of either the key or notes when she first studied them.

Mr Whyte told her that she had done well for a first lesson. She smiled, feeling inordinately grateful for the praise. He then gave Lillian some basic music sheets to practise at home.

'Like anything else in life, how quickly you will learn to play the piano, depends on how much you practise,' he advised.

When she went to bed later that night, she knelt by the side of the bed and said her prayers as usual. Afterwards, she lay in bed reading from her current book – *Great Expectations* – and it was only when she turned her bedside light out and closed her eyes that it occurred to her that today she hadn't thought about the orphanage or prayed that she was back in familiar surroundings. She felt a sense of achievement that she was adjusting to living in Rodney Street with her aunt, and that after such a short time, people were now regarding her as a normal girl instead of an orphan.

Already, she felt a distance from her old life.

Chapter Nine

On Saturday morning as they were having breakfast together, Lillian asked her aunt where the local Catholic church was and what time Confession was held.

'*Confession*?' Anna had repeated, as though she hadn't heard properly.

'It's Saturday and we always had Confession on a Saturday...'

Her aunt looked at her. 'You might as well know, Lillian, I'm not a practising Catholic any more. I lost faith in the church a long time ago.'

Lillian was shocked. How could her aunt have lost her faith? And how would this affect her? She and the other girls had all been warned by the nuns against mixing with those who were enemies of the true church. Countless times they had heard about the evils of the Protestant religion and even worse, atheists and heathens. Once you were a Catholic, Lillian believed, you were always a Catholic, and as such, you were therefore beholden to observe all the Catholic rituals: Mass on Sunday, Holy Days of Obligation and attending Confession on a regular basis. 'Lapsed Catholics' – those who missed Mass through slothfulness, being under the influence of drink or being prone to imagined illness – were regarded as the worst scourge of all; even worse than Protestants and atheists because they had been baptised into the true church and dared to reject it.

Lapsed Catholics were not to be entertained at any cost. They had no excuse to stay away from church because even those who had committed a mortal sin still had the benefit of Confession to wipe the slate clean.

The subject of a Catholic who had wilfully made the decision to leave the church, had never been raised in the convent... It was as though the idea was beyond comprehension.

When she saw the shocked look on her niece's face, Anna reached across and took her hand. 'I know it probably feels strange, and probably wrong, for you to hear that, but I have my own, very serious reasons for leaving the Church. I can imagine all the things that the nuns have told you about people who don't believe in the Catholic Church being damned to hell and all those frightening scenarios, but believe me, Lillian, it's all nonsense. I was fooled by it all too when I was your age. It's only when you get out in the world, and mix with people from all backgrounds, that you realise that we all have choices in what we believe – and that goes for both religion and politics.'

Lillian took a deep breath. 'I don't really understand...'

'You're young, Lillian, and you don't have to understand everything. It's only when you get older that things in life truly begin to make sense in all sorts of ways.' She held her hands out. 'I suppose what I'm trying to say is that we don't have to be told what to believe and how to behave – it's our choice how to live our own lives. We can be anything we want to be, if we make our minds up to do it.'

Lillian thought for a few moments and then she said, 'If you show me where the church is, I can go on my own.'

Anna looked at the clock, then her gaze moved to the tall Georgian window. 'From what I remember, Confessions are on late morning. I'm meeting a friend in the city centre at twelve o'clock, so if we leave here at about eleven, I can take you to St Nicholas Church; it's in Copperas Hill, up behind Lime Street Station. It's a lovely morning for the time of year, and the walk will do us good. I'll leave you at the church and you can make your own way home later.'

'Thank you,' Lillian said quietly.

Anna squeezed her hand. 'You are old enough to make up

your own mind about religion, and I am not going to sway you either way. You must decide what is right for you. While you are at the church for Confession, you can find out about the times of Masses for tomorrow.'

As Lillian went upstairs to get her hat, coat and rosary beads, she went over everything her aunt had said, and tried to take it all in. It was so alien to what she had been taught in the orphanage. She had believed everything because all the Bible stories – especially the New Testament about Jesus – had all made sense to her. He had been such a real person to her. Someone she could relate to. Apart from being able to perform miracles, Lillian felt Jesus, as a human being on earth, had done good in every possible way. And yet, as she listened, she could hear sense in what her aunt was saying.

As they walked down into the city centre, Lillian said, 'Lime Street Station is quite near the Adelphi Hotel, isn't it?'

Her aunt smiled. 'That's correct. I think you're getting to know your way around the city quite well by now, don't you?'

'Yes,' Lillian said, 'It's not easy, but I think I'm beginning to recognise all the different places and make some sense of it.'

'Good girl! I'm delighted to hear how independent you're becoming already. It's important for women to be able to do things for themselves. So many depend on men for everything, which, in this day and age, is ridiculous. We have to make sure we don't let down all those brave women – the Suffragettes – who fought for women's rights. We have to make sure we keep any independence we have gained, and work to get even more.'

Lillian said she didn't know anything about the Suffragettes; they hadn't been mentioned by the nuns in any of the classes.

'Interesting,' Anna said, 'especially since they live in an all-women community, and seem to have no difficulties making their own rules and regulations.' As they walked, her aunt gave her a quick, potted history of the political struggles of women in Liverpool and London. Lillian listened intently, and when she had finished, Anna asked. 'What do you think about the notion of equality for men and women?'

Lillian hesitated. 'I've never thought about it.' She could not remember being asked her opinion on anything in the orphanage. Quite the opposite had been encouraged, where the girls' role had been to accept everything the nuns said.

'I suppose you've had a lot of new ideas to get used to this week.' She held a gloved hand up. 'Art also came to my mind. Did you study anything about art in school? Look at pictures of paintings by famous painters like Michelangelo or Leonardo Da Vinci?'

'No,' Lillian said, 'but we had a lady who was an artist who came in to each of the classes last year, and she gave us special paper to draw on and some pencils. We did drawings of a vase of flowers that she brought with her.'

Anna slowly nodded her head. 'Well, next time you are in the library, find the art section. They have books with all sorts of paintings, and you will enjoy looking through them. We'll also take a visit soon to the main art gallery and museum in the next few weeks.'

The church came into sight and they could see people coming and going from Confession.

'When you come out of the church, you could go to the library and I'll come and meet you there. I'll be finished around two o'clock.' She looked at her watch. 'You will have a couple of hours now, so if you get hungry, go into a café and get yourself a sandwich or soup, and then go back to the library and wait for me. I'll find you in the area we were in last time, and then we can go shopping and look for a winter coat for you.' She took her purse out of her handbag and gave her a half-a-crown. 'That will be more than enough, and whatever you eat should keep you going until we get home later on.'

Lillian thanked her. 'It's funny,' she said, 'but since I came to live with you, I never feel cold or hungry ...'

'And hopefully, you never will feel hungry again.'

*

When they parted, Anna walked on a few yards, and then, when there was a reasonable distance between them, she paused to watch Lillian going up the steps into the church. She saw the erect, confident way she held herself, knowing that deep down the girl would be anxious at going into the church on her own, and probably confused about their earlier conversation regarding faith.

Anna worried that things were going too quickly. It was only a week since Lillian's life had been turned upside down. She wondered if she could have done things differently, slowed it down a bit, but every time she thought things through, she came back to the same conclusion. The transition from that wretched orphanage to Rodney Street had to be done as quickly as possible. And keeping Lillian busy with activities and lessons gave her less time to brood.

She watched until Lillian went inside, and then turned back to the city centre. The wind whipped at her face and ears, the morning chillier than expected. As she walked along, she thought of all the things that had still to be organised for Lillian. She had started with the material things that she needed, and now she would concentrate on her education and the general skills she would need for life.

At almost sixteen, there wasn't a day to lose. Lillian could, of course, have gone to a decent boarding school, but she would be behind the other girls in many areas. Questions would be asked that she did not want Lillian to have to answer. Anna also thought that the poor girl had had enough of residential places to last her a lifetime.

Her thoughts moved on to Gethsemane House. Now she'd seen inside the place, and heard a little from Lillian of conditions in there, she would have liked to have stopped the donations that went to the nuns immediately, but she needed to retain links with the place a little longer in case there was trouble over her taking Lillian out in such an unorthodox way. She also owed it to Lillian to let her see her friend one more time. Molly Power had been mentioned every day since Lillian had left the orphanage, and Anna knew that she wouldn't settle properly in Rodney Street and her new life until she had said goodbye to her friend properly. The thought of contacting the nuns again filled Anna with dread, but, after everything Lillian was doing to please her, she owed the girl that at the very least.

As she walked along past the Adelphi, her heels tapping on the pavement, she wondered for a fleeting moment whether she had done the right thing. A cold hand clutched at her heart as she thought about it. After all the years of searching for her, bringing Lillian to live with her had been one of the hardest decisions she had ever made.

At the back of her mind she wondered if it was too late for a bond to form between them now. In truth, they knew nothing about each other and Anna had to think long and hard about the strains it could put on either or both of them; how taking Lillian from the orphanage to live in an imposing house would be a massive change for the girl, and how being solely responsible for Lillian would impact on herself.

With icy tears streaming down her beautiful face, Anna walked quickly towards the city.

Chapter Ten

As she knelt at the back of the church, having said her five Hail Marys and an Our Father as penance, Lillian didn't have the feeling of lightness that she usually experienced after Confession in the orphanage.

The priest she had just confessed to had been nice, and she had told him her usual list of small indiscretions, including her malicious thoughts about Mr Guthrie. The real sin she should have confessed was that she was knowingly living in a house with a relative who was a lapsed Catholic. How he would have responded she had no idea. He might quiz her about how she had come to live with her aunt, and where she had been previously. Being in a confessional box, she would have to tell the absolute truth, and the priest might make the link to Gethsemane House and the nuns.

It was common knowledge that priests were bound by God not to reveal anything they heard in Confession, but Lillian thought that they still might be able to follow up information indirectly without revealing where they had got it from. She could only imagine how Sister Agnes or Mother Superior would react if they knew that she was now living with an aunt who had no regard for religion. The fact that it was a house in a prestigious area and the people were privileged would make them even more enraged, she guessed.

As she walked up towards the library, her attention was diverted by the busy traffic and the other pedestrians. Just being out in the world still felt overwhelming, and the tranquillity of the library was welcome. Lillian went to look for the art section as her aunt had suggested. There were shelves of art books, some very big and heavy. She lifted some out, and came upon a book containing paintings of nudes, which she quickly put it straight back on the shelf, blushing and embarrassed in case someone had seen her.

One book she particularly liked had beautiful scenes by an artist called Claude Monet and she took it over to a table to study it. One painting caught her eye – a woman and child walking through a field of poppies. It was one of the most beautiful things she had ever seen.

'A Monet fan, I see,' a familiar voice said.

When she lifted her head she found she was looking into the smiling face of Andrew Whyte.

'Hello,' he said, giving a sweeping bow, 'we meet again.'

Lillian smiled back at him. 'Hello,' she said, in a whisper.

He pulled a chair out and sat down beside her. 'Well?' he said, his eyebrows raised. 'What are you doing here? And all unchaperoned?'

'Looking at books,' she told him, 'and waiting for my aunt.'

He held out a book with racing cars on the front. 'I'm busy studying history, as you can see...'

Lillian started to laugh. She shook her head and whispered, 'Your grandfather isn't going to be very happy with you.'

He shrugged. 'All work and no play makes Jack a dull boy.'

Lillian noticed a man at a table further down the room looking at them and shaking his head.

'You better go and get on with your exam studies,' she whispered, 'or you will be in trouble.'

'I do enough studying at school and home. My mother would have my nose permanently in a book if she had her way. That's why I come up to my grandfather's so often, to get away from all of that.'

'What are you doing in the library then?' she asked. 'It seems the wrong place to come to if you are trying to escape from books.'

His eyes narrowed. 'Oh, you're a sharp one. I came here for an alibi, to be seen working for an hour, and then I can go off "gallivanting" as my grandfather refers to it. So,' he said, mimicking her whisper, 'you're interested in art? Are you planning on becoming an artist?'

'No ... I am just looking at some books.' She could tell by his manner that he was only teasing her, but she was afraid he might start asking questions about her subjects at school. 'I arranged to spend some time here, and then go for something to eat before meeting my aunt at two o'clock to go shopping.'

'So you're free until then?' He took out a small pocket watch. 'It's only twelve o'clock.' His eyes lit up. 'I was just thinking about lunch myself ... I'm probably going to go to The Phil, if you would like to join me. Sorry, that's the Philharmonic Dining Rooms – I'm forgetting you've just arrived in Liverpool.'

Lillian caught her breath at his suggestion. 'Thank you for asking,' she said, her voice low, 'but I don't think my aunt would like it, as we hardly know each other.'

'We have been officially introduced,' he pointed out. 'And our families know each other, so who is going to complain?'

'I would have to check with my aunt before making any arrangements.'

'She doesn't need to know,' he said. 'If I don't say anything to Grandfather, how is she going to find out?'

Lillian looked up at him, thinking how blue and friendly his eyes were, and how she liked his tousled blond hair. She knew nothing about boys or about how she should behave around them. 'I can't,' she said, shrugging. 'I just can't ...'

Lillian suddenly became aware of a tall, cross-looking woman with a grey bun and spectacles coming briskly towards them. She came to a halt at their table.

'I was informed that there are two people having a loud conversation and distracting others from their studies. I didn't need to look far – I could hear you both as I came into the section here.' She put her hands on her hips. 'Quieten down or kindly leave.'

'I do apologise,' Andrew said in a low voice. His face was serious and all laughter and frivolity gone. 'I had no idea we were disturbing anyone. It was my fault entirely, I was the loud person.' He indicated to the art books on the table. 'We were having a discussion about Renaissance painters and I must have got carried away ...'

The librarian studied him for a moment with some suspicion, then turned, eyes narrowed, to look at Lillian.

Lillian was grateful to Andrew, but felt she could not let him take the entire blame. 'I'm very sorry ... I didn't realise we were disturbing anyone ...' She halted as another figure appeared.

A familiar female voice said, 'Is there a problem, Miss Nelson?'

Lillian suddenly realised it was Miss Moran, and her heart sank even further.

'We have had a complaint,' Miss Nelson said, her voice high and trembling, 'about these two young people talking loudly and disturbing some of the other library users. I've told them that they either quieten down or they will have to leave.'

Miss Moran raised her eyebrows and nodded her head. 'I'm sure they will be taking on board what you have said. If you don't mind going back to help out at the front desk, I'll take over from here.'

'Of course,' Miss Nelson said, giving a final, stern glance at the offenders.

There was silence as the tall, thin librarian made her way down through the bookcases and out of the Art section. Then Miss Moran turned with wide, questioning eyes to look first at Lillian, then Andrew.

'Well,' she said, in a muted voice, 'I must say I am surprised to find out who has been causing all the commotion. Very surprised. But,' she said, smiling now, 'I think you have both got the message.'

'Yes,' Lillian said quickly. 'I am very sorry ...'

Andrew nodded in agreement. 'I do, of course, sincerely apologise.'

The librarian shrugged. 'Well, it's not exactly the crime of the century,' she said in a whisper, 'but people do take the silence rule very seriously, especially Miss Nelson.' She paused. 'I didn't realise you two knew each other so well.'

'We don't,' Lillian said quickly. 'We met when I was over at Mr Whyte's for piano lessons, and then Andrew happened to be in here today and so was I.'

'So you didn't arrange to meet up?'

'Not at all,' Andrew said, 'I was just having a wander around and I came upon Miss Taylor, leafing through a pile of art history books, and we started talking.' When he saw her face darken again, he said quickly, 'I know we shouldn't have talked in here, and in my defence I suggested we go outside for lunch or a coffee – '

Miss Moran shot him a glance. 'Have you asked Lillian's aunt for permission?'

'I didn't think . . .'

'Well, Andrew,' she said, 'you really should think. Your grandfather and Mrs Ainsley would be very disappointed if they heard you had asked Lillian to accompany you anywhere without asking permission.'

'Well, Lillian did point that out to me, but I'll be going back to London tomorrow so it's immaterial now.'

'Okay,' Miss Moran said, 'I shall leave you in peace now, and you needn't worry about me telling tales to anyone.'

'That's jolly decent of you,' Andrew said. 'And I'm grateful.' He turned to Lillian. 'I'm off to lunch somewhere now, and you may be gone when I get back . . .'

'Goodbye,' Lillian said, 'and thank you, Miss Moran.'

As she watched them both disappear behind the long row of bookshelves, Lillian felt a stab of disappointment at hearing that he was going away so soon. She had never met anyone like Andrew Whyte before. She liked the funny things he said and the way he made her laugh. He made her feel interesting – he wanted to know her opinions and the sort of things she liked. He made her feel good about herself.

Chapter Eleven

The following week, Anna came into their private sitting room, where Lillian was busily engaged with a new piece of embroidery.

'I have just had a phone call from Mother Superior,' Anna told her, 'and she has agreed to allow your friend, Molly, to come out with us next Sunday afternoon.'

Lillian's face lit up at the news. 'Oh, thank you!'

'We will take her out for something to eat, and have a walk down by the docks if it's not too cold. I'll collect the coat and dress that we got her from the laundry tomorrow, and I'm sure we can pick up a pair of warm boots for her from that same second-hand shop we found.'

Anna had phoned the convent on several occasions and had almost given up hope of them being allowed to see the girl, when the head nun had finally relented. She was sure that the offer of an extra donation at Christmas had something to do with it.

'Molly will be delighted with anything,' Lillian said, 'as she only has her uniform.' She put her embroidery down. 'I'll leave my sewing until I finish off the scarf I was knitting for her. She will need that more with her bad chest.'

As they set off in a taxi on Sunday afternoon, Anna was quite sure that Lillian would already see a world of difference between herself and the girl, but better to find that out for herself. Anna was unsure how being back in the place would affect Lillian. She was preparing herself for the worst case, in which Lillian might decide that she wanted to go back to be with her friend.

If she did, Anna thought, she wouldn't stop her. She would at least know she had done the right thing bringing her out and giving her the choice.

Although she was excited at the prospect of being reunited with Molly again and telling her all her news, Lillian was filled with dread at the thought of seeing the nuns. Her aunt had told her that there was no need for her to come into Gethsemane House if she didn't want to. She could wait in the taxi while Anna went and collected Molly.

By the time they reached Gethsemane House, an idea had formed in Lillian's mind. Given the right length of time and the right circumstances, she would ask her aunt if Molly could come and work at their house. She had initially wondered if there was a chance that Anna might even adopt Molly, but something told her that it was too extreme to expect her aunt to take another girl – a total stranger – under her wing.

Having her living and working in the house would suit both Anna and Molly better, as her friend could feel she had earned her place there through hard work, and the girls could continue their friendship and do things together when Molly had days off work.

The current maid Lucy was older, and quite a pretty girl, so there was every chance she might get married at some point, and her aunt would need someone to replace her, Lillian decided. Or perhaps, even if Lucy stayed on, maybe her aunt would know someone else in Rodney Street or the surrounding areas who needed a parlour or scullery maid.

She knew Molly was small and not that physically strong, but hopefully, in a year or two she would be fully grown and able to manage some sort of household work. She was aware there would be differences between them, and in some ways there always had been, but it had never mattered, and as her aunt had taught her, the right clothes would change Molly. Lillian, in turn, could teach her all the things that she herself was now learning. There was no reason why they couldn't go to places like the cinema together or even dancing.

The idea brought a smile to Lillian's face and she couldn't wait to get a chance to speak to Molly on her own about it.

Anna was surprised when Mother Superior opened the door of Gethsemane House. 'Please come in,' she said, her face grave. 'If you wouldn't mind stepping into my office for a few minutes…'

Anna had expected the girl to be waiting for her, and immediately felt something was amiss. They walked in silence along the cold corridor, Mother Superior's black skirts swishing as she moved along.

When the office door was closed, the nun turned to face her. 'It's not going to be possible for Molly Power to go out with you today. She's been taken ill…'

'Ill? In what way?'

The nun turned and walked towards the window. 'She fainted about an hour ago,' she said, looking out into the garden, 'and she has been taken down to the sick room to recover.'

As Anna looked at the back of the nun and her arrogant stance, something told her that this was a very deliberate act to sabotage their plans. She thought quickly. 'Lillian is outside in a car, perhaps if she came in to visit her friend?'

'I don't think that is a good idea,' Mother Superior said, turning around slowly to look at Anna. 'Lillian has gone now, and things are probably better just left at that.'

'But she's very fond of the girl,' Anna said, in a deliberately quiet and calm tone, 'and she didn't get to see her before she left to say goodbye.'

'That might be just as well. Molly Power is not a suitable friend, and the nuns did not realise they were so close. It was a total surprise to us all when you rang and asked about them meeting up.'

Realising what this would mean to Lillian, Anna's voice took on a more authoritative note. 'I have been trying to organise a day which suits for the last week. We came out in a car to collect the girl, to make the most of the few hours we had agreed on. I thought it would do her good to have a day out in the outside world, in a carefully chaperoned way of course...' She stopped, realising she sounded as if she was rambling on. 'Surely Lillian can see her for a few minutes?'

There was a silence before the nun said, 'I don't think you realise the sort of girl Molly Power is. She's not at all like Lillian, who was sadly orphaned but from a respectable, Catholic family. Molly Power was brought up in the worst slum dwellings you could imagine, and her mother was no better than a prostitute.' She closed her eyes and shook her head. 'The girl could have had any number of fathers, and that is borne out by the fact that her brother was fathered by a black man. I'm sure Lillian would be shocked if she knew her background and wouldn't be so keen on her.'

'Lillian is quite an innocent girl, and I'm sure she wouldn't think any less of her unfortunate friend...' Anna was struggling to keep her voice steady, and trying to carefully pick her words so as not to rile the nun into being more awkward. 'I would appreciate it,' Anna said, lifting her head higher, 'if you would be kind enough to let Lillian see the girl for a few minutes?'

Mother Superior pursed her lips tightly together and then looked Anna up and down with great disapproval. 'I know you and your associates have been generous with donations, but it does not give you the right to make demands. It behoves those who are in a privileged position to help the poor and needy, and do not forget that people like myself and the other nuns have devoted our whole lives to helping these poor wretches.' She rolled her eyes to the ceiling and then she strode across to the door. 'Let me just check how things are,' she said icily, 'but I am promising nothing.'

Anna paced up and down the office. Occasionally she went across to the window, wondering if Lillian was all right in the taxi on her own. She was afraid to go back outside to speak to her, as she thought it might be hard gaining entry to the convent again.

Eventually, the door opened and a younger nun stood holding it ajar. 'Mother Superior said I have to bring you and Lillian up to the sick room, but you are only allowed five minutes.'

Anna's face lit up. 'She's out in the car – I shall fetch her immediately.'

Chapter Twelve

Lillian watched from the safety of the taxi window, her eyes fixed on the heavy front door of Gethsemane House. She had been so excited about seeing Molly that she had not fully imagined how it would feel to be back at this place. She knew that she had only dark memories of the place, and her early homesickness for the orphanage had been nothing more than a panicked reaction to the strange world outside its gates.

As she looked at the grey building, she realised she had put a greater distance between herself and the orphanage than she had imagined. After a few weeks of living in Rodney Street with her aunt, she had unconsciously become a part of that new world. The things that were initially alien had quickly become familiar. Her palatial surroundings, the people she was living amongst and the new routines were not just part of her present life; they were also pointing to a future very different from what awaited most of the orphanage girls.

As she sat in the black leather-covered seats of the hired car, the minutes ticking by, the thought crept into her mind that Mother Superior or Sister Agnes might be inside arguing with her aunt and demanding that she was returned to them. If that were to be the case, her aunt wouldn't give in easily, she reasoned. Every so often she glanced fearfully back to the heavy door, wishing for it to open, and for her aunt and Molly to come out, and then for the car engine to rumble into life and carry them away from this place.

Eventually, the door opened, but only her aunt came out, with no sign of Molly. Lillian sat on the edge of the seat and waited until her aunt opened the car door. In the background, holding the door open, she could see Sister Ignatius.

'Molly is not well and won't be able to come with us,' her aunt said, her voice clipped and a little higher than normal, 'but Mother Superior has said you can go in to see her in the sick room for a few minutes.' She opened the door wide to let Lillian climb out, then went around to the driver's side of the cab to speak to the driver.

As she followed her aunt to the door of the convent, Lillian felt her legs trembling. She had not been prepared for this, had not thought she might have to go inside, or how she would act if she met any of the other girls. She imagined how they would view her in her smart, expensive clothes. How they would feel about her disappearing one afternoon, without as much as a goodbye or backward glance at the place?

All her anticipation had been focused on Molly, and what she would say to her when they first met. How she would first help her friend to feel at ease with her Aunt Anna, and then how she would tell her of the big outside world waiting for her after all her years of confinement.

Sister Ignatius pulled the door wider to allow them to enter. Lillian smiled and opened her mouth to greet the young nun – the only one who had been kind to her – but Sister Ignatius just turned away.

For a moment, Lillian wondered if the young nun had not recognised her. She knew she looked different in the new clothes and her hair was loose, which might have deceived anyone. But something about the tilt of Sister Ignatius's head and the quick movement of her eyes told Lillian there had been no mistake.

Sister Ignatius walked in front of them and silently guided them along the main corridor past the empty classrooms, and then down smaller corridors to rooms at the rear of the building, which Lillian had only been to a few times during all her years in the orphanage.

She held her breath now as Sister Ignatius went in. There

was a moment's hesitation before her aunt ushered her in. All the excitement about seeing her friend had been replaced by an anxious feeling.

The room looked different to what she remembered. The walls were still grey and the window high, but there was a comfortable chair, similar to the chairs in the nun's drawing room, and a small side table with a lace covering, which held a lamp, a glass of water, a prayer book and Molly's rosary beads.

Lillian's heart quickened as her eyes moved over to the bed where her friend lay underneath the familiar threadbare orphanage blankets which were, surprisingly, topped by a plump, pale blue eiderdown. Eventually, her fearful gaze came to rest on the thin, pale-faced Molly, who was propped up against two starched white pillows. One eye was closed tight, while the other was flitting anxiously around the three people in the room.

Lillian was startled by how strange her friend looked, as she had forgotten all about the problem with Molly's eye. Somewhere, at the back of her mind, she had thought it was temporary and would have righted itself.

Sister Ignatius stared up towards the window, like a person engrossed in viewing a painting. 'Mother Superior said someone will be back in a few minutes to show you out of the building.' She left, quietly closing the door behind her.

Lillian felt an immediate sense of relief, and quickly moved over to sit on the chair at the side of the bed. 'Hello, Molly...' she said, reaching out to squeeze her friend's hand. 'How are you?'

Molly's hand lay impassively in hers, although her good eye was fully focused on Lillian. 'I'm okay, I'm getting better...' Her voice was distant and unsure.

There was a silence during which Lillian felt a sense of panic. It was as though they were strangers. She wondered now if she had imagined the depth of her friendship with Molly, or if it had been irreparably damaged by her sudden disappearance. 'I'm sorry I didn't see you before I left,' she said, 'but you weren't too well that day... I asked Sister Ignatius to tell you. Did she give you my message?'

'She told me that yer were gone... that yer auntie had come to take you away. She told me yer would be havin' a lovely time and she even held me hand and told me not to be sad.'

For the first time, Lillian noticed how guttural her friend's Liverpool accent was. 'I didn't know anything about it until the very day,' Lillian told her. 'It was as big a surprise for me. I couldn't believe it...' She turned to look behind, then gestured towards Anna, who had remained silent since coming into the room. 'This is my Aunt Anna.'

Anna came forward now and stood at the end of the bed. 'Hello, Molly,' she said, smiling warmly. 'It's nice to meet you.' She waited for a few seconds to let her respond, but when she realised she was too nervous, she carried on. 'Lillian has told me all about you, and what good friends you are.' A little light suddenly appeared in the poor child's eye. 'She has been worried about not saying goodbye to you, and we've tried to get permission to visit you, but this is the first time that suited the nuns.' She raised her eyebrows and nodded. 'I expect they are busy with so many girls here...'

Molly gave an awkward little smile, then turned back to Lillian. 'It wasn't just me bad chest this time... it was the accident with me leg.'

'Your leg? What happened?'

'I was washin' down the stairs and... and...' The effort of speaking sent her into a convulsion of coughing, which Lillian recognised only too well. Everyone waited until she finished, and then she took a deep breath and said, 'Sister Agnes shouted at me to hurry up and I went to lift the galvanised bucket but it was too heavy and I tripped over it.' She closed her eyes and swallowed hard. 'My knee went down on the handle and it cut it open real bad.'

'And how is it now?' Anna asked.

'The nuns said it's gettin' better, but it feels a bit hot and sore like.'

'Did they take you to a doctor?'

Molly shook her head. 'Sister Teresa has been checkin' it and she says it'll heal up by itself.' She looked over at Lillian. 'I would 'ave let yer see it, but it's all bandaged up like.'

Lillian tried to think of something nice to cheer her friend up. 'We were going to take you out to a nice café for your lunch, and go for a walk around the town. If I'd known you were sick, I'd have brought you a present – some chocolates and maybe a book or a comic – something like that.'

'Never mind. You know wha' it's like in here, I probably wouldn't 'ave been allowed to keep them, like the girls that get stuff from their Sunday visitors.'

Lillian looked around her. 'The room is nice. They've done it all up...' A vision of her bedroom in Rodney Street flashed into her mind and a wave of guilt washed over her. She had been planning on describing it all to Molly in great detail but something told her now that it wouldn't be the right thing to do.

Molly gave a little laugh. 'They only did it when they knew youse was comin' to visit me like. Mother Superior got some of the girls to get this fancy cover for me from the nuns' laundry. She had them runnin' around the place just before youse came in.' She pointed to the chair and the table. 'They got them out of the nuns' drawing room. Don't you remember them?'

'I thought I did...' Lillian said, 'but at least it's made the room really nice for you... Does Sister Ignatius come to see you often?'

Molly shook her head. 'No, I hardly ever see her now. When I asked her if she had heard anything more about yer after yer left, she told me she wasn't allowed to mention yer name.'

'Did she?' Lillian gasped.

Molly nodded. 'I think one of the nuns heard her talkin' to me about yer, and she must have been reported to Mother Superior for showing fondness.'

Lillian felt a wave of guilt about the young nun. Then, as she glanced at her friend, she noticed her eye flickering again. 'Are you still having trouble with your eye?'

'Yeh,' Molly said. 'A doctor looked at it, and he said the muscles around the eye might have got kind of paralysed or somethin'. He said he heard of soldiers getting it in the war when they got a shock.' She gave a little shrug. 'He said it might get better after a while.'

Lillian guessed that hearing her mother had suddenly died must have caused poor Molly's problem. Even though she had acted as though she didn't care about her mother, she must have had some feelings for her.

'What's it like bein' outside?' Molly asked. 'Do yer like it?'

Lillian suddenly felt awkward with her aunt sitting there listening to everything. 'It just took me a little bit to get used to it ... all the traffic and the noise and things. But I like the house we live in ... and I've met some nice people.'

Molly nodded enthusiastically. 'I remember the traffic that day me and our kid were out at me ma's funeral. The noise, it would 'ave bursted yer ears until yer got used to it.' Her good eye widened and she suddenly smiled. 'Remember the priest took us for the fish and chips?'

'I do,' Lillian said. 'And I'd asked Aunt Anna if we could go to a café like that today because I knew you enjoyed it so much.' She was delighted to hear Molly sounding more like her old self.

'We'll go another day when Molly is feeling better,' Anna said. 'She can look forward to it.'

'Oh, I will,' Molly agreed. 'Could you maybe come again next week?'

'We'll see,' Anna said, guardedly. 'It will all depend on Mother Superior ...' She looked at her watch. 'They will be coming for us soon.' She went to the door. 'I'll wait outside and give you a few minutes on your own. Goodbye Molly, and I hope your leg gets better soon.'

'Ta very much for bringing Lillian to see me.'

'You're welcome, and next time we will go to the café that Lillian told you about.'

When the door closed behind her, Molly turned to her friend and said in a loud whisper. 'Yer auntie's nice, but I never imagined she'd be so posh!' She looked Lillian up and down. 'And you look dead posh too, in yer nice fancy clothes. When yer first came in, yer looked so different I didn't know what to say to yer. Even your hair looks different, it makes yer look older.'

'Do you really think so?' Lillian asked, not sure whether to be pleased or worried about it.

'Definitely... you look really nice. She must have spent a fortune on those lovely clothes.'

'She has been really good to me,' Lillian told her. 'I still can hardly believe it. I never even knew I had an aunt anywhere.'

'What's it like livin' with her? I bet she has a big posh house?'

'It's nice,' Lillian said, lowering her voice, 'but she's not as rich as you would think, because she takes boarders in to help her out.' She glanced towards the door. 'I was thinking, when you get out of here, maybe you could come and live with us.'

Molly's eyebrows shot up. 'Do yer mean it? Yer really think she'd let me come and live with yer?'

Lillian nodded, thinking fast. 'I think she would, but I need to give it a bit of time before asking outright. I need to give her time to get used to having me around.' She was afraid of promising things that her aunt wouldn't agree to. 'You might have to get a job though – maybe helping out in the house...' Lillian felt awkward even suggesting her friend come and work for her keep, but Molly seemed delighted at the thought.

Molly sat up straight now, her good eye wide with excitement. 'I'd love it. I can help in the kitchen or do the cleaning or anythin' like that.' She gave a little giggle. 'Can you imagine us together in the house? You an' me! It would be the gear, wouldn't it?'

'We'll have to wait a while,' Lillian said, whispering. 'As I said, I'm only there a few weeks myself, and I don't think Mother Superior would let you go as quick as they let me... She wasn't a bit happy about it, but my aunt went to see her and I don't know what she said, but she let her take me.' She leaned in close to Molly. 'I was afraid to come in here, in case Mother Superior changed her mind and made me stay... but I wanted to see you.'

Molly reached out now to take Lillian's hand, but as she moved, the bedcovers touched her sore leg and she winced at the pain.

'Are you all right?' Lillian asked.

'Yeah, it's just me leg...'

They both stopped as the door opened and Anna beckoned to Lillian. 'The nun has come to take us to the door.'

Lillian turned back to her friend. 'I'm sorry... we have to go.'

'I'll see yer again soon though,' Molly said, her voice sounding upset now, 'won't I? An' when yer get the right time, make sure to ask yer aunt...'

Lillian put her finger to her lips to shush her friend in case her aunt overheard. 'I will,' she whispered, 'I promise.'

As they sat in the back of the taxi going back home, Lillian said to her aunt, 'I feel much better now that I've seen Molly, and explained things to her face to face.'

'That's good,' Anna said. 'She seems a nice little girl.'

There was a short silence, then her aunt asked, 'And how did you feel being back in the convent?'

'As soon as I stepped inside, I knew I could never go back there,' Lillian told her.

'So you feel you are beginning to feel settled in our house in Rodney Street?'

'Yes, I am, thank you.'

Lillian suddenly felt very grateful for her new situation, but wasn't quite sure how to express it. She was still getting to know both her surroundings and her aunt, and she was still afraid that something might suddenly go wrong. That something bad might happen; and if she could not live in Rodney Street, where else could she go? She wasn't old enough to get a job that would pay the sort of money she would need for lodgings and clothes and everything else.

'I'm very lucky you came for me,' Lillian said now, 'but it

makes me feel very sad about Molly. I'm sure that living in that cold building isn't helping her chest. And she really shouldn't be doing all the heavy work she's made to do at times.' She paused, choosing her words carefully. 'It would be different if she was working in an ordinary house, doing the sort of work that Lucy does for you. Molly is a very good worker, and she might not sound it – the way she speaks and everything – but she is clever in her own way. If someone would give her a chance, just even as a maid in the kitchen or parlour.' She paused, waiting for her aunt to say something, which would give her an idea of whether there was any hope about her coming to live with them. But her aunt just nodded her head.

As they reached the city centre, Anna leaned forward and said to the driver, 'Would you take us to the Philharmonic Dining Rooms please?'

She turned to Lillian and said, 'I told Mrs Larking we would be out for lunch, so we'll eat here instead.' She smiled. 'It's a place I had planned on bringing you to soon.'

Anna looked out of the window wondering what she would say when the subject of Molly Power came back up again, as she knew it undoubtedly would... She was sure it would take some time for Lillian to forget her years in the orphanage, but she had not imagined that she would want to drag anything from that past into her new life. A sense of foreboding crept up on Anna, and she wondered if she had been mad to think this would all work out as easily as she had hoped.

So far, Lillian was showing great promise. Her assimilation into her new world had gone well, but this issue with Molly would undoubtedly throw up questions about their shared past. There was no way she would get rid of that guttural Liverpool accent, and even if she did, her whole demeanour spoke of her disadvantaged life. Sad though she felt for the poor child, the years of poverty and neglect were stamped on her undernourished body and could not be denied. No matter how desperate Molly was to join Lillian in a better life, the girl wasn't in any way equipped for it.

As the taxi moved up Renshaw Street past the Adelphi Hotel, Anna decided that she would just avoid the subject of Molly as long as possible. In another few weeks' time, Lillian herself might have changed. Who knows, Anna thought, she might make friends with some of the girls she met who lived locally, at her dancing classes or when she started tennis lessons in the spring. In time, she hoped, the girls would invite Lillian to social occasions and introduce her to the right sort of boys.

With Molly close by and depending on her, Lillian wouldn't be free to mix with young people in her social circle. She would not be free to become the person she should have grown up to be.

Anna turned towards Lillian now and squeezed her arm. 'I know the day hasn't gone exactly as you'd hoped, but at least you got to see your friend and let her know you hadn't forgotten her.'

Lillian smiled and nodded. 'Hopefully next time Molly will be able to come out for the day with us.'

'Hopefully she will.'

There was no point in saying anything about the future. They would just wait and see. Fate, Anna knew, had a way of sorting things out, and she would rather let things run their natural course as opposed to being seen to intervene. But if she found there was no other option, and the obsession with Molly became a problem, she would quickly sort things out – and without Lillian being any the wiser. She decided that as soon as Molly came of age, she would find a place for the girl to work in another city, a position with a good employer where the girl would be well looked after, but at a safe distance from Lillian, too far for them to meet up often. Anna herself had overcome many difficult situations in her life, and had learned hard lessons along the way. She would do everything she could to avoid Lillian going through the same things, and to make life kinder to her in the future.

She glanced again at Lillian, and was once more moved by the beauty of the girl: her hair, her eyes, the straight way she held herself. She hadn't imagined she would have such natural good looks and grace, something which she herself had lacked and had to work at.

A steely determination ran through her. She would do everything possible to give the girl the place in society that she deserved and the inheritance that was rightly hers. Molly, and anyone like her, had no place in Lillian's future.

Chapter Thirteen

'Excellent!' Mr Whyte said, smiling and nodding his head. 'You have mastered that piece perfectly. You can tell that all your practice is making a difference.' He lifted a pile of music scores from the top of the piano and, his forehead creased in concentration, started to riffle through them.

As she waited for him to choose another new piece, Lillian felt a little glow of satisfaction. She was gratified with the praise as she spent hours each day practising. Initially, she had been very self-conscious about being heard, and only used the piano when all the paying guests were out at work. Gradually, as her skills improved, she became more confident and began to practise in the evenings as well, when the library was free, although she made sure to close the door properly.

A tap was heard at the door, and the young parlour maid came in to give Mr Whyte a message. 'The message boy said he was to wait outside until you read it,' she told him.

Mr Whyte opened the envelope and looked at the message for a few moments, then looked up at the maid. 'Ask the boy to wait and I shall give him a letter to take back.'

He turned to Lillian and handed her a well-used music score. 'I'll only be a few minutes, and in the meantime, see how you get on with this.'

When he left, she opened the piece and studied it, and when she felt she was ready, she propped it up and started to play. Mr Whyte appeared fifteen minutes later, by which time she had mastered over half the piece.

'You must be spending hours practising every day to make this much progress,' he said, clearly impressed. He paused, his brow wrinkling. 'I hope you are not putting yourself under too much pressure? You are only young once, and I would not like to think you were missing out on more enjoyable pursuits?'

'I do lots of things,' Lillian told him. 'I have my sewing and reading and dancing...' She had been about to mention her elocution and etiquette classes when she stopped herself. These particular activities her aunt had suggested she kept quiet about, as it only raised curiosity about her previous education.

'All very worthy pastimes for a clever young lady,' he said. 'And I'm sure your aunt must be greatly entertained by your company. It's always nice to have younger people around.' He smiled. 'I must admit I enjoy having young Andrew to visit, he fairly livens the old house up. It can get very quiet here. I feel it since I lost my dear wife.'

Although Lillian's attention was taken with the mention of his grandson, she felt upset that Mr Whyte looked so sad about his wife. 'I'm sorry to hear that,' she said.

'Thank you, my dear,' he said, 'that's kind of you. I suppose things could be worse. I'm lucky that I have my music to keep me occupied.

'Your aunt, of course, was left in a similar position, and I think at times it can be worse for a female. Most others would have found running a house on their own very difficult, but instead Anna set about making hers into a profitable business. Even though she is financially secure, she refused to sit back on her laurels. She is a remarkable woman.' He raised his eyebrows. 'A remarkable woman indeed.'

'She is,' Lillian said, 'and she has been very kind to me.'

'Of course she has,' he said, smiling warmly at her. 'You are her closest relation, and very dear to her. It's the same way I feel about that scoundrel, Andrew.' He paused. 'He's spending time here after Christmas when his parents are up in Scotland – perhaps we could get tickets to the theatre or to a pantomime.'

Lillian looked at him, not knowing what to say. She had never been to the theatre, but the thought of more time with Andrew brought a glow to her.

'I shall speak to your aunt about it. I'm sure we can organise something.' He picked up the piece of music and gave it to her. 'I shall hear this again and then I have another piece for you to practise at home that might be a little more challenging.'

As she walked across the street to the house, Lillian felt a lightness inside her, a kind of excitement, every time she thought of seeing Andrew Whyte again. So far, he was the only boy she had been introduced to since arriving at her new home, and she wondered if she would feel the same way if she met any others.

'You look very happy,' her aunt said, when she came to Lillian's bedroom shortly after she arrived home. 'You're doing very well apparently – Mr Guthrie tells me you have a real talent for the piano.' She looked at the white material in Lillian's lap that she was carefully embroidering with flowers. 'What are you making now?'

Lillian looked up from her sewing. 'I'm embroidering a hand-kerchief,' she said. 'Do you think the stitches are neat enough?' She handed it to her aunt to let her examine it.

Anna looked at the flowers, and then she noticed the initial 'M' on it. 'It's lovely,' she said, 'and perfectly done.'

'It's for Molly,' Lillian said, her voice faltering a little. 'I think she would be allowed to have them, although I'm not sure, because I've never seen any of the other girls with their own personal handkerchiefs. If I give them to her when we see her next time, then at least she will see them and know that I made them for her. If we post them, the nuns might decide not to give them to her.'

Anna stifled a sigh. Even though things were going so well for Lillian, and she was growing in confidence every day, she always seemed to have Molly at the back of her mind. 'I didn't get a chance to tell you earlier, but I got a letter in the afternoon post from the head nun...'

'What did she say?' Lillian's eyes widened. 'Is she allowed to come out for an afternoon with us?'

'Yes,' her aunt told her, 'but not until Christmas.'

Her face fell. 'But that's weeks away...'

'Mother Superior said that Molly has only just recovered fully, and that it would be best to wait until nearer Christmas.'

Lillian pursed her lips together and looked as though she might cry. Then she slowly nodded her head. 'I suppose there's nothing we can do, and it will be more exciting for her to have a lovely day out then, won't it?'

'Yes,' Anna said, 'I think it will.'

Chapter Fourteen

The following week Lillian was given great praise by Miss Churchill for the improvement in her pronunciation and etiquette. Lillian was pleased, but as the session went on, she felt the teacher seemed to be acting a little strangely and at times couldn't tell when Miss Churchill was addressing comments to her or talking to herself.

When she had arrived at the teacher's house, Lillian noticed that she was dressed even more flamboyantly than usual, in a long, brightly printed dress and a blue turban. Miss Churchill listened as Lillian went through all her vocal exercises and lists of word pronunciations. When they finished, she presented Lillian with a copy of a poem, *The Highwayman*, to read aloud, but before Lillian even got a chance to look at it, she snatched it back, saying, 'I think if I read it out to you first, you will have a better idea of how it should be performed.'

Miss Churchill had paced up and down the room a few times, then come to a halt. Her voice was slow and dramatic, and her hands were waving about demonstrating the movement of the trees, her arms outstretched as though she was trying to balance.

Lillian suddenly remembered what her aunt had said, and it dawned on her that Miss Churchill was drunk. She forced herself to look serious, as though she was concentrating, and then she realised that Miss Churchill seemed oblivious to the fact that she was even there. She was now imitating a rider on a horse, cantering around the room. She went around the table in the middle of the room and then came to a halt in front of Lillian. She handed Lillian the poem.

'Lillian,' Miss Churchill panted, out of breath from all the exertion, '*The Highwayman* is one of the most romantic poems you will ever read. It is a great lesson in love and passion, and it is timeless.' She shook her head sadly, and as she did so, her turban dislodged itself and came down over one eye.' When true love grips, we are all fools, Lillian...' She put a hand up now to straighten the turban. 'You will find that out soon enough.'

She took a step back and then suddenly lost her footing and landed squarely on the floor.

Lillian rushed forward to help her back up. 'Are you all right? Can I help you?' she asked, putting an arm under Miss Churchill's arm. The teacher made a few moves to get up, and eventually with the help of her pupil and a chair, she got into a kneeling position.

'I'm quite all right, dear.' She sat back on her heels and smiled benignly. 'I'm still very supple for my age. When I was a young girl, I could do the splits. Of course, it wasn't very seemly for a young lady, but it was...' She paused and looked around her. 'What was I saying?' She leaned on the chair and with Lillian's help pulled herself into a standing position. 'I think, my dear,' she said, straightening her turban again, 'that I am a little under the weather, and perhaps I should go to bed.'

'Would you like me to call for your maid to help you up the stairs?' Lillian asked.

'My maid? She's gone, my dear girl,' Miss Churchill informed her. 'She left last week.' Her brows came down. 'Didn't you notice that I opened the door to you myself? Apparently she found a better situation in a bigger house.'

'Your cook?' Lillian ventured.

'Mrs Maloney only comes in a few times a week.' She waved her hand dismissively. 'I have no real interest in food, and it's a waste of money paying a cook for the small amounts I eat. She's getting on a bit, so I imagine she will go next and then I shall be fending for myself.'

Lillian found herself helping Miss Churchill up the stairs and along the cold and dimly lit corridor to her bedroom. She was taken aback when the door opened to reveal a rather untidy, colourful, bohemian-style bedroom. Every corner of the floor seemed to be filled with plants, while clothes and hats were draped over chairs and hung outside the wardrobe. Piles of books and magazines were on her bedside cabinet and around the room. A mannequin stood in one corner, adorned with numerous silk, velvet and decorative stoles topped with a variety of necklaces and strings of beads. Lillian guided Miss Churchill over to the bed, where she flopped down on top of the exotic bedspread. Within moments she was fast asleep and gently snoring.

Lillian crept out of the room and down the stairs, a feeling of hope building up in her. This, she thought, would be perfect for Molly, and only a few streets away. If the cook left, Miss Churchill was soon going to have no staff, which would be most unusual for a lady in her position. From what her aunt had confidentially told her, the teacher was already struggling to run her house and pay her bills, so she could probably not afford to hire anyone else. Molly could do the work of both the cook and the housemaid, and save Miss Churchill the wages of two employees in return for a room in a nice house.

The household chores would be nothing compared to what she was doing in the orphanage, and both she and Molly had spent many hours in the kitchen in the orphanage and knew all the basics required for cooking. Of course it had all been very plain, but Molly would know how to make toast or porridge, boil eggs or potatoes. They knew how to make soup from the skeletons of chickens which had been picked clean by the nuns, and then chop carrots and turnips to give a bit of body to the pale liquid. It wouldn't be as fancy as the food Miss Churchill would be used to, but she was sure the teacher would help and guide her as she was doing with Lillian now.

The greatest asset that Molly had if she came to work for Miss Churchill, Lillian thought, was that Molly was more than capable of handling a drunken woman, as she had spent her early life doing it. As she let herself back into her own house, a little thrill ran through Lillian as she imagined it all falling into place. She would need the intervention of her aunt.

Lillian knew she would have to be careful how she approached her aunt with this new idea. She could tell by her aunt's demeanour every time Molly was mentioned that she wasn't comfortable with their friendship. It would take her aunt time to accept a girl like Molly, who had come from the court housing slums. It wasn't either of their faults that they were so different, and it wasn't her fault that she was caught in the middle of them both. Lillian had given it great thought, and understood that it was a big enough change for her aunt to have her niece living in the house, and dealing with any more than that was bound to be asking for trouble. She wasn't used to young girls, though she had put a huge amount of work into preparing for Lillian's arrival.

She decided that she would go down to the church in the morning and light a candle, then say a prayer to the blue and white statue of Our Lady. She would ask her to intervene on her and Molly's behalf, and help them find a way to be together in the not-too-distant future.

Chapter 15

Lillian found that her weeks were now falling into a pattern. She no longer thought of the orphanage the minute she woke, nor did she mentally follow the daily routine of Molly and the other girls. There were days when she didn't think of her friend for hours at a time, and then a great feeling of guilt would wash over her.

But new routines had brought comfort to her life. She continued to say the Rosary every evening and she went to Confession at St Nicholas Church every Saturday. She had also made a habit of going from there to the Central Library. Some weeks she saw Rose Moran there, who always came to have a whispered conversation with her, and often had books saved under the counter that Lillian had requested. On one occasion, Rose had asked her if she had heard from Andrew Whyte, and Lillian felt herself blushing at the mention of his name.

'I think he was very taken with you,' the librarian had whispered, smiling in a conspiratorial manner. 'He spoke about you to me on a number of occasions, asking about the books you read, and the sort of thing that shows interest.'

Although she had light-heartedly brushed it aside, Lillian had been secretly delighted with what Miss Moran had told her, and found herself thinking about Andrew more often. The following week – after Mr Whyte had mentioned his intention to invite her and her aunt to the pantomime when Andrew was next home – Lillian blurted the news out to Rose. 'I'm just not sure how Aunt Anna will feel about it,' Lillian said, sounding a little anxious.

'I'm sure she will be fine, especially since she and Mr Whyte are old friends. I was at a concert in the Philharmonic Hall a few months ago and they were there together, and on another occasion – just before you arrived – I saw them go into the Adelphi Hotel for a big charity ball.'

She suddenly stopped when she saw the frown on Lillian's face. 'Oh, gosh... maybe I've put my foot in it. Really, it's none of my business, and I shouldn't have said anything. I was just trying to reassure you that your aunt would be fine about an invitation from the Whytes.' She lowered her voice further. 'I would be grateful if you don't say anything to your aunt about this. I would hate her to think I was a gossip...'

Lillian had smiled and said, 'Of course I won't say anything, I knew you were just being kind.' Miss Moran had gone off then, in case a queue was building up at the main desk.

Lillian was thoughtful for a while afterwards, and she wondered if there was a romance between her music teacher and her aunt. It was something she would never have considered, even though she liked Mr Whyte. The thought of her having a husband and a different sort of life was something Lillian found hard to imagine. Her aunt was so strong and independent, and seemed to manage the house and her business so very well on her own, that she found it hard to envisage her with a husband.

From what she had gleaned, it seemed her aunt's marriage had been relatively recent, and short in years. She wondered why Anna had not got married at the usual younger age that most women did. She was still very attractive and elegant, and must have been even more so twenty years ago, and Lillian thought she could not have been short of admirers. She tucked the thought away in her mind, along with the other questions she longed to ask her aunt.

Along with going to church and the library, another part of her new routine was that every Saturday, her aunt gave her ten shillings to use for any small personal items she might need and for buying cups of coffee or cocoa and a sandwich when she was in the city. Lillian was grateful for it, and in the beginning felt obliged to tell Anna everything she had spent the money on.

'It's your own money,' she said, 'and I know you will use it sensibly, so there is no need to account for everything you buy. All I will say is that if you have anything left over, try to save it. It's a good habit to get into early, and it's very important that you learn how to manage money. I had no idea about finances when I was young, and I had to learn the hard way.'

A shadow seemed to cross her face for a few moments but then she smiled. 'It reassures me to know that you will not be in that position, because you will share everything I have worked for, and hopefully, in the future, you will make a good marriage and have a husband who will protect and provide for you. But, in the meantime, it will serve you to learn the basics of finance, so you are not ignorant of how the world works in these matters, as many women are.'

Anna had then gone on to explain about the smaller properties she owned in various parts of Liverpool, and the rent that she derived from them.

Lillian was quite astonished to hear that her aunt owned more houses than the large one in Rodney Street. It must have shown on her face because her aunt then went on to explain in a low, serious voice.

'It's a monthly income,' she told Lillian, 'and an investment which I can sell if I ever need to.' She had paused. 'The only house I will never sell is the one Mr and Mrs Larking live in, out in Anfield.'

When Lillian had looked at her curiously, she went on to tell her that she felt bad when they first came to work for her and she found out they were living in a very old and damp house nearby, and paying an exorbitant rent for it. It had only two rooms and they had four children so there was little room for them all. 'Not as bad as some houses,' she said, 'but bad enough.'

'It was just after I got married,' she explained, 'and my husband was looking for property to invest in, and I suggested we buy a decent house in a better area, and rent it out to them. I knew they would keep it well maintained for us, and we would feel better knowing they weren't being taken advantage of. It worked out very well, and they were meticulous in every way with paying their rent and looking after the house. As you know, Michael Larking is very good with his hands, and as time went on, Edward asked him to take over the maintenance of a house he'd bought down in the city centre, so he has always worked between the two houses.'

She lowered her voice. 'After Edward died, I stopped the Larkings paying the rent, and I deduct a token amount each week from their wages to cover it. They are very hard-working and deserve to get on in life, and I know they could have made more money if they had worked in a factory or somewhere like that, but they have been loyal to me, especially since Edward passed away. Not paying a big rent has helped balance things for them, and they know I will keep them both in regular employment until they retire.'

As Lillian listened, she began to see the Larkings in a very different light. She had only thought of them in relation to the work they did in the house, and although Mrs Larking referred to her children regularly, she had given no real thought to their lives beyond Rodney Street.

'In the next few years,' her aunt went on, 'I intend to sign the deeds over to the Larkings so they own the house legally.'

'I think that is very kind of you,' Lillian said.

'They are very decent people, and I'm delighted to see that their children are benefiting from the situation. Their oldest son, Paul, is training as a tailor with Lewis's, and by all accounts is doing particularly well.' She reached over and squeezed Lillian's hand. 'Remember this, Lillian: money and how you use it is very, very important. Money buys you freedom and choices; it opens doors and can take you to all sorts of places. It also enables you to help others in a less fortunate position.'

Lillian wasn't exactly sure what her aunt meant about money

buying freedom – freedom from what, she wondered – but she did understand about it letting you help other people.

At the beginning of each week, her aunt worked out a time-table for Lillian's studies, and Lillian was constantly surprised by the wide range of subjects she had both knowledge of and an interest in. Over the weeks, Anna had taken her around the city museums and art galleries, and encouraged Lillian to focus on particular artists or sculptors she was interested in. Her aunt frequently brought novels and non-fiction books home for her that she bought in local bookstores or in a good second-hand bookshop she knew. She also bought magazines, and after reading them would give them to Lillian, and a few days later she often had afternoon tea brought up to their sitting room and she would then encourage Lillian to discuss the various articles with her.

One wet and windy afternoon, as they sipped tea and ate slices of Mrs Larking's fruit cake, her aunt asked if she found the problem pages in some of the magazines interesting. She noticed a hesitation and the pink circles that appeared on her niece's face.

'I take it you have read the pages?' She smiled. 'They're very popular with women, and I presume even more popular with curious young girls of your age. I just wondered if some of the problems married women write in about seem strange or confusing to you? Problems with their husbands... or perhaps about being intimate, that sort of thing.'

Lillian took a deep breath. 'Yes,' she admitted, not wanting to lie. 'I have read the page a few times.'

'And?' her aunt prompted. 'Is there anything you might want me to explain to you?'

'I'm not really sure...' She shrugged. 'I don't really know much about it.'

'I don't suppose the nuns ever mentioned anything about the facts of life? How babies are born and that sort of thing?'

'No,' Lillian said quickly, her cheeks flaming with embarrassment. The nuns had continually warned the older girls against sins of impurity and impure thoughts. They had also referred to 'wanton women' as those who encouraged men to have impure thoughts, and described women like Molly's mother who had gone with men for money. Exactly what 'gone with' men meant, Lillian was very unsure. She knew it had something to do with men and women going to bed together and women getting drunk and allowing men do things to them in dark laneways for money.

From the magazines, Lillian was shocked to realise that 'going with men' wasn't just something that happened to bad women, it was also an act that took place between decent, married people. She knew it involved taking your clothes off and allowing your husband to touch you, but beyond that, she had no real idea.

'Well,' Anna said, 'I've been thinking about it, and I feel it's something that you should know about sooner rather than later. In the next year you will be legally old enough to be married, and I don't want you waiting until your wedding night to discover what goes on between a man and a woman.'

Lillian bit her lower lip.

'I would rather you were prepared and understood about it because it's a very complicated thing. I don't want you totally ignorant, and I'm afraid of you hearing things that are not true and might frighten you, because that's exactly how I was introduced to it. Some women and girls have a very dark view of men and sexual intimacy, and enjoy nothing better than to tell horror stories about men demanding their marital rights from them. They would have you believe that it is an act that has nothing at all to do with them.'

Lillian then listened while her aunt went on to explain in a matter-of-fact way about how the sexual act was a natural and normal act between two loving adults. With her eyes lowered, she had briefly described the physical act itself, so Lillian was left in no doubt as to what actually happened.

'Now you understand the word, it's nothing to be afraid of, in itself. But some people, men in particular, have urges that are not always kept under control, so I would warn you to be on your guard as to the type of men you associate with as you get older.'

Lillian nodded slowly, trying to digest all that her aunt had said. She hadn't realised that relationships between men and women could be so complicated. And although she couldn't imagine herself in any sort of romantic relationship for the foreseeable future, she would bear in mind her aunt's advice if and when that time ever came.

Chapter Sixteen

On Sundays, Lillian continued to go to eleven o'clock Mass at St Nicholas Church. She had found a pew near the back and went into the same one each week. Gradually, she had got to know some of the people who sat around her – a few elderly couples and some families with children – and they now smiled in greeting when she arrived. One little girl of around four years old, blonde with curls, seemed to have taken a shine to her and had started to move along the seat to sit next to her.

On one drizzly Sunday, as Lillian was coming out of Mass, walking down the outside stairs and chatting to the little girl, she heard her own name being called. She turned around and saw it was a girl with curly red hair whom she recognised from her dancing classes. Lillian had only spoken to her on a couple of occasions, and wasn't sure of her name. She said goodbye to the little girl and then she turned back to the redhead.

'I thought it was you,' the girl said, smiling warmly at her. 'I said to my mum, I'm sure that's Lillian from the ballroom dancing class.' She turned back to a woman with blonde hair cut in a bob, wearing a fur coat and hat and red lipstick. 'Mum, this is the new girl I was telling you about. We are in the same dancing group.'

'Sure I know this young lady,' the woman said, smiling warmly at her. 'Aren't you Anna Ainsley's niece?'

Lillian looked at the woman, and for a few moments she was flummoxed. Then, the Dublin accent rang a bell and she realised it was the woman she and her aunt met the first morning she had arrived in Rodney Street. The woman had been friendly, but she remembered that her aunt had not stopped to talk to her.

Lillian smiled and nodded, 'Yes, you're right,' she said.

'Pleased to meet you, love.' The woman stretched her hand out to shake Lillian's. 'I'm Freda Flanagan.'

'It's very nice to meet you, too,' Lillian said. They all started moving down into the street so as not to obstruct the other people who were coming out of Mass.

'Anna is a real lady,' Freda said, 'always was, since the first time we met. Always turned out beautifully.' She paused. 'And I hear you've come to live with her?'

'Yes,' Lillian said.

'I'm not a nosey-parker or anything like that,' she laughed. 'I only know because my housemaid, Grace, knows your house-maid, Lucy, and she mentioned it. She was very complimentary about you, said what a lovely, clever girl you were.'

'Oh, that was kind of her,' Lillian said, smiling benignly. 'Lucy is very nice.' She remembered her aunt's advice to say nothing if anyone asked her anything about her background. She looked up at the sky, feeling a drop of rain hitting her hat.

Freda hesitated for a few moments, then said, 'Well, isn't it a small world, that you and Irene go to the same dance class? Irene loves it, and according to what Billy Gibb told me, she's a natural at the waltz.' She turned to her daughter now, beaming at her. 'And here's me thinking she had two left feet.'

'Thanks Mum!' Irene said, laughing.

Lillian laughed along with them, relieved to hear the girl's name.

'I said to her, you better learn how to dance properly or you're never going to meet a nice fella. I'd thought about her going to Irish dancing classes, but what good would that do her? It's mainly girls that go to it, and they end up spending all their time in competitions and the like.'

Lillian was already warming to the woman; she seemed very open, friendly and down to earth, like Mrs Larking.

'Besides, she would only meet other Irish people at these

things, and she meets plenty of Irish when we have family get-togethers.' She paused, her face more serious now. 'And how is your Aunt Anna?'

'She's very well, thank you.'

'She doesn't go out much now, since her poor husband died, does she?'

'Not really, I think she keeps busy at home.' Lillian was now feeling out of her depth; she knew nothing about her aunt's husband, and she could tell that Freda Flanagan presumed she knew all her history.

'I can understand it,' Freda said, 'it's not easy when you've been part of a couple and then you're on your own. I know that well enough.' She looked over at Irene and gave a little sigh.

Lillian felt some heavy drops of rain on her hat and was glad of the excuse to say, 'I think I had better move or I'll be soaked by the time I get home.'

'Are you walking home?' Irene said. 'You can have a lift with us in the car if you like, can't she, Mum?'

'Of course you can, love,' Freda said. She pointed to a car across the street. 'John is there waiting for us. He helps me out in the house and in the garden, and drives the car as well.'

Lillian was very surprised to realise that Mrs Flanagan owned a motor car because she had heard her aunt and some of the paying guests saying how expensive they were to buy. And although she was very pretty and well-dressed, Lillian didn't think that Mrs Flanagan's voice and way of speaking sounded like someone who came from a wealthy background.

Freda laughed. 'John's always saying I need to learn to drive myself, but could you imagine me behind the wheel of a car?' As she shook her head, Lillian noticed that her blonde bobbed hair stayed perfectly in place. The rain suddenly came on heavier now, and Freda said, 'Come on, girls, we'd better run or we'll get soaked.'

Irene linked her arm and as they went down the stairs, she wondered if her aunt would mind if she took a ride in the car with them. They seemed very nice and when she thought back to the day she first saw Freda, she guessed her aunt was just self-conscious because she was wearing her orphanage boots and didn't want to invite any queries about them. Lillian knew she was dressed as well as Irene now, so her appearance would not draw any negative comments or queries today. As they came closer to the green, shiny car, she thought what harm could it do to accept a lift home? The driver's door opened and she was surprised again when a very handsome, casually dressed man with dark hair came out to open the door for them. Lillian thought he looked like one of the film stars in her aunt's magazines. He was very polite and pleasant and asked in a light Liverpool accent where he should drop Lillian off.

Freda directed him to the house at the end of Rodney Street and when the car pulled up outside, Lillian thanked her for the ride home.

'Oh, you're welcome any time we're at Mass, love,' Freda said. 'And I was just thinking, wouldn't it be nice for you and Irene to go to the cinema together some time? Especially with Christmas coming up, because they usually show some great films around then.'

'Oh, that would be lovely!' Lillian said.

Irene leaned forward. 'We can have a chat about it on Wednesday at the dancing. Have a look at any newspapers that tell you what films are coming.'

'I will,' Lillian said, 'That would be great.' She had enjoyed discovering the delights of the cinema with her aunt, but the thought of going with a friend her own age seemed even more exciting and grown-up.

She thanked Freda and the driver again and then waved as they pulled away from the kerb. As she turned towards the house, she had the feeling that Irene might become a real friend, just like Alice and Molly had been. Having friends had made life much more bearable in the orphanage, and to have a friend to share all the lovely things she had in Rodney Street, Lillian thought, would be just wonderful.

Chapter Seventeen

One Monday in late November, Anna had to go down to London on some business. She explained to Lillian that she would be gone overnight, and back the following afternoon. She checked that Lillian had plenty to keep her occupied during the time she was gone and reminded her that Mrs Larking would be on hand for anything she needed.

Lillian kept to her usual routine, doing her studying, piano practice and sewing, and in the afternoon she walked down into the city to a haberdashery shop. After checking through the knitting section, she bought a deep V-neck cardigan pattern and chose some four-ply wool in a lovely shade of blue. The size was for a twelve-year girl, which she felt would be a perfect fit on Molly.

The following day when Anna returned home, she gave Lillian a six-inch square, black and gold metal cash box with a lock and key. 'Every week,' she advised, 'try to have something left over from your allowance to put in it.' She had glanced over at the blue knitting and said, 'Another little gift for Molly?'

'Yes,' Lillian said. 'It's a simple enough cardigan, and I thought it would be nice for her to wear when we have our Christmas day out. I know she won't be able to keep it, but I thought I could save up all the things I have for her in a cardboard box, and when she finishes with the orphanage, I'll have all those nice things for her.'

Lillian was delighted with the money box, and that week she started saving, even if she only had just a shilling or sixpence left over. With Christmas coming in a few weeks' time and her day out with Molly, it meant she could buy some little gifts for her friend. She also wanted to buy something special for her aunt, although she wasn't at all sure what, as her aunt seemed to have everything.

Just over a week later, Anna came to Lillian's bedroom to tell her that she was going down to London again.

'It's for a small female operation,' she confided. 'The only problem is that I will be gone for three or possibly four nights. The appointment letter was waiting for me when I arrived home, so I thought I would let you know immediately. Will you be okay on your own for that length of time?'

Lillian looked at her with frightened eyes. 'Are you okay? It's not serious, is it?' She couldn't imagine what she would do if her aunt was seriously ill, as she had grown to really care about her and would be devastated if anything happened. There was also the worry that if Anna wasn't there, she might have to go back to the orphanage. She could not imagine how she could go back to a life with the cold, heartless nuns after discovering what it felt like to be so well cared for and cherished.

'It's fine,' Anna said, registering her niece's anxiety. 'It's something that will be quickly and easily sorted, so there's no need for you to worry. We'll make sure you have plenty to do while I'm away, and if you have any little problems, you can go to Mrs Larking or either of the two ladies in the house.'

She then took a brown-wrapped package from her bag and gave it to Lillian. It was a large, heavy book: a *Blackie's Girls' Annual*.

'I spotted this today and I thought it was perfect for you. It has all sorts of stories and poetry, which I think you will love, and bits from Shakespeare. There are also some excellent non-fiction pieces. It's like an encyclopaedia, but more interesting, because there are activities too, like sewing patterns and crafts, and it even explains how you would construct a tent!' She laughed. 'Not that I imagine you have any plans to go camping yet, not at this time of the year anyway.'

'Oh, that's very kind of you,' Lillian said, looking at the bright cover, which had a picture of a girl cycling in the countryside with books tied to the pannier of her bicycle. She flicked through the pages, nodding her head and smiling. 'It's lovely. I will really enjoy this, thank you so much.'

'I'm glad you like it,' Anna said, delighted with the reaction. 'I thought we would go through the contents properly tomorrow and work out a little project for you to do on it while I'm away.' She paused. 'I know you have your piano lessons and ballroom dancing two of the evenings, so that will help to pass the time. And maybe we could ask Miss Moran or Miss Dixon if they would accompany you to the cinema another night?'

Lillian looked at her. 'Would it be okay if I went to the cinema with a friend from my ballroom dancing class? Her mother said she would make sure we get home safely, as they have a car that will collect us.'

Anna raised her eyebrows in surprise. 'Well, that sounds just lovely,' she said. 'Of course it would be okay. Do they live near?'

'Yes, I think they said they lived in Hope Street.'

'Ah, that's only a few streets away. What's the girl's name?'

Just as Lillian went to answer, a knock came on the door and Lucy came in.

'Mrs Larking says can yer call down to the kitchen when you get a minute, Ma'am?' the maid said. 'Her son, Paul, has called in, and she says you were askin' about him recently and thought you might like to see him.'

'Please tell her I'll be down in five minutes.' When Lucy went out, she turned to Lillian. 'If you come down with me, I'll introduce you to Paul. He's a nice young man, and I think Mr and Mrs Larking would be pleased if came down to say hello.'

When her aunt called for her a few minutes later, she was pleased to see Lillian sitting on the side of her bed, already engrossed in her new book.

'Are you finding it interesting?' she asked. When Lillian looked up, Anna was taken aback to see tears in her eyes. 'What's wrong?' she asked.

Lillian wiped a tear from her cheek, and then took a deep breath as though to stop herself from crying. 'Nothing...' she said, 'it's just something stupid.'

'What is it, Lillian?' her aunt said, coming over to sit beside her.

'I was just reading something and it made me think ... it made me think about my mother and father...'

'What is it?' Anna's face was suddenly pale.

Lillian held the book out to show her a chapter entitled *Children's Games and Their Origins*. 'I remembered my father playing games with me before he was sick. I was thinking about my mother too... about her teaching me the words of *Oranges and Lemons*. We had oranges at home, but I kept asking about the lemons, and I remember her one day, when we were in the greengrocer's, showing me what a lemon was.' Her voice faltered. 'I asked her to buy it and she did, and she made a sort of hot drink with sugar and the lemon squeezed into it.'

'And did you like it?' Anna asked in a soft voice.

'No... not really.' Lillian gave her a weak smile. 'It wasn't just Mum and Dad the book made me feel sad about. It was reading about the ordinary lives that other children had... all the things they did at home.' She looked at Anna. 'Apart from the games I remember from when I was little, I don't know any others. We never played any games in the orphanage; the nuns said girls like us needed to be praying and not playing.'

Anna's heart sank. She could not cope with her overwhelming guilt at not realising the situation that Lillian had been in for all those years – and for not rescuing her sooner. But she had done everything in her power to rectify it, and bringing her here to Rodney Street had been at great risk to her reputation. She knew that Lillian arriving as she did would invite lots of questions. She had gone ahead regardless, and had done her very, very best to make up for what had happened to the girl. And yet she was now realising that all the plans she had made were no guarantee that things would go as she had expected. The past was clinging on.

It was not Lillian's fault. Anna swallowed hard and tried to steady herself, then she turned towards Lillian and put her arms around her. 'I'm so sorry you have all these awful memories, Lillian. All the things that happened to you are terrible – losing your parents and then being sent to a place that wasn't what it should have been... but I had hoped that coming to live here would help make up for all of that.'

Tears were now streaming down Lillian's face, and Anna was at a loss over what to do.

'What can I do to help you?' she asked, holding her now at arm's length so she could look into her eyes.

Lillian took a deep breath. 'It's not you,' she said, 'you have been so good to me. I'm sorry that I'm being so stupid...'

'Stupid is the least thing you are! You're a very clever, sensible girl.' She drew her into her arms again and gave her a final squeeze. She paused and then said, 'Would you like me to take the book back to the shop and change it for another one? It would be no trouble.'

Lillian shook her head. 'Oh, no, I really like it... it's a lovely book...' She shrugged and tried to smile, but it didn't reach her eyes. 'I don't know what came over me. I was perfectly happy one minute, then I read that page and suddenly I began to think...'. She searched in her skirt pocket for her hanky and then rubbed it to her eyes, which were still a touch rimmed with red. 'I'm fine now, and Mrs Larking will be waiting for us.'

Anna moved to her feet. 'Let's go into my bedroom quickly and we'll dab a bit of powder on your nose and around your eyes.'

A few minutes' later, Lillian was back to her usual self and went down to the kitchen. As they went along the lower hallway they could hear voices and laughter, and she felt herself relax a little more. She often heard Mr and Mrs Larking chatting and laughing in the kitchen with Lucy, and Anna always seemed brighter and easier in their company too.

Michael and Nan Larking were sitting opposite Lucy, and seated comfortably in the carver chair at the top of the table was a dark-haired young man dressed in a smart suit and tie. They all looked up as Anna and Lillian came in, and then Michael and his son pushed their chairs back and stood up.

'Paul! How lovely to see you,' Anna said, going over to shake his hand. 'I hope you are keeping well?'

'I'm very well, thank you, Mrs Ainsley,' he said, smiling and nodding his head. 'And I hope you are well too?'

'Yes, still ticking over as usual, I'm glad to say.'

Lillian was surprised at how well-spoken he was, and at his obvious confidence, because her aunt had told her he was just turned eighteen. His parents were confident in their own way, but even when they were all relaxed in the warm kitchen, there was always a slight deference in manner when speaking to her aunt and even to herself.

As she looked at Paul through lowered eyelids, she could see an immediate resemblance between him and his father. He was, she thought, only a year or so older than Andrew Whyte, but Paul seemed almost like a grown man, whilst Andrew was still very boyish.

Anna turned to Lillian now. 'Paul, I would like to introduce my niece, Lillian, to you.'

Paul turned towards Lillian, his hand outstretched. 'I'm very pleased to meet you, Lillian,' he said, smiling warmly at her.

'Pleased to meet you,' Lillian replied, smiling back at him.

A picture of Miss Churchill flew into her mind, as she had made a huge issue of the fact that people on first meeting should just say, 'How do you do?' She had discussed it with her aunt and they had both agreed that Miss Churchill was being a bit pedantic and they thought it much more polite to repeat the greeting that was offered to them.

Paul smiled at Lillian again and asked, 'How are you settling here in Rodney Street?'

Lillian glanced shyly at her aunt, who quickly said, 'Oh, she's settled in very well, haven't you, Lillian?'

'Yes, I have, thank you.' Lillian hoped no one had noticed her red eyes.

Mrs Larking moved out of her chair over to the small table placed under the window, where she left freshly baked things which needed to cool. 'I've just taken a batch of scones out of the oven,' she said. 'Would you like to have one with us?'

Lillian looked over at her aunt.

'That would be lovely,' Anna said, pulling a chair out from under the table.

Paul immediately moved to help her and then pulled one out for Lillian.

'You're a gentleman, Paul,' Anna said gratefully. 'And how is life in the tailoring world?'

'Very good,' he said. 'We've been particularly busy lately. Our type of customers haven't been hit by the slump.'

His mother came over to the table with a plate of the warm scones and set them down in the middle, then asked Lucy to get the side-plates and knives, and tiny individual dishes for butter and jam. 'Tell Mrs Ainsley your good news,' she urged. 'That's what you came to tell us.'

'Ah, Mam, you're embarrassing me now,' he said, smiling and rolling his eyes. 'I just dropped in to catch you and Dad.'

'No good in hiding your light under a bushel, and Mrs Ainsley is always asking how you're getting on, so you can tell her your latest news yourself.' She watched as Lucy distributed the plates, then cut the butter into squares and put one in each small dish, then spooned the jam into more of the dishes.

'You must tell us, Paul,' Anna said, cutting her scone in two. 'We could all do with hearing some good news.'

Paul gave a little embarrassed sigh and said, 'I did well in my last exams, and I was told this morning that I've been moved on to train as a tailor's cutter, measuring the client, laying out patterns and cutting the material.'

'A big move on from when he started,' his father said. 'He was picking up pins from the floor, taking out tacking threads for the tailors and finding the right buttons, then sweeping up all day long.'

'Ah Dad,' Paul said, laughing, 'you make it sound like it was slave labour. When you're young you have to learn to keep the workplace clean and tidy.'

Michael winked at him now, enjoying getting a rise out of him. 'You complained enough at the start,' he reminded him.

Paul laughed. 'True, I admit I was desperate to get my hands on the scissors but they wouldn't let me near the material for the first year. Looking back, I can see they were right. The material is expensive and if the patterns aren't laid out properly, or the cutter isn't experienced, you can ruin a whole garment. Thankfully, that has never happened to me.'

'He's the youngest cutter they've ever had in the store,' his mother interjected.

'Really?' Anna said, her eyes bright and interested. 'That's terrific news. I'm so pleased for you, Paul.'

He shrugged. 'Lewis's are very good employers. They'll even help me with lodgings in the city centre.'

'That sounds excellent,' Anna said, clearly impressed.

'They said he's very good with the customers as well,' his father said. 'Got a way of getting on with all different types of people.' He nodded his head gravely. 'Oh, he'll have his own shop one day, nothing surer. Mark my words.'

'I'm more than happy where I am for the time being,' Paul said, 'and you see the world and his mother at Lewis's. You learn a lot about life working in a big place like that.'

'Well, it's good to be ambitious,' Anna said. 'It's a good trade to be in, clothes never go out of fashion, and those who can afford to buy top-quality, handmade suits will always buy them.'

'Enough about me!' Paul said laughing and reaching out for a knife. 'I've talked so much I haven't even started my scone yet!'

Just then, the bell upstairs rang, and Lucy automatically moved from her chair to answer the door.

Anna held a hand up. 'I'll get it, Lucy,' she said, 'please finish your tea. I'm expecting an order from Blackler's and I need to check it's exactly what I asked for. I'll be back in a few minutes.'

Lillian noticed that the atmosphere seemed to relax a little as soon as her aunt left. It made her feel self-conscious, and she wondered if the staff would feel more relaxed if she left too.

'Yer aunt's a great woman,' Michael Larking suddenly said to Lillian. 'If it wasn't for her, we wouldn't have been in the position to let Paul do his apprenticeship. She's been more than kind to us.'

'She certainly has, in more ways than one, and when she does something for you, she won't let you say a word about it,' Nan Larking said, 'but Paul never forgets, do you?'

'Of course not,' he said, looking over at Lillian and smiling. 'She's a lovely lady, and was always encouraging to me. She knew one of the managers in Lewis's and I'm sure she put in a good word for me to get a start there, although she would never tell you. You're a lucky girl to have come to live here with her; she's got a better business head than a lot of men, and she'll help to keep you on the right track.'

'She is a wonderful woman,' Lillian agreed.

There was a little pause as everyone took a sip of tea or ate their scones.

Paul looked over at Lillian again, his eyes narrowed in thought. 'Have you any idea what you want to do when you're ready to work?'

Lillian looked up and realised he was speaking to her. Work was something she had never even contemplated. Lillian herself had had no thoughts of the future further than Christmas – and so far, that had all been centred around her day out with Molly. She could see the expectant look on Paul Larking's face, and she realised that she was amongst people who all worked very hard for a living, as it was their only means of survival. It dawned on her now that it was something she had never considered. In the orphanage the only talk about the future had been dire warnings about the terrible wake-up call the girls would get when they were cast out into the real world. There had been no proper discussion about what they might do when they left.

Since arriving at Anna's lovely house, she had gone along with her aunt's plans to work on the education she had missed. She knew she was lucky that there was no need to go out and earn a living for the time being, and so far there had been no mention of what might happen when she had finished with her studies.

'I'm not sure . . .' she said, trying to sound as though she was answering an ordinary question, 'but I suppose I'll have to think about it quite soon.'

'Maybe yer aunt will send you to one of them posh schools in Switzerland,' Lucy said, spooning jam onto her scone. She looked at Mrs Larking. 'Finishing schools they're called, aren't they? Where you go learn all the things for when you get married to a real gentleman.'

Lillian felt startled now. The last thing she wanted to do was move away and have to start all over again, amongst girls she had nothing in common with. Meet more strangers she would have to hide her orphanage past from, and try to pretend she had grown up in an upper-class family like they had.

Mrs Larking must have seen the confused look on her face because she suddenly said, 'That's enough talk now about Lillian's plans for the future,' she said, 'and I'm sure her aunt wouldn't like us gossiping about it.' She cast a withering glance at her son for opening up such a controversial conversation. 'She'll know what's best for a young lady in Lillian's position, and it's not for the likes of us to be talking about it.'

Lillian took a drink from her teacup to help calm her racing heart and when she lifted her head she saw Paul Larking gazing intently at her. For a moment she felt as though he had been reading her mind, and as if he knew how scared she was.

'I'm sure Lillian doesn't mind, Mam,' he said unconcernedly. 'The world is changing, and there are plenty of young women like her now working in the city in all sorts of jobs. Some people think it's old-fashioned for a woman to be stuck at home doing things like needlework and giving afternoon tea parties.'

Michael Larking looked up at the clock, then drained the contents of his cup. 'I think I need to get moving now. I need to walk down to the ironmongers for some screws for the back gate.'

'We can walk down together,' Paul said.

Nan Larking looked at her husband. 'Can you give me and Lucy a few minutes' help with a wardrobe upstairs before you go?'

Lucy finished her tea off and all three went upstairs.

Lillian was about to leave with them, but she still had half her scone to eat. She thought if she left it, it might look as though she didn't want to talk to Paul.

She took a bite of her scone, then, as she went to swallow it, she suddenly caught her breath and began to cough. She reached for her cup and took a mouthful of her tea to help it go down, but the crumbs seemed to have lodged in her throat and she began spluttering.

'Are you okay?' Paul said. 'Will I get you some water?'

Lillian closed her eyes and tried to swallow again, but it just set off more coughing. Paul quickly rinsed out one of the cups and filled it with water and then rushed back to her.

By this time, Lillian's face was beetroot red and tears were streaming down her face with the effort of trying to suppress her coughing. She took a drink of the water and then held her breath for as long as she could to let it all subside.

'This might help dislodge it,' he said, coming around to the back of her. Lillian felt him leaning over her to firmly clap the middle of her back with the heel of his fist. Whether it was the action or the shock of him touching her, the coughing suddenly stopped.

'Are you okay?' he asked, pulling the chair out beside her.

Lillian finally managed to take a shuddering deep breath. 'Yes, thank you,' she said, feeling mortified. 'I don't know what happened ... it must have gone down the wrong way.'

'It's probably my mother's fault,' he said, smiling at her. 'I'm always telling her that she puts too much baking powder in them.'

Lillian felt a stray tear on her cheek and embarrassedly wiped it away. 'No, no,' she said, 'the scone was lovely ...'

He raised his eyebrows. 'I'm only joking,' he said, quietly.

Lillian thought he must think her very immature not to recognise a joke. She felt stupid, as the nuns had often told her she was.

He leaned a little closer now. 'Don't say a word to my mam,' he whispered. 'She would clout me over the head with the frying pan if she heard me criticising her baking. She still sees me as eight years old instead of eighteen.'

Lillian caught the devilish glint in his eye and an unexpected bubble of laughter came up in her throat.

'You are terrible,' Lillian said, giggling. She looked down at her plate and said, 'I'm not touching any more of this in case I show myself up by choking again.'

'Ah, don't worry about it, I'll just tell Mam you didn't like her baking. She's not the sort to take it personally or anything; she'll probably just put a bit of arsenic in the next one she gives you.'

Lillian started off laughing again, and he started to laugh heartily too. It was only when the sound of footsteps were heard on the stairs that they both straightened up, and Paul got to his feet and walked towards the window.

'Sorry I took so long,' Anna said, coming in and then making back to her place at the table, 'but there was a problem with the order and I had to wait until the man went through every parcel in his van.' She looked at Paul. 'Your mother kindly told me that she had left the scone for me to finish.'

Lillian suddenly gave a little snort of laughter at the mention of the word 'scone' and her aunt stared at her. 'Are you all right?' she asked anxiously.

'Yes,' Lillian said, 'I'm fine ...'

Her aunt's brow was furrowed and she didn't seem reassured. 'It's just that you look ...'

Lillian realised that her face and eyes must be red again, and that her aunt thought she had been crying again. 'We were actually just laughing ...' she said, not wanting to cause her aunt any more worry. '

Paul came towards the table. 'I made a daft joke about my mother's baking and we both started laughing.'

Anna's shoulders immediately relaxed. "'It's so much better to laugh than cry...' She took a mouthful of her lukewarm tea, then she took a few bites of her scone before Mrs Larking and the others appeared back in the kitchen, with Mr Larking already in his overcoat.

'Lovely to see you again, Paul,' Anna said, 'and good luck with your new position.'

'Thank you,' he said, shaking her hand. He turned to Lillian. As he took her hand in his, he gave it a little squeeze and when Lillian looked up at him he gave her a conspiratorial wink and said, 'Lovely to meet you, Lillian.'

When the men left, Anna turned to Nan Larking and said, 'You must be very proud of him. He'll make a good husband for somebody in a few years' time. Is he courting yet?'

'Not that I'm aware of. He was going out with a nice girl called Edie for a few months in the summer, but she left to go to Newcastle to train to be a teacher.' She shrugged. 'Whether they'll pick up again when she comes home at Christmas, I don't know.'

Back up in her bedroom, Lillian lifted her embroidery and started working on it again. Every so often she put it back down, thinking about the events in the kitchen earlier. Each time, she found herself smiling. It was strange after all the years of living in a female-only establishment that she should now find that she enjoyed the company of the opposite sex. She had now met two very different boys: Andrew Whyte and now Paul Larking. Although she supposed most girls would find them both good-looking and well-dressed, what she found most appealing about them was the fact they could make her laugh.

And whilst she had the odd little daydream about a future romance with someone like Andrew, Paul Larking was older, and his worldly-wise confidence was a little intimidating. She wasn't surprised to know that he had already started courting.

Although her aunt had prepared her for what would physic-ally happen if she ever got married, and she no longer thought of it as being frightening, she knew it would be a long time before she was ready to embark on any real kind of relationship.

She looked back down at her embroidery and thought of the things she would make for Christmas. Her aunt had told her that they would take the train across to Manchester one day, and do some Christmas shopping in a popular store called Kendal Milne. Anna planned to buy them both a new day outfit and an evening dress for any functions they might be asked to.

Lillian wondered about Mr Whyte's suggestion that she and her aunt go out with him and Andrew one evening. She presumed that was one occasion she might get to wear an evening dress. An *evening dress!* Who would have thought it, when only a short time ago she was in an orphanage wearing drab uniforms every day?

Her glance fell on her *Blackie's Girl's Annual* again, and her throat tightened when she thought of the fuss she had made earlier in the day about her time in the orphanage. Apart from Molly, it was all over and done with, and she had a bright future to look forward to. Hadn't Paul Larking asked her what she planned to do? He obviously thought she was capable enough of finding work somewhere.

Liverpool was a big city and she was sure there must be lots of openings for girls around her age. When she got the chance, she might even chat to Irene about her plans for the future. She was sure she would know what opportunities there were. In the meantime, she would just keep busy improving herself in as many ways as she could without the need for a finishing school.

Chapter Eighteen

On a frosty Thursday morning in early December, a hackney cab pulled up outside the house. Lillian came out of the house with her aunt to wave her off. They had had an early breakfast together, then Anna had gone to prepare for the taxi to take her to Lime Street Station to catch the train to London.

'You should have nothing to worry about,' Anna said, as they walked towards the vehicle. 'Lucy will be here every night to make you supper, and both Rose and Jane Dixon have said they will keep an eye on you.'

'I'm not worried about being on my own,' Lillian said. 'I just hope you are going to be okay. I don't like you going all the way down to London on your own.'

The taxi driver came to take Anna's bags.

'I'll be fine. I have lived in London and I've chosen to go to the hospital there because it's the best. The procedure I'm having is fairly routine for women my age.'

Lillian clasped her hands together. 'You'll let me know as soon as you have had it all done?'

'Yes, I promise. The minute I am awake and able to organise it, I will make sure that a telegram is sent here to let you know all is well. The operation is early tomorrow morning, and the surgeon said I can expect to be awake and bright by the afternoon, so hopefully I'll organise the telegram then. I'll spend the weekend recuperating and I expect to be home on Monday.'

Lillian nodded her head, taking it all in. She thought she had been unconcerned about her aunt going, but now it was actually happening, she felt strange, almost as though her aunt was abandoning her forever – which she knew was silly.

The driver held the passenger door open.

'I've got to go,' Anna said, 'and I'll be home before you even have time to miss me.' She opened her arms wide and then encircled Lillian in a big hug. 'I love you, Lillian... and I can't tell you how happy I am to have you in my life.'

Lillian felt a surge of emotion so great, she initially could not speak. She hugged her aunt back tightly and then kissed her on the cheek. Then, as they moved apart, Lillian whispered, 'And I love you too... and I'm very happy that you brought me to live with you.'

She waved her off, and as she walked back into the house, she realised she was crying again. Three times recently she had cried: the first time out of sadness, the second with laughter, and now she had cried because for the first time in years she knew she was loved.

The following morning, Lucy came up to Lillian's bedroom with a letter for her.

'Someone must have stuck it through the letterbox,' the maid said, ''cos there was no stamp on it and only yer name.'

It was the first letter Lillian had ever received and as she took it from the maid, she couldn't think who might write to her. For a fleeting moment she thought it might be from Andrew. When she slid the torn sheet of paper out, she gasped with delight when she recognised Molly's childlike handwriting. It was only one page, but she couldn't stop smiling as she read it.

Dear Lillian,

A nice girl from outside the convent called Gretta has started work in the laundry. She is eighteen years old and she lived in the same street that we did when my mother was alive. She remembers me and our Daniel, but I don't remember her. She is very friendly and when I told her about you she said if I wrote you a letter, she would hand it in to your house. I remembered your address and when I told her, she knew where it was and said it was in a posh part of the city.

Everything else is the same here, day in, day out. I miss talking to you and the laughs we had. My leg is nearly better now and my chest is better than it was when you came to see me, so I never had to go back to the sick-room, thank God.

We have been doing a lot of knitting and sewing, as there is a Christmas Fayre in one of the churches and the nuns said we have to make things for them to sell. I had made a lavender bag and tried to keep it for you, but Sister Dominic had them all counted and I had to hand it in to her.

I am looking forward to seeing you when you come before Christmas. I have been quiet and keeping out of trouble, so as not to give Mother Superior any excuses to stop me going. I heard her talking to Sister Ignatius when she thought I was asleep, and she seems a bit afraid of your auntie stopping some money coming to the convent. She said they needed to keep on her good side, and that's why they let you go to live with her. They said other things I didn't understand, but as long as she lets me out to see you for Christmas, I don't care. It is the only thing that keeps me going in this place. I can't wait until I am sixteen to get out.

Gretta said if you want to write back to me, you can leave a letter at her house and she will smuggle it into me. I will write her address at the bottom of the letter. She says it is right behind the library and the Walker Art Gallery if you know where they are. If you write back to me I won't be able to write again until after I see you as I'm afraid of getting Gretta into trouble. The priest got her the job and she says her family need the money as her mother is very sick.

  See you soon,

    Yours sincerely,

      Molly.

Gretta O'Brien, 12 Clayton Street. She said if you can't find their rooms, ask any of the neighbours outside and they'll tell you where they live.

Lillian was overjoyed with the letter and throughout the morning kept reading it over and over again. Although Molly's handwriting was that of a younger child, she was surprised that the content of the letter was perfectly worded and spelled. At least it was one good thing about their basic 'Three Rs' education in the orphanage – English and spelling had been drummed into the girls along with arithmetic and religion. Being good at writing, she thought, would stand Molly in good stead when she got away from the nuns. If there were no openings for her as a maid, perhaps she might get a job in a shop or one of the factories.

At one point Lillian sat down to write a reply, but after a while she laid it aside as she felt it was too soon, and once it had gone, she would have to wait weeks before she met up with Molly. She decided instead she might write a longer letter, adding bits to it over the weekend when she might have more interesting news.

That evening, Rose Moran came up to Lillian's sitting room to ask her if she would like to join the guests for dinner while her aunt was away. Mrs Larking and Lucy brought up a lovely dinner of roast pork and crackling, which Lillian had said was her favourite meal, and she guessed that it had been especially organised for her.

There were only the two women and Mr Collins, and Rose Moran told Lillian that Mr Guthrie wouldn't be joining them as he had gone to visit the family of a colleague who had recently died of flu.

'A fit and healthy man by all accounts,' Noel Collins said, shaking his head. 'He was fine one day and then went down with flu. By the time they got him to hospital he was dead within hours.'

Rose clapped her hands together. 'Right, we could do with

something to cheer us all up, so why don't we have a game of cards?'

Lillian enjoyed the game and afterwards, she went into the library and did half an hour of piano practice.

When she came back upstairs, she went to her wardrobe and lifted down a cardboard box from the top shelf. It contained Christmas presents she had been buying and wrapping in festive paper for Molly.

She had started collecting them in mid-November, and had added to them as the weeks went by. Some of the gifts she had bought and some she had made. She had found an excellent second-hand clothes shop at the top of Renshaw Street, and any time she was passing she called in to see if she could find something suitable for her friend. She had bought a couple of plain skirts and carefully altered them until they were the size she estimated that Molly was. She had also picked up some girls' shoes with a small heel and a lovely dark brown handbag for seven shillings, which she thought wasn't too showy for her friend, and would be suitable for everyday use. She had almost been put off the bag when the elderly saleslady told her it was made from alligator skin.

She explained that the bag was a gift for a friend, and the saleslady had smiled and said, 'Alligator and crocodile skin bags are very popular at the moment with young middle-class ladies like yourself.'

As the lady wrapped the bag up for her, Lillian spied a navy blue and silver beaded evening bag, which depicted two colourful peacocks. It was small with a long silver chain, but it felt very heavy. 'How much is this, please?' she tentatively asked.

The woman came over to examine it. 'It's marked at fifteen shillings. The lady who brought it in said she had bought it in a big department store in New York. You won't find anything like it in the shops here.'

Lillian looked at the bag and thought she would have to take money from her savings to be able to afford it. She gave a little sigh and put it back on the shelf.

The lady looked at her. 'I can let you have both of the bags for a pound.'

Lillian thought for a moment. 'I have enough for the alligator bag now.'

'Well, if you pay me for that, I'll hold the American bag for you until next week.'

'Oh thank you,' Lillian said. 'It's for my aunt's Christmas present. I think she would like it for going to the theatre or places like that.'

Along with the bag and clothes, Lillian had a lovely nightdress case she had made for her friend using the pattern from her Blackie's annual, and a handkerchief holder she had embroidered. She had also some stockings and underwear she had bought from Marks and Spencer's on Church Street, as she wanted Molly to have all the basic things for coming out of the orphanage that her aunt had been kind enough to give to her. She had read in a magazine advert for underwear that a special allure comes from knowing you are wearing pretty things underneath your clothes. She wasn't quite sure what it meant, but she felt that anything that gave Molly confidence could only be a good thing.

Chapter Nineteen

The following morning was cold but bright. After breakfast, Lillian thought that since the part-time housekeeper, Mrs Magill, would be cleaning their bedrooms and changing the bedding, she would go into the city early.

She decided to go the Walker Art Gallery first as she'd agreed with her aunt to work on an art project while she was away. On her way out of the house, she spied Mr Guthrie in the library. He was more formally dressed than usual and when she saw the black armband he was wearing, she remembered he was going to a funeral. Miss Churchill had recently discussed with Lillian the correct way to offer condolences to people who had been bereaved, so she stopped briefly to commiserate about his colleague.

The art gallery was quiet and an hour flew by as she went around the various rooms hung with paintings. For her project, she picked three different paintings that she would like to write about. The first was one was painted by an artist called William Frederick Yeames entitled *And When Did You Last See Your Father?*

She liked the little boy dressed in blue in the painting, and after reading the short information piece about it, decided it would be interesting to research. The second painting she liked was called *A Street in Brittany* by an artist called Stanhope Forbes, depicting a scene with local women wearing clogs, and sitting outdoors in the sun, knitting and making nets. It was painted in lovely blue tones, and it made her think about how differently people lived in other countries. As she stared at the painting, her thoughts turned to her friend Alice in Canada. A sadness washed over her as she knew she would never see her friend again.

She moved on to another room to choose her third painting, *Dante's Dream* by Dante Gabriel Rossetti. Although she thought it was a darker painting in many ways than the others, something about the women – dressed in green flowing gowns – and the crimson-robed angel caught her attention, and made her think there would be an interesting story behind it all.

She had moved forward to get a better look at the poppies at the bottom of the canvas when she became aware that someone was standing close to her. She turned and found herself almost face to face with a smartly dressed man, wearing a bowler hat and a striped tie, and who smelled strongly of cologne,

He raised his eyebrows and smiled at her. 'Interesting, isn't it?'

Lillian instinctively stepped back. 'Yes,' she said, 'it is . . .'

'And which part of the painting appeals most to you?' he asked.

Lillian suddenly thought he must be one of the gallery staff. She smiled at him and then looked at the painting. 'I like the colours,' she said, 'the colours and the lovely flowing clothes.'

'Personally,' he said, moving closer to her again, 'I always prefer ladies without their clothes.'

Lillian looked away for a moment, trying to work out what he meant.

When she looked back at him she noticed his eyes moving from her face to her breasts and back up again, smiling all the while, and it dawned on her that he was one of those awful men that her aunt had warned her about. A hot feeling of indignation rose up in her. She gave a loud, disgusted sigh and turned on her heel and walked quickly back into the main area towards the stairs.

As she went quickly down the grey stone stairs, a mixture of fear and anger raced through her. She was glad her aunt had warned her about strange men, but she had never imagined things like this happened in public places.

When she came out of the gallery she decided to walk across to Lewis's tearoom for tea before going into the library to write up her work about the art. She also thought that getting away from the area would also lessen the chances of running into the horrible man again.

The day suddenly seemed much colder and the sky had gone from blue to dark grey. She pulled her hat down over her ears as she crossed William Brown Street, to cut through John's Gardens and from there walk down to the busy Ranelagh Street to the department store.

She was just halfway through the gardens when heard footsteps coming quickly behind her. Her heart lurched at the thought of the man following her. She whirled around to face him and found herself staring at the smiling face of Andrew Whyte.

'I thought it was you,' he said, looking delighted. He was dressed in a navy overcoat and had a black hat on with a navy band, and had a leather document holder under his arm. 'I called out but you didn't hear me.'

He paused, waiting for a reaction, then something about her made him ask, 'Are you all right? Did I give you a fright or something?'

'It wasn't you ... I thought you were someone else.'

He put his arm on her back and guided her over to a bench. 'Come on, you have to tell me what's wrong.'

When they were sitting down, she explained what had happened.

'What a creep!' Andrew said. 'And you gave him the correct response.' He stood up and walked a few steps forward, looking to the left and right. 'Can you see him anywhere? If you point him out, I'll give him a piece of my mind.'

She shook her head. 'It's not worth it. I just got a fright when I thought it was him coming up behind me again.'

He held his hands up. 'Thankfully, it was only me.'

'I didn't know you were coming to your grandfather's – he never mentioned it.'

'He didn't know,' Andrew said. 'It was a surprise for his birthday. I came up with my parents. They've taken him out in the car to visit an old friend in the Wirral.' He tilted his head to the side, his eyes looking straight into hers. 'I saw you leave the house on your own earlier on, and I guessed you might be down around the library area as usual.'

As she looked back at him, she felt both surprised and pleased that he was happily admitting that he had actually followed her down into the city.

'Well, you were right,' she said, trying to sound casual.

He held his document case up. 'I'm supposed to be studying in the library for my Christmas exams, but I'm in no rush to get there. Where are you going now? Not home, I hope?'

'I was on my way to Lewis's tearoom to have a break before doing some art history work.'

He stood up and crooked his arm for her to put her arm through his. 'Allow me to escort you, Madame,' he said, 'and if you will allow me, tea will be my treat to apologise for my clumsy greeting.'

'You didn't do anything at all, and I do have money of my own.'

'I insist,' he said. 'Besides, my father gave me two pounds to get rid of me for the afternoon. He knew I would be bored listening to all the old guff they talk about the orchestra and the war and everything.'

Lillian started to laugh. 'You are terrible,' she told him.

'Do you fancy going to the Adelphi instead of Lewis's?' he suggested. 'They have lovely coffee and a terrific variety of cakes in there.'

She hesitated for a moment, thinking about the awful man in the art gallery. Her aunt had warned her about men like that and she guessed that she would prefer to be with Andrew than take a chance on bumping into him again.

'Okay,' she said. Anna had said they would go to the Adelphi

Hotel soon, so she was sure she wouldn't mind her going there with Andrew, especially now she knew Anna and his grandfather were such good friends.

The hotel was much bigger, grander and surprisingly quieter than she had imagined. A uniformed doorman welcomed them at the entrance and showed them inside. As they walked along she took in the beautifully decorated walls and ceilings, the pillars and exotic plants, the elaborate velvet curtains, the tapestries and the glittering chandeliers. It was the fanciest place she had ever been in, and a little voice inside told her that she was moving into unfamiliar territory and shouldn't have come here without her aunt.

Andrew moved alongside her and quietly asked, 'Where would you like to sit?'

She tried to remember Miss Churchill's advice, but her mind was racing too quickly to think properly. 'I don't mind,' she said. 'I haven't been here before, so I'll let you choose.'

He gestured towards the stairs, which she could see led up into a huge room.

'I think you'll like it in here,' he said. 'This is where I usually come for tea with my grandfather or my parents.'

When they went into the huge lounge area, she noticed that less than half the tables were occupied and she was glad. She would have felt more self-conscious walking across the floor of such a formal place, with a young man by her side, had it been full.

A waiter appeared and found them a table over by one of the tall windows. He took their coats and whisked them off to the cloakroom.

'You are still thinking about that incident in the art gallery, aren't you?' Andrew said, smiling sympathetically. Lillian glanced over at him and he leaned forward and whispered, 'Your gloves.'

'You're right, I'm not thinking straight,' she said, shaking her head and smiling. 'I hadn't even noticed I still had them on.'

The waiter came back to place napkins in their laps, then handed them menus and stood to the side while they decided.

Lillian wondered if she should take her hat off, but imagined that her hair might look tousled if she did. She decided to leave it on.

She looked at the menu, and found it hard to focus on the tiny, elaborate writing. Everything suddenly felt complicated without her aunt to advise her.

'Well?' Andrew said, rolling his eyes and trying to be funny. 'Have you decided yet?'

'A scone, please,' she said.

'You'll have to go for something more exciting than that,' he told her. 'The pastries are fantastic here.'

The thought of eating a fancy cake made her feel worse. 'Just a scone will be fine,' she repeated, her voice sounding strained even to her own ears.

Andrew checked his watch. It was quarter to twelve. He widened his eyes in mock horror. 'My darling mother would have a fit if she thought I was having cake at this time, but it's what I fancy and she's not here to tell me off.' He looked at the waiter. 'Coffee for two please, and a scone for the young lady...' He halted, still deciding. 'And I will have... a chocolate éclair!'

When the waiter left, Lillian shifted uneasily in her chair, wishing she had stuck to her original plan of Lewis's tearoom.

'So, tell me,' Andrew said, staring intently at her, 'what have you been up to since I last saw you?'

She shrugged. 'Nothing much... just the same, studying and practising music... I'm sure you have more interesting news than me.'

'School, school and school!' he sighed. 'But thankfully, this is the last year.'

'What will you do after that?' Lillian asked.

'Law,' he sighed. 'Probably Oxford or Cambridge. It's all organised for me. The plan is eventually to take over my father's practice in London.'

Lillian bit her lip. 'I'm sure it will be a very good career for you...'

'I don't know,' he said, 'I really haven't given it much thought.

It all seems to be so dark and serious, that's why I want to enjoy any freedom while I have it. And you? What's all this studying about? Is it just to continue your education and general knowledge or are you an independent, scholarly lady and planning to go into one of the professions?'

Lillian gave what she hoped was an elusive smile. 'I don't know yet,' she said. 'I'll be sixteen soon, and I'll start to think more seriously.'

'Maybe you have plans to get married?'

Lillian's head jerked up, and when she looked at him she could see he was grinning at her. 'Married? I certainly don't have any plans for that,' she said, looking appalled. 'I'm sure there are plenty of other things that a young woman can do besides getting married.'

'Gosh, Lillian, you are very serious today. I was only joking.'

He grinned and rolled his eyes. 'I was told off at breakfast by my mother for what she called my "bizarre sense of humour". I don't mind driving her mad now and again as she can be very pompous, but it looks as though I might be on rather shaky ground if you share her opinion.'

He clasped his hands beseechingly. 'I really was joking, and I agree that it is only right that women should have far more options now.'

'I'm glad to hear it,' Lillian said, smiling now.

'You have a good example with your aunt, who is a very independent lady,' he said. 'My grandfather has huge admiration for her. Apparently she has made a great success of her boarding house.'

Lillian shrugged. 'I don't really know much about the running of the house...' She suddenly wished she hadn't met Andrew Whyte today. Every topic he brought up seemed to be a minefield. She felt out of her depth in this place.

She was glad when the waiter appeared with their coffee and food. The waiter fussed around for a few moments, and then they both sipped at their coffee.

'What paintings did you look at this morning?' Andrew asked.

Lillian looked up at him expecting another silly conversation, and was surprised to see he was serious. 'I looked at quite a few,' she said, 'and then I picked three to study this afternoon.'

'I would love to know which ones you liked.'

She told him about the paintings, and was pleased when he didn't know one of them, *When Did You Last See Your Father?* It meant they weren't too obvious.

'I must make a point of going over to the gallery to see it,' he said. 'It sounds an interesting one.' He raised his eyebrows. 'There are times when I could ask when I last saw my own father. He spends a lot of time at work, and then he is away at the weekends in the car visiting my married older brother or sister, or going to race meetings or playing golf. My mother complains about him being away all the time, but it doesn't seem to make any difference.'

Lillian kept glancing at him, expecting him to make a joke, but his face remained almost grave.

'Another bone of contention is travelling – she hates getting into the car with him because she thinks he drives too fast.' He rolled his eyes. 'That's why I'm happy to escape up to Liverpool to my grandfather's as often as I can.'

Three very smartly dressed men came down from the hotel's upper floors, and stood talking at the open doorway. When Lillian heard the voices, she looked across the room and saw one of them staring at her. She immediately lowered her eyes, but as she did so, she registered something familiar about him. When she glanced up again, the three men had gone.

Andrew finished the last mouthful of his chocolate éclair, politely dabbed his mouth with the napkin, then sat back. 'You seem to get on very well with your aunt,' he said, 'and she doesn't seem too strict with you. Compared to most girls I know, you seem to be allowed to do pretty much what you like.'

Lillian was taken aback. 'In what way?'

'The fact that you could join me without having to ask permission,' he said. 'My mother would never have allowed my older sister to go for coffee with a boy without an adult being there, but she is very strict and old-fashioned.' He raised his eyebrows. 'Miss Moran thought we should have been chaperoned even in the library. I don't know what she thought we might get up to on our own.'

Lillian suddenly felt a little stab of alarm. Had she judged things very wrongly coming to a hotel for coffee with him this morning? The advice she had had from her aunt and Miss Churchill now swirled around in her mind. She didn't think there had been any rules about friendship between boys and girls, and she now realised she had just treated Andrew as though it was a female friend who had asked her to go for a coffee. Her stomach started to churn now at the ramifications of it all.

She took a drink of her coffee. 'I think I am sensible enough to make a decision when I am on my own.' She looked up at him. 'I actually decided to join you because I was afraid I might meet that awful man again, and I thought you asked me for the same reason – to look after me. And I'm sure if something like that happened to your sister, your mother would prefer her to be safe rather than caring about old-fashioned rules.'

'Of course,' he said, looking flustered. 'I didn't mean it to sound as though I was criticising you. It was meant as a compliment to you and your aunt for being so modern in your thinking.'

'If my aunt is not happy when she hears about it, then I will abide by her rules until the time comes when I make my own decisions.'

'Gosh, I hope that doesn't happen,' he said earnestly. 'I really enjoy being with you, and it would be very boring if I didn't see you.'

Lillian didn't answer. She lifted her handbag and started to search inside for her purse. She was so engrossed that she didn't see the figure approach until he spoke.

'I hope you don't mind me interrupting?'

She lifted her head and found she was looking into the eyes of Paul Larking. A very smart, well-dressed Paul Larking.

'I was here a short while ago meeting a client who is staying in the hotel, and I saw you. I just thought I would come and say hello and check you weren't choking on anything today.'

Lillian smiled embarrassedly. 'I'm fine thanks, no choking today.' She looked over at Andrew who was now sitting up straight in his chair, looking from one to the other.

'Andrew,' Lillian said, 'I would like you to meet Paul Larking. Paul, this is Andrew Whyte.'

Paul went around the table to shake hands with Andrew, and said, 'My mother works for Lillian's aunt.'

'And Andrew's grandfather is a friend of my aunt's,' Lillian explained. 'We met when I was having music lessons.'

Paul nodded his head. 'Well, I'm sure that's nice for both families that you are stepping out together.'

'We're just friends,' Lillian said quickly. 'I was going to Lewis's and we bumped into each other.'

He held his hand up. 'You don't have to explain a thing to me,' he said. 'I only came over to say hello. I'm with a colleague and I have to get straight back to work.' He signalled with his hand to Andrew. 'Nice to see you both.'

Andrew watched the young tailor with narrowed eyes until he went out of the lounge. He turned back to Lillian. 'You seem to know each other well... Where does he work?' he asked.

'He works in Lewis's, he's a tailor.'

He nodded his head thoughtfully. 'He's very confident...'

'Yes, I suppose he is.'

'Especially when you consider his station in life. Considering he's only the son of one of the household servants.'

'He's a very successful tailor,' Lillian said, 'and obviously very talented.'

'Of course,' Andrew said, 'but he's still trade, whichever way you look at it, and his sort won't ever be recognised in certain circles.'

'But that's ridiculous,' Lillian said, a dark feeling coming over her. 'People shouldn't be judged on their background. How can anyone help the situation they are born into? Any judgement should be based on their character and how they treat other people.'

Andrew looked at her now. 'I'm not saying it's fair or right, but unfortunately that's how life is.' He shrugged. 'People judge other people on their status in life, they always have.'

'Well, it might be how life is for you,' she said, 'but that doesn't mean it has to be like that for everyone else. I certainly don't judge people on how much money they have.'

He smiled now. 'Ah, that's because it's not an issue for you: you live in the best area of Liverpool and you have your family's financial support.'

Lillian wondered what he would think of her if he knew she had been in an orphanage for most of her life. And if he looked down on someone like Paul Larking, what he would think of someone like poor Molly? She took a deep breath, trying to control the anger she felt building up inside her at the injustice of it all. 'My aunt has worked hard, you said so yourself earlier. Is she to be judged for trying to better herself?'

'Not at all,' he said, shaking his head in a bemused fashion. 'It's different for women – they're expected to improve themselves by marriage, and anyway, your aunt has hardly come from the same background as Mr Larking, has she? She's to be admired for all she has accomplished with her little boarding enterprise and her property portfolio. My grandfather said her husband left her comfortably set up, especially with the property she owns in London too.'

Lillian felt as though her head was spinning now with all this information. If he was correct, Andrew Whyte knew far more about her aunt's background than she did. She had no idea that her aunt owned property in London, and she wondered why she hadn't told her. What else didn't she know?

Andrew suddenly gave a wide grin and he leaned forward and touched her hand. 'I must say, Lillian, I truly admire your spirit and your social conscience.'

She pulled her hand away from him. 'I'm glad you find my views so entertaining...'

'Oh, don't be cross,' he said, 'I really do admire your attitude, it makes people think.' He lowered his voice. 'It's made *me* think. I shouldn't have said what I did about your friend. I suppose attitudes are ingrained in us from home and that sort of thing, and until someone else challenges them, we think they are right. You're like my grandfather; he has always had a social conscience and is involved with a number of charities.'

'Well, that's good to hear,' Lillian said, her attitude softening a little towards him now. His comment about attitudes being ingrained in people from childhood had also struck a chord within her, and she was wondering what had been instilled within her.

'My grandfather is also involved in fundraising for a local orphanage.'

Lillian caught her breath now. So many things that had been said had opened her eyes to the difference between them, and Andrew's last comment had just underlined it all.

'I need to go,' she said, looking down at her handbag which she still held in her lap. She lifted her purse out. 'Can you see the waiter to ask for the bill please?'

Andrew stretched his arm to signal to the waiter who was clearing a table nearby. 'I don't care how cross you've been with me, I insist on paying. Your aunt and my grandfather would both be shocked if I didn't, and I don't want to give him any more reasons to be disappointed in me.'

Lillian sat back. 'Okay,' she said, giving a weak smile, 'and thank you.'

As they walked down the stairs from the lounge and through the foyer, Andrew asked Lillian when they would meet up again.

'I don't know,' she answered. 'I have a lot of things on over the next few days...'

She wasn't sure if his grandfather knew her aunt was away, and she didn't want to bring up the subject in case they asked what was wrong, with it being a 'female matter'.

As they went out into the street, she could tell Andrew was

uncertain about what to say or do next, and she felt guilty for having been so sharp with him earlier.

'I actually have a piano lesson tonight with your grandfather,' she told him, 'but he will probably cancel since your parents are visiting.'

'Well, hopefully I'll see you when I'm back in Liverpool in a few weeks' time, during the Christmas holidays?' He sighed. 'I don't want to sound like a pathetic limpet, but I don't really know any other people here near my age.'

Lillian felt almost sorry for him. 'That sounds like a great idea.' She smiled. 'Has your grandfather mentioned anything about organising an evening with my aunt and me?'

His eyes widened and his usual happy grin came back. 'Tell me about it,' he said.

Lillian was in the middle of explaining when a taxi pulled up alongside them, and they moved to give the passengers room to alight. Four or five men, all formally dressed, got out, arguing good-naturedly about who was going to pay.

'It's your turn, Williams,' one of the men said, 'and be sure to give the chap a tip this time.' They all laughed and then another said, 'And the first round of drinks are on Guthrie after his little win on the horses yesterday!'

The name caught Lillian's attention, and when she craned her neck to look, she saw Mr Guthrie in the middle of the men. She quickly turned away, but it was too late, as she spied him out of the corner of her eye coming straight towards them.

'Miss Taylor...' he said, beaming brightly and lifting his hat to her, 'and if it isn't young Master Andrew Whyte. A match if ever I saw one.' He clapped his gloved hands together. 'And what are you two youngsters up to, coming out of the Adelphi Hotel, might I enquire?'

Lillian stayed silent and watched as Andrew confidently put his hand out to shake Mr Guthrie's hand.

'We were having coffee,' he replied. 'Lillian had a nasty experience in the art gallery with a man... around your age. He quite frightened her, and she came running out through the gardens...'

He pointed across. 'Luckily, I was passing and recognised her as my grandfather's music student. I brought her into the hotel to have a hot drink to get over the awful incident.'

Mr Guthrie's earlier high spirits drained away. 'Oh dear,' he said, looking most solemn. He turned to Lillian. 'Are you well recovered now, my dear?'

'Yes,' Lillian said in a low voice. 'I'm fine now...' She looked over towards the library. 'In fact, I have to go. I have a lot of work to do in the library this afternoon.'

'I'll walk you over, and see you safely in,' Andrew said, 'just in case the man is still loitering.'

'Good man!' Mr Guthrie said, 'I would accompany Lillian myself if you weren't here.' He gestured back to the men who were now walking towards the hotel entrance. 'If you will excuse me now, I have lunch booked with some of my colleagues.' He held a fist up to Andrew. 'If you come across the reprobate again, give him a bunch of fives from me.'

As they walked through St John's Gardens again, every so often Lillian and Andrew glanced at each other again and started laughing.

'I keep thinking of him holding up his fist as though he was a bare-knuckled boxer wearing a bowler hat,' Andrew chuckled. 'He was so funny.'

Lillian nodded, giggling at the memory. 'Although I am glad you let him know that we bumped into each other and why we went to the hotel, because otherwise I think he would have made an issue of it to my aunt.'

'You're right,' Andrew said. 'If we go anywhere else together, we will ask your aunt and make sure you're not put in an awkward situation again.'

When they got to the library entrance, Lillian looked at him and then smiled warmly. 'Thank you for the coffee, Andrew, and I'll probably see you again over Christmas.'

He had stared at her, his face serious. 'I'll look forward to that, very much.'

As she went upstairs to find a quiet place to work, she thought back over the last hour in the Adelphi Hotel. Being in such a luxurious place had been uncomfortable, and the conversation about class had not helped. But, she gave a relieved sigh, she had not only survived the experience, she had learned from it.

Chapter Twenty

When Lillian came in from the library, Lucy brought up a telegram for her, along with a sandwich and a glass of milk.

'This was delivered an hour ago, and I also have to let yer know that Mr Whyte sent his maid over with his apologies, but he has to cancel yer lesson tonight as he has relatives visiting.'

Lillian thanked her, relieved that she didn't have to see Andrew again this evening. As soon as the maid left, Lillian quickly opened the telegram, hardly able to believe she had received mail two days running.

She read the message.

```
EVERYTHING HAS GONE WELL AND I AM MAKING A
GOOD RECOVERY.
LOOK FORWARD TO SEEING YOU ON MONDAY.
    LOVE ANNA
```

It was the first telegram that Lillian had ever received, but more importantly, it was bringing good news. She felt a surge of relief and she realised how anxious she had been about her aunt's operation

When she had finished her sandwich, she checked through her music folder to find her most recent sheets, then went downstairs to do her practice. She was engrossed in a complicated piece when there was a tap on the library door and Mr Guthrie entered the room.

'I hope you don't mind me checking on you,' he said, his

voice sounding more formal and strangely halting than usual. He closed the door and then stood with his back to it. 'I hope you didn't come across that person who was so vile to you?'

'No,' Lillian told him. She was surprised to realise she had forgotten all about the incident now. 'And I'm fine now. Thank you for asking.' She turned back to her book.

'I'm so glad, especially with your dear aunt being away . . .'

Mr Guthrie stood up straight, then moved across the room towards the piano, to lean on it. Something about his movements reminded her of Miss Churchill, and she suddenly realised he had been drinking.

Lillian lifted her book from the holder. 'Do you want to use the piano now?' she asked. 'I can come back later.'

He put his finger to his lips and then started to wave it about. 'No . . . no,' he said, 'you carry on, my dear. I enjoy listening to you. You carry on . . .'

Unsure what to do, she settled her music book down again on the wooden holder and started to play. Mr Guthrie closed his eyes as though listening intently. She hoped he might become bored listening after a while and go upstairs or find Mr Collins to have a chat to. She went through one of the easier pieces, halting once or twice, but then continuing on through to the end.

'Well done,' he said when she finished, nodding his head in approval. 'You have really improved. Practice makes all the difference, doesn't it?'

Lillian smiled at him. 'Yes, it does.' She lifted the book again, looking for another piece.

'I was surprised . . . initially . . . to see you with young Master Whyte today,' he said, 'but when I thought about it, I'm sure your aunt would think you a perfect match.' He tapped the top of the polished piano with his forefinger. 'I just wondered what Mr Whyte's family would make of it?'

Lillian's forehead creased. 'We are only friends, Mr Guthrie,' she replied, 'so there is nothing for anybody to be concerned about.'

'Oh, indeed, indeed...' he said. 'But by the looks of young Andrew, I would say he is quite smitten with you.'

'Not at all,' Lillian said. 'He is just a friend, and I am much too young to think of boys in that way. I have no interest and my aunt certainly has no intention of trying to match me up with anyone.'

'Ah, but that makes young men all the more keen,' he said. 'They love the chase. I remember it well myself...'

Lillian suddenly felt uncomfortable with the way the conversation was going. She lifted her book. 'I have to go, I have things to do upstairs...'

Mr Guthrie stepped out, barring her way. 'Before you go,' he said, his voice slurring, 'I want to give you a piece of advice because Andrew might just run into a little trouble with his family if they hear where his interests lie. Certain families do not care to mix with others of a different background – let's say those of background unknown.'

'Mr Guthrie,' Lillian said, finding it difficult to keep track of his ramblings, 'I have no idea what you are talking about, and I don't think my aunt would be happy with this personal discussion.'

'But your aunt is not here,' he said, 'and according to what I have heard, she won't be back for some days. I therefore feel that it falls to the people in this house to care for you while she is away.' He moved now to stand with his back against the door again.

'I really don't understand...' Lillian felt her legs begin to tremble, as his words became more deliberate and pointed. Did he know about the orphanage, she wondered. Had he made some investigations or found something out about her?

'I think you may be confused...' she began.

Mr Guthrie's eyes suddenly lit up. 'I can assure you that I am not in the least confused. I see things all too clearly, and I have seen this scenario many times over the years. It's the ultimate cliché: ambitious parents or relatives plotting to move the offspring up the social ladder.'

He suddenly smiled. 'Unfortunately in your case, regardless of your undeniable looks and talents, your indeterminate background just won't cut the mustard.'

'I don't think my background has anything to do with you, Mr Guthrie.'

'I am only trying to advise you, my dear,' he said, smiling benevolently at her. 'All the evening classes in the world are not going to change the circumstances of your birth and it is naive of Mrs Ainsley to set you up for such humiliation and failure. Perhaps if her husband had still been alive, and he had endorsed you as part of the family... But a single woman rescuing a niece in unknown circumstances raises many questions.'

Hot tears of indignation sprung into Lillian's eyes. 'Mr Guthrie, you seem to have drunk too much, and don't know what you are saying...'

'But that's where you are wrong, my dear, I know perfectly well what I am saying. It is sadly you who has been left in the dark. Your aunt – as you refer to her – has been very clever in covering up her own background, hiding it under the cover of widowhood. But the fact is she was unmarried for a much longer time than she was ever a legal wife. Furthermore, during that time, she was the mistress of a married man for years – the wealthy man who owned this house and various others. She owes everything she has to him.'

Lillian shook her head in disbelief. 'My aunt is going to be very angry when she hears all these awful things you have been saying about her... I think she will ask you to leave.'

'I am already leaving, my dear,' he said airily. 'Since I heard about your aunt's background, I decided I no longer wanted to live in a house with a woman of ill-repute. Today while I was in the Adelphi, I secured arrangements to move into a house without scandal attached to it.'

'How dare you?' she said, pushing past him now to open the door. 'Whatever lies you have heard, my aunt is a very respectable woman...'

Mr Guthrie kept his grip on the door handle for a few seconds longer until he delivered his parting shot. 'Your dear aunt is neither respectable – nor is she your aunt.'

Lillian froze.

'You see, Lillian, this is the nub of the situation. Everything else about her background – her morals – could be glossed over, if she were indeed only your aunt.'

Lillian's heart and mind were racing now, trying to make sense of his words. 'You are drunk and talking nonsense, Mr Guthrie.'

Mr Guthrie smiled and waved a finger. 'Indeed I am not. What I am explaining to you, in the most delicate manner that I can, is that Anna's morals would not impinge on a match with a decent family as long as *your* birth credentials were in order.'

'You are a very heartless man... bringing up the fact I was orphaned...'

'If only you were orphaned, my dear,' he told her. 'It's the fact you are *illegitimate*, and that your dear aunt is actually your mother.'

Lillian looked at Mr Guthrie now with disgust. He was as bad if not worse than the nuns. They had always chosen the girls' backgrounds as the most vulnerable area to target, and the worst insult to hurl was usually about the mother and her morals. There was nothing that Lillian hadn't heard before.

'Lies!' she hissed. 'A pack of evil lies. When my aunt comes back she may well take out a legal case against you for defamation of character.' Lillian had read about this many times in her Dickens books, and knew it was a crime.

'I think you will find that she has a number of people to sue then,' he laughed. 'Because you could say it is more or less public knowledge, thanks to an aggrieved former servant...' He gave a little laugh and then he opened the door wide. 'You have it all now,' he said. 'Your so-called aunt won't be quite so quick to threaten me or anyone else with eviction in the future. Had she been more civil to me when you arrived from the orphanage in your hobnail boots, I might have chosen to keep the information I heard to myself. You're a nice enough girl given your situation, and I'm sorry if this comes as a shock to you, but better to hear the truth now than have it thrown at you by the Whytes.'

Lillian pushed past him and ran out, his drunken laughter echoing down the hallway after her.

Chapter Twenty-One

When Lucy brought her dinner that evening, Lillian apologised and said she had a stomach ache and wasn't hungry. She stayed in her bedroom all night, not venturing downstairs in case she ran into Mr Guthrie again.

She took a long time getting to sleep, and then woke every two or three hours with a sense of alarm. Each time she lay staring up at the ceiling and trying to make sense of the information that Mr Guthrie had thrown at her. Was it possible that her Aunt Anna was actually her mother? And, if her 'aunt' had given birth to her illegitimately as Mr Guthrie had said, to whom had she been given away? Why also had she let her go into an orphanage after the woman who brought her up died?

If her aunt had been there, she would have gone to her immediately and asked her to defend herself against all these terrible accusations. But Anna wasn't here and Lillian had to get through the weekend in the house on her own.

In the morning, Lillian woke just before six o'clock. She was relieved that the night had put some distance from the incident with Mr Guthrie. The worst, she thought, had happened. In the orphanage, she learned that waiting for something to happen was often worse than the actual event.

As well, there would be no big row to worry about between her aunt and Mr Guthrie, as it sounded as though he would be gone by the time she returned.

However, the truth about her background concerned her greatly. It had been difficult enough hiding the fact that she had been in an orphanage, but if Anna was her mother and she was illegitimate, she would have to carry that stigma too. Lillian felt sick to her stomach at the thought.

Anna had been open about religion and sex, so she would now have to be open about Lillian's birth and background. She would be confronted as soon as she arrived back home, Lillian decided.

She had eaten nothing since the afternoon before and now felt light-headed. She got out of bed, put on her dressing gown and went downstairs to the kitchen to get a drink and a piece of bread. She was just filling a glass of water when she heard someone unlock the kitchen door, and then she recognised the voices of the cook and her husband.

'Lillian! You gave me the fright of me life,' Nan Larking exclaimed, clutching a hand to her chest.

Lillian tried to say she was sorry, but the words wouldn't form properly in her mouth.

'Are you all right, love?' the cook asked. 'You've gone very pale...'

'I'm sorry...' Lillian's voice was a small croak. 'I don't feel very well...' She suddenly felt dizzy and gave a little stagger.

'Come on,' Mrs Larking said to her husband, 'we need to get her back up to bed.'

They took an arm each and supported Lillian along the corridor and up the two flights of stairs. At one point the cook whispered in her ear, 'Is it your monthlies?'

Lillian couldn't think. 'I don't know...' she whispered back.

When they got her into bed, Mrs Larking said, 'What did you eat last night, love?'

'I wasn't very hungry...'

The cook turned to her husband. 'Michael, go downstairs quick and get two sweet biscuits and some lemonade, before you get the fire going and the kettle on.'

When her husband left, Mrs Larking brought a chair over to the bed and took the girl's hand. 'What's wrong, love? Is there something worrying you?'

The warm and gentle tone of the older woman's voice made Lillian want to lean into her arms, but she knew that it wouldn't be appropriate. 'I'm all right, thank you,' she said.

'Is it because your aunt's down in London? Are you anxious about her being in hospital?'

'Maybe ... I just didn't feel well.'

'Your aunt is going to be okay, it's not that serious.' She paused. 'Has someone upset you?' She squeezed her hand. 'You can trust me, Lillian, and your aunt asked me to look out for you when she was away. I wouldn't like to think you were worrying about anything ...'

Lillian was about to say no when she thought about Mr Guthrie again, and it struck her that he said he was leaving, and she wondered if he had told anyone else.

She took a deep breath. 'Mr Guthrie was drunk last night ... and he said some terrible things about my aunt ...'

'Did he now?' There was a silence. 'And what did he tell you?'

Lillian hesitated, then the kindly cook's hand tightened around hers reassuringly again, and she felt she needed to unburden herself. 'He said ... he said Anna is not my aunt – she's my mother ...'

Mrs Larking's eyes widened in shock. 'Oh, dear God ...' She put her hand to her mouth. 'The wicked, wicked man! Pay no heed to him. He's a fool of a man, and I don't know how he got to be so educated. I'll say he'll get his marching orders from Anna after this, and it's not before time. I've told her before that he was nothing but a snake in the grass – and all his drinking and gambling.'

In the midst of her misery, Lillian noticed that the cook called her aunt by her first name – and did it very naturally.

'He said he is leaving ... that he's found somewhere else to go.'

'I'm delighted to hear it. Good riddance to bad rubbish!'

Lillian was silent for a few moments, then asked, 'Mrs Larking, do you know anything about what he said? He told me that it was one of the servants who found out about me. Is there any truth in what he said?'

The older woman leaned forward and brushed a strand of Lillian's dark hair back out of her eyes. 'The best thing you can do, love, is put it all this nonsense out of your mind until your aunt comes home.' Then, as Lillian's eyes looked deep and searchingly into hers, her voice faltered as she said, 'This is nobody's business but yours and Anna's.'

Lillian lay back in the bed and closed her eyes. It was true, then. If it hadn't been, Mrs Larking would have denied it and been more shocked than she was. Mrs Larking knew and so did other people. She had to face the fact somehow that Anna was her mother and she was illegitimate.

Chapter Twenty-Two

Saturday morning was usually busy as Lillian and Anna normally walked into town and looked around the shops, then went for lunch. Today, Lillian did not feel like leaving her bedroom.

Under the watchful eye of Mrs Larking she had forced down some scrambled eggs with toast and two cups of milky tea. Afterwards she had a bath, and as she lay with the warmth of the water enveloping her, she looked down at her naked body and wondered how she had come to be.

Her aunt was over forty now, so she had had her when she was in her mid-twenties, which wasn't very young. Who, she wondered, was her father? Had Anna really been the mistress of a married man? Lillian found it hard to imagine it, given the upright woman Anna seemed to be. All the indoctrination that had been put in place by the nuns – the automatic adherence to rules and regulations, the fear of reprisal, the meekness and compliance, the acceptance that her life was in the hands of others – slowly began to dismantle inside her. Lillian now wanted answers about her life.

She dressed and sorted her hair, and as she stood in front of the long wardrobe mirror to put the last pins in the back of her hair, she studied her reflection and tried to see a resemblance between Anna and herself, or between herself and the mother from her early years. She stared for so long her own features started to look strange, and she turned away from the mirror, no wiser.

Mrs Larking came up to her room around two with a cup of

hot chocolate and a scone and sat chatting to her about light, random issues like the funny things her grandchildren said and did, and about the decorations they would soon be putting up in the house for Christmas.

After a few minutes, she reached over to take Lillian's hand. 'Whatever happens to us, love, life has to go on,' she said. 'We all go through good and bad times. Look at what happened to all the poor men during the war, the ones that were killed and their families that were left behind. And there are ones that came home wounded in body and mind, some poor souls who will never be the same again.' Her eyes filled with tears. 'I have a brother who lost a leg and was also blinded...'

As Lillian listened, she felt heart-sorry for the poor soldier – and all the other soldiers like him, but it didn't make her feel any better.

After a while Mrs Larking had to leave to get on with her work, but she stopped at the bedroom door and advised Lillian to go out for a walk. 'The fresh air will do you the power of good, but make sure you're wrapped up well.'

As she was getting ready to go out, a card was delivered from her aunt. It had a picture of a girl and a little dog walking past Buckingham Palace. It said that she was feeling even better and was up on her feet and moving around a little. Tears filled her eyes again as she looked at the card. Everything was different now. She was of course still glad, but Anna was now a stranger to her. In twenty-four hours it had all changed. She put the card alongside the telegram, then went to collect her handbag and the books she wanted to take back to the library.

As she walked down Rodney Street, the snow that had been threatening for several days started to fall. By the time she reached Renshaw Street it was coming down thick and fast. St John's Gardens was a beautiful all-white scene as she passed, but she gave it little thought as she hurried through on her way to the library.

Over the last few happy weeks, Lillian had imagined everywhere being white and festive for Christmas, almost like a

Christmas card scene. She had imagined watching it from her bedroom window, delighted that her first Christmas in her new home would be as traditional as the ones she read about in her books and magazines. She had pictured so many happy scenes in her mind: Christmas trees, decorations, wrapping presents in colourful paper. She had planned to make little personal things for the guests, like embroidered handkerchiefs for Miss Moran and Miss Dixon, and pairs of white initialled handkerchiefs for the men. She had even planned to give a pair to Mr Guthrie. All the little things she had so enjoyed were now obliterated by what he had told her.

When she was settled at a library table in the upstairs room, she took her writing pad out of her handbag and started to read what she had written to Molly so far. She read all the glowing things she said about her aunt, about how kind she had been, how understanding and thoughtful she was. Everything she had written was true, but it was no longer relevant.

She stared at the paper and then very slowly and deliberately, she ripped it in two – then again and again until the page was in tiny pieces. She sat for a while, her mind turning over and then she started a fresh letter.

My dearest Molly,

I hope you are well. It is not long until we meet again, and I am so looking forward to it.

I have been making plans for you coming out in a few months' time, and I have started collecting things for you like nice clothes and shoes. I was going to keep it as a surprise until you came out, but I think it is better if I tell you so you can be more prepared.

I am going to start looking for work for both of us in a big house in a new place, maybe Manchester or London. I will try to find jobs with accommodation for us. I know you are not sixteen until April, but I think it is best to start checking what is available so I can try to plan ahead.

I am sad to say that things have not worked out as well with my aunt as I had hoped. She has been kind and generous, but she isn't the person I thought she was. I have found things out that make me think I would be better off without her. I will try to get some time on my own with you when we meet up, so I can explain things properly to you. I will just have to do my best to get on with her until you come out.

I am planning to take any kind of job in January when I turn sixteen, and I will save every penny I can to help us start off our new life in a new place together. I will be going to Manchester for a day out soon with my aunt on the train, and I will see if it is the sort of place we might like to live in. If not, I have heard there are lots of big houses in London where they might need two maids. Who knows, when we get settled we might be able to help Daniel get work too, because I know you will want to keep in close contact with him.

I have seen a magazine in the library called _The Lady_, which advertises posts for live-in servants, and I will buy a current copy soon to see what is on offer. The staff here in my aunt's house seem very happy in their work, as do the staff in some of the surrounding houses, so it is possible that we could be lucky enough to get good positions.

We have survived a very hard life with the nuns and we have learned all kinds of domestic work, so nothing will be too difficult for us. I am confident that we can survive on our own with employers who might even kinder to us.

If it is safe for you to reply to this, I would love to hear what you think of my suggestions. Don't take any risks

*with the nuns, and I will give your friend Gretta a
shilling for bringing it into you, as a thank you to her
for being so kind.*

With great affection,

Your friend,

Lillian

She sealed the envelope and wrote Molly's name on the front and put it in her bag. She felt that the words she had written had helped to clarify things in her own mind. The only person in the entire world she could rely on now was her friend Molly. She also knew when she told her the whole story, that she was the one person who wouldn't judge her or think her less for being illegitimate.

A short while later, Lillian went down into the main library section. She remembered Miss Moran recommending *Pride and Prejudice*, so went over to the shelves which held the books by Jane Austen and found a copy. After scanning through it, she thought it was the sort of book that might help lift the dark mood that seemed to have overtaken everything.

Outside, the snow was still falling, but the flakes were lighter and she felt there was a calming gentleness to it. She stood at the library entrance for a few minutes, just staring out at the whiteness. It was only when she felt herself shivering that she realised she needed to move. She wasn't ready to go back to the house yet where she would have to talk to people, and where the kindly Mrs Larking would be fussing around her.

She wondered if it was a good time to walk around to Clayton Street to Gretta O'Brien's house to drop the letter off for Molly. It was only a few minutes' walk away. The quicker she got the letter away, the quicker she might hear back from her friend.

She walked back out onto William Brown Street and turned right and headed down to Byron Street. Even though the snow was lying on the ground, the area suddenly seemed somehow darker, and as she went along, she heard voices and shouting which made her feel more apprehensive, and she hoped she was going in the right direction. Then, she felt a wave of relief when she saw the sign for Clayton Street, and she knew she was in the right place. She turned into a passage and walked down a short way and then she saw the opening for what she knew were the court dwellings.

The shouting and arguing continued as she walked towards the buildings, and she wondered if she dared go any further. Two tall buildings were on either side, with steps leading to each of the bleak-looking houses. There were women, young and old, dressed in filthy aprons and wrapped in black shawls sitting outside on the steps, some nursing babies or young children. She could see a group of around a dozen people – adults and barefooted children, raggedy, rowdy and shouting – gathered outside a small outbuilding at the bottom of the yard. A man wearing a cap and trousers tied at the ankles with cord was banging on the door with a thick stick, and shouting to whoever was inside to get out.

Lillian sucked her breath in as her eyes took in the depressing sight, and her nose wrinkled as the most awful foul smell seemed to envelope her. She looked to her left and saw the main cause of the odour, a row of overflowing bins. This close-up scene was worse than anything she had imagined.

She started to walk backwards out of the yard, back to the safety of the streets behind. One of the older children spotted her and shouted something and then a group of them came running in her direction. She turned quickly to get away and ran headlong into two women who were walking into the place.

'Oh, I'm sorry!' she stuttered, her heart racing so quickly she could hardly speak. She looked up to see two gaudily made-up women, dressed in clothes that looked as though they had come from a pantomime.

'Yer all right, love,' one of the women said in a cheery voice. 'Are yer from the welfare or the charities? Are yer lookin' for somebody?'

The children raced up to them, then started circling around Lillian and the two women, chasing each other in a game of tag.

'Gerrout of here!' the younger woman shouted, her arms flailing around. 'Fuck off or yer'll get my toe up yer arses!'

One of the men came quickly towards them, and herded the children back to the bottom end of the yard. 'No need for the language in front of the kids, Tessie,' he said, in a soft Irish accent. 'They're only playing.'

'Sorry Jim,' the older woman said, holding her hand up. 'We've had a bloody bad night. A man took Tessie down to the docks and then wouldn't pay her. He roughed her up and then cut her leg with a knife. It were nothin' terrible but she needed four stitches. We've been down the police station and then at the 'ospital half the bleedin' day.'

Lillian listened in horror, realising the women were prostitutes. She wondered if she should just make a run for it.

'We've had nowt to eat,' the woman said in a weary voice, 'an' we just need to get to our beds.'

'I understand,' the man said. 'I just don't like the kids hearing things they shouldn't. Your business is your own. I know you're good helping out some of the worst off here.'

'I wish somebody would've helped us out,' Tessie said. 'We went to a café near the police station, an' they friggin' threw us out. Wouldn't even let us have a cup of tea...'

The man's eyes fell on Lillian now, and the older woman noticed and suddenly seemed to remember her. 'What did you say you was here for, love? Was it the Welfare?'

Lillian shook her head. 'No,' she said, shaking her head. 'It doesn't matter...' She stepped backwards. 'I can come back another time...'

'What did yer want, love?' the older woman repeated. 'We know everybody here. Have yer brought somethin' for somebody?'

There was a kind note in the woman's voice that surprised Lillian. She suddenly realised that if she didn't find Gretta today she would have to come back another time, and she didn't think she could face it. 'I was looking for Number Twelve,' she said, 'A girl called Gretta...'

'Gretta O'Brien?' the man asked.

Lillian nodded. 'Do you know where her house is?'

'What d'you want her for?'

'I have to give her a letter...' She suddenly remembered her manners. 'I should have said, my name is Lillian Taylor.'

'Gretta is my daughter,' the man said. 'But she's not here. She's at the convent she works in.' He put his hand out. 'If you give me it, I'll see that she gets it.'

Lillian hesitated, not sure what to do.

'You can come back later if you want to see her yourself,' he said understandingly.

The older woman straightened up, and took on an air of dignity. 'You've nowt to worry about there with Jim O'Brien. You can trust him,' she said. 'He's a decent man.'

Lillian could see the slightly injured look in the man's eyes. 'I'll let Gretta know you'll call again later...'

She suddenly thought that by not trusting him because he lived in poor housing, she was unwittingly taking on a similar attitude to that of Andrew or even Mr Guthrie. She, above all, had no justification for judging people's backgrounds.

'If you don't mind giving it to Gretta,' she said, quickly taking her glove off to searching in her bag for the letter. She handed it to him. 'I'd be very grateful. And if you could ask her please, to pass it on to my friend,' she said, handing it to him.

Jim O'Brien nodded his head. 'I'll make sure she gets it the minute she comes in.'

Lillian suddenly remembered the shilling and delved back into her bag. She found the silver coin in the little inside pocket, where she had put it in to find it quickly. 'Would you give her this please, with my thanks.'

'No, no...' he said, waving it away. 'Our Gretta wouldn't be looking for anything.'

'Please...' Lillian said, holding it out, 'she's doing me a great favour. I could never get the letter to my friend any other way.

It means a great deal to me and I am really grateful to her. She also took the trouble to deliver a letter to me, and it's a bit of a walk, especially in this weather.'

He looked at her and then his face softened. 'In that case, I'm sure she'll be delighted, although she would have done it for nothing.'

He looked up towards the sky as he felt the snow starting again. He tipped his cap at her and smiled. 'Mind your step on your way home, Miss, it's bound to be getting slippery.'

'I will,' she said, smiling back at him. 'And thank you again.'

As she walked back down the passageway and out into the streets again, she felt strangely calmer than she had felt at any point in the day.

Chapter Twenty-Three

The snow continued for the rest of the day and when Lillian woke the following morning, Rodney Street was a carpet of white. She was still in bed at nine o'clock, thinking about Molly's reaction to her letter, when Lucy came in to make up the fire in her bedroom. As she cleaned out the grate, she told Lillian that Mr and Mrs Larking hadn't arrived yet as the buses weren't running as normal due to the snow.

'I'm runnin' late with the breakfasts,' she said, all flustered, 'because the fires need doing first, and Mr Larking usually helps me to bring in the firewood and the coal. It's harder too with it being Sunday, because we always do a good fried breakfast.'

'I can help you,' Lillian said, throwing the covers back. 'If you just tell me what needs to be done.' It would give her something to do until it was time for Mass, and it would stop her mind going over everything. It would also give her practice in the sort of chores that had to be done by servants in houses. She went over to lift her dressing gown from the back of the door. 'I'll just go to the bathroom first, and I'll be ready in a few minutes.'

Lucy sat back on her heels, looking startled. 'I don't think Mrs Larking would be very happy, Miss. It wouldn't be right...'

'We can't have you doing everything. It's an emergency,' Lillian said, 'so I'm sure she won't mind in the slightest.'

By the time Lillian was dressed, Lucy was back down in the kitchen and she had laid out the sausages, bacon and eggs along with mushrooms and tomatoes.

189

'If you put the sausages in the oven, Miss,' Lucy said, 'I'll separate the rashers of bacon and start frying them.'

Lillian was then instructed to wash the mushrooms, take out the middles, then cut the tomatoes in half. Within twenty minutes all was going well, and most of the items were cooked and warming in the oven. Lucy had run upstairs to check everything was on the table, and when she came back down, she started to make toast under the grill.

'We only have the eggs to do, and it's all sorted,' Lucy said, more relaxed now. 'I've still a few fires to do, but at least the one in the guests' sitting room is going fine, so they will be warm enough while they are having their breakfast and reading their Sunday papers.' She paused. 'Are you joining them this morning, Miss?'

Lillian shook her head. She wasn't in the mood for small talk with the other guests, and she did not want to get into a big discussion about Mr Guthrie having left.

'At least I won't have to do Mr Guthrie's fire,' Lucy commented, as though having read her thoughts. 'He left with his bags when you were out yesterday. I wonder what yer aunt will have to say about him disappearing so quickly? He left a note for her, so he's probably explained about it.'

Lillian raised her eyebrows. 'I'm sure she won't be too disappointed…'

While Lucy was upstairs, Lillian made the decision not to go to Mass this morning. She had become aware of a dull ache down in her stomach, and discovered that her monthly period had arrived. As it seemed heavier than normal, she decided it might not be wise to walk all the way to the church without eating or drinking as she normally did. Instead, she decided to take things a little easier and have breakfast in the kitchen with Lucy.

They were just clearing up when the back door opened and Mrs Larking came in followed by her husband. She looked taken aback to see Lillian down in the kitchen. 'I'm so sorry, Miss, but the early trams and buses were off on account of the heavy snow. They're only movin' now.' She quickly took her hat and coat off and lifted her crossover apron from its usual hook behind the door.

'I'll get the fires started,' Michael said, taking his outdoor clothes off and rolling up his sleeves.

'I've the main fires going, Mr Larking,' Lucy said. 'There's only the guests' bedroom ones still to be done. She then turned to the cook. 'And the breakfast is all served upstairs.'

'Served?' Mrs Larking's voice was high with surprise. 'And how did you manage all that on your own?'

'Miss Lillian insisted on giving me a hand...'

Seeing the disapproval on the cook's face, Lillian said quickly, 'I enjoyed helping and I couldn't leave poor Lucy to do it all on her own.' She raised her eyebrows. 'Besides, it gave me something to do. Now, why don't you and Mr Larking sit down at the fire and have some breakfast? You must be frozen and in need of a cup of tea to thaw you out.'

'But what about them upstairs? Do we need to check on them?'

'They're all fine,' Lucy said, 'I've just been back up with more toast and fresh tea and coffee, and they all said they've had enough.'

'And we have eaten too,' Lillian said, 'so really, there's nothing much to be done apart from the washing-up.'

'I'll just go up and check the fires in the sitting room,' Michael Larking said, 'and I'll be straight back down.'

Mrs Larking looked most perplexed by the disruption to their usual routine, but she allowed Lillian to guide her over to the armchair by the range, while the young maid went to get the hot plates of food they had kept in the oven for the couple.

As she sank down into the armchair, Nan Larking grasped Lillian's forearm gently and asked, 'How are you managing, love?'

'I'm fine,' Lillian said. She leaned closer and said, 'You were right, I got my monthlies this morning. I wasn't feeling a hundred per cent so I decided not to go to Mass.'

'You were dead right, love,' Mrs Larking said. 'We usually go to half-seven Mass out in Anfield on our way to work, but I said to Michael there's no way we were going to fight our way through the snow to the church. The last thing we want at our age is to break a hip or an arm or something.' She pulled a face. 'Our Paul wasn't happy with us comin' out this morning at all, but we don't work every Sunday and I'd told yer auntie I'd be here while she was away.'

Lillian could just imagine Paul Larking feeling protective of his parents, but she also knew Anna was caring towards them.

'She wouldn't have known about the snow when she asked you,' Lillian said. 'And I'm sure she wouldn't have wanted you to take any risks.' Her aunt had so many, many good points, and Lillian wished she could turn the clock back to the episode with Mr Guthrie and she would have got out of the library before he had got the chance to spill out all the terrible things he had said.

Mrs Larking made a little waving gesture. 'Sure, what would we do stuck indoors all day?'

Lillian went back for a bath and washed her hair. She had enjoyed being downstairs with the staff and it had distracted her mind from imagining what would happen when her aunt came home and all the changes that were going to take place in her life.

She had just got dressed when the front doorbell rang, and a short while later she heard Lucy coming up the stairs. She tapped at her bedroom door and came in to tell her that she had visitors. 'It's a lady with a girl who goes to yer dancing classes.'

Lillian thought for a few seconds. 'Would you please show them up to my aunt's sitting room?' She guessed her aunt might not be very happy about it, but soon her aunt would have nothing to do with her decisions. Lillian liked Irene, and her mother had seemed kind when they met last week. When she and Molly were out in the big world on their own, they would need all the friends they could get, and they might even need help from the Flanagans.

She heard them come up the stairs and gave them a few moments to get settled and then followed them into the sitting room. Both were dressed beautifully as usual, Freda looking very glamorous in a light-coloured fur coat with brown boots with the same light fur trimming. Irene had a lovely blue coat and hat with a fur muff.

'I hope you didn't mind us calling?' Freda Flanagan said, 'but we had hoped to see you at Mass and when you weren't there, we thought we would drop in. Irene mentioned that your aunt was away for the weekend, so I knew we wouldn't disturb her.' Freda smiled. 'We wondered, if you have nothing planned, if you would like to join us for supper at home tonight? We can send the car around for you, so you don't need to worry about walking in the snow or the dark.'

'That's very kind of you . . .' Lillian quickly thought. Sunday nights were usually quiet, and with her aunt gone she presumed she would eat upstairs on her own, a supper of cold cuts of meat and bread and butter. No one would miss her. 'Yes,' she decided, 'that would be lovely.'

'The car will collect you at seven o'clock, if that suits you?' Freda said.

'That sounds lovely,' Lillian said. 'I'll look forward to it.'

As she was showing her visitors out, Freda commented on how lovely the house was, and stopped to look at pieces of furniture and paintings. 'I've often wondered how this house looked inside,' she said. 'I was sure it would be very nice, as your aunt is so elegant in every way, and always was, even when we were young and both had hardly anything.'

Lillian looked at her, questions suddenly forming in her mind. Freda had known her aunt for years, and she might know things about Anna that could help her build a picture up of her early years.

As she opened the front door for them, she saw Freda's shining car parked a little further down the street, and she heard the car engine start up. John had been sitting waiting for them, and she watched him climb out of the car to see them safely in the back. Freda Flanagan had obviously done very well for herself. She also noticed with some surprise that Andrew's father's car was still parked outside the house. With all the things that had happened over the last few days, she had hardly given Andrew a thought, and, at the back of her mind presumed he had gone back to London by now.

Lillian waited on the doorstep until the Flanagans' car pulled away, and was just going inside when Mr Whyte's door opened and Andrew called out to her. She waved to him and turned back towards the door, but he came across the road as quickly as the snow would allow.

'We're getting ready to leave after lunch,' he told her. He rolled his eyes. 'My father was out late last night and only got up recently.' He paused. 'I've been watching out for you the last few days, but I didn't see you go out at all. I was watching for you going to church...'

'I haven't been out much,' she said, 'and this morning I was helping in the kitchen as the Larkings were late because of the weather.'

His eyes narrowed. 'That's the chap's parents who we met in the Adelphi?'

'Yes, that's right.'

There was a silence. 'I wanted to apologise to you about that again... I'm afraid I came across as rather pompous. All that talk about trade and professions... I was stupidly echoing my mother's views... and I am sorry for the things I said.'

'Really?' Lillian sounded unconvinced.

'Yes,' he said. 'After I came back to the house on Friday, I spoke at length with my grandfather, who has a much broader view of things. My mother's family are very traditional and old-fashioned in their thinking, and they actually think she married down with my father. They don't have much to do with him, and I think my mother feels that he hasn't done much to prove them wrong.' Lillian noticed that he looked embarrassed. 'He's a kind enough man, but I suppose in some ways he can be irresponsible and he doesn't always behave very well as a husband. It is difficult for my grandfather and he tries to advise my father because there are even times when he agrees with my mother.'

Lillian looked at him and said sympathetically, 'That must be difficult for you as well.'

'I'm used to it.' He noticed her shivering. 'I don't want to keep you but I won't see you for a few weeks now . . . and I just wanted you to know that I thought a lot about our conversation.'

'I can tell.'

Flakes of snow started to fall again, and they both looked up to the sky.

'Look Lillian,' he said, taking a step closer, 'I know it's the wrong time . . . but the thing is, I like you. I like you a lot and I was hoping that we might get to spend more time together when I come home again. I told my grandfather, and he said he will get that evening organised with your aunt. You're almost sixteen, so hopefully she won't have any objections.'

'That would be very nice,' Lillian said, nodding. There was no point, she thought, in telling him that there was no future in their friendship, and that their lives were to take very different paths in the next few months.

Although she liked him very much, she didn't think that he would feel the same about her when she moved out of Rodney Street to take work as a live-in servant. And whilst he liked the girl he had met in the library, the niece of the quiet and elegant Anna, he might not be so keen if he knew of her history in the orphanage and met her best friend, Molly. And even if he could deal with all of that, it would pale into insignificance when he discovered her illegitimate background.

She looked back at the house now and then gave him a smile. 'I have to go . . .'

'Of course, I'm just so glad I got the chance to see you before I go.' He gave an almost theatrical sigh. 'And I will count the days until I see you again. I'm going to ask your aunt if we can start writing after Christmas,' he said, stepping backwards, '…and I'll write every single day.'

Lillian nodded and held her hand up in farewell. As she turned towards the door, her eyes welled up and she rushed upstairs, threw herself on the bed and sobbed her heart out.

Chapter Twenty-Four

Lillian busied herself for the rest of the day, finishing off the stitching on two handkerchief holders for Irene and her mother. Since it was a Sunday, there were no shops open to buy flowers or a box of chocolates, so she had decided to give Mrs Larking's and Lucy's holders to the Flanagans, as she had almost finished them. She would easily make more for the staff in the next few days.

When the car pulled up outside the house, Lillian was watching from her bedroom window, and was already dressed and ready. She wore a blue calf-length dress in georgette, which had a bolero jacket which tied in a little bow at the front. It was the first time she had picked her own clothes for an outing, but she felt confident from the discussion Anna had had with the sales assistant that it was suitable for an evening in someone's house. She put on her warm coat with a cloche-style hat and picked up her evening purse and the gifts, which she wrapped in paper with red poinsettias printed on it.

She quickly went down the flights of stairs to the kitchen to tell Lucy that she was going out, and would take her key as she wasn't quite sure when she would be back.

When John opened the car door for her, she was delighted to see a smiling Irene sitting in the back, waiting for her. As she climbed in, she made a promise to herself to enjoy the evening and forget all about her problems until tomorrow.

The car drove up the few streets towards Falkner Street, and pulled up outside a house at the opposite end from Miss

Churchill's house. As they went up the steps, Lillian though how lovely it looked with all the matching lamps lit at the various windows, and when she stepped inside, she could see it was decorated in a more dramatic and feminine style than her aunt's house. Where Anna had the classic wooden panelling in the hall, Freda's had been painted in a pale blue with a white trim, and the marble floor was light and bright. A most unusual art deco console table stood against one wall holding a large figurine of a dancing lady on it, with a mirror styled like the sun with a silver ray surround above it.

Freda Flanagan came down the marble-tiled hallway towards them, all smiles, and ushered Lillian into the elegant drawing room where a maid wearing a white frilled apron and cap was there to take her coat and hat. As she glanced around, she could see that Irene's mother had obviously had a hand in choosing the pale pink walls and the cream, tulip-shaped sofa and chairs. Tables and cabinets were dotted around the room, all holding gold or silver figurines or similar style lamps.

In one corner, Lillian spied a most unusual gramophone, with the box and interior of the horn decorated with delicate pink flowers. 'Your house is beautiful,' Lillian said. 'It's so light and bright. I really like it.'

Freda was delighted with the compliment. 'I changed it all after William, Irene's father, died,' she said. 'He was more old-fashioned and liked things as they were. It needed doing badly, and it gave me something to do for the first year after he had gone.'

'I didn't realise...' Lillian said. 'I'm sorry to hear that.'

'It was a few years ago,' she said, 'one of the flu epidemics.' She put her arm around her daughter. 'William spent a lot of time down in London with work, so we often didn't see him for weeks and we were used to being on our own. We've muddled along okay since, haven't we, Irene?'

Irene shrugged and looked sad.

Lillian handed over her little gifts, apologising for not being able to buy chocolates or flowers as it was a Sunday.

'You shouldn't have brought anything,' Freda said. 'It's just a little supper night with the three of us, and I didn't expect you to come with gifts.'

Irene and her mother opened their presents and Lillian was delighted to see how well the handkerchief holders were received.

'Much better than flowers or chocolates,' Freda said. 'These are things we can keep for years.' She smiled fondly at Lillian. 'I will think of you every time I use them.'

The maid knocked on the door and came in with three glasses of sherry. Freda told her that she would come down in a few minutes' time to let her know when they were ready for the food.

She then turned to Lillian who was holding her glass, unsure what to do as she had never been given alcohol before.

'I'm sure your aunt won't mind you having a little aperitif,' she said. 'I told Irene that since she is sixteen in January, that this Christmas I would allow her to start having the odd little sherry on special occasions like tonight, and a glass of wine with dinner.' She raised her eyebrows. 'I believe it is much safer to learn how to drink moderately at home than make a mistake out on a social evening. Nothing worse than seeing a woman falling down with drink.' Freda smiled and held her glass up. 'Cheers,' she said, 'and welcome to our home, Lillian, and we want you to make yourself at home with Irene and me tonight.'

The girls held their glasses up and then Lillian took a sip of the sweet, amber-coloured drink and was very pleasantly surprised at how nice it tasted. She wasn't sure how her aunt would react to her drinking alcohol, but she felt it would have been impolite to refuse. She also didn't know how she would react to the news about her even visiting Irene's house while she was in hospital, but how her aunt felt about either situation no longer troubled her.

Irene complimented Lillian on her lovely dress and jacket and they all talked about the winter fashions. As they had a discussion about the lovely handbags in Lewis's, it crossed Lillian's mind how easily she had learned how to talk about clothes and bags and shoes in the space of only a few months. In the orphanage all the girls wore the same thing, and clothes were never discussed other than when they were due to go to the laundry. In her new world, she learned about clothes and fashion by walking around stores and looking at people in the street. It had been the same with current affairs, which she knew nothing about, and could now read about in the newspapers. Food, too, which had been rationed and repetitive, was now plentiful and varied. Her aunt had talked her through every meal they had eaten in restaurants and cafés, making sure she knew which cutlery to use and how to eat anything unusual.

So far she had managed to pass as respectable in the house, and even in the hotel with Andrew Whyte. And tonight, she was in the most beautiful house, and appeared to be accepted as though she had always been as used to this privileged lifestyle as Irene seemed to be.

Everything, Lillian now knew, could be learned and unlearned.

After a while Freda left the two girls chatting while she went down to the kitchen to let the maid know that they were ready for the supper dishes to be brought up. When she came back up she asked Irene to put some music on the gramophone and Lillian went over with her while they looked through the selection of records. Irene was adept at working the machine and showed Lillian how to do it.

They picked several popular songs like *Carolina Moon* and *Tiptoe Through the Tulips*, and then they sat back down to listen to them. The maid came in with several long dishes with salads and tiny bite-sized sausage-rolls, pinwheel sandwiches with various fillings, individual soufflés and a variety of rolled-up cold meats and cheeses. She then brought a bread basket filled with slices of different sorts of home-made bread and tiny biscuits.

When they were seated at the table, the maid came around with a bottle of white wine and poured each of them a glass. She checked if Freda wanted her to stay to pass around the food but she smiled at the girl and said they were fine, and to go back downstairs and have her own supper.

'This is a very casual night,' Freda said to Lillian, 'so just help yourself to whatever you like.' She laughed. 'As we used to say in Dublin: "Eat up, you're at your auntie's!"'

Lillian found herself laughing along, and after the glass of sherry and a few sips of wine she felt more relaxed than she had felt in days. When they had finished eating and Lillian had drunk her glass of wine, the maid came back to clear the table.

While she was going back and forth with the crockery, Irene took Lillian upstairs to show her her bedroom. Lillian wasn't surprised that it looked as lovely and glamorous as the rest of the house. It had framed photos of film stars on the walls and her wardrobe and dressing table were painted in white and trimmed with gold. As she looked around, admiring all the lovely things, it struck her that considering she seemed to have everything, Irene was a nice girl and had not let it go to her head.

She knew from some of the things Irene had said that she was in a private girls' day school and was due to finish school that summer. She wondered if Irene planned to find work, but kept away from the subject lest Irene started to ask her similar questions.

When they came back downstairs, Freda showed them a Cole Porter record that she had bought a few days previously. The girls were delighted as they had heard it played at their dance classes, and they sat quietly listening to it. Freda asked the girls to show her some of their dance moves, and she sat back in her tulip-shaped chair, smiling and making encouraging noises as they moved around the room, giggling and chatting.

When Lillian said she thought she should go home soon, Freda went to let John know that he would be needed soon. The girls played the Cole Porter record again and then a funny Eddie Cantor one called *Making Whoopee*.

As the girls danced, Lillian was glad she had accepted the invitation to come to the Flanagan's house tonight, rather than sitting in the silence of her own bedroom with her torturing thoughts. The music, the dancing and the laughter with Irene had really lifted her, and taken her mind a million miles away from her troubles.

As she went to collapse onto the sofa beside Irene, Lillian thought she might use the bathroom before she went home and asked her friend for directions.

'There's one at the top of the stairs, the first door on the right,' Irene told her.

Lillian went slowly up the stairs, looking around at the lovely mirrors and pictures on the walls. Just as she reached the top, she heard Freda's voice coming from the kitchen area and she stopped to check if she was talking to her. She saw her coming up to the ground floor and walking towards the reception rooms. Everything about Freda was lovely, Lillian thought, and she was so friendly and such good fun. She seemed too young to be a widow, and was more like an older sister to Irene than a mother.

Lillian leaned over the banister, and had just opened her mouth to say she wouldn't be long, when she saw the handsome John moving quickly behind Freda to grab her around the waist. Lillian was wondering what on earth he was doing, and then she saw Freda turn to face him. There was a moment when they just looked at each other and then he reached to fondle her breasts. Lillian held her breath, waiting for Freda to push him away or shout at him. Instead, she put her hands on either side of his face and pulled him towards her and they started kissing.

Lillian stood like a statue, frozen to the spot and afraid to move in case they saw or heard her. John whispered something in Freda's ear and she heard the sound of low, intimate laughter. Freda moved out of his embrace and after only a few steps he moved quickly and caught her by the waist, and started kissing her again. She watched as Freda lay back in his arms, almost like an elaborate dance move, and they kissed again, passionately.

An astonished Lillian tiptoed up the last few steps and made her way stealthily along to the bathroom. When she got inside, she quietly closed the door and then stood with her back against it, her heart thumping as though it might come out of her chest. What, she wondered frantically, was Irene's mother up to with man she wasn't married to? A man who worked for her?

She remembered Irene saying that John lived in one of the rooms in the basement, similar to Lucy's accommodation in Rodney Street. Was Freda having an affair with him, she wondered? She wondered if Irene knew, and if so, how she felt about it.

Lillian spent longer than usual in the bathroom, and then when she could not stay away any longer without arousing concern, she came out quietly and went to the top of the stairs to look down. Thankfully, there was no sign of Freda or her driver. She went quickly down the stairs and took a deep breath before tapping on the drawing room door and then going in.

Freda was back in the drawing room, over at the gramophone with Irene, chatting and going through the records as though nothing had happened.

'We have the music for the Charleston, Lillian,' she said, sounding delighted. 'So we can have another quick dance while John gets the car going!' She gave a little whoop. 'You and Irene will be the belles of the ball when you start going to proper dances to meet eligible young men! You'll be able to do all the latest dances along with the waltzes and the foxtrots.' She laughed. 'Men love a woman who loves dancing; it shows she isn't stuffy and old-fashioned.'

Lillian found herself going through the motions of the dance with Irene and her mother, trying to ignore the images of Freda and John which kept floating into her mind. But she found the more she moved, the lighter and less concerned she felt, although it was hard to escape the guilt about enjoying herself in the company of a woman of loose morals. But, she reasoned with herself, it wasn't Irene's fault that her mother was like that, and it wasn't fair to punish her by being judgemental.

When the maid came with her coat and hat, Freda asked her to bring her fur coat and hat. 'I'll come for the ride in the car,' she said, smiling at Lillian. 'It's snowing again, and I want John to drive me down into the city centre to see what it looks like covered in white.'

As they pulled up in front of Lillian's house, Freda got out from the back seat and moved to sit in the front passenger seat saying, 'I'll have a better view of the streets from here.' She waved Lillian off, calling out from the window, 'We'll arrange the cinema night soon, and please ask your aunt if she would like to come with us.'

Lucy picked her steps carefully through the snow to the front door, and then had to stop to return Freda's gay wave as the car swept onto Upper Duke Street and down into the city centre.

Lucy was still up and when she heard Lillian coming in, she came rushing up the kitchen stairs to meet her in the hallway. 'I've kept the fire going in the bedroom for yer, Miss,' she said, 'and I'll bring yer hot water bottle up in a few minutes. Would yer like me to bring yer anything to eat or drink?'

'Thank you, Lucy,' Lillian said, 'that's very kind of you, but I've already eaten.' As she continued on up to her bedroom, Lillian felt an unexpected wave of emotion wash over her, and she had to steel herself against breaking down crying again when she felt the warmth of the glowing fire and saw her curtains drawn and her bed turned down. She hadn't thought about her comfort on this cold and snowy night, and for some reason didn't feel she deserved it.

She felt tired and overwhelmed with all that had happened during the entertaining but strange night at Irene's home. Lucy's concern and kindness underlined the lovely life and the people she had grown so attached to in this house in Rodney Street, the life she was about to lose when she confronted her aunt about her lies and deceptions.

Chapter Twenty-Five

Lillian felt the cold air on her face as she walked along Rodney Street on her way down towards St Nicholas Church. A weak sun was beginning to melt the top layers of snow, and there were men working with shovels to clear the mounds from the main road and the footpaths, and she had to constantly watch her step as she went along.

She had woken in the morning with the realisation she had committed a mortal sin. She had missed Mass yesterday for the first time, and for what the nuns would count as no good reason.

She was aware that she had already become lax in her religious duties, because she has no one to answer to as her aunt was not a churchgoer. After years of going to Mass in the orphanage every single morning, she now only attended on the main day in the week, as did most of the other parishioners.

'Sunday Mass,' the priest at St Nicholas constantly reminded the congregation in a grave tone, 'is only one hour out of every week, and surely not much to ask of people, when we think how much love and support Jesus gives back to us. And when we are tempted to turn over in the bed, we should remind ourselves that missing our weekly duty of Mass is a mortal sin. And if anything disastrous should befall us in the week between missing Holy Mass and getting to Confession on Saturday to beg for absolution, we only have ourselves to blame. The fires of hell are full of people who were too lazy to make the effort to go to Sunday Mass.'

Whilst Lillian was unsure about Jesus or Our Lady condemning people to the pits of hell for missing one Mass, this neglect of her religious duty – this shift in her attitude – was something which didn't feel right to her. She felt she needed to do something to redress the balance, so today, as she ate breakfast, she decided that she would feel better if she went down to church and lit a candle and said some prayers. She would talk silently in her head to Jesus and the Blessed Virgin, and beg forgiveness for not making the effort to attend Mass the previous day. Afterwards, she would explain her dilemma and ask for guidance in how to handle the difficulties that lay ahead. Just the thought of sharing her anxieties made her feel less burdened, and helped her concentrate on the small and ordinary details of her morning routine.

While she was finishing off the remainder of her pot of tea, Lucy came up with a telegram from Anna, saying she expected to arrive at Lime Street Station around two o'clock that afternoon, and would catch a taxi up to the house. The news brought a heavy feeling to Lillian's chest, and she pushed aside the tea to get ready to go out.

As she walked up Copperas Hill towards the church, Lillian wondered if Molly had received her note yet and what her reaction to all her suggestions had been. Hopefully, she would know soon.

She went up the outside steps of the church and into the inner vestibule. She halted at the door to take her gloves off and dip her fingers into the holy water fount and then went into the main body of the church. There were only a few other souls inside, praying privately in various pews around the church. Lillian found a seat up near the front, and after saying her initial prayers, which she directed at the almost life-size statues of Our Lady, The Sacred Heart and St Joseph – who always, as a carpenter, seemed kindly and human to her – she went over to a side altar to light her candles. She then returned to the pew to kneel and say more prayers, and after a while she got up and left the church.

She knew nothing would change instantly just because she had been to church and prayed. But she hoped that within a reasonable length she would be living a life which she could be honest about her background, and with people who were truthful and fair with her; a place where she felt she was equal to others – and where she felt in control of her own life.

She had walked past the Adelphi and Lewis's and then had to wait at the next junction until there was a gap between the buses, vans and cars to safely cross over. There were still mounds of snow in various parts of the road which needed careful negotiating, and slushy, melting piles that were black from the traffic.

Several times she made to cross the road and then had to quickly step back as a vehicle came flying around the corner. She was still watching when she heard a male voice call her name and she turned around to see Paul Larking coming towards her. He was very smart in a navy coat over a grey tweed suit, and a dark grey bowler hat and wine leather gloves.

'Are you heading home?' he asked her. 'I just saw you trying to cross over – the traffic is really busy this morning, isn't it?'

'It is busy,' Lillian smiled, trying to hide her embarrassment.

'I think the snow has held up some of the delivery vans and they're rushing now, trying to make up for lost time.'

'Are you working today?' Lillian asked, for something to say.

'I'm actually heading your way,' he said. He held a square leather bag up. 'I have a customer on Upper Canning Street who asked me to bring out some samples for a suit.' He laughed, showing even white teeth. 'It gets me out of the shop for a while. What have you been up to?'

'I went to church,' she said. 'I didn't go yesterday so I thought I would walk down this morning.'

'I didn't go yesterday either with the snow, but I have to be honest and say I never gave it a thought this morning, although my mam was fretting about having missed it. When it comes to religion, I say "each to their own".' There was a silence and then he shook his head and grinned at her. 'I can't believe we've bumped into each other again, with all the people who are in the city.'

'I was thinking the exact same thing,' she said. 'It's a real coincidence, isn't it?'

'Well, it's a nice coincidence,' he said. 'It's quietened down for a bit – shall we make a go for it?' He moved his case to his right hand, and with his free hand he took Lillian's arm and guided her halfway across the road, where they had to stop to let a lorry past.

When she glanced at him their eyes met and he winked at her. She could feel her cheeks starting to burn, then he suddenly moved to stand in front of her as the wheels on the lorry sprayed lumps of dirty snow in their direction.

'I don't believe it!' he exclaimed, looking down at his coat and shoes. By shielding Lillian, he had taken the worst of the soaking and was covered in dirty slush. 'I'm going to have to go back to the shop to get cleaned up.'

Lillian felt bad that he was drenched because he had protected her. 'Why don't you come up to our house and get sorted there? Your mother will have everything you need to clean your coat.'

He thought for a moment. 'That might be best,' he agreed. 'At least if I get cleaned up at your house, I've only got a short walk to the client.'

They eventually got across the road and very carefully made their way towards the house. As they went along, Lillian asked him about his elder sister in Ireland and about her children. She often heard his mother talking about them and felt it was a safe enough subject.

'Eleanor – or Nell as the family often calls her – lives in a small town in the middle of Ireland.' He laughed. 'It's funny when you think how full of Irish Liverpool is, that she's the one who moved over there. It came out of the blue really – she'd only been seeing her now-husband for a few months when his father suddenly died and he inherited the farm.'

'Does she like Ireland?'

'Oh yes, she's very settled now. Her husband Terry has a

good-sized farm in Tullamore. I've been twice and I love it. Great being out in the fresh air and helping out on the farm. Mam misses her of course, especially with her being the only girl. She'd just lost my older brothers, who had gone to New York, and there was just the two of us left at home. Mam and Dad didn't know what to do because she was only sixteen at the time, and it was around her seventeenth birthday when Terry came back to ask her to marry him.'

Lillian's eyes widened. 'That is young. It's only a year older than I am.'

'They knew what they were doing, I suppose,' Paul said. 'They get on great and they have a lovely little family now, two girls and a boy.' He smiled.

Lillian shook her head. 'I couldn't imagine getting married so young…' The way her life was going, it was unlikely to happen. Not too many eligible young men would want to take on an illegitimate bride.

'Oh, I'm sure you'll be snapped up soon enough, a nice-looking, well-educated girl like you.' He raised his brows and smiled. 'The young man you were with in the hotel looked fairly struck on you. I don't think he took too kindly to me interrupting you.'

Lillian felt her face flush. 'We're just friends,' she said. 'Andrew lives in London. He just comes up to Liverpool to visit his grandfather.'

'You never know, he might start coming up more often to see you. Look what happened to our Eleanor. In a year or two's time you could be living in a nice big house down in London.' He nodded. 'I could just see you there, with a fancy car and driver. Dad said that young Whyte's father has a car that they travel up and down to Liverpool in.'

'One of these summers,' he said, when they were safely across another street, 'I'm going to take Mam and Dad over for a holiday to Ireland. I fancy taking my bicycle over and exploring.'

'You have a bicycle?'

'Yes, I love cycling. It gives you great freedom. Last summer I went cycling in the Lake District with a friend.' He smiled at the memory. 'It was terrific and it's a great way to see the country.'

'That sounds really exciting,' Lillian said, 'but I suppose it's different for boys doing those sorts of things.'

'It would surprise you the number of young women who are cycling now,' he said. 'And proper young ladies like yourself.'

Lillian felt a little knot come into her stomach; he obviously believed the story about her privileged background. 'Do you cycle to work?' she asked.

'No, the bicycle would only ruin my clothes with the oil and everything.' His eyes lit up. 'What I would really love is a car, but I reckon I'll have to wait a few more years for that.' He shrugged. 'No doubt your young Mr Whyte will be driving about in his own car soon.'

Lillian caught her breath. 'He is *not* my young Mr Whyte!' she said, in a high, indignant tone. 'And I would be glad if you stop referring to him as that.'

'Calm down,' he said, laughing, 'I'm only teasing you...'

'Well don't,' she said, 'it's not a bit funny.'

'Anyway,' he said, obviously amused by her outburst, 'I still go cycling on Sundays and my afternoons off, so I see plenty of farms, although you have to be careful as there's usually a sheepdog that comes tearing out after you, trying to catch the hem of your trousers.'

'Good for the dog!' she laughed. 'I'm sure you deserve it.'

'What a thing to say!' he exclaimed. 'And here's me thinking what a young lady you were.'

Lillian could tell by the devilish glint in his eye that he found it as funny as she did.

She felt a sense of disappointment as the house came in sight. They walked along in companionable silence, then a thought suddenly occurred to her. 'Do you remember when we were talking in the kitchen and you asked me if I was planning to work? Well, I was just wondering about Lewis's. It looks a lovely place to work. Your mother mentioned that they sometimes organise accommodation for staff...'

He halted, a serious look on his face. 'You're thinking of getting a job in Lewis's?'

'Well, anywhere really ... I'm sixteen on the tenth of January, and I thought it was time I started looking for work.'

'Does your aunt know about this? If she allows you to go out to work, she might be thinking of something a bit more upmarket than working in a shop.'

'But it's a lovely shop,' she said, 'and you enjoy working in it, don't you?'

'Yes,' he said, 'but you and I are from very different backgrounds.'

She took a deep breath. 'Can I trust you? You won't discuss it with your parents or anything?'

'No,' he said, 'not if you ask me not to.'

'I need a job with accommodation,' she said. 'I can't live with my aunt for much longer. I want to move out of her house as soon as I'm sixteen.'

'I don't know what to say ...' There was shock and concern in his voice. 'Maybe you need to talk to her.'

'Will you find out for me if there are any vacancies?' she asked, 'and if it's true that they have accommodation?'

He put his hand out and touched her arm. 'I'm getting worried about you, Lillian, all these things you're saying. My mother has said from when she first met you, what a lovely girl you were and how your aunt adores you. Everyone seems to think you have settled in so well – I don't know how your aunt will react when she finds out that you're planning on moving out on your own. It doesn't make sense to me at all ...'

'I won't be on my own,' Lillian said. 'I have a friend, but she can't join me until she's sixteen in March. I was hoping to get myself settled, then I would be able to help her when she is free ...'

He looked at her and then sighed. 'Well, that makes me feel a bit better, to know you're not going out into the big world all on your own. It's not safe in the city for a young woman alone, but if there are two of you, you might stand a better chance ...'

Lillian felt a wave of relief. Her plan didn't sound so ridiculous as he had obviously first thought, and something told her that when she and Molly were all settled and out in the world, that Paul Larking might be someone that she could look to for advice.

'Promise me you won't breathe a word,' she whispered. 'Promise me?' She had no one else to turn to who could find out the information that she needed to help her and Molly set up on their own.

He nodded. 'Okay, but you must promise me that you will think this all through very carefully, and that you won't make any daft decisions until you are really sure what you are doing.'

She looked at him now and suddenly felt so lost and weary that she wished she could lay her head on his shoulder. 'I promise,' she said, attempting a smile.

'All I will say is: give it time,' he advised. 'Let Christmas and New Year come and go, and see how you feel then. A lot can change in a short time.'

'I know that already,' she said wistfully. She could only guess his reaction if he knew the different world she had travelled from in the last few months.

When they got to house, Lillian started up the steps.

'I usually go around to the back entrance at Pilgrim Street,' he said.

'But that's silly when I'm going in this way,' she said. 'Come in the front entrance with me.'

'I don't think so,' he said. 'Your aunt might not like it.'

'My aunt isn't here,' she said. 'She's not back from London until later.'

He halted, weighing up her offer. 'My mam won't like it either. She'll think I'm taking advantage of the fact your aunt is out, and that you're only a young girl who doesn't understand the differences.'

'This whole thing is ridiculous,' Lillian said. 'If we're to believe all the things we learn in church, then everyone should be equal.'

He raised his eyebrows. 'I like you, Lillian,' he said, 'but I'm afraid you've a lot to learn. You'll soon find that out if you do go off into the big wide world.' He pointed his leather bag at the end of the building. 'In the meantime, I'd rather not risk getting a frying pan over my head from my mother, and so I'll head around to the back entrance.'

'I'll come downstairs in a minute and explain to your mother how good you were helping me,' she said, 'and what a gentleman you were.'

'Do that,' he said, laughing. 'That should keep me in her good books for a while longer.'

They both suddenly stopped on hearing a female voice calling out, 'Miss... Miss!'

Lillian turned around to see a young woman coming towards them. She was dressed in an oversized, threadbare coat, and wearing a brown, faded shawl which covered her head and came almost down to her ankles. She had ripped stockings on and her ancient shoes were burst at the seams.

She looked from one to the other. 'Are you Lillian?' she asked.

'Yes,' she replied, wondering who on earth the girl was.

'Well, I'm Gretta O'Brien.' Her wary eyes darted from Lillian to Paul Larking.

It took Lillian a few seconds to work out who it was, and then she suddenly realised. 'Do you have a letter from Molly for me?' she asked eagerly.

Gretta slid the shawl back from her head, to reveal greasy-looking strands of red hair. 'No...' She brought a grubby hand out of her pocket and handed an envelope to Lillian.

Lillian looked down at the envelope. It was the one she had given Gretta O'Brien's father the day she had been down at the awful court dwellings. 'I don't understand... Didn't you give it to her?'

'I couldn't, Miss,' the girl said, stepping backwards. Her eyes suddenly looked huge in her thin, pale face. 'When I went out to the orphanage this morning, I heard that Molly was dead.'

There was a silence during which Lillian thought she had misheard the girl.

'What did you say?'

'I said she were dead... Molly Power's dead.'

'But she can't be...' Lillian said. Thoughts were now running madly in her mind. 'It's the nuns... they must have found out about Molly writing to me and they are saying it just to punish us.'

Paul stood just a few yards away, unsure what to do.

Gretta shook her head. 'No, Miss. It's true... She were very sick a few days ago and the nuns took her to hospital. I only heard today...'

The girl's words were echoing in Lillian head.

'They are sayin' she had something bad wrong with her leg... that it never healed right. One of the older girls told me she got another knock on it when she was scrubbin' the stairs and it all swelled up. One of the other orphans told me she heard Mother Superior sayin' it was a kind of blood poisoning, and with her chest so bad she weren't able for it....'

'No!' Lillian screamed. 'Molly can't be dead... she can't be dead!'

Hearing the piercing scream and then seeing her legs crumple under her, Paul dropped his leather bag on the ground and rushed forward to try and catch her, but he was too late.

She banged her head off the railing as she fell, and lay motionless on the ground.

Chapter Twenty-Six

Lillian opened her eyes to see anxious faces bending over her. She could feel someone stroking her hand, and when she looked to see who it was, she realised it was Mrs Larking. Her gaze then moved to the end of the bed she was lying on, where she could see Paul Larking looking very concerned.

'Are you all right, love?' Mrs Larking said. 'We've sent for the doctor and he'll be here shortly.'

Lillian went to move her head and felt a shooting pain at her temple which made her wince. 'What happened?' she whispered.

'You had a fall outside,' Mrs Larking said, 'but luckily our Paul was near and he managed to call us and then Lucy ran over to Mr Whyte's to use the phone to get the doctor. He was in his surgery just at the end of the street, and he'll be up when he's finished with his patient.'

'You gave your head a bit of a bang,' Paul said. 'That's why we thought you should see the doctor.'

His voice suddenly reminded her that something had happened to her before the fall. She closed her eyes, and after a minute or so, it all came flooding back. *Molly*, she thought, *it can't be true*... She moaned aloud now, and turned her head from side to side. 'It can't be true...' she said, in a fractured, slightly incoherent voice. 'Molly can't be dead... she can't be dead...'

Mrs Larking turned to Lucy. 'Go downstairs like a good girl, and get me a bowl with warm water and a clean cloth.' She then turned to her husband. 'And if you could top up the fire here with a bit of coal, Michael. I think Miss Lillian is going to be in bed for the day, so we'll want to have the bedroom nice and warm for her.'

When her husband and the maid left the room, Mrs Larking looked down at Lillian. 'What really happened, love? Did that girl with the shawl do something to you? Was she trying to steal your bag or something?'

Lillian closed her eyes. 'No... no...' She suddenly thought of poor Gretta being taken to a police station or something dreadful like that. She took a shuddering breath. 'She was only bringing me a message. Paul was there, he knows what happened.'

Mrs Larking now looked at her son, raising her eyebrows in question. 'And what kind of message was that?' she asked in a low voice.

He was silent for a few moments. 'It's not our business,' he eventually said.

Lillian looked over at Paul, and in the midst of her misery, she knew he would feel bad lying to his mother.

'It was a girl who knows a friend of mine,' Lillian said, 'and she had come to tell me that my friend...' Her voice faltered and she found herself engulfed in tears and unable to speak.

'What happened to your friend, love?'

Paul looked at his mother and shook his head.

Mrs Larking mouthed the word 'dead' and when he nodded, she said, 'Oh, dear God...' She turned to the crying girl, and managed to pull her into a sitting position on the bed so that she could put her arms around Lillian and try to comfort her.

After a few minutes, Lillian's sobbing eased, and the cook turned to her son and motioned with her head for him to go on downstairs.

Chapter Twenty-Seven

Lucy was waiting by the drawing-room window and the minute she saw the taxi, she rushed out into the hallway and called down to Michael Larking, then rushed back down the hallway to open the door.

By the time Anna had paid the driver, and he had lifted her luggage from the back, Michael was there waiting to take the bags into the house.

'I hope you're well, Ma'am?' he said.

'Yes, thank you, Michael,' she said, smiling at him. 'Is Lillian around?' She then started to carefully move up the stairs to the house.

'Yes, Ma'am,' he said. 'Nan is with her, and she has asked if you would go upstairs as soon as you arrive.'

Her brow deepened. 'Is everything all right?' she asked.

Michael hesitated. It wasn't his place to start telling stories he knew nothing about. 'Yes, thank you, Ma'am.' Unwittingly, he had given the same oblique reply that his employer had just given him.

Slowly and with great care, Anna went up the stairs, then along to Lillian's bedroom. She tapped on the door and went inside. Lillian was lying in the bed fast asleep, her face as white as the sheets that covered her. Mrs Larking was in the armchair beside her. She rose when she saw Anna, and then pointed back out to the hallway.

They went down the corridor to Anna's private sitting room, closing the door behind them. Nan Larking gave her the story of what had happened – about the girl in a shawl giving a message to Lillian. 'Seemingly,' the cook said, 'she came to give Lillian bad news about a friend.'

She saw the startled look on her employer's face.

'From what Paul heard, it seems that a girl Lillian was friends with has died. Molly, I think Paul said her name was.'

'Oh no ...'

As she watched Anna's face, which was now as drained of colour as Lillian's, Mrs Larking could tell that she knew at least part of the story. She went on in a low voice. 'Lillian tried to tell me about it herself, but the poor little mite was too upset to get it out.' She paused. 'Now, the worst thing about it all was that Lillian got such a shock with the news that she fainted, and when she went down, she gave her head a bang on the railings. We got the doctor in and he's had a look at her, and he thinks she'll be all right.'

Anna gasped and said, 'Thank God!'

'She has a bit of a bump that's come out at the side of her head, but he said that's a good thing, rather than something you can't see. He checked her eyesight and everything and gave her something for the pain and something to help her sleep after the shock.'

Anna closed her eyes and shook her head. 'Dear God,' she said. 'All this happening while I was away ...' She looked at the door now. 'I had better go to her ...'

'I'm sorry that you've to come home from London to news like this, and especially with you just out of hospital.'

'I'm fine,' Anna said, 'there's no need to worry about me.'

'Are you sure?'

Anna nodded.

'Well, if you are ...' Mrs Larking sucked air in through her teeth. 'I wish I didn't have to give you more bad news, God knows you have enough ...'

'What is it?'

'Mr Guthrie has gone, he left at the weekend. He's found a place somewhere else.'

'Well, I can't say I'm sorry about that,' Anna stated. 'It's actually a relief.'

'It would be fine if that's all it was...' Mrs Larking sighed and shook her head. 'The thing is... he caused trouble before he went. He was at a funeral, came back blind drunk and took it out on Lillian... He told her things that left her in a bit of a state over the weekend.'

'What?' Anna gasped. 'What did the wretched man say?'

Nan Larking held her hands up. 'I'm not right sure; I just know he said things about where she had been before she came here and about...'

Anna sunk her head into her hands. 'Oh no,' she moaned. 'Please God he didn't tell her what I think he did.'

Mrs Larking slowly nodded. 'He more or less told her that you were her mother... and that she's illegitimate. I did my best to comfort her, but I didn't get involved beyond that. I thought it best for me to say nothing.'

There was a prolonged silence, then Anna eventually said in a thin, weary voice. 'This was exactly what I prayed wouldn't happen. I was giving her time to settle in, to find her feet in this new home – this new life. I wanted to build up her confidence before telling her all the things she has a right to know. I was going to tell her a few weeks ago, but she was so excited about Christmas, I thought I would wait until nearer her birthday.' She looked at the cook. 'Was there ever going to be a right time and a right way to explain to her how she landed in that godforsaken place?' She closed her eyes, bowed with the enormity of it all. 'And now the friend who meant the world to her, little Molly, has died. How is Lillian going to cope with all of this?' Anna suddenly felt as though the walls in the room were closing around her.

'And are you okay?' Mrs Larking continued. 'We need to get you a cup of tea or brandy or something before you go into her... Something to pick you up a bit.'

'Nothing is going to do that, Nan, I'm afraid. Nothing is going to pick me up after all of this.'

Chapter Twenty-Eight

Anna sat in the chair by Lillian's bed until she awoke three hours later. Lucy had brought up several cups of tea and a sandwich, which were hardly touched. Mrs Larking came up at one point with a mug of sweet hot brandy, and in a whispered tone insisted that she drink it, and waited until half of it was gone.

Anna watched as Lillian stirred and then went still again. And she watched as she opened her eyes, looked around and then closed them again. Eventually, Lillian started to move and her eyes opened wide.

'How are you?' Anna said in a quiet voice.

Lillian looked over at her, her eyes filled with tears and she turned her face to the pillow.

'I'm so sorry about poor Molly,' she said. 'And I'm sorry for you that you've lost her.'

They sat in silence for a while, then Anna said, 'I'm also sorry about all the things that Mr Guthrie said to you.' When there was no movement from Lillian, she continued. 'I will say at once, there was some truth in what he said, but there were also malicious lies. I had every intention of telling you the whole truth after Christmas, when you were sixteen. I felt it was too much to tell you when you had just arrived. You had too many other changes to get used to... I was worried it would overwhelm you.' She halted. 'I also thought you were so happy making plans for Christmas and for seeing Molly, and I didn't want to spoil things...' She halted, trying to be so careful in the words she chose. 'I don't know where to start, so maybe it would be best if you ask me anything you want to know, and I will tell you the truth.'

'Are you my mother?' Lillian suddenly asked, without turning around.

'Yes, I am.'

'Why did you leave me?' Lillian's voice was plainly hostile now.

'I didn't leave you...' Anna took a great breath. 'You were taken from me.'

There was a silence. 'Was it because I am illegitimate?'

'No,' Anna said, 'that's not the reason, and you are not illegitimate. I was married to your father, but he was killed before you were born.'

Lillian slowly turned around now, and tried to sit up. Anna moved quickly to help her, and was grateful when she didn't pull away.

'What happened?' Lillian asked.

'It's a long story,' Anna said, 'and some of it isn't easy for me to tell... to speak about it.' She swallowed hard. 'Are you sure you want to know now, with everything that has happened... when you have just found out about Molly?'

'Nothing can be worse... and nothing can bring her back to life again. It's been in my head all the time since Mr Guthrie said it, and I need to know why I was in an orphanage when you could have looked after me. I need to know if there is anyone left in the whole world who cares about me.'

Anna had hoped that now Lillian knew she wasn't illegitimate, that she would feel a little better, but she could now tell that was not the main cause of her upset. 'Lillian, I have always cared about you, and always loved you...'

'You wouldn't have given me away or left me in the orphanage if you loved me.'

The accusation was too much. 'I did not give you away!' she exclaimed.

Lillian shrunk back in the bed. It was the first time she had ever heard Anna raise her voice.

Anna's hands came up to cover her mouth as though holding back an avalanche of emotion. 'Oh, Lillian, I'm sorry...' She moved now to put her hand on Lillian's shoulder. 'I don't mean to sound so defensive, but what I've gone through all these years worrying about you... It would have been easier if I could have forgotten you, but I loved you so much I couldn't. You were with me night and day...'

'Tell me what happened.'

Anna lifted her head and then breathed in as much air as her lungs would take, then slowly let it out. Reliving her life, detail by awful detail, was something she had hoped never to have to do.

'I left Ireland at sixteen to come to Liverpool,' she began. 'There was no work for girls in the small town I came from, and even if there was, I had to get away from my mother who never had any feelings for me. I had two older brothers, Martin and Mossy, whom she adored, but she never showed me any affection or interest. I knew it from a young age because she told me when I was very little. She always said that I was a nuisance and a burden, and that having me had ruined her life.'

'What about your father?'

'He was a quiet man, and he agreed with everything she said just to have a quiet life. He had a bit of a farm, and he was out in it from morning until night, probably to get away from her. The boys helped my father, so it was often just me and my mother.' She shook her head. 'There was nothing I didn't try to make her love me or even just like me at times. When I was very young I tried not to talk much as she said my voice annoyed her, and she would slap me because the sound of it grated on her nerves.'

She gave a small bitter laugh. 'Then if I was quiet and didn't speak, she would slap me and say she knew I was thinking bad things about her. From an early age she had me doing things around the house – she hated to see me sitting reading or sewing. When I was old enough to work out things that made her happy – or less unhappy – I would plan things to do things to help. Just so that she would get a surprise and be pleased with me. Little things like getting up early in the morning to have the kettle boiled or the floor swept and washed after my father had emptied the cold ashes from the grate and set a new fire. I would even go down the yard to our freezing outside toilet and empty it to save her doing it, put disinfectant in it – I would do any chores she complained about having to do. She never once said I was good for doing anything, she just then expected me to add anything new I managed to do to the list of other things.' A faraway look came into her eyes.

'There was one afternoon when I realised no matter what I did, she would never love me. She was across the road talking to a neighbour, Mrs Curtin, and I was doing some washing in the sink. Towels and dishcloths and old rags for washing the floor or polishing – that kind of thing. Anyway, when I had finished, I took them outside to hang them up on a bit of a washing rope we had strung between two trees. A short while later, when I was peeling vegetables, she came flying through the back door and grabbed me by the hair and dragged me outside. The rope had snapped and the cloths were lying on a patch of muddy ground from the rain that morning. She got me to pick them up, and as I was doing so, she took the end of the rope from the tree and she came up quietly behind me and whipped the back of my bare legs with it until they bled.'

As she listened, Lillian's heart was racing. She recognised the descriptions of cruelty only too well.

Anna lifted the mug and took a sip of the sweet, lukewarm brandy. 'Mrs Curtin was still outside her own house, brushing leaves and tidying the garden, and she heard me screaming. She came rushing over and saw me lying on the ground and my mother beating me with the rope, and she went over and took it off her.'

Lillian's eyes were as wide as saucers. 'What happened ... ?'

'Well, my mother pretended it was the first time, and that

I had given her cheek and told the neighbour a pack of lies. Afterwards, she continued to be as cruel to me as before but she did it more carefully.'

'She sounds like some of the nuns.'

'The change in me came when Mrs Curtin managed to speak to me on my own after Confession a few days later. She advised me that as soon as I could, I should get away from my mother as she wasn't right in the head and could seriously injure me.' Anna could see the curiosity in Lillian's eyes, and although it was painful to recall her childhood, she knew she owed her as much of an explanation as she needed.

'As I got older and started developing, she became more critical of my hair and my skin and my figure. She would laugh and say my hair was thin and stringy or that my breasts were uneven. She also continued to hit and slap me, but the cruel, personal comments I found even harder to take. That's when I started to plan my escape from her and from Ireland. At fourteen I got a job in the local hotel, and although I had to give her most of my money, I saved every tip I got, and anything I could keep for myself to pay for my boat fare over to England. Kitty Curtin kept my savings box in her house and when I got the chance I gave her money to add to it.'

'I was saving for nearly two years,' Anna continued. 'But every penny I put away made it easier to bear living at home because life had become even harder after Martin and Mossy emigrated to America. They had been as kind to me as they could be, but they were like my father and just kept quiet.' Tears came into Anna's eyes again. 'I was very upset when the boys went because I think my father and my brothers did love me in their own way but couldn't show it in front of my mother.'

'Did she mind your brothers going?'

'She was heartbroken, although they couldn't wait to get away either because of her moods. Kitty Curtin was a great help too – she got me the address of people she knew in Liverpool, and said I could lodge with them until I found my feet. She also constantly told me none of what happened was my fault, and that I should try to feel sorry for my mother because she had some kind of mental illness that made her behave the way she did.' She gave a sad smile. 'I still don't understand that or know if it was true, but her behaviour wasn't normal, and I just wanted to get away from her. I planned to leave as soon as I had the fare saved up, which I had just before my sixteenth birthday. When it got nearer the time, only weeks away from me booking the boat, I told my father what I was planning.'

Lillian asked. 'Did he try to stop you?'

'He went straight to my mother and for the first time I can remember, he stood up to her and said that things had to change. He said that it was hard enough losing the boys, and he didn't want to lose me as well.' Tears came into her eyes, which she fought back.

'She was okay for a week or two. Then, on the morning of my sixteenth birthday – when my father was out – she came into my bedroom and told me she wanted me out of the house or I would be very sorry. She said she would pay for the ticket and give me twenty pounds if I went when I had planned, without telling my father. She said if I didn't go then, she would take back the offer of the money, and would make life so hard for me that I would be sorry I hadn't gone.'

'So you had no choice?' Lillian said quietly.

'Exactly . . .' She dabbed her eyes and cleared her throat. 'I knew that the time had passed for me to have a proper relationship with my father . . . He was weaker than her, and no matter how strongly he felt, she would always undermine him. I also thought I deserved the money as I'd given her most of my wages since I had started working, and I needed it to make a decent start in Liverpool.'

'How did you manage on your own? Were you frightened?' The fears Lillian herself felt about leaving this house she had been so happy in, and striking out on her own with Molly, now rose up again within her.

'Now, Lillian, I don't want you thinking that I'm hiding anything, but if I go into every detail about what happened me after I came over to Liverpool, we're going to be here all night. So, if it's okay with you, I'll try to tell the next part quickly.'

She cleared her throat again. 'The people Mrs Curtin sent me to were very nice, but they lived a good way out of the city centre, and it wasn't easy to find work. So I spent a few days walking around the main streets, going into shops and hotels and different places asking if they needed anyone. I was good at English and Mathematics at school, and learned quickly, and I was very lucky that a saddlers' shop took me on within my first week. I had to help serving and taking orders, and then after a while the owner sent me to night classes to learn accounts so I could do all the books. It was a really thriving business because back then there were horses everywhere pulling carriages and carts, not like now where we have motor cars and buses, and delivery vans. People needed saddles and bridles for work and for sport.'

She smiled. 'I really enjoyed working there; I met all sorts of people from every walk of life. And after about six months, I got my own room in a house like this on the other side of the city.' She smiled. 'The following year, just after war broke out, I met your father. His family had a small ironmonger's business which specialised in the metal parts used for harnesses and riding crops and those smaller items, so he often came to the shop with deliveries. His parents were Irish as well, from Dublin, although he was born in Liverpool. We started seeing each other, Sunday afternoon walks, the theatre, that sort of thing, and then he took me to meet his parents.'

Lillian hesitated for a few moments, then asked. 'What was his name?'

'Loman – he was their only child. They were very nice people and they made me welcome. His mother was kind, although shocked when she realised I was living on my own, as it wasn't the done thing then for young women. She invited me out on Sunday afternoon for dinner. She was very religious, and she said that it had given her the strength to get through when she lost five babies before having Loman.

'I felt I was getting to know her well, and when she asked me about my own family I told her about my parents having the farm and my brothers in America, but I didn't say anything about my mother. Gradually she became more curious, and after a few months I confided in her about my mother. She was shocked, and could not imagine a woman being so hateful towards her own daughter.'

'It is hard to imagine,' Lillian said.

'When your father and I said we were getting married, she was happy, but she found it strange that I didn't want to go back to Ireland to be married from home. She asked me to visit a priest with her for advice, who also said I should write to my mother and sort things out. The thought of it made me ill, and I was so anxious about it all I lost weight.'

Anna gave a great sigh. 'Loman was angry about his mother interfering so much, and when she realised that it was causing a rift between us, she let it drop and agreed we should just get married in Liverpool. With the war and everything, we just had a very small, quiet wedding in St Nicholas Church with a few friends and Loman's family.'

Lillian's mouth opened. 'You were married in the church I go to?'

Anna nodded. 'Yes... 'We rented a small house in Bootle, and we were saving hard to buy a place when I became pregnant, but I lost the baby at five months.'

Lillian listened carefully, trying to take it all in. Trying to fit all the pieces of her own life together.

'It took me a while to get over losing the baby, but I was delighted when I found out I was pregnant again. I was three or four months pregnant when the war became more serious and they brought conscription in. It was all people talked about, but we knew your father was safe because it was just for single men or childless widowed men. But within months they were taking all the men they could get – married or not. They were so desperate they raised the age limit from forty to fifty, and I think it went even higher than that.'

'I've read about it,' Lillian said, 'and the nuns told us about it during some of the history lessons.'

A silence fell between them now at the mention of the orphanage, and Anna bowed her head, as more tears welled up in her eyes. She lifted her hanky and wiped her eyes again and then took another sip of brandy.

'Your father was called up and before we knew it, he was in an army uniform and heading out to France. We were told that it would be a short fight which the British and French would quickly win, that they would all be home for Christmas. We believed it, and I was so happy thinking about him being home for the baby coming. He was only twenty-one, a young man who had only started to live his life.' She closed her eyes. 'He was killed on the very first day of the Battle of The Somme. He was one of over nineteen thousand men who died.'

Lillian looked at Anna – at the slumped shoulders and the face drained of colour – and was shocked to see that she looked years older than she had looked just last week.

'You can imagine how life suddenly changed for me – for everyone. Loman's parents were devastated, especially his mother. She spent half her days in church. His father was gone to work early in the mornings and didn't come home until late.'

'What about you?' Lillian ventured.

'After the funeral I spent most evenings up at his mother's house, and then we got involved helping out at a big house down near the docks that was being used to rehabilitate wounded soldiers.'

She lifted her mug and drained the remains of it. 'They had all sorts of injuries: lost limbs, blinded, deafened, their faces disfigured. Working there helped both of us, and took our minds off Loman for a while. I couldn't do any heavy work being pregnant, but there was always something to do in the kitchen or reading newspapers or books out to the blinded men. The weeks passed, and I moved in with Loman's parents as my time came nearer. The midwife was organised and everything was in order. Then, one night my waters broke...' She looked at Lillian, not sure if she knew what that meant, 'but things did not go as well as they should, and the midwife sent for a carriage to take me to hospital. There's no point in going into a lot of details Lillian, but in the end I had to go into hospital for a caesarean section. You were perfect... absolutely beautiful, but I was very ill afterwards. Your grandmother took you home and organised a young neighbour who had lost a child to be a wet nurse for you, until I was well enough to be released from hospital.

'At first I thought I was all right, but as the days and weeks went on, I was still bleeding heavily and could not sleep. I was feeding you and lying awake between feeds unable to stop thinking about Loman and imagining the horrors he had been through. At other times my mind took me further back in time and I relived the cruel mental torture I had undergone with my mother. The lack of sleep took its toll, and truthfully... I was in a daze a lot of the time.

'Then, the family I had lived with when I first came over – Mrs Curtin's relations – came to me at Mass one Sunday to say they had received a letter from Kitty to say that my father had died and had been buried the previous week. My mother had not even tried to contact me, although she knew he was ill and wouldn't recover. I believe she knew I was in Liverpool and could have tried through the church to find me, as many families do. The knowledge that she didn't even want me to be present at my father's funeral brought back all the overwhelming feelings of rejection. Then, on the day of your baptism, I collapsed in the church and had to be taken back into hospital with an infection and had to be operated on. Again, your grandmother had to look after you...'

'Is she who I thought was my mother?' Lillian asked. 'Betty, the woman who brought me up until I went to the orphanage... was she really my grandmother?'

'Yes,' Anna said, 'Betty was your grandmother – and she absolutely adored you. You were the only thing that kept her going after Loman's death. She lived and breathed for you...

At the time, I don't know what I would have done without her – but I paid a very high price for her help.'

'What did she do?'

'I was in and out of hospital for months, and when I came out I was very fragile. Again, I lived with her, so I was with you for almost the whole first year of your life... but I was still struggling with depression, or melancholia as they often called it. The doctors said it was the trauma of losing your father, exacerbated by a difficult childbirth.' She sighed heavily, as though the memory itself was causing her great pain.

'I was getting a little better, then one of the doctors suggested that it would be good for me to get involved again helping the soldiers, that it would get me out of the house and take my mind off my anxieties. I went to a different place this time – out near Fairfield, where there were quite a few big houses in use for rehabilitating the soldiers. It all went fine for a few weeks and getting out of the house and the walk there and back was helping me.' She smiled over at Lillian. 'On one occasion I even took you out with me in the pram, to let the staff and the soldiers see you. I was beginning to feel I was ready to go back to our own house in Bootle when something terrible happened...'

Lillian looked at her with concern as Anna's face crumpled, and then her whole body started to shake.

'Just thinking about it...' she said in a strangled voice, 'just thinking about it brings it all back...'

As she looked at her mother, Lillian turned over in her mind all the information that she had so painfully imparted to her, and she suddenly realised that worse things could happen to people than life in the orphanage. Anna had experienced a childhood as bad if not worse than her own, and at the hands of the person who should have loved and protected her. She had then suffered the loss of her husband and then all the difficulties of giving birth and subsequent illness. Anna seemed almost broken now, and Lillian wondered if her own determination to know the truth was worth the pain she was inflicting on her. From what she had been told so far, she could see that Anna's tragic experiences had left her fragile and struggling to survive herself, added to which she had the responsibility of a young baby.

She could now see how she might give the care of the child over to its grandmother. What happened afterwards – her grandfather dying, and then later her grandmother, Betty, dying – wasn't something Anna could have envisaged happening.

Lillian sat straight up in the bed now, suddenly feeling a painful throbbing in her temple as she moved. She waited until it subsided, and then she reached a hand out to touch her mother's. 'I think I understand,' she whispered. 'You don't need to tell me any more… I know it's hard for you…'

Anna grasped her hand and held onto it like a drowning sailor would with a lifeline. 'I need to tell you the rest,' she said. 'You're entitled to hear it. If I don't explain why you ended up in that dreadful orphanage, you're going to resent me for the rest of your life.'

Their eyes met and Lillian saw the unbearable guilt and grief that her mother had carried with her all the years they were apart.

Anna closed her eyes and forced herself back to the night when her life changed forever.

Chapter Twenty-Nine

Liverpool 1917

Anna looked at the sleeping baby still attached to her breast. She moved slightly, and the baby, inch by inch, slipped away from the nipple, a small dribble of milk running down the side of her lip.

'She'll be grand now,' Betty stated firmly. 'If you put her down in the cradle, you can go and sort yourself, and I'll mind her from now.'

Anna hesitated. 'Maybe I should leave it for another day... They won't mind. They said to come when it suited me.'

'The doctor said you should get out in the fresh air as soon as you are able, and when Lillian is settled, so you're not worrying about her.' She looked over at the sleeping baby and smiled. 'She is well settled now, and won't need feeding for the next five or six hours. If she wakes before you come back, I'll give her a rusk and some cows' milk.'

Anna looked down at the baby again. In her heart she knew the child was fine, she was healthy and thriving and eating solid foods. But all the weeks of separation had left her anxious about Lillian, left her frightened that her baby daughter had been affected in some way by the terrible tragedy that had befallen the family. Breastfeeding the child made her feel closer to her and as though she was doing something useful and good, but this she knew wouldn't last much longer.

Whilst she had been in hospital, she had expressed her milk

every day to ensure that it would still be coming through, so she could still feed when she was well enough to go back home. She was grateful to have succeeded and kept her milk, and every day that she now fed Lillian, she felt she was making up for her absences when she was born. It also, she thought, underlined the fact to both herself and everyone else that the child was hers and hers alone.

Very gently, she stood up now, and moved across the floor to place the child in the cradle, then covered her up with the hand-knitted blanket her grandmother had lovingly made for her.

'You get yourself ready now,' her mother-in-law whispered. She looked over at the clock, which said two o'clock. 'If you hurry you'll be there to help them with the evening meal. They always need a hand feeding the men.'

Anna filled her rose-patterned jug with warm water from the kettle and went down to her bedroom to get freshened up for going out. She stripped out of her working day clothes and apron, and poured the water into the matching basin. She lifted her Yardley's lavender-scented soap, and then standing in just her undergarments she washed her face, under her arms and her intimate parts. When she had dried herself thoroughly with a rough towel, she then lifted the bowl onto the floor and washed her feet.

Her ablutions complete, she then dressed in a blue dress with a bow at the neck and a cream cardigan with embroidered flowers. She brushed her hair and then put cream on her face, wishing she didn't look so pale and wan. Some fashionable women were now wearing powder and rouge which might have made her look brighter, but Anna was too afraid of being thought fast and cheap.

She came back to hover at the sitting-room door, her grey coat belted and green felt hat on top of her pinned-up hair. 'Are you sure it's okay for me to go? I'm worried that she will be fretful...'

Her mother-in-law smiled at her. 'You don't need to worry, isn't she as used to being with me as she is with you?'

The little reminder of her absences hit the target, and as she walked down onto the main road, the familiar feeling of being a useless, incompetent mother washed over her. She walked on quickly, breathing in the fresh air, telling herself that she would be back to her old self and that things would continue to improve.

She focused on the house in Bootle, and the little changes she would make when she and Lillian were there living peacefully on their own. Somehow, she had managed to keep paying the rent, regardless of Betty's disapproval, who wanted them to stay indefinitely. The money her mother had given her to leave Ireland, plus her steady savings, had kept this one symbol of her independence. She and Loman had dreamed of owning their own home, but like all Anna's other dreams, that had turned to dust too.

She thought longingly of the garden at the back where Loman had planted rose bushes for her, and where she could imagine Lillian toddling around. Her father-in-law had checked the house regularly and kept the grass cut, and had weeded and tidied up the flower borders. As soon as she felt able, she would move straight back in. Her feelings of melancholy, she thought, were lessening, and the fact that she was now heading out to the soldiers' care home in Fairview was a huge move forward.

After the thirty-minute walk, her cheeks were pink again and her spirits somewhat lifted. She went up the long tree-lined drive, and as the rambling old house came into view, she squared her shoulders and mentally prepared herself to greet the other staff and the men who needed her help.

When she called into the office, the staff nurse told her she was assigned to the kitchen for the first two hours, and then she was to go to the men's restroom to read the newspapers to the blind men. She also told her that four new soldiers had been admitted for assessment, three with missing limbs and one badly shell-shocked.

'We can do nothing for him at all,' she told Anna sadly. 'He's in a room on his own at the bottom of the corridor. He can hardly stand without shaking all over. God love him, his arms and everything keep moving. The worst of it is, he's the finest looking fella you could ever lay eyes on. A proper waste of a man.'

Tears immediately filled Anna's eyes. These poor men were supposed to be the lucky ones – the ones who survived. From what she had seen, they were in a living hell. And she felt particularly sorry for the shell-shocked soldiers, as many people didn't understand their distress. She turned away, willing her mind not to go back to her imagination of the trenches and what poor Loman had gone through.

Anna was happy to be in the company of the other women in the kitchen, as it tended to be light-hearted, full of chat about their families along with stories and gossip. There were plenty of incidents to relate about women taking advantage of the chaos that had descended on the city to behave badly. Sex before marriage had become common, as both male and female sought comfort and a little excitement before the men were shipped off in their army uniforms. With husbands gone, babies of uncertain paternity were often conceived, which gave great fodder for gossip.

Whilst listening to the women took her mind off her anxieties, she had little to add to the conversation as her life was centred on Lillian and feeling well enough to care for her. She guessed the other women speculated about her and men, but she made it clear that it was the last thing on her mind. She could not imagine ever replacing Loman, although strangely, Betty had made a few similar comments herself. She said that Anna was still only a young woman, and that she might in the future remarry and give Lillian brothers and sisters.

After her stint in the kitchen, Anna went down to the men's recreation room. Several men were at a long table quietly reading, and at one end of it sat two men playing chess. Anna quietly greeted them, then went to a table and lifted a copy of the

Liverpool Echo, which the men preferred. A few moments later a nurse came down wheeling a chair with one of the blind men, who also had a missing leg. An older, voluntary nurse came behind leading another man.

Anna spent an hour reading selected pieces from the paper, being careful to avoid any articles that mentioned the current war situation. If the men particularly asked for news about the troops, she carefully edited what she read out to them. Afterwards, she went back to the kitchen and helped distribute the evening meal, first to those who were able to sit or bring their wheelchairs to a dining table, then to carry trays down to the bedrooms.

She was walking down the corridor to one of the bedrooms when the last door opened and two nurses came out with the young shell-shocked soldier, his arms flailing around and making unintelligible noises. He only looked around eighteen, with thick blonde hair and was as handsome as the staff nurse had described. The sight of him brought a lump to her throat and she quickly turned into one of the other bedrooms, which she found thankfully empty. She put the tray down on a bedside locker and then she stood with her back against the door, trying to get a deep breath and trying hard not to cry.

As Anna was finishing off her duties, she felt her breasts becoming tense and hard and she knew she needed to get home quickly to feed Lillian. She went to the cloakroom to collect her coat and hat, and looked in at the office to say she was heading home. Usually she left feeling good that she had helped out the poor soldiers in some way. Today, though, the melancholia had intensified, and she hoped walking briskly home would help it lift.

As she set off down the driveway of the big old house, the evening sun was sinking into an orange halo in the sky, but she timed it so that she would be home before dusk settled in. The lovely grounds took her interest as usual, the tumbling roses and ivy on the walls, the bushes and trees now in full bloom, their fallen petals making pink, yellow and white patterns on the grass and pebbled path.

As the large stone pillars and iron gates came into view, Anna felt her breasts start to leak, and she quickened her step. Hopefully, Betty wouldn't have given Lillian too much to eat or drink, and she would have a full milk feed before settling for the night. She still woke at least once during the night, which Anna could cope with, but she found it draining if it was two or three times.

Then, a scuffling noise broke into her thoughts and she turned back to look over to the right where it had come from, but she saw nothing. She walked on, guessing it was one of the cats from around the house, or perhaps a rabbit or a large bird. She heard it again, but this time when she turned around there was a man behind her. A man with a red silk handkerchief tied over his face, standing with his coat open and his trousers unbuttoned to reveal his private parts in an obvious state of arousal.

'Come on!' he said in a low, well-spoken voice with the barest Liverpool accent. 'Come on, you want it too...'

Anna froze to the spot, trying to make sense of what she was seeing, then she suddenly realised what was happening and she turned to started to run. As she moved, her shoe caught in the gravel and her ankle gave way, and she fell face down on the ground. Before she could even move to get up, the man caught her by her hair and one arm and started to drag her off the path and into the bushes.

Anna suddenly found her voice and started to scream and kick at him, making her coat and skirts ride up to her thighs. A hand clamped over her mouth and she was dragged further into the greenery until all she could see were branches and leaves which scratched at her face and exposed skin. He threw her down and then quickly sat astride her, his penis pushing between her swollen breasts. She continued to fight him off, but still he kept his hand over her mouth and nose making it difficult to breathe.

At one point she went limp, trying desperately to take in air

237

through her nose, and he took the chance to reach back with one hand to take a knife out of the back of his trousers.

'I'll use it!' he hissed, 'and you'll be found here dead in the morning with your insides ripped apart. Do you want that?'

Anna's eyes widened with terror and she shook her head back and forth. *Lillian,* she thought, *Lillian. What will happen to her?* Then she closed her eyes and made a silent prayer to Loman.

'Open up!' he demanded, using the hand with the knife to open his trousers further to expose his rigid penis. 'I said open your legs!'

Anna took a deep breath and then she summoned up every ounce of energy she possessed and, screaming 'No!' as loud as she could, she lunged forward with both hands to push him off her. He threw the knife to the ground and then grabbed both her flailing arms by the wrists and pushed her back to the ground, her head making a dull thud as it hit the mossy mound.

His hands were around her neck and he pressed his thumbs hard against her windpipe. 'Another word out of you and I'll strangle you!' As she gasped for breath, he moved a hand to rip at her underwear, and before she could move again he gave an almighty push and forced himself within her.

Chapter Thirty

Anna looked at her daughter with sad, grief-filled eyes. The biggest part of the jigsaw puzzle had been put in place. 'That horrific attack was the thing that finally broke me, and set into motion all the circumstances that would result in me losing you.'

Lillian was horrified at what she had just heard. 'Did they catch him?' she whispered.

'No. When Loman's father took me down to the police station, they were having a bad night in the city with a crowd of sailors from a ship that had just docked and some soldiers who were home on leave.' She shrugged. 'It was the worst possible time to go in complaining about... about a rape... Since his face was covered I couldn't give them any great details about him apart from height and how he spoke and that sort of thing. The police said they would go out to the nursing home the following day and see if anyone had seen or heard anything. They did say that there had been two other attacks in the last few weeks, both in parks outside of the city, and the man was of a similar age and height and had also used a knife. 'Investigations went on for a few days and they interviewed the staff and any of the able-bodied soldiers, but nobody heard or knew anything. The man just seemed to have disappeared into thin air and within a week it seemed as though any further investigation was disappearing too.

'I was back in the same cycle of not being able to sleep and when I did, waking up terrified that the man was in the room or in the house. I was terrified of going outside in case I met him, and of course I never went back to the soldiers' care home. Even the mention of it sent me into a state of nerves, but I kept fighting it all back, determined not to let it overtake me. A month afterwards I started to worry I might be pregnant...' She looked over at Lillian. 'When you are breast-feeding, you don't have your usual monthly cycle, so I couldn't tell. I became convinced I was pregnant, and Betty took me to the hospital to be examined, but when the doctor put his hands on me I became hysterical. All the pent-up fear and anger came rushing out and I ended up being held down by two doctors and being sedated, and when I woke up I was in hospital again. Thank God it turned out I wasn't pregnant as I was almost suicidal as it was and I could never have coped.'

'It's all terrible,' Lillian said, shaking her head. 'It's much, much worse than anything I could have imagined happening to you... I'm so sorry for you.'

She moved to put her arms around her mother. 'What a brave woman you are to be leading such a normal life now. Many women wouldn't have survived after that attack. I don't know how you coped,' Lillian said, almost whispering.

'I barely survived,' Anna whispered. 'I was in the hospital for months, and when I was eventually released Betty told me that she had been given legal advice and that she was now your next of kin and guardian by law. She said that the doctors thought I had inherited my mother's mental illness, and that the best thing I could do would be to leave you with her, and let you have a normal family life with two parents.

'The thing is, I believed it. The same thoughts had gone through my mind as I lay in hospital, and I was terrified that I would do the same things to you that my mother had done to me. I imagined myself living in a house on my own feeling exhausted and pushed to the brink with a young child...' She shook her head. 'I loved you too much to take the chance, whereas I knew Betty would do everything right for you. And of course, I had no choice because your grandmother had the law on her side and all I had was a pile of medical records declaring me an unfit mother.'

Lillian and her mother held onto each other as Anna then told the story of how she moved to London to try to build a new life for herself.

'It was always with the plan that I would come back when I was truly well and able to be the mother I wanted to be. I took a little time to plan my departure and got references from the leather company I had worked in to validate my office and accounting skills. The staff nurse at the soldier's hospital gave me a reference, too; she had been so kind, visiting me regularly after the rape. She knew I wasn't well enough to work with groups of soldiers again, so she advised me to look in the classified advertisements for situations vacant in *The Lady* or similar magazines for a private position working for a family with a disabled soldier.'

Lillian sucked in her breath at the reference to advertisements for positions, thinking that it was only days ago that she was making similar plans for herself and poor Molly. How her life had turned upside down once again. Nothing was as it had seemed any more.

Anna described her move to London, hoping to survive on her widow's pension and what was left of her savings to tide her over until she found work. She took a room in a small hotel and spent a week answering advertisements and finding her way around the city. 'And that was when life started to improve for me,' she said. 'I answered an advertisement for a live-in companion and head of household for a couple in Victoria called Edward and Violet Ainsley. They were both in their mid-forties and childless.'

Lillian eyebrows shot up.

'Yes,' Anna nodded. 'That's where I got my name from. A long time afterwards Edward became my second husband.' She paused, recollecting her thoughts.

'Edward had been an officer during the war, and was also out in France. He had been wounded in the leg and stomach, and when I arrived, he still had a nurse attending him on a regular basis. From the moment I walked into their beautiful house to be interviewed, Violet and I immediately bonded. She was a most unusual woman – upper-class of course – artistic, vivacious and interested in every area of life, unlike anyone I had ever met before. Although tall and broad-shouldered, she was feminine in her dress with flamboyant hats and jewellery, wearing large rings and a multitude of bangles and bracelets. When she rode her bicycle, she shocked everyone by wearing trousers.

'She was very sympathetic about your father, and was intrigued by my experience working with the blind soldiers, and wanted to know every little detail. She explained that she needed someone who understood what soldiers had gone through as I would have to spend a lot of time with Edward, who was still recovering from his wounds and at times used a wheelchair. "I am out a lot in the evenings and occasionally away at weekends," she had explained, "and I need someone to provide company and even a little entertainment for Edward – playing chess or maybe even getting him out to the theatre."

'When she saw my references,' Anna explained, 'Violet clapped her hands in delight and asked if I would move in immediately – and I did! Edward was much quieter, but equally nice in his own way. The other staff were easy to work with, a cook and a couple of maids, and a handyman who came in when needed.'

She smiled. 'Much like the set-up we have here with the Larkings. I learned a lot from the Ainsleys. They taught me so much about every aspect of life – but most importantly, they gave me a home, a purpose, and in their own way, they gave me my life back. They equally felt I was invaluable to them; Edward could unburden himself about his experiences during the war, knowing that I understood, being a war widow myself. He often broke down when he told me about how he sustained his injuries and the horrors he witnessed in the trenches. He cried about the officer friends he lost and those who were dreadfully maimed or psychologically traumatised, and he described the awful fear and dread they lived with whilst having to keep a brave face for the morale of his troops. He taught me to play chess and we had days out in London going to museums and art galleries.'

Lillian looked up at her mother and smiled. 'All the things you have passed down to me.'

'Exactly,' Anna said, squeezing her hand. 'I went to London an Irish country girl and within a few years, I'd learned about different food, fashions, and begun to appreciate all the finer things in life that were kindly given to me. I never forgot my ordinary background and the basic first home your father and I had – and I never will forget it – but by God, I certainly appreciated my new home and lifestyle, and experiencing all the lovely things I didn't even know existed.'

Anna went on to describe the years that followed, during which she got to know the couple and became an integral part of their life. She travelled around England with them, often staying at old country houses belonging to friends. 'The lifestyle was unbelievable,' Anna said, 'like nothing I ever had imagined. Some of their friends were on the fringes of aristocracy; Violet explained she was from a very mixed background where there were relations to royals and also products of scandalous affairs.'

Anna gave a wry smile. 'All the fears we have about illegitimacy, and yet they both talked about it quite easily. They had friends who were poets and artists and sculptors. Some of the women were quite bohemian, but Violet didn't mind and often spent time with them.'

Sometimes Anna wondered if her female employer was more comfortable with her odd female friends than with men, but she said nothing of this. There was no point in opening up the more complicated areas of life, things that didn't directly affect her. Violet's private life hadn't affected Anna and she could see that Edward and his wife had been absolutely devoted to each other. The only affection Anna felt from Violet was maternal, and she wished her own mother had shown a fraction of her kindness.

Anna went on to describe how after the war was over, and Edward was recovered enough to walk again, how she had travelled with the Ainsleys to Paris, Rome, Florence and all the major cities in Europe. 'At one point we even stayed for six months in a chateau in France as Edward wanted to go back to Normandy to visit the graves of some of the soldiers. He offered to take me to see your father's grave, which was something I had only dreamed of doing. It had always unsettled me that I did not know where he was buried, and Edward found out all the details for me. It was ironic as we discovered that one of Edward's close friends had been the commanding officer in Loman's regiment, and there is a possibility that their paths crossed in France during the conflict.'

'Did you ever tell them about the terrible things that happened to you?' Lillian asked.

'Not for a long time, but eventually I did when Violet got sick and had to spend a lot of time in bed. She loved to talk, and it was then she asked me to tell her about my childhood...' Anna suddenly felt a wave of exhaustion. The past held so many difficult places for her and revisiting it was taking its toll. She rolled her eyes up to the ceiling and let out a big sigh. 'Have you heard enough about my life now? Enough to know you were not illegitimate as Mr Guthrie so nastily implied – not that I'd have loved you one jot less, even if you had been – and that I did not abandon you or anything like that.'

Lillian lowered her head. 'I'm so sorry all those terrible things happened to you.'

'I'm sorry too...' Anna said, her voice weak and exhausted. 'But there's not one thing we can do about it. It's something I've learnt to live with, and I hope and pray you can live with it too.'

She looked at her mother. 'I feel much better now I know the truth, but there are still things I'm confused about... but I think we should wait until another time. And I'm sorry for being so angry with you, when you have been so good to me. It was the shock of hearing what Mr Guthrie had said...'

'And of course I wasn't here,' Anna said, nodding understandingly. 'The reptile waited until I was gone to catch you on your own. That awful man, he was determined to cause trouble one way or another.'

Lillian looked closely at her, noticing the dark shadows under her eyes. 'You're tired and you're just back from hospital ... hearing all this must be terrible for you.' She paused. 'Are you all right? Maybe you should go to bed for a while.'

'Maybe later ...'

They heard heavy footsteps coming down the hallway and both moved to sit up straighter, then a tap on the door and Mrs Larking came in.

Her face was full of concern. 'How are you both?'

Anna turned towards her. 'I think we both feel a little better in one way ... but very tired and drained in another.'

'It's not been an easy day for either of you,' she said, shaking her head. 'I have some chicken soup, and I think a bowl of that with some nice crusty bread would do you both the power of good.'

After the cook had gone bustling off, Lillian looked at Anna again. 'Was your operation serious? I didn't like to ask before you went.'

Anna made herself smile. 'It could have been worse,' she said. 'I'll be fine in a few days. How is your head?'

'It's sore where the lump is, but I'm okay if I don't touch it.'

'Well,' Anna said, laughing, 'you know the answer to that – *don't* touch it!'

As she saw Lillian's face lighten a little, Anna thought it was better they laugh than cry. This was not the time to tell Lillian about her operation, or the lasting damage that had been done by the depraved man who had raped her, then used his knife to inflict further internal injuries on her.

Whether the time would ever come that she would want to share those darkest details, Anna did not know. What she did know was that they had done enough crying for today.

After they had had their soup, Anna suggested they both have a rest. 'Afterwards,' she told her daughter, 'I'll get in touch with the convent and find out about Molly's funeral. 'I don't know if they will allow us to attend; I suppose it all depends on where it is.'

'I would like to go,' Lillian said, 'if you would come with me. I don't think I can face seeing the nuns on my own...'

'Of course I'll go with you,' Anna said. She didn't feel up to it for a number of reasons, but she owed it to Lillian to go.

A few hours later the matter was taken out of their hands. After she had rested, Anna went across the street to Mr Whyte's and used his private phone to call the convent to be told that Molly Power's funeral had already taken place that morning.

As she came back to tell Lillian the news, she had a mixture of feelings: relief, sadness and guilt. Molly had been at the back of Lillian's mind, and her constant planning to get Molly out of the orphanage had hampered Lillian settling properly into her new life. In the long run Lillian would be better off without her friend. Anna didn't want to seem unfeeling about the poor girl, but from her own bitter experience she knew that life would undoubtedly be uncertain enough for Lillian herself, without her constantly feeling responsible for Molly's well-being. But first, Lillian needed to grieve for the unexpected loss. Afterwards, time would eventually help to heal things. Anna also knew that from long experience.

Later that evening, after dinner, Lillian was given the final part of the story, which now gave her the full picture of her life until she entered the orphanage.

Anna explained how after a year or two working for and living with the Ainsleys, she gradually returned to her old self, and even began to flourish. As soon as she was settled, she sent a letter to Betty with her new address, and started to send money back every week to her mother-in-law to help to pay for Lillian's keep. She wrote letters, which her mother-in-law replied occasionally to at first, giving little details of Lillian's progress walking and talking, but the gaps became longer between them.

When Lillian was around five years old, a short letter came from Betty informing Anna that Loman's father had died suddenly – another fatality in the flu epidemic – and that she was moving house. When she was settled, she promised she would send on her new address.

Anna waited a short while and then sent a letter to her mother-in-law care of her old address, but she heard nothing back. Every few weeks she wrote again, asking for the new address, then she started received her own letters back saying 'Not known at this address'.

Sleepless nights began to creep in again, and one bright April day, when it looked as though spring had finally arrived in London, Anna decided she needed to take a trip back to Liverpool to find out where her daughter was.

A few weeks later Anna took the train from London up to Liverpool Lime Street Station. She walked confidently along the platform, dressed in a fashionable navy dress with a matching cross-over coat, a white cloche hat and navy and white T-bar, heeled shoes. She was carrying a new leather weekend bag, which Violet had given her as a gift. As she came out into the familiar landscape of Lime Street, all the memories she had fought so hard to leave behind began to gather in her mind and she felt her legs starting to tremble. The trembling continued as she walked down onto Renshaw Street, and she had to stop on the corner of Coppras Hill to catch her breath before she could continue. As she stood there, her gaze moved up the narrow hill to St Nicholas Church where she and Loman had been married, and where Lillian had been baptised.

She took a taxi out to her mother-in-law's house in Anfield. She asked the driver to wait in the cab while she went and knocked on the door of the semi-detached house. A smart young woman around the same age as herself opened the door, and after a short conversation, Anna went to knock on the doors of the houses on either side to speak to the women there. She got the same answer from all of them. They had no idea where Betty Taylor had moved to. She had disappeared without a word to anyone, and no one had seen her since.

The elderly neighbour in the next semi along, Mrs McCabe, was still there, and Anna had felt anxious knocking on her door, not knowing what reaction she would get as she had no idea what Betty had told people.

Mrs McCabe didn't recognise her immediately with her new hairstyle and clothes, but when she did, she was very pleased to see her. Anna explained quickly that she was looking for her mother-in-law and wondered if she had left a forwarding address.

'Not with me, she didn't,' Mrs McCabe said. 'And I was surprised because we'd always got on well. Betty was very private, she would only let you in so far, and I'm not the sort to ask questions, but I still thought she'd have told me that she and Lillian were moving.' The old woman shrugged. 'She had no "For Sale" sign up or anything; she and Lillian just went off in a taxi and then an hour later a van came with two men to take her furniture. I went out and spoke to them, and they said they had been booked weeks ago.'

Mrs McCabe shrugged again. 'It wasn't my place to ask where she'd gone, but I kind of hinted to the removal men about where they were taking the furniture and they just said it was out the other side of the city, so I suppose that could have been anywhere. Again, I'm so surprised she would do such a thing because she was full of praise for you, working away in London to make a better life for Lillian.' Mrs McCabe paused. 'I think losing Frank so suddenly knocked her back – she didn't seem the same afterwards. Now, she was always very good with Lillian – she doted on her as you know – and still took her down to the shops and to church as she always did. But anytime I was talking to her after Frank died, she didn't have the same go in her. I think it brought back all the sadness of losing Loman.' She sighed. 'Maybe she decided that a new start would be the best thing for her and Lillian. Plenty of people uproot after that kind of thing happens. You know what it was like during the war...'

Anna continued with her story. 'I went back to my hotel room and thought back to all the places I knew Betty went to in town, and after I had eaten I went out again. I went straight to the ironmonger's workshop where your father and grandfather worked, and met the new owner. He told me your grandmother had sold the business a few months after your grandfather died, and knew nothing else about her. I then spent the next few hours walking around all the shops like George Henry Lee's and Blacklers and Lewis's. I sat in a café in Church Street, which had a window looking out into the street, hoping I might see you both.

'The following day was a Saturday so I went down to St Nicholas's to Confession and sat at the back of the church until the priest had finished with the last person. I asked the priest there too, but he was only a young curate and he didn't have a clue who I was talking about. Of course I went back to St Nicholas on the Sunday. I went to the first Mass at eight o'clock, then went back to the hotel for breakfast, then I went back down to the ten o'clock Mass and then back to the twelve o'clock. I prayed and prayed and prayed that I would see you, but there was no sign of you anywhere. Not one prayer was answered.'

She shook her head. 'Is it any wonder I have no faith left in religion? After all the terrible things that had happened over the years, and then, when things were improving for me, and I could see a time coming when you and I could be living together again, this happened. My mind was back to being good and healthy, and I was saving money so I could eventually buy a nice house for us in Liverpool or London – I thought my life had turned a corner. Instead, on the Monday I had to go back on the train thinking I had lost you forever.'

'How did you eventually find me?' Lillian asked.

'I travelled up to Liverpool again the following year but had no further luck, and I started to sink back into a depression. I knew I had to block it all out of my mind or I would become ill again. It must have been four or five years later when Violet helped me start the process off again. She was ill and was forced to stay at home more.

'Violet developed serious kidney problems, which eventually killed her several years later. During the time Violet was confined to bed, she talked to me about her own early life and bit by bit she managed to get me to talk about mine. She told me she had a very distant and cold mother, and how it had affected her, and hearing it helped me to open up to her about my own mother.'

Anna's eyes grew moist with emotion. 'She was a wonderful woman in many ways, and her honesty helped me face all the other awful things that had happened. She knew I had been married of course and about Loman, and one night we sat up late talking and I told her about you and how my nerves had been very bad afterwards, and then I told her about the man who had raped me and how your grandmother took over your care.'

There was a silence as Anna took a few deep breaths to compose herself. 'Violet was so understanding about everything, but was most shocked of all by Betty's disappearance with you. The following afternoon, she brought Edward and me into the library and after quickly explaining the situation to him, she showed us a plan she had worked out to track you down. She had managed to get hold of a list of all the Catholic churches and schools all around the Liverpool area, and she suggested I write to them. I spent weeks and months writing and copying letters, but I got little response, and then Violet was taken into hospital in central London, and my time was devoted to visiting her and caring for Edward before she died.'

Lillian bit her lip. 'That was another loss for you...'

'One of the biggest,' Anna said ruefully, 'but that wonderful woman was determined that you would be found and that we would be reunited. On her last Christmas Day, which was weeks before she passed away, after our meal when we were sitting having a drink, she told Edward and me that she wanted us to get married.'

Lillian's mouth opened in a circle of shock. 'What? She wanted you to marry her husband?'

Anna smiled and nodded. 'It sounds very strange, doesn't it? But that's exactly what she wanted.'

'What did you say?'

'Well, I was as shocked as you are now, and Edward was too. First of all, he said that he had never planned on marrying again, and then said I was much too young and lovely to marry an old codger like him.'

In the midst of her sorrow and confusion at all this news, Lillian found herself giggling at Edward's response. 'He sounds a bit like Mr Whyte,' she said. 'He makes me laugh at the things he says about himself and Andrew.'

Anna smiled and raised her eyebrows. 'I suppose there are similarities between them. Anyway Violet went on to say that it would be the best possible arrangement for both of us, as I would be there to look after Edward as opposed to some gold-digging woman making a play for him, plus I knew all his medical history and things would more or less continue as they were.'

She looked over at Lillian. 'I suppose you are old enough to hear this now, since you have heard probably worse things already. It might also help you understand why the age difference and everything else didn't matter as much as it might have. You see, Edward's war injuries meant that he would never be able to have a proper marriage with a woman again.'

Lillian was now back to being serious, and hoped that Anna wouldn't go into too many embarrassing details because she just couldn't envisage an elderly man being involved with anyone romantically. Sex and intimacy, she had imagined, were only for young people. Surely that all disappeared after people were married a few years? She wondered now how Anna felt about this because she was sort of in between. Neither young nor old. The image of Irene's mother with her driver suddenly flew into her mind and she felt unsure about the whole thing. Relationships, she was beginning to find out, could be very complicated.

Anna went on, oblivious to Lillian's uncomfortable thoughts. 'Violet explained that having no children, they had planned to leave their property and money to charity. She said that after all I had been through, and especially what you had been through, she would rather they left half to the charities and the rest to us. The easiest way to do it, she said, was if Edward and I married. 'You have been like a daughter to me,' she said, 'and I know you will make a lovely, kind partner for Edward when I'm gone. Lots of marriages are not based on physical relationships, and plenty are only matched because of money and land benefits. Taking all the unusual circumstances into account, I think you two have as much chance of having a happy marriage as anyone else.'

'I can see you have it all worked out,' Edward had said, 'and it does seem advantageous for me... so I now have to leave the decision in Anna's hands.'

'What did you do?' Lillian wanted to know.

'I said I would have to think about it, but to be honest, it didn't take me long. It was the most wonderful opportunity I had ever been given, and I loved both Violet and Edward dearly, so it made absolute sense to agree.' She took Lillian's hand now. 'And it meant our future would be secure. When I eventually found you and brought you here, I told you that your life in this house was your future. Thanks to the kindness of Edward and Violet, I inherited both property and money.' She gestured with her hand around the room. 'And everything I own will one day be yours.'

Throughout the rest of the evening, Anna filled Lillian in on the latter part of her life with Edward after Violet had died. How they were married six months later, how that summer they travelled back to the same place in France for several months, revisiting Loman's grave and the other graves they had been to before. They had a few weeks at home when they came back to England, and not long after, Edward told Anna that he thought they should book a week in the Adelphi Hotel in Liverpool, and go and view property there.

'But we're not moving to Liverpool, are we?' Anna had asked.

'Not permanently,' Edward had said, 'but I like Liverpool, it's a nice city. I thought maybe we could spend a month in London and a week or two here on a regular basis. It would give you more time to see if you can track your daughter down.'

One of the first houses they viewed was the house in Rodney Street, which Edward thought was a bargain compared to London. Anna explained to Lillian how she was initially reticent about giving her opinion because she had no experience of buying property and she also didn't feel entitled to spend money that wasn't hers, but Edward was insistent that she should buy the house she thought would be ideal when she eventually found Lillian. It was also he who came up with the idea of having it as a boarding house at some point in the future, when she didn't need to spend time in London. After checking it over carefully, both Edward and Anna thought the Rodney Street house was exactly what they were looking for. By the time they left for London at the end of the week, the wheels were in motion to buy it.

'Edward also decided it would be a good idea to take on a couple who could do the general running of the house: a woman to do the cooking and housekeeping while we were staying, and a man for the heavy work. Someone who lived nearby and could be there to keep a general eye on the house while we were away – and that's how we came upon Mrs and Mrs Larking.'

She looked at Lillian now. 'Do you want to have an early night? You must be exhausted having listened to all this...'

'I'm really happy to know the truth,' Lillian said, 'and I really do understand now, and I don't feel angry with you any more or even upset. You did your best and you couldn't help being ill after everything that had happened to you.'

Anna put her hand on Lillian's bedspread and moved it around, smoothing the satin material. 'And I don't want you to blame Betty for what happened. She thought she was doing the right thing giving you a settled home and a routine and the things mothers do. She loved you very much, and was afraid to lose you...

'The thing I took a long time to forgive her for was that she didn't plan what was to happen to you if she died, which unfortunately is what happened. She never in a million years imagined that she would suddenly suffer a heart attack and you would be left entirely alone with no relatives. When she moved out to Wavertree after your grandfather died, she told her neighbours and the teachers at school that she was your real mother, and that she had had you late in life. There was only one person she trusted with the truth – a priest. From what I learned later, she had told him that I was locked up in a mental asylum in London because I was dangerous, and if I ever got out, I would come looking for you. She made the priest promise never to tell anyone you were actually her granddaughter.'

Lillian eyes filled with tears. 'It's very sad,' she said, 'because I know she did love me, and would never have deliberately done anything to harm me.'

'You're right,' Anna agreed, 'but by shutting me out, even though she knew I was recovered from my nervous breakdown and doing well in London, she wouldn't let me into your life again. And that, Lillian, is how you ended up in the orphanage all those years. The priest believed you had no one else, and that was the only place they could find for you.'

'How did you find me?'

'Edward hired a private detective who spent months going over every little detail, and visiting all the school and churches again until he came upon the priest your grandmother knew.'

'A consulting detective?' Lillian repeated, her voice full of amazement. 'I didn't know they really existed. I've read the Sherlock Holmes stories, but I can't imagine one looking for me.' She smiled. 'Edward must have been very keen to help you find me if he hired a detective.'

'Oh, he was very determined,' Anna said, smiling back. 'He needed to visit the orphanage to be sure there were girls of your age there, but he couldn't let the nuns know who he was or they would never have let him onto the premises. Edward came up with the plan that he and the investigator would become bene-factors of the orphanage and donate money, which of course Edward provided.'

She took a deep breath. 'He was so delighted when we had found where you were, and we were making plans to go out to the orphanage together when he became ill. His old war problems with his stomach started up again and he had to go into hospital in London for several operations, and then there was the recovery afterwards which took months. I couldn't leave him, so we had to put things off until he was well enough to come with me – but that never happened. He was ill for a long time, unable to leave the house without a wheelchair, but he was the sort of man who managed things from the house, writing and by telephone. By the time of his final illness, he had transferred everything into my name – the house in London, the house in Liverpool and other smaller properties. He had arranged for me to visit exceptionally well-run boarding houses in our area of London, so that I knew what would be expected if I returned to run the house here in Liverpool. And that is exactly what I did when he died.'

Lillian had a final question for now. 'Why didn't you come for me earlier?' she asked. 'When you moved up here.'

'I didn't want to bring you back until I was certain I was settled here again, and could cope with all the difficult and sad memories. I also needed to wait until I had the guest business running properly. It had to be the perfect situation to bring you here because I knew we would need time to ourselves to get to know each again, just as we did. I wanted to have all that time to help you to adjust to your new life when you arrived.' She squeezed Lillian's hand. 'Do you understand that now? It's very important to me that you do.'

'Yes, I really do – you did it the best way you could.'

Anna bowed her head. It had been a long, hard journey getting here and reliving it all again had not been easy. 'Thank you,' she said. 'Thank you.'

Chapter Thirty-One

Lillian woke just after eight o'clock the following morning and lay looking up at the ceiling for a long while before she moved. She had slept well all night despite the events of the previous days. The lump on her head had gone down a bit and she felt surprisingly lighter and brighter than she had in days. There was an awful ache in her chest every time she thought of Molly, but it was balanced by the peaceful feeling she had now about Anna being her mother, and knowing the truth about her background. She found some of the future implications hard to take in – knowing that she was heiress to this house and the property in London.

But then, she thought, it was almost as strange as looking back to her life in the orphanage, which was only a few months ago. It seemed much longer than that, and with Molly gone, the link to it now seemed to have faded even further into the past. She was relieved that she didn't have to leave Rodney Street. Her future, she now knew, belonged here with Anna.

She pushed the covers back and padded barefoot over the fringed rug to stand by the window to look out. She smiled now, remembering the time that Andrew Whyte had waved up to her. There would be no sign of him now, of course, until Christmas. The snow had disappeared, and the sky looked clear and bright.

After her bath, she brushed her long dark hair and put clasps in either side to hold it tidily in place, and put on a pleated navy skirt and a blue and white sweater, which came down over her hips. She went into the sitting room next door, where there was a bright fire burning, and Lucy was just finishing brushing the rug in front of it.

'Are you feelin' better, Miss?' Lucy asked, looking a little uncertain.

'Yes, thank you,' Lillian said, smiling at her. 'I feel much better. Is my aunt up yet?'

'Yes, she were down in the kitchen with Mrs Larking just now. Do yer want me to bring yer porridge or do yer want something liked boiled eggs and toast?'

'If it's no trouble, a boiled egg with tea would be lovely. And would you let my aunt know I'm in here?'

As she waited, it crossed Lillian's mind that there were still some things she and Anna needed to talk about, and one of them was what she should now call her. It might be easier for both of them to continue calling her 'Aunt Anna'.

Anna arrived up a short while later, and, although she was wearing a cheery red dress and was smiling when she came over to kiss her good morning, Lillian could tell by the shadows on her pale face that she hadn't slept well.

She looked at Lillian. 'How are you feeling?'

'Better, my head is just a tiny bit sore now. I was just thinking I might go down to the church today – it looks dry out and the fresh air would do me good.'

'I was thinking the same thing,' Anna said, 'and if it is okay with you, I'll come with you.'

Lillian looked at her. 'I think it is too soon as you only came out of hospital yesterday – I think you should have a rest today. It would make me feel better if you did.'

Anna thought for a moment. 'Maybe you are right. What if I come to Mass with you on Sunday? It might help to make up for missing the funeral.'

Lillian nodded, her face sad now. 'That would be nice,' she said in a quiet voice.

'I was downstairs talking to Mrs Larking...'

'Oh, I was thinking about that earlier...' Lillian interrupted.

'Do the Larkings know about me? When I spoke to Mrs Larking yesterday, I got the feeling they knew...'

'Before you came, I spoke to both Michael and Nan, and told them the basic facts about you. I felt they needed to know the most important thing, that I was your mother. I know and respect her too much to pretend to her. I told them both about your father being killed in the war, and you being brought up by your grandmother while I went to work in London, and about us very sadly losing touch. They know you were in a place with nuns, but at the time I thought it was a good place, so I haven't really gone into all that detail with them. They are not intrusive people and they didn't ask for more information; they were just very sorry to hear that you and I had been separated.'

'And what about the guests?'

'I don't intrude on their lives and they don't intrude on mine, so there was no need to tell them anything.' She took a deep breath. 'Unfortunately, Mr Guthrie wasn't like the other guests, and he took delight in meddling in other peoples' business. A few years ago when Edward was in the house with me, Mrs Larking was off sick at one point, and we had a very odd woman who took her place for a few weeks. She not only eavesdropped on Edward and I discussing the private investigator looking for you in orphanages, but she then went through papers and documents from priests and schools that we had written to.'

'Why?' Lillian asked. 'Why would anyone do that?'

'Some people feel better about themselves if they think others have problems. Later, Mr Guthrie came across her serving in a hotel bar somewhere in the city, and they got chatting and discovered they had both been in this house. She must have told him about her findings. He would have been delighted to hear about it all, and he added his own speculations and concluded that you were illegitimate. He made several shrouded comments to me about knowing the woman, but I just cut him off, hoping she hadn't spread malicious rumours.' She waved her hands. 'We've had enough about Mr Guthrie and all the unfortunate things that have happened. We need to start looking forward to happier things like Christmas and New Year – and your sixteenth birthday!'

Lillian's face lit up. 'I must finish off my gifts for the staff and...'

'I was thinking that you might like to give the things you collected for Molly to a charity...'

'I thought I could give them to the girl who came here with the letter from Molly – I know where she lives.'

'If that's what you want to do, and if it makes you feel better, then do that.'

Molly's brother, Daniel, was also at the back of her mind. She would have liked to have got in touch, and maybe given him something for Christmas, but from what she knew, the nuns in the boys' orphanage were as unlikely to pass anything on to him as the nuns in Gethsemane House. She would wait, she decided, until it was time for Daniel to leave the orphanage, and maybe she would be in a position to help him then.

Lillian looked at Anna now. 'There's just one other thing I want to ask you,' she said. 'Now I know you're my mother, what should I call you?'

'What do you want to call me?' Anna asked. 'It's entirely your decision.'

'Well, I'm used to calling you aunt, and I just thought people in the house, and my tutors like Miss Churchill or Mr Whyte, might think it strange if I started calling you anything different. They might ask me questions...'

'I thought that too, but I want you to feel happy about whatever you decide to call me.'

'For now, I'd rather keep calling you Aunt. Maybe in the future...'

'As long as we know who we are to each other, that's all that counts.' Anna's eyes crinkled as she smiled. 'When the right time comes, maybe if you meet a nice young man and want to get married, and you want to explain our relationship...'

Lillian laughed. 'I can't imagine getting married! Who would want to marry me?'

'You're a beautiful, intelligent girl,' Anna told her. 'So I think it's a distinct possibility.' She halted. 'I hope you don't feel less about yourself because of your years in the orphanage? Lots of families have sensitive situations that other people know nothing about, and it really is no one else's business.'

'Life can be very complicated,' Lillian said. 'I had no idea about all this when I was with the nuns. They told us what to think and say, and they also told us that most people were sinners and bad.'

'Life is very complicated,' Anna agreed, 'but there is always something good around the corner. Sometimes you have to wait a little bit longer, but the good eventually comes and is worth waiting for.'

Chapter Thirty-Two

Lillian checked herself in the mirror, then smoothed down the fur collar of her coat and straightened her black felt hat. She went into the sitting room, where Anna was quietly reading by the fireside.

'Do you need anything while I'm near the shops?' she asked.

Anna thought for a few moments. 'Would you pop into Lewis's and get me some gift vouchers please? They make such useful presents.'

Later, as she walked through the festively decorated department store, Lillian felt delighted that she had a valid reason to be there. She stopped to admire the massive Christmas tree hung with glass baubles and candles, and all the beautifully wrapped parcels beneath. She went straight to the desk that sold the vouchers and bought them before walking upstairs to the men's department. She looked around, unsure where to go, when a young smartly dressed salesman came over to ask if she needed help.

'I wonder if Paul Larking is here today?' she asked. 'He works in the gents' tailoring department.'

He smiled at her. 'Yes Madame, Mr Larking is in. I just saw him go through to the cutting room a few minutes' ago.' He held a finger up. 'I'll just get him for you now, Madame.'

Lillian was surprised to be addressed as Madame, as she had only been addressed as Miss before, and she wondered what age they thought she was. As she waited, a little anxious knot formed in her stomach, and she wondered if Paul Larking would mind her calling at his place of work like this. She had no other way of contacting him and she wanted to speak to him alone.

She looked around the gents' gift area for a while, and then, aware she was the only female on the floor, she went over to a quiet corner where there was a full-length mirror. She was checking her hair and hat when she heard low voices coming towards her, and she whirled around – embarrassed to be caught at the mirror – to see Paul coming towards her. He turned to the sales assistant and made a little gesture with his hand to thank him, and the assistant went off.

He gave her a warm smile. 'Well, I'm relieved to see you up and about. How are you feeling today?'

Lillian touched the side of her head. 'Apart from a bump and bruise, I'm fine, thank you.'

'What brings you here?'

'I wanted to thank you,' she said. 'And I feel I owe you an explanation...'

His face became serious, and he shook his head. 'You don't owe me any explanation. It's your own business.'

He seemed so grown up and serious, and Lillian suddenly felt self-conscious. 'Well, you were very kind and...' She was blushing and stuttering now. 'I didn't know when I would see you again, and I wanted to thank you personally without everyone else being about. You were very nice walking me back to the house in the snow, and then helping when I got the bad news about my friend...'

He looked grave as he listened. 'I did nothing really,' he said, 'only what any other fellow would do in the same position.'

There was a silence and then she straightened herself up as Miss Churchill had told her to do when she needed to appear confident. 'I also wanted to tell you that everything has changed since yesterday. I've sorted things with my aunt, so I'm not planning on moving out or looking for work just now. And my friend...' She sighed. 'I'm going down to church to light a candle for her after I've finished my business here.' Tears suddenly flooded her eyes.

'You poor girl.' He moved forward to take her hand in his. 'Wait here for a minute, please,' he said, 'I'll be straight back.'

Lillian got her hanky out from her handbag and dried her eyes, and by the time she composed herself, he was striding back towards her.

'Okay,' he said, 'I've organised to take an early break. Let's go down to the tearoom and have a cup of tea, and you'll feel better.'

Lillian's heart lifted a little. Even though he was quite formal at times, she felt comfortable and safe with Paul, as she did with all the Larkings. 'Are you sure? I don't want to take you away from your work.'

'It's fine,' he said, 'I would be stopping in an hour anyway.' He put his hand under her elbow and they walked out onto the landing and got the lift to the upper floor. Paul found a table for them and ordered tea and biscuits for Lillian, who had told him she wasn't hungry, and a beef and horseradish sandwich for himself.

As they drank their tea they chatted about Christmas coming and Paul told her he was looking forward to a few days off, as he had been working longer days than usual due to the festive late-opening hours.

'It's a lovely place to work,' Lillian said, looking around her. 'Even though I'm not thinking of moving out any more, I am still thinking about finding a job. I think I would enjoy being here every day, and it's only a ten-minute walk from Rodney Street. There are a lot of girls like me working in the different departments. What do you think?'

Paul gave a sidelong smile. 'Talk to your aunt,' he said. 'Get her blessing first.' He lifted his teacup and took a drink from it.

'I'll be sixteen in a few weeks,' she reminded him, 'and I can't stay at home all day forever.'

Lillian lifted her cup and took a small sip, and then she looked him straight in the eye. 'I feel I can trust you,' she said, 'and you're the first person I've told, but Anna is actually my mother . . .' The way Paul's head jerked up at her statement told her that he knew nothing about it. 'I only found out yesterday. Your parents know, but they've obviously kept it confidential.'

'I don't know what to say ... Was it a shock for you?'

'It was, but in a lot of ways it's a nice shock.' She then went on to explain the situation.

Paul sighed and nodded his head. 'I've a young neighbour who thought the same thing, but it turned out that his oldest sister was really his mam. She'd had a fling with an American soldier during the war, and he went back to New York before the kid was even born. It's the way things go sometimes.'

A warm feeling passed through Lillian, hearing how open and understanding he was.

He looked thoughtful for a few moments, then took another sip of his tea.

'But you know, Lillian, things like that don't count for the gentry. Life will always be easier on people from your background whatever happens. That kid I was talking about has a hard time because his mother wasn't married, and they are living on practically nothing. The other kids in the street throw his illegitimacy at him every time they're fighting.'

'That must be awful for him. My friend Molly was in a similar situation, and the nuns were cruel to her about it, so I do understand.'

'You might think you understand,' Paul said, 'but you live in a very different world from ordinary people now. No matter how hard we work and how far up the ladder we climb, we're still never really accepted. Even when you think you're doing well and have improved your position in life, there's always somebody who will let you know that you're only tradesman and you still don't count.'

'What do you mean?' Lillian was taken aback at this sudden turn in the conversation.

'What I mean is, there's a law for the rich and a law for the poor.' He shrugged. 'Look, I don't mean it personal to you or anything, but there are people in Liverpool who are living in real slums with six or seven of a family all in one room. There are men who are lining up at the docks twice a day for a few hours' work, and their wives and kids are hungry every minute of every day because they haven't got the money for basic food. There are people in terrible situations you would never even dream about.'

'But I do know,' Lillian said, her voice indignant. 'I was in the court housing in Clayton Street the other day. That's where the girl who brought me the message lives.'

He held his hands up. 'I'm not going to agree and say that you've got things hard when you have a lovely home and everything that goes with it. Your problems are minuscule compared to most other people's.'

A searing sense of injustice rose up inside Lillian. 'You know nothing absolutely nothing about my life before I came to Rodney Street...' she said heatedly. 'For your information, I spent years locked up in a miserable orphanage with nuns who hated me and all the girls, I had to scrub floors and toilets every day...'

Lillian suddenly halted as she noticed a well-dressed, pretty young lady with red curls coming towards their table.

'Edie!' Paul moved his chair back to stand up. 'I didn't know you were back home...'

'I just arrived last night. We finish early for the Christmas holidays.' She looked at Lillian and smiled.

Lillian took a deep breath, trying to still her racing heart. She felt like getting up from the table and running out of the tearoom, but she knew it would look ridiculous to both Paul Larking and this lovely-looking young lady.

'Oh, Edie, I would like you to meet Lillian.' He looked over at Lillian again, his eyes checking hers. 'Edith is a friend of mine; she's training to be a teacher in Newcastle.'

Lillian remembered Paul's mother telling Anna about a girlfriend he had been seeing over the summer.

'Lovely to meet you, Lillian,' Edie said, smiling warmly at her. She put her hand out.

Lillian somehow managed to return the smile and shake her hand.

Paul pulled out a chair beside him. 'Sit down,' he said, 'and have a cup of tea with us. I'm on my break, I have another half an hour.'

Edie looked at him. 'I didn't mean to interrupt...?' She sat down and then looked from one to the other. 'So, you two are friends?'

There was a small silence. 'Sort of,' Paul said. 'My mother works for Lillian's family.'

'Ah,' Edie said, her eyes widening, 'in the lovely house in Rodney Street?'

Paul's eyes darted towards Lillian. 'Yes, that lovely big house...'

He turned back to his friend. 'So, how is the teaching going?'

'Okay, I think,' Edie said, her face lighting up. 'I was out on teaching practice in Gateshead for a week before we finished up.' She rolled her eyes. 'A very poor area, the slump has really hit everywhere, every bit as bad as Liverpool.' She smiled. 'But the kids are lovely and the teachers do their best to make things a bit easier for them.'

'You'll make a fantastic teacher,' Paul said.

Lillian could tell by the look in his eyes and the sound of his voice that this was the sort of girl he admired. She could understand why he would be drawn to her, as Edie was very attractive and friendly. As she listened to them talking about each other's families, Lillian suddenly felt an outsider, and in the way.

She took another sip of her lukewarm tea and then she lifted her bag. 'If you'll excuse me,' she said, 'I've got to go.' She looked at Edie. 'It was lovely to meet you and I hope you have a nice Christmas.'

'And the same to you,' Edie said.

Paul stood up. 'I'll see you out...'

'Thank you, but there's no need,' she said quickly, without looking at him. 'Stay and chat to your friend.'

Lillian walked straight out of the tearoom and caught the lift down to the ground floor, then exited the store towards the church, which she found empty. She walked up the aisle to the main altar, genuflected and went over to the small side aisle where the candle stand was, put her coin in the box and lit a candle for Molly.

She came back down the aisle to kneel in a pew halfway down the church, then closed her eyes and forced herself to push the memory of her argument with Paul Larking out of her head, and to concentrate on saying prayers for her dead friend. She started with the *De Profundis,* a Catholic prayer for the dead, her lips moving with her silent, ancient words, *Out of the depths I have cried to Thee, O Lord; Lord hear my voice. Let Thy ears be attentive to the voice of my supplication...*

As she prayed, her mind was filled with images of Molly, talking and laughing with her in the orphanage, working with her in the laundry; and then darker images of Molly lying sick in bed mingled with ones depicting Molly lying dead in a coffin. When the worst pictures came to mind – of Molly shut in a coffin and buried under the cold, winter ground – Lillian quickly sat up on the edge of the pew, and fixed her gaze on the statue of the Blessed Virgin.

She sat for several minutes, concentrating her eyes on the statue as her mind eventually found some sort of stillness. She sat there, staring ahead until she became oblivious of her surroundings, and didn't even notice someone else entering the church until she felt a hand on her shoulder. She turned quickly, to find Paul Larking had slid into the pew behind her.

'I hoped you would be here,' he said quietly. 'I wanted to catch you to apologise for earlier. Something happened this morning when I was out doing a home measurement, and I suppose I was feeling a bit slighted.

'I was told by the customer to come around to the front door of the big house. He sent for coffee for us while I was measuring him up, and everything was all nice and friendly. He was a pleasant man, and he asked me all about my training, and seemed very interested; and basically treated me as though we were on an equal footing.' He sighed and shook his head. 'Then, just as I was leaving, his wife came and said in a very high-handed manner that she'd noticed I had arrived by the front door, and that she would prefer me to leave by the tradesman's entrance at the back, as she had a friend arriving for lunch.' He put his forefinger and thumb together and measured about an inch. 'I felt that size ... and I realise I was still annoyed about it, and took it out on you.

'I'm sorry for being so rude, Lillian, especially when you were pouring your heart out just before Edie arrived and it might have looked as though I was ignoring what you had said, or hadn't heard you, but there was nothing I could do, I didn't want to snub her. Her arrival was bad timing.'

He leaned over the back of her pew and took her hand in his. 'Are you okay? I could kick myself for being such a big mouth and only thinking about my own situation.'

Lillian looked at him. 'I'm okay.' She spoke in a low voice, conscious that although they were alone, they were still in a church.

'I really am sorry; I thought you were in one of those privileged boarding schools run by nuns. I had no idea it was an orphanage. I'm not even sure my mam knows that.'

'It doesn't matter. Aunt Anna – my mother – believed the same thing. You can't imagine nuns treating young girls so badly.' She lowered her eyes. 'It was awful ... that's where I met Molly. I was in there for years, with girls from the saddest backgrounds, and up until a few months ago, when my aunt turned up, I thought I had no relations in the whole world.'

Paul let out a long, low breath. 'Oh God,' he said. 'I had no idea. The last thing you needed was an idiot like me mouthing off...' He went along to the end of the bench, and then slid into the same pew beside her. Their eyes met, and he shook his head and said sorry again. Then he gently moved forward, gathered her into his arms and held her close to him.

Lillian froze, unsure what to do. The closeness of him seemed strange. The texture of his woollen jacket, the light citrusy smell of soap or cologne, the feeling of strength in his arms were all unknown territory to her, having lived most of her life in a female-only environment. But her uncertainty seemed to evaporate, to be replaced by a subtle but pleasant feeling, which ran through her like little ripples.

When she laid her head on his shoulder and closed her eyes, the ripples grew stronger, then began to centre around the lower part of her stomach. She stayed in the comfort of his arms for as long as she thought was decent, especially in the holy confines of a church. Slowly and reluctantly, she eased herself into a sitting position, surprised but happy to feel his arms still around her.

They were silent for a little while, and when she tilted her head to look at him, he was looking straight at her. 'I wish things were different,' he said, his voice sounding a little hoarse.

She felt his hold loosening on her and she had to stop herself from moving closer to him again. 'What do you mean?' she whispered.

He reached a hand out and touched her hair. 'You're a lovely girl, Lillian, and I would love to spend more time with you, to listen properly to all the things you were telling me about your past, but I can't think of a situation in which that can happen again. It just wouldn't go down well with your aunt.'

'But what's wrong with us talking to each other? I know my aunt likes you...'

'Yes, I'm sure she does in a certain way, but it's because she's fond of my mother and father, and they all get on well together in a work situation. She thinks I've done well given my background.' He shook his head. 'It was different you coming to see me today, after I helped you yesterday, but if we started to see each other, meet up as proper friends, it would cause all sorts of problems.'

'Why can't we be friends?' she asked. 'I really like talking to you, I can be myself with you, and I feel you are very honest with me.'

'I like talking to you as well,' he said, 'but believe me, it's more complicated than that.' He took his watch out of his jacket pocket. 'I have to go back to work...'

'Can I walk back down to Lewis's with you?' she said, slightly petulantly. 'I have to buy gift vouchers for my aunt from there. Surely nobody can see anything wrong with us walking together?'

'Of course,' he said. Their eyes met again, and then he gently touched her hair with his hand. He hesitated, and then he gave a little sigh and moved out of the pew. He waited while she genuflected, then they walked out of the church together.

Just before they parted in Lewis's at the perfume counter, Paul took her hand and said, 'You're a lovely, clever girl, Lillian, and I'm sure everything will work out for you. If I don't see you, I hope you have a lovely Christmas.'

Before Lillian could reply, a very glamorous young woman came from behind the counter and tapped Paul on the shoulder.

'Mr Larking,' she said, smiling brightly at him as he turned around, 'I'm on the social committee, and I'm just checking if you've got your ticket for the staff Christmas Ball yet?'

'Yes, Sadie,' he said, smiling back at her, 'I have.'

She raised her eyebrows, then looked at Lillian. 'And are you bringing a partner with you or shall I tell the girls you will you be footloose and fancy free?'

'I already have *two* tickets,' he said, 'so I have a partner coming with me.'

'Aw,' she said, shaking her head in mock disapproval. 'There will be a few disappointed young ladies.'

He laughed. 'Oh, I'm sure they'll get over it. There will be more fellas than me at the dance.'

Lillian felt her stomach clench, realising that Paul Larking inhabited a very different world from her. Not only had he organised a partner to take to his Christmas party, but he was obviously seen as a great catch with lots of the other glamorous girls working in Lewis's. He could probably have anyone he wanted.

A customer arrived to check out the range of expensive

perfumes, so Sadie said a quick goodbye and moved quickly back to her counter. Paul smiled after her and turned back to Lillian. 'I have to go,' he said, 'so have a lovely Christmas and New Year, and don't do anything I wouldn't do.'

Lillian smiled back at him. 'You have a lovely Christmas as well,' she said, 'and thank you for ... for everything.'

She stood for a few moments watching him weave through the crowds of Christmas shoppers and then she turned away, suddenly feeling bereft. Being with Paul Larking, talking and joking with him, felt the most natural thing in the world, and she did not want their friendship to end. But she understood all he had said about how it would be inappropriate for them to see each other, and knew she would just have to get over it.

She also now understood the difference of friendship between girls like her and Molly, and friendship and romance between males and females. She had been bemused at Andrew Whyte being so adamant about keeping their friendship going, but having experienced for herself what it was like to feel close to someone of the opposite sex, it now all made sense.

She suddenly realised that, at almost sixteen, she was now entering a big, new world. A world full of rules that she would have to learn.

Chapter Thirty-Three

When Lillian arrived back at the house, she found Anna having a cup of tea in the guests' drawing room with Miss Dixon. She stopped to exchange a polite few words with them, then headed upstairs. Her aunt followed her up a short time later and gave her a note which had been handed in earlier on. 'It was delivered by a man in a car.'

Lillian opened it and read it, then she looked up at Anna. 'We have been invited to go to the cinema with my friend and her mother.'

'The girl from the dancing?'

'Yes,' Lillian said. 'I forgot to tell you with everything that has happened. I was at their house for supper when you were away.'

'How lovely!' Anna said, 'I'm delighted to hear that you're making new friends, and of course we will join them for a night at the cinema. I shall look forward to meeting them.'

Lillian caught her breath. 'Irene's mother seemed to know you already ...'

'Do you know her name?'

'Mrs Flanagan ... She told me she is originally from Dublin and that she knew you years ago.'

Anna thought for a few moments, then her eyebrows shot up. 'Freda? Is Freda the mother's name?'

'Yes,' Lillian said, 'they live near Miss Churchill.'

'Oh ...' Anna sighed. 'She's a lady whom I know from a long time ago. I met her in hospital when I had you, and she was in having her daughter. I used to see her when I was down at the shops, when you and her little girl were in prams.' She took a deep breath. 'Since I came back here, I have come across her on a number of occasions, but I have had to give her a wide berth because I didn't want to have to explain about our situation. It just didn't occur to me that you would get involved with them.'

'I met Irene at dance classes, and when you were away, they saw me at Mass and offered me a lift home in the car because it was raining. It was then her mother realised who I was.'

Anna nodded her head. 'And after that she invited you to their house?'

'Yes, they picked me up and saw me safely home in the car.' She paused. 'It was after Mr Guthrie had said all those things to me about being illegitimate, and I was upset. I thought if I went out it might take my mind off it.'

Anna sighed deeply. 'Well, you did the right thing,' she said. 'I would much rather you went for a lovely night with your friend than sit here on your own worrying.'

'I don't want to put you in an awkward position going out with them if you're not keen, or if you have some kind of problem with her.'

'When I think about it rationally,' Anna said, 'the problem is actually with me. And after what you just said about Mr Guthrie and how much he upset you, I realise I'm being very unfair to Freda and her daughter.'

'How?' Lillian asked.

'If I tell you, will you promise to keep it to yourself?'

Lillian nodded. 'I promise I won't say a word.'

'Well, when I was in hospital after having you, we were in the same ward and it was very awkward.' She could see the confusion on Lillian's face now. 'The thing is, Freda wasn't married then, and I'm ashamed to say it now, but I felt uncomfortable with the fact she had an illegitimate baby.'

Lillian sucked her breath in at this information.

Anna shrugged. 'Who was I to judge anyone? But at the time, I was leading an ordinary life and my mother and the priests

– everyone really – thought having an illegitimate baby was the biggest sin you could commit, next to murder.'

'Poor Irene...'

Anna held her hands up. 'You don't have to tell me, I can see it now... I was wrong for thinking badly of her, but it's the way most people felt then, and still do.'

'I know how I felt after what Mr Guthrie said – I really did believe I was illegitimate and I was ashamed of it because the nuns had always told us how bad it was.'

She looked Anna straight in the eye. 'It made me feel very angry with you for putting me in that position. How does poor Irene cope?'

'She might not even know,' Anna said. 'People keep things like that secret. And the thing is, Freda did actually get married sometime later. I'm not sure when, but I met her a few years ago when I was in the Philharmonic Dining Rooms with Edward. She caught me in the ladies' room and she told me she had got married to Irene's father some years back. It seems he was a Protestant and his family wouldn't let him have anything to do with Catholics, and her family were equally as bad. When she became pregnant, she left Ireland to come to England to have Irene. I think she was on her own for a while, and then whatever happened, Irene's father must have stood up to them and come over to Liverpool and they must have got married after the war.'

'He's dead now,' Lillian said. 'They mentioned that to me.'

Anna nodded. 'Freda did tell me that another time I met her. She always tried to be friendly, but I didn't want to get too involved with her. It wasn't just because of Irene; I also didn't want her to question me about you. Anytime she asked, I just gave vague answers about you being at your grandmother's or...' She halted. 'I said you were boarding with nuns.'

There was a silence.

'I suppose you had to say something, but it seems as if everything about our life is all secrets and lies. It must be hard to make friends when you have to watch every word you say.'

'And that's all my fault,' Anna said, 'and I'm sorry about it.'

She was reminded again that losing Molly had left a huge gap in Lillian's life. She was a young girl and it was only natural she would want to share things with a friend. 'I am not going to stop you choosing your own friends. Soon you can go to the cinema or dances on your own with your friends, but in the meantime if you would like us to spend some time with Irene and her mother, that will be fine. I could ask them to afternoon tea or supper...'

'I don't want to put you in an awkward position.'

'I'm sure we can work out something that will satisfy any questions they might ask of us.'

'They made me really welcome, and I enjoyed it, especially the music.'

'Well, I think we need to accept their kind invitation and hopefully you will have lots of enjoyable nights with them.' She smiled. 'When the summer comes, it will be lovely for you to have a partner for tennis or to have day trips with.'

Lillian's face brightened, although she now felt in a bit of a quandary because she had not mentioned about Freda Flanagan's relationship with John, her live-in driver. To bring it up now might prejudice Anna against her, and cause an awkwardness between herself and Irene. It wasn't Irene's fault how her mother behaved, Lillian thought, and apart from that incident, she had really liked Mrs Flanagan. She decided for the time being to leave well alone.

A note was dispatched by Lucy to the Flanagans and the reply came back, and it was arranged that they would go to the cinema the following Thursday night to see a film called *Juno and the Paycock*.

On Tuesday, since the weather forecast was for a cold but dry day, Anna decided it was a perfect day for their trip to Kendal Milne in Manchester. She thought that the journey on the train would be something different for Lillian. They had an early breakfast at eight o'clock, and then dressed in warm clothes and their heaviest coats and hats, and set off walking down to Lime Street Station to catch the ten o'clock train.

Lillian was entranced by the steam train, enjoying watching people getting on and off and reading the names of all the different stations. They got a taxi from the station in Manchester straight to the front door of the department store.

As they walked through the gift department on the ground floor, Lillian didn't know which way to look as her attention was caught by glittering Christmas trees and decorations and beautifully arranged perfume and cosmetic stands. They took their time examining and choosing some small gifts, and then went upstairs to the ladies' clothes department to start their earnest business of selecting outfits for the festive season.

They were assigned a sales assistant who checked sizes with them and she walked around the floor with them suggesting coats and dresses that she thought would suit them.

Lillian enjoyed trying on the evening gowns Anna said she would need for Christmas, and eventually settled on a lovely, bias-cut wine chiffon dress with beaded patterns and a hand-kerchief hem. She turned around to let the assistant and Anna check the back.

'You have the perfect figure for it,' the assistant said admiringly. 'It's lovely on the bust and hips and falls beautifully.'

When she came out of the changing room, Anna said to her, 'You really have filled out since you arrived, and you look tremendous in it. You could almost pass for twenty!'

Since Anna's open discussion with her about her finances, Lillian felt easier accepting gifts from her mother, and understood that it helped her feel she was making up for all the years she hadn't been able to buy her anything. She also thought that when the right time came, she would have a serious discussion with Anna about finding work to make her more independent and able to help to pay for things herself.

An hour or two later they left the store with several shopping bags each and went to a nice restaurant Anna knew for lunch. Both were delighted with new day and evening dresses and it felt like the Christmas season had truly begun.

*

On Wednesday night Lillian met up with Irene at their ballroom dancing class, and when they partnered up for some of the dances, Irene told her excitedly that she was going over to Dublin in February to be a bridesmaid at her cousin Emily's wedding.

'My mother is invited too, and is travelling with me to Dublin and staying with her brother while I stay at my grandparents' house in Ballsbridge.' She lowered her voice. 'Father's family are all Protestants, and they were never keen on my mother because she's Catholic and my father married her in a Catholic church and brought me up Catholic too.' She shrugged. 'But they have always kept in touch with me, and send me birthday and Christmas presents. They live in a huge, old rambling house with quite a few servants. I love going to it because they really spoil me, but I can't say too much to my mother about that. She thinks my father's family are all a bit stuffy, but I quite like them, especially Emily's mother. I think my mother will be relieved that after this wedding I will be old enough to travel over to Dublin on my own.' She grinned at Lillian. 'Maybe I'll even be allowed to bring a friend. There are lots of really good places to go in Dublin.'

The idea of travelling appealed to Lillian, but when she got home she didn't mention Emily's trip to Dublin to Anna, as she didn't know how she might feel about her going to Ireland. It was a place that seemed to have only bitter memories for her, and not somewhere she had ever mentioned they might visit. There was nothing concrete in place and she felt there was no need to make her feel uncomfortable. Anna had recently said they might have a weekend in London to celebrate Lillian's birthday, and to show her where she had lived with Edward and Violet, and all the places of interest that a tourist might visit.

Although she was still raw about Molly's death, the new openness between herself and Anna had brought a closeness which had helped to ease the pain of her friend's loss. Her burgeoning friendship with Irene and all the plans she had over Christmas were also helping to direct Lillian's thoughts to more positive things. The mist surrounding the memories of the orphanage had grown denser until looking back to those dark days became like trying to see through an impenetrable veil.

Chapter Thirty-Four

When the car pulled up outside the house, Lillian went out first, excited about seeing her friend and feeling quite elegant in her new green velvet coat. John held the door open for her, and as soon as she entered the car both Freda and Irene were full of compliments about her outfit, which she returned as they both looked glamorous, as always.

'Isn't it lovely to get a night out where you can get dressed up?' Freda said, almost as excited as the two girls.

Anna followed and when she got inside, Lillian felt a small tension in the car. She was relieved when Anna smiled and thanked Freda for the invitation, saying, 'Isn't it a great coincidence that the girls know each other, after all those years ago when we first met?' She smiled and said, 'I never imagined I would be travelling in your new motor car either.'

'You're not the only one!' Freda said, smiling. The car was rattling along the cobblestones of Rodney Street. 'It was all trams back then when we first arrived, wasn't it? A different world to the one the girls are enjoying now.'

Lillian could tell her mother was still a little anxious about how the conversation might go, and she was pleased when Freda kept it very general and asked nothing personal. When they arrived at the cinema, Freda said she had already organised and paid for tickets to be collected at the box office, and Anna thanked her and insisted on buying the refreshments at the interval.

As they passed the long snaking queue to buy tickets, and

headed for the pre-booked collection booth, Freda looked at Anna and made a little face. 'I've no idea what the film is about,' she said, 'I only glanced at it in this month's *Picturegoer* magazine, and it had very good reviews from the opening in London.'

Anna smiled 'I haven't heard of it at all, but I'm sure it will be very entertaining.' She smiled. 'Even watching the newsreels on film is more interesting than reading about it.'

When they got inside the lavishly decorated blue and gold auditorium, an attendant led them down the aisle with a torch to a row about halfway down. They all took a few minutes taking coats off and folding them in their laps and generally settling down. Lillian glanced at Anna, and she thought how different in personalities the two women were, and wondered if it had been such a good idea that they had come out together.

The orchestra struck up and after a few minutes of music, the curtains lifted and the newsreels started, and after a few minutes the big event itself, *Juno and The Paycock*, started.

The whole auditorium watched in silence, broken only by the odd bout of coughing or murmur of voices as latecomers were shown to their seats. At the break, all four gathered their coats and bags and headed upstairs to the tearoom.

'I had no idea it was an Irish film,' Freda said. 'It was funny seeing all those places I knew in Dublin on the screen.'

'I thought that myself,' Anna said, 'I must say, I'm thoroughly enjoying the film.'

While the two women ordered tea and small sandwiches and cakes, the two girls went off to the powder room. On their way downstairs, chatting about the film, Lillian got a shock when she turned a corner and almost bumped into Paul Larking, who was arm-in-arm with Edie.

Remembering her last conversation with him, Lillian felt self-conscious, but she made herself smile and said a friendly hello to both of them, and then seeing Irene's inquisitive stare, she quickly introduced her friend.

'Your outfit is beautiful,' Edie said, her eyes moving from

Lillian's green velvet hat to her long-sleeved gold dress, which had an overlay of tulle with tan embroidery.

Lillian thanked her. 'You look very nice too.' She looked quickly at Paul, deliberately avoiding his eye. 'I hope you enjoy the film and the rest of your night.' Then she turned back to Irene. 'We'd better hurry or our tea will be cold.'

In the privacy of the powder room, Irene whirled around to Lillian. 'Wow! Who was he?'

'Do you mean the fellow we just met? Paul Larking?'

'He's like a film star! How do you know him?'

Lillian laughed. 'Do you think he's that good-looking?' she asked. 'His mother is our cook. He's a tailor in Lewis's.'

'He is gorgeous! I was admiring his suit as well, so now I know why he's so well dressed.' She made a little face. 'Do you think tailors make much money?'

Lillian's eyebrows shot up in surprise. 'I haven't a clue...'

'I need a man with money,' Irene laughed. 'My mother is always joking that she's not handing over my father's fortune to some penniless fellow to squander away. I have to find a good eligible bachelor with his own fortune. I'm sure your mother must think the same thing?'

Lillian suddenly froze. 'Do you mean my Aunt Anna?'

Irene's hand came up to her mouth. 'Oh, I'm sorry Lillian...' She looked genuinely shocked. 'I didn't mean to put my foot in it. Oh God, my mother will kill me...'

'You didn't,' Lillian said. Her heart was beating quickly, but she forced herself to sound normal. 'Anna is my mother, but I was brought up by my grandmother and just ended up calling her aunt.' She shrugged. 'My grandmother is dead now and it would be funny suddenly changing it.'

'Of course,' Irene nodded, her eyes wide and understanding. 'As long as you are not offended?'

'No,' Lillian said, smiling back, and surprisingly not feeling awkward at all. She had half prepared herself for this arising in the future, and stating the fact had not been as earth-shattering as she had imagined. Besides, she reasoned, Irene had been open with her about the fact that there were difficulties within her own family.

When they went back in to the tearoom, Lillian was surprised to see her aunt and Freda not only chatting, but laughing heartily together.

When the girls sat down, Freda dabbed the corner of her eye with a handkerchief and said, 'I haven't had a laugh like that in a long time. I was just telling your aunt there was a woman I knew when I was growing up in Dublin, who discovered some old Chinese vase that was worth a lot of money. She went out and bought a load of drink and invited the neighbours in to celebrate her good fortune.' Freda started laughing again and then Anna joined in too.

'What happened?'

Freda was laughing too hard to talk, so Anna explained. 'The woman got drunk and when she went to show it to somebody, she tripped over and fell on top of the vase and it smashed into smithereens!'

The girls laughed too, although not as heartily as their mothers.

'It just reminded me of the great Irish sense of humour,' Freda said.

Anna raised her eyebrows and smiled. 'As only another Irishwoman would appreciate.'

The waitress made her way over with their tea and food, and as they were eating, Lillian said to Anna, 'I met Paul Larking just now.'

'Ah, did you?' Anna said, smiling warmly. 'Was he with a young lady?'

'Yes, the same one I met in Lewis's.'

'Oh, that's the student teacher. I think he's fairly serious with her this time, according to his mother. She's delighted about it and feels it's a very good match for him.' She then turned to explain to Freda who he was. 'He's very talented. When he's fully trained he could go on to open his own business, but I think his parents are encouraging him to stay with Lewis's, as they think it's safer.'

'Sometimes you have to take a chance,' Freda said. 'We wouldn't be as well off now if Hugh hadn't taken a chance on the car business. Everyone told him it was a fad that would never catch on. We were lucky with the men we married that the financial disasters didn't hit us. That's what I'm always telling Irene: you have to make sure to marry somebody who will give you a good standard of living, wouldn't you agree?'

'Absolutely,' Anna said. She smiled at Lillian. 'It's a case of them now meeting the right one.'

'I'm so pleased the night went well with Irene and her mother,' Lillian said afterwards, when they were taking off their coats in the sitting room.'

'It was lovely,' Anna agreed. 'And I will invite them to the house sometime soon.'

'I hope it doesn't worry you,' Lillian said, 'but Irene referred to you as my mother. She did it by mistake, and when she went to correct herself, I just quickly said it was fine as you were actually my mother.' She shrugged. 'I just explained about being brought up by my grandmother and how I called her mother instead and you aunt. Irene didn't ask any more.'

Anna nodded her head slowly. 'I did the same with Freda, just gave her bare details, and she understood too.' She smiled. 'It was a good evening, and I'm pleased you have a nice friend like Irene.'

'I'm pleased too,' Lillian said. Slowly, she felt, after the shock of Molly dying and finding out about Anna, things were beginning to settle back into place.

Chapter Thirty-Five

The week before Christmas, after her last lessons of the year, Lillian gave Miss Churchill and her dance teachers sets of four nicely wrapped white linen napkins, which she had embroidered with flowers. After seeking Anna's advice, she gave Mr Whyte a bottle of wine. She had made pink satin nightdress cases for Mrs Larking and Lucy, and she gave Michael Larking a block of his favourite War Horse tobacco, in a special festive tin. The paying guests were all going to their respective families for Christmas, so Lillian gave them their presents early.

Mr Whyte had been delighted with the wine, and after her lesson he accompanied her back across the street to her aunt's house to discuss with Anna a suitable date for an evening out at a pantomime when Andrew came home.

'I would be most grateful if you would both join us,' he said, 'as I think after a while Andrew finds my company a little dull. It's Christmas after all, and I know he will enjoy having a younger companion there, and I'm sure Lillian would enjoy a night at the pantomime as well.' He looked at her. 'Have you seen *Aladdin*?'

Lillian suddenly felt a little moment of anxiety, as she had never seen any pantomimes.

'I don't think you have seen that particular one,' her aunt quickly intervened, 'but I'm sure we will enjoy it.'

The days flew by, and, a few days before Christmas, Lillian took a box to the post office filled with Molly's clothes and gifts, plus a fruit cake and sweets, and sent them to Gretta O'Brien. She had thought about taking them to the house herself, but was afraid it would look too much like charity to both the family and the neighbours. The gesture towards the girl and her family made her feel better, and it also helped not to have to look at the little pile of clothes and things she had imagined Molly wearing in her new life. On her way back from posting them, she decided she would do this every year for the O'Briens, and would start knitting items and collecting things for Gretta to give to some of the children she had seen in the court dwellings.

On Christmas Eve, a tall tree was erected in the hallway by Michael Larking, and Lillian and Lucy then helped him to hang it with bells, glass baubles, and lengths of tinsel. Later that night Anna accompanied Lillian to Midnight Mass and they had happily accepted a lift back from the Flanagans.

When they arrived back at their quiet house, Anna went down to the kitchen to make them mugs of cocoa and cut a couple of slices of fruit cake and brought them back up to the coffee table in front of the fire.

She went over to her bureau and brought out a small, slim box wrapped in Christmas paper. 'I think this is the right time to give you this.'

Lillian carefully opened the heavy little box to reveal a gold Rotary watch with a gate bracelet strap and a mother-of-pearl face. She looked at Anna and bit her lip, unable to speak.

'Miss Dixon helped me choose it. We decided that a plainer watch would be best for you.'

'It's not at all plain, it's beautiful,' Lillian finally said. 'But you have already given me so much...'

'I want to give you things; after all, I'm your mother. Having you back has changed my life in every way, and I'm so grateful for it.'

Lillian looked up at her and saw tears in her eyes, and she put the watch down and moved over to her mother's chair to put her arms around her. They hugged each other tightly and quietly cried on each other's shoulders.

*

Christmas Day itself was quiet as Anna had given Lucy two days off and told the Larkings that they could come in for a half-day and then have a few days off as well. Anna was delighted with the beaded evening bag, saying it was a work of art. She was also very pleased with the handmade gifts Lillian had given her, along with a small bottle of perfume.

Anna then said, 'I want you to come downstairs, I have an extra gift for us both; well, for the whole house really. I thought it might keep us busy over Christmas.'

Lillian was intrigued and followed behind, wondering what on earth it could be. When she walked into the library, there, in a space by the window was a gramophone player. She clapped her hands together in delight, saying, 'Oh, that's wonderful!'

'I was thinking about buying one,' Anna said, 'and after you mentioned the great enjoyment you all had at Freda's house, I decided it was time we had one too. I took advice from both her and Oliver Whyte.'

Mr and Mrs Larking came to the library to look at it too, and then Lillian showed everyone how it worked and played a Cole Porter record on it for everyone to hear. It started off blaringly loud, and Lillian turned the volume dial down lower.

'Our Paul would love one,' Mrs Larking said. 'He was going to buy one but I told him they were too noisy, that he should wait until he was married and buy his own.' She pulled a face. 'I might have been a bit hasty with him. I didn't realise you could turn the sound down.'

'I told you that,' Michael said, 'The older ones only had things you put over the horn. These new models can be turned down.'

'Maybe he could get one and keep it in his bedroom,' Mrs Larking conceded.

'Paul is welcome to come and have a look at this, and play records on it and see what he thinks.'

As the day went on, Lillian thought how relaxed and lovely it was to spend Christmas Day in a real home with kind people. A shiver went through her as she remembered the miserable

Christmases she had spent in the orphanage with Molly and the other girls, grateful for any little treat that came their way.

Mrs Larking cooked a goose for Christmas lunch, with roast potatoes and vegetables, and served it for them in the guests' drawing room. Afterwards she brought out a homemade trifle.

'Have you your own goose at home?' Anna checked, when they were drinking coffee. She had ordered two nice-sized turkeys and two joints of pork, one of each for the house and the same for the Larkings along with their Christmas gifts and bonuses.

'I left it on a low heat this morning when we left for early Mass,' Mrs Larking said, 'and I warned Paul to keep an eye on it when he got back home.'

'Is there just the three of you?'

'Yes, just us and Paul.' Her face tightened. 'Hopefully next year we'll have our Eleanor over with her family. It would be lovely to have the children around, and to take them to see the Christmas things in Lewis's and Blacklers.'

Lillian suddenly felt sad. She thought of her and her aunt sitting there eating Christmas dinner on their own, and the three Larkings getting ready for dinner in their home. It crossed her mind that, lovely though her first Christmas day with Anna was, how much livelier the table would have been if the five of them had eaten together. But that, she knew, would not happen due to the social constraints that seemed to bind everyone to their own place.

'Lillian was saying she ran into him and his young lady at the cinema the other night.'

'He mentioned it all right,' Mrs Larking said, smiling. 'Paul has brought Edith to the house a couple of times, just casual like, when they've been out cycling together. She's a quiet enough girl, not as much of a talker as he is.' She shook her head. 'He could talk for England when you get him going. He's been invited out to her house tomorrow night – a fancy Boxing Night do – so I'm thinking it must be getting serious if he's meeting the family.'

'Well, she's a lucky girl,' Anna said. 'I'm delighted to hear he's met someone nice and is doing so well.' She looked at the clock. 'You go and get ready now, Nan. The taxi will be here for you in ten minutes.'

'Sure the bus would have done us fine as usual.'

'Not on Christmas Day,' Anna said. 'It's the least I can do for you. Get ready now and go home and relax for the next few days.'

Lillian and Anna had a quiet evening after they went, reading and sewing, and then they went downstairs later and Anna listened while Lillian played the piano. They had a supper of cold meats and cheeses with bread and pickled dishes, then listened to both the records they had several times.

Boxing Day followed a similarly quiet routine, although Anna, since the staff were away, cooked the potatoes and vegetables and organised smaller meals throughout the day. Michael Larking had left buckets filled with coal for them both in the kitchen and in their sitting room and bedrooms to keep the fires going.

On 27 December, Anna asked Mrs Larking and Lucy to make food for a small cocktail party. They spent the afternoon filling trays with dainty sandwiches and small tasty bites such as devilled eggs and stuffed mushrooms, along with platters of cold meats, homemade breads and a variety of cheeses.

Mrs Larking had a bit of a cough, which grew worse as the afternoon went on, and Anna told her and Michael to go home early, saying that Lucy would manage to put the food out on her own.

'I'll be fine,' Mrs Larking said, 'Michael got me a bottle of cough medicine from the chemist this morning and I'll take it tonight again with a hot toddy going to bed, and it should get rid of it overnight.'

The guests were due at eight o'clock so Anna and Lillian got dressed just after seven o'clock in the outfits they had purchased in Manchester. Anna put on a navy satin slim-fitting dress, with a low, crossover neck and a large diamante brooch, and Lillian, for the first time, wore her sleeveless wine chiffon dress with the long, floaty handkerchief hem. Earlier in the day she had copied a new hairstyle from a magazine, and now had her dark hair coiled up at the back, which her aunt and both the servants said made her look very elegant.

When she saw how lovely Lillian looked, Anna said, 'I think a little touch of make-up will just finish your outfit off.' She went into her bedroom and came back with a new powder compact and a light pink lipstick, which Lillian had to agree looked perfect on her.

As she looked in the mirror, her eyes widened. 'If the nuns could see me now with make-up on, they would be horrified...'

Anna sighed. 'There are a lot worse things in the world for them to worry about than a bit of lipstick.'

As it got nearer the time for their guests' arrival, Anna went around about making sure that Lucy had the fires well filled with coal, and had put out all the necessary crystal glasses and small dishes for nuts to have with the drinks. She was working on the place settings at the dining table when she called out to Lillian, who was checking the gramophone in the library.

When Lillian appeared, Anna handed her two white porcelain salt and pepper dishes. 'Would you mind going down into the kitchen for the silver salt and pepper shakers please? They are much nicer; I brought them from the London house to use for special occasions. They should be in the cupboard to the right of the cooker.'

Lillian went off down the hallway, holding the hem of her dress in one hand. As she descended the stairs she smiled to herself, as Anna had said she looked like one of the film stars in the *Picturegoer* magazine. She didn't for a moment think she looked like a grown woman, but she looked much better than she could ever have imagined.

She went into the kitchen and over to the cupboard, and was just reaching up to the shelf when she heard a tap on the back door. She turned around to see Paul Larking coming in, dressed in a heavy brown tweed jacket with a matching waistcoat and cap.

He stopped dead when he saw her, then he slowly took his cap off and stood holding it in one hand.

Lillian thought he looked just as handsome in his casual clothes as he did in his smart suits. She wondered what on earth he was doing in the house at this time, especially since his parents had gone, but she said nothing, in case he took it the wrong way. Instead, she smiled brightly at him and said, 'Hello Paul.'

She turned fully towards him, but he was still standing staring at her. 'You look beautiful, Lillian,' he suddenly said. 'Absolutely beautiful.'

Lillian felt herself blushing, and for a moment she didn't know what to say. Miss Churchill's etiquette training took over. 'Thank you, that's very kind of you ...'

He came over to stand closer to her. 'It's not kind, it's true.'

She suddenly noticed that he was dressed in cycling clothes. 'You came on your bicycle,' she said.

He nodded. 'My mam left her cough medicine here, and she's going to need it for tonight, so I said I would cycle over and pick it up for her.'

Lillian looked around, and saw the bottle on the window ledge. 'It's over there,' she said, and, as she went to pass him by to get the bottle, Paul caught her hands in his. 'You are absolutely beautiful, Lillian,' he said, his voice low. 'And all those things you told me about the orphanage ... don't let anything make you feel less about yourself. It doesn't matter what happened before, just keep being the lovely, kind girl you are. Always remember you are as good as anyone else.'

'You are very kind, Paul,' she said, grateful for his reassuring words. As she looked back at him, the same feelings she had in the church enveloped her again. She looked down at their intertwined hands and she instinctively moved closer to him. She put her arms around his neck and laid her head on his shoulder.

There was a short hesitation and then his arms encircled her waist and he pulled her towards him, and he stood holding her. There was silence, with only the sound of their breathing. Lillian felt her heart racing, and she was sure she could feel his heart beating too.

Then, Paul gently moved back and released his hold on her, then took a step away. 'I'm glad things are fine now with you and Mrs Ainsley,' he said. 'And I am glad that you and I can be friends whenever we come across each other here or in town.'

Lillian felt that sounded too vague. She really enjoyed talking to him and felt very comfortable when he was around. 'Maybe we could meet up again, go for tea or...'

Paul shook his head, and his gaze was directed above her head somewhere. 'No, we can't do that, Lillian. It wouldn't be right for us to be out together alone and it would cause talk and trouble.' He cleared his throat. 'Apart from anything else, I don't think Edie would be happy. We've been courting for a while now, and it wouldn't be right for me to be seen with another girl.'

'But if we're only being friends...'

'No, no,' he said. 'It just won't work. Believe me.'

Footsteps sounded and Paul moved back to stand at the end of the table. Lillian went over to get the cough medicine and as she turned back, her aunt came into the kitchen.

'Paul!' Anna said, her voice high with surprise. 'Have you just arrived?'

'Yes,' he said, and went on to explain about the cough medicine.

'I've got it here,' Lillian said, giving the bottle to him.

'Oh, I do hope your mother improves,' Anna said. 'If she doesn't feel well in the morning, tell her she's to stay at home. We can manage with Lucy until she feels well enough.'

'I will,' he said, smiling at her. 'I must say, you are both looking very elegant tonight.'

'Oh, thank you,' Anna said, looking delighted. 'We have some friends coming so we've made an effort.' She paused to look at her watch. 'Did your mother mention that I bought a gramophone?'

'Yes,' he said, 'that's terrific.'

'I hear you're interested in getting one.' She turned towards the door. 'We have nearly half an hour before our friends arrive, would you like to come up to the library and have a look at it? Lillian is very good at operating it, and she'll show you how it works.'

He glanced over at Lillian. 'I don't want to keep you back...'

'You're not, you're very welcome,' Anna said. 'I was just going to pour us a sherry, so come up and join us. Oh, and Lillian, don't forget to bring the salt and pepper with you.' She hurried back down the corridor.

Lillian turned to Paul. 'Please come up for a little while.'

'This isn't a good idea, us being like this. It's too close.'

She suddenly said, 'But I really like you...' and then, embarrassed at blurting such a thing out, she corrected herself, 'I mean, I really like *talking* to you.'

Paul pressed a finger to his lips. 'It's because I know what you've gone through, that you feel you can tell me anything. It's because my mam knows bits about you as well, and it all makes you feel sort of close to me.' He sighed. 'The thing is Lillian, it's not real. Our lives are so different. And don't forget about Edie. We've been going out for some time now.'

'Surely you can come upstairs and see the gramophone?' she said. 'That's just a normal thing anyone would do.'

He thought for a few moments. 'Okay, but I'm doing it just to please you, and because Mrs Ainsley might think I'm acting very ignorant. I don't feel comfortable about it.'

She touched his arm and his eyes met hers.

'Okay,' he sighed, 'five minutes.'

Anna met them in the hallway carrying two sherry glasses. 'A little festive drink,' she said, handing them one each. She walked towards the library. 'You show Paul the gramophone, Lillian, and I'll be through in a minute.'

Paul went straight over to the instrument. 'This is really lovely...'

'We only have a few records so far,' she said. She lifted the small pile and handed them to him.

Paul took a mouthful of his sherry, then put it down on the table to examine the records. 'This is a nice one,' he said, handing her one titled *Georgia on My Mind*. 'I've heard it in the music shop a few times.'

Lillian went over to the gramophone and put the record on. 'Your mother said you would love to have one of these,' she said over her shoulder.

'I would,' he said, lifting his drink. 'But there are a lot of things I would love, but can't have...' He lifted the covers of the records and began studying them.

The sultry music came on, and she turned back to him to make a light comment. As she looked at him, her pulse started to quicken, and she suddenly didn't know what to say. And she had a feeling if she did speak, she would say the wrong thing again. She took a drink from her glass.

'This is a lovely song, isn't it?' he said, not looking up. He moved over to sit down on a chair, whilst still examining the record covers and sipping his sherry.

Anna came in to stand at the door. 'Beautiful music,' she said. 'I'm delighted that I got the gramophone. Whether it's a fad or not, we're getting a lot of pleasure out of it for now.'

'I reckon that these sorts of things are here to stay,' Paul said. 'Like cars: there are more and more on the streets every day.'

The doorbell sounded, startling everyone. 'Gosh,' Anna said, checking her watch, 'Someone is early – hopefully Lucy will hear them.'

Paul immediately got to his feet. 'I must go,' he said, lifting his cap.

'There's no rush,' Anna said, distractedly. 'Finish your drink please, Paul. If you will excuse me, I'll go and see to whoever has arrived.' She went, closing the library door behind her.

Paul finished his drink in one gulp. 'Thanks,' he said, putting the glass down on the table, 'and I hope you all have a lovely night.'

'I'm sorry,' Lillian said. 'I wish you could have stayed longer to hear more of the music.' She went to the door. 'I'll see you out.'

'I'm fine,' he said, 'I know my way downstairs.'

As they went out into the hallway, Anna and Andrew Whyte were coming towards the library. Anna stopped to introduce Paul to Andrew.

Andrew came forward with his hand stretched out and smiling. 'Nice to see you again.'

Paul shook his hand and gave a similar greeting.

Anna looked at them in surprise. 'I didn't know you two had already met...'

Lillian realised that in the midst of everything that had recently happened, she had not told Anna about being in the Adelphi with Andrew. 'Yes,' she said quickly, 'I met Andrew when you were away, and then we bumped into Paul.'

'Well, Andrew kindly came over early,' she told Lillian, 'with some records that he brought up from London that he thought you might like to hear.'

'Oh, that was good of you,' Lillian said. She turned to Paul. 'Would you like to have a look at them?'

'Maybe another time, thank you.' He smiled politely around the assembled group. 'I have to rush now; I hope you all have a lovely night.'

'Please give my best wishes to your mother,' Anna said, 'and remind her not to come in tomorrow unless she feels well enough.'

'I will,' he promised.

Then, without even glancing at Lillian, he walked smartly down the hallway in the direction of the kitchen, heading for the back door where the servants entered and exited from.

Lillian suddenly noticed that all three of them, Anna, Andrew and herself, were all standing in the hallway, inadvertently blocking the entrance to the front door, as if there had been no question of Paul leaving the house that way. Lillian felt she had been party to him being almost dismissed like a servant. She looked at Anna, feeling perplexed. 'Should I have shown him out?'

'No, not at all,' she replied, 'Paul has been here plenty of times and knows his way around.' She smiled at Andrew. 'He is perfectly self-sufficient, and knows his own business.'

'Yes,' Andrew said, 'I rather got that impression on our first meeting.'

'Come into the drawing room,' Anna said, 'it's more comfortable.'

Andrew looked into the library. 'Are you leaving the gramophone here or would you like me to bring it into the drawing room for you?'

'Do you mind?' Anna said. 'I put it here for people to listen to it privately, but tonight it might be nice to have it playing while we are all in the bigger room.'

'It's no trouble at all,' he said. 'I carry our gramophone around the house in London all the time.' He laughed. 'In fact my mother tells me off for carrying it up to my bedroom. I have to sneak it back down when she's not around.'

As she watched them, Lillian noticed how relaxed Anna seemed with Andrew. And, whilst she had been friendly with Paul Larking, there had been a polite distance which she could now see was because of his class. She felt guilty now she hadn't just gone down to the kitchen with him, but then, he hadn't given her the opportunity.

As she thought about it, an embarrassing feeling crept over her. Paul hadn't wanted to be on his own with her again, and he had stated that quite plainly. He had been very nice to her when she was upset and had listened to her, but she was beginning to think now that he was only being polite to her, possibly treating her as he would a younger, emotional sister. He had also explained about his romance with Edie, and how he couldn't be seen meeting up with a young girl around the city, as it would get back to her. It must be serious enough, she now realised, if his mother was talking about Edie calling out to the house and saying that Paul was going to be introduced to her family. She felt foolish now, and realised that she had got the whole friendship thing wrong, and that apart from the occasions they would run across each other, they would only ever be polite acquaintances.

Shortly after the gramophone was put in place, Oliver Whyte arrived, and he was just settled in when Flanagans' car drew up at the front door. The introductions were all made and then Lucy went around with drinks. Anna checked with Freda about Irene being allowed alcohol, and both mothers agreed that the girls were old enough to have a few festive drinks.

The gramophone was a great topic of discussion and by the time everyone was ready to sit down to eat, Oliver Whyte and the two ladies were relaxed and chatting about cars, and Andrew and Irene were talking about learning to drive.

'I have my licence now,' Andrew said, beaming delightedly, 'and I even drove part of the journey from London up here. It's amazing how you get a straight road and can just fly along. My father is an absolute demon on the roads; he is totally fearless on bends and overtaking other slower cars.'

'You shouldn't encourage him to go too fast, Andrew,' his grandfather cut in. 'And certainly do not copy him.' He shook his head in despair. 'Every time he takes the car out, he thinks he is driving in the Grand Prix.'

'I'm definitely going to learn to drive as soon as I am seventeen,' Irene said. 'Why should the boys have all the fun? There are lots of women drivers now.' She looked over at her mother. 'My dad was one of the first in Liverpool to have a business selling cars – wasn't he?'

Freda's face was suddenly serious. 'Yes,' she said. 'And I was terrified, thinking they wouldn't catch on.' She looked over at Anna. 'He put every penny he had into the business, and luckily, for once, it was at just the perfect time, when people had money and were fascinated by automobiles.' She looked around the small assembled group. 'Frankly, Irene and I wouldn't be in the secure financial position we are in now if it hadn't been for David's firm belief in the future of the motor car.'

'You will love it,' Andrew said to Irene. 'The freedom and the speed is like nothing else I have experienced.'

'I'll have to ask John if he's brave enough to take you out driving,' Freda laughed. 'What about you, Lillian? Have you any interest in learning to drive?'

Lillian smiled and shrugged, feeling slightly uncomfortable as she remembered Freda and John's carry-on. 'I really haven't thought about it. Maybe... But first, I might get a bicycle. I read recently in a magazine that it's very healthy for you, and there are lots of cycling clubs with women members.'

'Good for you, Lillian,' Mr Whyte said. 'I applaud your sense of adventure and common sense.'

When they had finished eating, Anna asked Oliver Whyte if he would play the piano for them, and they all gravitated towards the library. They had a lovely hour listening and singing along to his tunes, and in between, Lucy went around filling glasses with wine. Mr Whyte then invited Lillian to play, and her first instinct was to refuse, but she was eventually persuaded to play a piece she was fairly confident about, Beethoven's *Für Elise*. She started off well, then had a little stumble, but when she continued, she played the piece better than she had ever played it before. She then played another easier piece, and was given a lively applause by her teacher and the others. As they were going back across the hall to the drawing room to play Andrew's records, Irene and Lillian asked if they could be excused for a short while as Lillian had promised to show Irene the pattern for the nightdress holders she had made.

As soon as they were inside the bedroom, Irene went over to lounge on Lillian's bed in a slightly ungainly manner. 'You didn't tell me how gorgeous Andrew was!'

'Do you think so? I know he's nice but I've never thought about him in *that* way.'

'Come off it!' Irene laughed. 'He's besotted by you. You can tell the way he looks at you and keeps trying to bring you into the conversation. Besides, he more or less told me he was. He's planning to spend more time in Liverpool when he's at university so he can see you. Rather than travel back to London at his breaks, he's going to come here more often.'

'Really?' Lillian felt a pang of alarm. The thought of Andrew planning his holidays around her felt almost like a responsibility. A responsibility or obligation that she wasn't willing or ready for. 'I'm not sure that's a good idea. I don't feel as though Andrew and I are close enough friends for him to start coming here because of me.'

'You're nearly sixteen, Lillian,' Irene reminded her. 'And my mother said if you don't meet the right man when you are young, it gets harder every year, and then the chances are you might never meet them. I bet your aunt is thinking the same thing. Why else do you think she invited Andrew tonight?' She grinned and jabbed her finger in Lillian's direction. 'And, he told me you're both going to the theatre tomorrow night as well.'

'With my aunt and his grandfather,' Lillian said.

'Well, they must both be keen on you two getting together, or they wouldn't be organising outings for you both, would they?'

'His grandfather just wants him to have a nice time over Christmas, and I'm probably the only young person he knows here.'

Irene raised her eyebrows and smiled. 'Well, if you're not interested in Andrew, I wouldn't mind spending time to get to know him a bit better.' She mused. 'I might get my mother to organise an evening at our house before he goes back to London...'

Lillian started to laugh. 'Please don't tell me we're going back to the days of *Pride and Prejudice*! You're making your poor mother sound like Mrs Bennett, organising events to try to find you someone like Mr Darcy.'

'You may well laugh, Lillian,' Irene said, wagging a mock-teacherish finger, 'but you won't be laughing in five years' time if you're an old maid on the shelf, and some other girl has snatched Andrew Whyte from under your nose.'

'I'm changing the subject,' Lillian said, laughing again as she went over to her desk to get the book with the pattern for the nightdress case.

*

Back downstairs, Andrew was engaged in a deep conversation with Irene's mother about her husband's car business, which it turned out Freda Flanagan now owned, and which explained her comfortable financial situation. She was telling Andrew about her plans to open another car showroom in Manchester, and he was asking her which makes of cars she thought she would be selling.

Lillian went over to the gramophone to put on a Cole Porter record. She put it on the turntable and as she waited to check that the needle was in the proper groove, she noticed how Andrew seemed at ease chatting to both Irene and her mother. He was enthusiastic and knowledgeable about the different makes of cars, and she could see how he and Irene might have some things in common.

It crossed Lillian's mind that one of the reasons she had been reluctant to get closer to Andrew was her mistaken belief that she was illegitimate. This was no longer an issue to her or a barrier to their friendship, and nor were her feelings about the orphanage. She now knew it hadn't been Anna's fault. It hadn't really been anyone's fault. She wasn't going to waste any more time feeling resentment or self-conscious any more.

As she watched Andrew now, it occurred to her that maybe she was being too quick to dismiss his friendship. Not that she wanted to become part of an official courting couple, but maybe it would be wise, and fair to Andrew, to take her time and get to know him better. She would probably see him a few times over the next week or so, and then it would be Easter before he was back up in Liverpool again. It might be nice for them to exchange letters regularly, and would help them to get to know each other better.

She would enjoy the rest of the evening with her friends and look forward to the pantomime tomorrow night. After that she would wait to see what happened.

Chapter Thirty-Six

January arrived and along with it came a bicycle for Lillian's sixteenth birthday, a present from Anna. It was the first birthday she could remember being acknowledged since she was a child living with her grandmother. She was thrilled with the bicycle, but more than a little nervous as she had never attempted to ride one before.

'Michael and Paul Larking came with me to choose it,' Anna said, 'as I really didn't have any idea what I was looking for. Paul suggested that you practise using it in one of the smaller, quieter streets behind, like Pilgrim Street, before you venture out into Rodney Street or any of the busier streets.'

Lillian was surprised to hear that Paul Larking had been involved in the buying of her present. She hadn't seen him since the night she had met him in the kitchen. She had not expected him to acknowledge her birthday, but she thought that he might call in to see if she was happy with the bicycle and give a little advice.

Andrew, on the other hand, had sent her a birthday card and a book voucher which she had been very pleased with. As she read the funny comment he had written about her getting very old, she thought back to the last time she had seen him, on the night of the pantomime. They'd had a great evening, and she had enjoyed his company very much. But, there were times when she wondered exactly what her feelings were towards him. Sometimes she imagined that as they got older they would become much closer romantically, and at other times she felt that they were too different to be anything more than friends.

Anna had arranged with Freda that they would take the two girls to a new French restaurant in the city for a birthday treat, and afterwards all four would go to the Adelphi. The Flanagans' car came to the house to pick them up, and although Irene looked lovely in her evening gown, Lillian thought her quieter than normal and somehow not her usual self.

When they took their seats in the restaurant, Freda surprised them by having a bottle of champagne brought to the table. As they held their glasses up in a birthday toast, Freda said, 'Sixteen is the age where you are now officially young women and your lives will change more in the next few years than they have ever before.'

Irene had raised her eyebrows and said in a cool tone. 'Does that mean we can make our own decisions from now on?'

'Within reason,' her mother said, smiling brightly back.

When they had finished their meal they walked along to the Adelphi. Lillian and Irene went to the ladies' powder room, while Anna and Freda were shown into the lounge, where a pianist was playing.

'Are you okay?' Lillian asked tentatively. 'You seem very quiet.'

'Oh, I'm sorry,' Irene said. 'It's just... well, my mother and I had words this afternoon and I'm still a bit upset.'

Lillian was unsure whether it would be intrusive to ask anything more, but then Irene smiled and said, 'I'm fine; I'll get over it, and I'll make sure to enjoy the rest of the night.'

They all had another glass of wine and Irene showed them the beautiful pearl necklace, earrings and bracelet which she had been given by her mother. The conversation then moved on to Lillian's bicycle.

Freda looked at Lillian. 'You're not going to wear those awful-looking knickerbocker things, are you?'

Lillian laughed. 'No, but I've been thinking about it, and I'm going to make a divided skirt, which can button into either a skirt or a kind of shorter, wide trouser that still looks like a skirt.'

'Lillian has become very good with a needle,' Anna said. 'I got a second-hand sewing machine after Christmas, and she has learned to follow patterns, and has already made a skirt and a blouse.'

'What a clever girl!' Freda said.

'I love it,' Lillian said, 'and I'm going to try making dresses and other things later.'

'I need to find more things to do,' Irene said. 'Since leaving school last year I'm finding I'm very bored at times. I was even thinking of going to work in the office of my father's car business.' Irene cast a glance at Freda. 'But my mother thinks girls shouldn't work.'

'I didn't actually say that,' Freda corrected. 'I said I wasn't sure that it would look well for you to work in that particular business. It would be working with all men, and there's already a man who does the paperwork.' She paused. 'We've a lot of plans this year for you to join tennis clubs and a ladies' golf club, so I'm not quite sure when you would get the time to go out to work.'

'You own the car business,' Irene said, 'so no one can argue with you if you decide to put me in the office.'

'We can talk about it later,' Freda said.

Lillian took her chance. 'I would love to work too – I was thinking of one of the department stores...'

Anna's head jerked up at the news. 'Really?'

'I was thinking that I might train as a dressmaker,' Lillian went on, 'but when I looked into it at the library, the training is very long and I don't think I want to spend all day at a sewing machine. So I thought that maybe I would prefer to work in ladies' fashion, maybe doing shop displays or window displays. I was reading about Selfridge's store in London in a magazine, and they have lots of women working there. They have specialists who decorate the windows, not just for Christmas, but all year round, and people travel from all over the country to see them. Isn't that amazing?' She smiled at the other three, who were all listening intently.

'Well,' Anna said, obviously taken aback. 'This is all news to me... We will have to have a serious talk about it. I hadn't really thought about you working as such...'

'I suppose since the war more women are working than ever,' Freda said, 'but the thing is getting the right sort of work.'

The waitress brought their drinks and everyone went quiet as the pianist started playing. At the end of the piece, Anna looked over at Lillian. 'You've reminded me mentioning Selfridge's; we must go down to London for a weekend soon. The beginning of February might be a nice time, when it's not too busy.'

'We're going to Ireland in February,' Freda said, looking over at Anna and rolling her eyes, 'but I'd much prefer to go to London.'

Lillian noticed a frown on Irene's face, and could see that there was still tension between her and her mother. She was sure that it would all blow over. In the meantime, she was delighted that Freda had brought up the subject of working, as it had been something she had been waiting to do herself. She guessed Anna would not be entirely pleased, but times were changing and Lillian was ready to take another step into her newer, bigger world.

Chapter Thirty-Seven

When they met up at breakfast the following morning, Anna asked Lillian if she could get something off her chest.

'Before we talk about anything else, I just want to clarify things.' She took a deep breath. 'I felt a little hurt in the hotel last night, when you announced your intention of finding work.' She held her hand up. 'Now, it's not the issue about work that is bothering me, it's the fact that you blind-sided me by saying it in front of Freda and Irene. To tell the truth, I felt a little silly as it was patently obvious that you hadn't mentioned the subject to me before. It made me worry if there were other things you haven't told me that I need to know.'

Lillian looked at her, not sure what to say. They had cleared the air about the past, but this was the first time they had clashed about their relationship. 'I had been hoping to talk to you about it soon, and when the subject came up, I thought it seemed the right time to say it.'

Anna was silent.

'I didn't mean to cause any awkwardness for you, and I'm sorry if that is what happened.' She caught her lip between her teeth.

'Is there anything else?'

'No, no...' Lillian's eyes suddenly filled with tears. 'I'm very happy here... happier than I've been in my life.' Her voice faltered. 'I've enjoyed all the lessons and have learned a huge amount, but I just thought that since I am now sixteen that it would be good to do something more serious to earn money rather than to take from you.'

'Well, I'm glad you're happy here because it means the world to me.' She reached over and covered Lillian's hand with hers. 'And I hope you'll always feel that you can talk to me about anything. I promise you that I will always listen and give serious thought to anything that's important to you.'

'Thank you, and I'll make sure to talk to you first about anything important.'

'Well, regarding work, if that's what you want to do, I'm not going to stand in your way,' Anna said. 'I actually know one of the managers in Lewis's fairly well, from when I was buying the new furniture and beds for the guests. If you like, I could have a word about any staff vacancies.'

Lillian's heart dropped at the mention of Lewis's. 'That's very good of you,' she said, 'but I was thinking of applying to Blacklers department store or maybe Bon Marché or George Henry Lee's. But if I don't have any luck there, I would be grateful for help with Lewis's.'

'Fine,' she said, 'whichever you prefer.'

Lillian could not contemplate the thought of meeting Paul Larking in the store every day. He might think she had picked there because of him, and she had too much pride to put herself in that position.

'Have you any idea how they take on staff?' Anna enquired.

'I think you have to go to their personnel department and ask for application forms.'

'Well, if you go down and get the forms, I'll help you to fill them in.'

Within two weeks, Blacklers and George Henry Lee wrote back to Lillian to say they had nothing at present, but had kept her name in a file, and if any vacancies came up in ladieswear or in window dressing, they would be in touch. She heard nothing at all from Bon Marché, and felt slighted they hadn't taken the trouble to reply.

'It is understandable with the Depression and so many people being out of work,' Anna said, 'so it might be best to continue with your programme of studying and then see what happens.'

Lillian was very disappointed, but glad that Anna didn't mention anything about Lewis's again. As the weeks passed, she continued to work on her sewing and piano skills, and still went to Miss Churchill and her ballroom dancing classes every week. She visited the library regularly, and devoured books and magazine articles related to fashion and department stores.

She received letters from Andrew Whyte at least once a week, and sometimes two or three times. She wrote back telling him about her idea of going to work, which surprised him at first, but then he started collecting and sending her any articles he read about department stores which she might find useful. He wrote well, and through his letters Lillian began to see a maturity growing and could see there was more depth to the giddy boy than she had previously thought.

When she told him that she and Anna were planning a trip to London, he immediately wrote back to say his mother had invited them to afternoon tea at their house in Great Cumberland Place in Marylebone. Lillian felt intimidated by the invitation and the thought of meeting up with Andrew's mother, and even the sound of their address made her feel anxious. Anna, on the other hand, was delighted.

'I think it's very nice of the Whytes to invite us,' she said. 'Andrew is a lovely boy and he spent a lot of time with us over the Christmas holidays. I'm sure his mother just wants to repay some of that hospitality on his behalf.'

'From what I've heard, she's a very socially conscious lady,' Lillian said, 'and I feel we won't be grand enough for her.'

'Well, there's only one way to find out,' Anna said, 'and that is to accept the invitation and see how it goes.' She halted. 'You do know that Andrew is exceptionally fond of you, don't you? His grandfather is too, so they will have spoken very highly of you to his mother.'

'We're just friends,' Lillian said, feeling awkward.

'I think he feels more than friendship towards you,' Anna

said, 'and he certainly wouldn't be writing all those letters to you if he just regarded you as a friend. He's over eighteen now, and after university, in three years' time, he will be thinking of settling down to get married.'

'That's a long way off,' Lillian said.

'Yes,' Anna agreed, 'but now is the time to find the right partner before they are snapped up by someone else.'

'Well, even if I had feelings for him, I'm much too young to tie myself down at the moment.'

'But that's exactly my point,' Anna said. 'You won't have to be tied in any way because Andrew will be studying. It gives you a few years to enjoy the life of a young lady, to travel and see a bit of the world before you settle down to married life and having a family. It give you time to build up a nice marriage chest and organise things.' She smiled. 'I will enjoy having you to myself for a while longer, but I would absolutely love to help you to plan a wedding in a few years' time.'

'I just cannot imagine any of that, and I'm glad he lives in London so I don't feel pressured into anything too soon.'

Anna had touched her cheek. 'When the time comes, you won't feel like that. And believe me, Lillian, the world is a much kinder place when you have the care and protection of a man by your side. Especially one who adores you and can afford to give you everything you need – someone like Andrew Whyte.'

In mid-February – leaving the Larkings and Lucy to look after the guests – she and Anna took the mid-morning train down to London, and booked into the Elizabethan, a small hotel near Victoria. The first night they were there they went to the ballet at Covent Garden, and the following morning Anna took Lillian on the Tube over to Oxford Street to Selfridge's. Although she had read about the store and seen some photographs in magazines, nothing could have prepared her for the amazing wonderland that it was. Viewing the huge building from the outside – and the variety of windows filled with mannequins wearing the latest fashions or showcasing displays of beautiful furnishings or jewellery – filled Lillian with awe.

The smell of exotic perfumes welcomed them as they walked through the cosmetic and gift department, heading for the elevator to take them to the upper floors.

'I think we should have a look around the ladies' fashion first,' Anna said, 'as it will let you see how London stores are operating now, as they are usually a bit ahead of the other cities.'

As they made their way around the floors, looking at the rails of clothes or stopping to study a display in the middle of the floor, Lillian decided it was exactly the sort of place she would love to work. They hadn't come for a shopping trip, as Anna said they would be wearing winter clothes for the next two months and they would wait until nearer Easter to buy lighter clothes for spring and summer. She was, however, drawn to a wall display of colourful silk scarves, each one mounted on a white wooden frame, as though it was a work of art. She bought one for herself and one for Lillian as they were so eye-catching and could be worn at any time of the year.

The young sales assistant who helped them choose the scarves was friendly and grateful for their purchases, because, she divulged, the scarves were a new line by a French designer whom Mr Selfridge had personally discovered and wanted to promote.

As she carefully wrapped the scarves, Anna asked the girl how she liked working in the store.

'I love it,' she stated. 'The very first time I walked inside Selfridge's I knew I wanted to work here.' She gestured with her hand. 'I loved the building and the glamour of the displays and everything about it, and I just wanted to be here every day.'

Lillian's eyes lit up. 'That's exactly how I felt when I walked into the store. Was it difficult to get a position?'

'Confidentially speaking, my aunt helped,' the girl whispered, looking around her to make sure none of the other assistants could hear. 'She works in the restaurant upstairs and she serves Mr Selfridge his lunch when he is in the store, and they get on very well. She put in a good word for me and when a vacancy came up they sent for me to be interviewed.'

'We live in Liverpool,' Anna explained, 'and Lillian, my daughter, is hoping to find a position in one of the big department stores there.'

'I would love to work in ladies' fashion,' Lillian said, 'and I'm really interested in learning to do things like window dressing and the lovely stands with displays on all the floors.'

'I'm sure the stores in Liverpool are nice,' the girl said, 'but Selfridge's and Harrods are amongst the very top department stores in the world. You must have a look around the whole store. When I was interviewed I was shown around all the departments and I was amazed there was so much. You could spend a whole day shopping and when you need a break there are lovely places for lunch, or tea or coffee. There's even a library and special reading and writing rooms if you need to write a letter or anything like that.' She smiled. 'They've thought of everything. There's even a Silence Room, for older customers or people who have been travelling and need to have a rest, with soft lights and lovely deep, comfortable chairs.'

'How clever,' Anna said. 'It means people don't leave the store because they are exhausted, and they can resume their shopping when they are refreshed.'

'Mr Selfridge thinks of absolutely everything,' the girl said, 'and he's always willing to listen to ideas from the staff, although he does expect very high standards.'

She looked at Lillian, and then said in a lowered voice. 'It's not for everyone because it can be very hard work and the department managers are strict. You are on from early in the morning sometimes until ten o'clock at night, so it's hard on your feet. On special days we have to be in from eight o'clock to wait in line at the hairdressing department to have our hair perfectly curled so we look immaculate.'

'But you still enjoy working here?' Lillian checked.

'Absolutely,' the girl said, 'I couldn't imagine spending a long boring day at home when I can be in an exciting place like this, where you meet all sorts of people from all over the world.'

'Well, you are certainly the example of a very valuable staff member,' Anna said.

'And I'm very grateful you bought the scarves,' the girl said. 'I hope to see you in the store again next time you visit London.' She paused. 'If you have time later and the weather isn't too cold for you, do go up to see the terraced gardens on the roof. You can see right across London from there.'

When they were in the book department, Lillian bought a new notebook and when they stopped later for lunch upstairs, she made notes of all the things that had caught her attention, such as displays, stands with the latest household equipment, and details of the window displays.

They had dinner that night in the hotel, and then went for a walk around Victoria, and when they came to Belgrave Road, Anna stopped outside a row of imposing white-stone Georgian houses. She pointed at one of the houses. 'That will be yours one day.'

Lillian looked at her, confused. 'How?' she asked.

'That's where I lived with Edward and Violet, and it's where I lived after I got married again. I still own it. It's managed by a property company who have rented all the rooms out individually.'

'It's huge,' Lillian said in a low voice, 'much bigger than Rodney Street...'

'Yes,' Anna said, 'it's a lovely house, and it gives me great pleasure knowing that you will have it to sell or do with it what you wish when you are older.'

She took Lillian's arm, and started walking back up the road. 'I couldn't bear to look at it now, knowing that it's full of strangers and wondering what sort of state it is in. But, I can't complain because I receive a very good rental for it every month. That's one of the reasons for me thinking you would never need to work, but after seeing you in Selfridge's I can understand it's more to do with you being independent. When I was young, women like me had to work to survive, and I imagined that you would have a different life, something akin to the independent way Violet lived, where you could travel and just enjoy yourself without worrying about money.'

'I think times are changing for women,' Lillian said. She gave a little laugh. 'Don't forget I'm now a brave lady cyclist.'

'Oh, don't remind me,' Anna said. 'My heart is in my mouth every time I see you cycling off into the middle of the city now.'

'Whilst I am hugely grateful to know that I don't have to worry about money,' Lillian explained, 'I feel there are so many things out in the world that I have to see and do. And I want to mix with all sorts of people rather than a small privileged group.'

'The main thing is that you have choices,' Anna said. 'And hopefully, things will be much easier for you in life than they were for me.' She paused. 'And will make up for what you went through before.'

Chapter Thirty-Eight

Lillian woke with a sense of trepidation around eight o'clock the following morning, realising it was the day they were to visit the Whytes' house.

They had breakfast in the hotel, and then left around ten o'clock for a walk to Buckingham Palace, and after they had stood for a while watching the changing of the guards, they walked on down to St James's Park. Afterwards they headed back to their hotel to change into their smarter outfits, Lillian wearing her green velvet hat and coat with a cream woollen dress and pearls underneath, and Anna in a blue fur-collared coat with a matching dress. Anna had bought a bouquet of flowers to take, and Lillian had a box of handmade chocolates which they had bought on their walk that morning. Lillian had enjoyed everything about her trip to London so far, and whilst she was nervous about meeting Mrs Whyte, she was looking forward to seeing Andrew.

The black hackney cab turned at Marble Arch and then slowly bumped its way down over the cobbles down Great Cumberland Place. Anna paid the driver and checked they were at the right house. The houses, Lillian noted, were as big as the house Anna owned, but these ones had taller windows and somehow seemed more imposing.

The door was opened by an elderly maid with a limp. As they were shown into a wide hallway with rooms on either side, Andrew came rushing down the stairs towards them. Lillian thought he looked more handsome than she remembered, dressed smartly in a blazer with a navy spotted cravat and a plain silk handkerchief in his top pocket. His fair hair was cut in the latest floppy style as worn by some of the film stars.

'I'm so delighted you made it,' he said, smiling and shaking both their hands enthusiastically. 'You both look particularly well, if I may say so.' His eyes lingered on Lillian for a few moments and then he gave her a conspiratorial wink, before turning to lead them down the hallway, gesturing with his hands in a way that made Lillian think he was nervous too. 'My mother is waiting for us in the drawing room.'

They went into a large room with panelled walls and an imposing fireplace which went almost up to the ceiling. The furniture was polished mahogany with chintz-covered armchairs and sofas, and dotted around the room were individual tables holding tall plants. A round walnut table and four matching chairs stood by the window. It was set for tea for four, with plates and folded linen napkins and a silver jug and sugar bowl with small tongs.

Lillian had seen Andrew's mother from a distance when she was getting out of the car or standing at the door of Mr Whyte's house in Rodney Street, but she had never seen her close up. She had guessed her to be around Anna's age, but now, as she walked into the large room and saw the thin, upright woman in the armchair, Lillian thought she looked older than she had imagined. Her face was quite drawn and there were lines evident around the sides of her face.

Sybil Whyte's fairish hair, noticeably streaked with grey, was tied back in a severe bun, and her dress was dark and formal. Her whole demeanour seemed formal. She rose from her chair as Andrew brought the guests to be introduced, and Lillian was relieved when she smiled sweetly as she greeted both herself and Anna. The maid came to take their coats and Sybil urged them to sit down and make themselves comfortable.

'I hope you are enjoying your trip to London?' she asked, looking from one to the other.

'We are indeed,' Anna said. 'I always enjoy it, and we have been lucky with the weather given the time of year.'

'I should imagine that it's a good deal milder than Liverpool?'

'It is,' Anna said. 'We had quite a lot of snow this winter, but thankfully, it has eased off.'

'I believe you lived in London for some years?'

'Yes,' Anna said, 'in Victoria.' She wondered now if Sybil Whyte was going to quiz her on her background, and thought she should furnish some quick details to save a long drawn-out inquisition. 'I moved back to Liverpool when my dear husband died.'

Sybil Whyte nodded thoughtfully. 'But you still have the London property?'

'Yes, I have a letting agent who looks after it for me.'

'Indeed. And you run a boarding house in Liverpool, I believe?' Sybil gave a small, terse smile, which gave no indication of her views on this. 'My father-in-law mentioned it.'

'Yes,' Anna said, 'I have a few paying guests, all professional people. I enjoy it and it helps keep me occupied.'

Anna asked how long had the family been living in Great Cumberland Place.

'Since I was a child,' Sybil answered. 'It was my parents' house, which was left to me. Andrew's father and I lived in Belgravia for some years, then we moved back here when I inherited it.' She turned to Lillian. 'And you, my dear girl? Andrew tells me you are being educated at home.'

Anna moved to the edge of her chair. 'She spent some years in a convent school,' she said, 'and is now continuing her education at home.'

'And she has become very accomplished on the piano,' Andrew said, smiling cheerily. 'Grandfather says she is one of his better students.'

'I see… Both Andrew's sisters went off to Paris for a year, and we found it very helpful for them.' She paused then looked over at Lillian. 'I suppose you will be planning a coming out party soon?'

Lillian looked over at Anna, who smiled and said, 'These sorts of parties are not so popular in Liverpool since the Depression. They are regarded as too ostentatious for the current times. Whilst not everyone has suffered as badly as others, there is a certain sensitivity around celebrations when there are people who are struggling to feed their families.'

The conversation halted as a maid appeared with a platter of sandwiches in one hand, and carrying a large silver cake stand in the other, filled with a variety of colourful confections.

Sybil Whyte sat forward in her chair, 'Now,' she said, 'I have heard this argument before here in London, but the poor people themselves have shown great disappointment at the thought of the debutante season being discontinued. They love to gather outside the places where functions are being held to view the fashions and wish the girls well. It helps brighten up their dull lives.'

Lillian's stomach clenched as she listened to Andrew's mother, and she thought of Lucy and the Larkings, and thought how patronising her comments were.

'Our servants and our friends' servants all love the lead-up to the party season,' Sybil went on, 'and love to be involved in the organisation of them. When Imogene and Helen came out together, we had wonderful fun organising parties and our maids loved it. The usual routine of the house was totally disregarded as we dressed to go out for lunches and dinners every other day.'

She shook her head smiling at the memory, and looked over at Andrew. 'Don't you remember the splendid summer we had, rushing from one party to another? Utter mayhem, but glorious fun.'

Lillian thought that Mrs Whyte, so doleful and serious, didn't look like a person who had ever had fun in her life.

Andrew shrugged. 'I think you have forgotten that I was much younger than the girls,' he said, 'and was mainly regarded as a bit of a nuisance having to be fed whilst they were rushing back and forth to have dresses fitted.'

'Of course,' his mother said, giving a small laugh, 'you

probably didn't understand half of what was going on.' She sighed. 'Oh, they were lovely days, I quite miss them now.'

'I'm sure you do,' Anna said, smiling brightly. 'As I said, it is different in Liverpool now.'

The maid brought the teapots in and gravitated towards the table. Andrew held out chairs for first his mother, and then Anna, then the one next to him for Lillian.

When they were settled with sandwiches, Anna again took the chance to direct the conversation and asked Andrew about plans for university.

'It looks as though it will be Cambridge, Oxford, York or St Andrews,' he said. 'A move from home in any case.'

'And then it will be several years of solid study,' his mother said. 'No tomfoolery or gadding about. Serious work will be required now, Andrew.'

'Well, I shall have to make sure that I enjoy my last summer then,' he said, smiling at Lillian.

'Lillian, have you any plans to travel this summer?' his mother asked.

'I think we might be going to Paris, but we have nothing organised yet.' She looked directly at the older woman. 'In the meantime, I am hoping to find work in Liverpool.'

'Work?' Sybil's voice rose an octave. 'Really? And in what field?'

Lillian could tell by her face and tone that she disapproved. 'In the fashion department of a department store,' she said, smiling. 'We had a lovely day yesterday in Selfridge's, and I really enjoyed looking around the various departments.'

'Shopping in Selfridge's and Harrods is very enjoyable,' Sybil said, 'as a *customer*. I'm very surprised you feel the need to go out to work.'

'There is no need,' Lillian explained. She smiled. 'In fact, I've had to work very hard to convince my aunt to let me apply for positions.'

'I'm not going to hold you back,' Anna said, 'if it means so much to you. I read recently that in life we regret more the things we wished we had done, rather than the things we did.'

Sybil shook her head and gave a pained smile. 'Extraordinary...'

'I think I would eventually be bored at home doing the same things,' Lillian told her, 'whereas I can work and then fill my evenings with music practice or sewing and reading.'

'Lillian has a great energy and zest for life, Mother,' Andrew intervened, 'and while she is young and unattached, she might as well use that energy to broaden her experiences. There are more women in the workplace now since the war.'

'I think I may be old-fashioned,' Sybil Whyte said, sighing. 'In my opinion, it was much better when everyone had their own place and work was left to the men.'

Andrew grinned at Lillian. 'How are you getting on with the bicycle? Have you mastered it yet?'

'Yes,' she said, with pride in her tone. 'I'm much more confident and I cycle down to the library and to the shops. I even cycled to church on Sunday.'

'Which church do you attend?' Sybil asked. 'Church of England?'

'Saint Nicholas,' Lillian told her, 'Roman Catholic.'

'Oh really?' Sybil's voice was strained. 'I hadn't realised.'

The maid came to serve them scones and cakes now, and replenish cups of tea.

Andrew then asked if anyone would mind if he took Lillian across the hallway to the main dining room where the gramophone was.

'Off you go,' his mother said, with a wave of her hand. 'But keep the volume down if you please.'

When they got into the dining room, Andrew closed the door behind him and then he looked at Lillian and started to laugh. 'My mother is an absolute nightmare!'

Lillian looked back at him, and tried to think of something polite to say. Then she found herself laughing too. 'She is a very strong-minded woman...'

He reached for her hand. 'I hope you're not offended by all the questions she asked? And I hope she's not put you off being friends with me?'

'It's not your fault...' She didn't know what to say, as anything that sprang to mind about his mother could not be interpreted as anything but critical.

Andrew rolled his eyes. 'Most of mother's friends have the same old-fashioned views, whereas my father couldn't give two hoots what anyone does.' He paused. 'He's not here as usual; he's gone off to some horse-trial event in the country.'

He took Lillian's hand and led her over to the corner where the gramophone was, and they spent a few minutes going through the pile of records.

Lillian lifted out a Marlene Dietrich and looked at the cover. 'I don't think I've heard this one before.'

He took it from her and then took it out of the sleeve. 'If there are any particular records you like, you can borrow them until I'm next in Liverpool,' he offered.

'No, no,' Lillian said, 'it's good of you, but I would be terrified of breaking them on the journey home.' She was touched by his kindness, and, as she watched him put *Falling in Love Again* on the turntable, she thought how kind he always was to her, writing and sending her articles, letting her know she was on his mind. She was reminded how struck Irene had been by his good looks and his lively personality, and wondered if she could see him as more than a friend.

He turned and caught her looking at him and his face suddenly became serious. Then, as the music began to play, he moved towards her, his eyes still fixed on hers.

'I'm so glad you came to London,' he said, 'it seems ages since I saw you...' He caught his breath. 'I think of you all the time, wanting to tell you about things I've seen and done. Every morning I'm home, I come downstairs the minute I hear the post arriving, hoping there's a letter from you. If there's not, I start to think about writing another one to you.'

'I'll have to start writing more often,' she said. 'And hopefully, I'll soon have more interesting and fascinating things to tell you.'

He took her hands in his. '*Everything* about you is fascinating. I have never met a girl like you...'

She looked up at him and smiled. 'I don't think your mother has met anyone like me either! I hope she's not too shocked?'

'Forget Mother.' He pulled her towards him. 'Can I kiss you?' he asked in a low voice. 'Please?'

Lillian's heart started to beat quickly, and she was unsure what to do. She looked back towards the door. 'What about...'

'We'll hear the drawing-room door open,' he said, holding her tighter now. 'Just a little kiss... I've been imagining it for so long.' He bent his head towards her, and his lips touched hers.

Lillian caught her breath as his lips pressed against hers, and as the kiss grew more passionate, she felt a tingle in her stomach starting to grow.

Andrew moved back to hold her at arms' length. 'That was even better than I could have hoped for...' He pulled her close to him again and they kissed again until a creaking floorboard sounded from somewhere along the hallway, and they sprang apart.

Lillian felt herself trembling as they stood by the gramophone. She had enjoyed the kiss – her first passionate kiss – and she wondered again if her feelings of friendship could grow into something deeper.

At five o'clock the hackney cab pulled up outside, by which time they had rejoined Andrew's mother and Anna in the drawing room. Sybil Whyte rose to see them off and smiled warmly at Lillian as they shook hands and said goodbye.

As the hackney pulled away from the kerb, Lillian looked at Anna and said, 'Thank goodness that's all over. What a dragon Mrs Whyte is. I couldn't go through that again.' She shook her head. 'She obviously thinks I'm totally beneath him. Did she say anything more when I was out of the room?'

'Yes, she said quite a lot,' Anna replied. 'She really liked you.'

Lillian looked at her in amazement.

'She told me she thinks you are a lovely, down-to-earth girl, not like some of the flighty pieces she's met, although to be truthful, I think the property in Victoria has helped her opinion of us both enormously.'

Anna halted. 'She said that Andrew is besotted with you, and is mooning around the house all the time, obviously thinking about you.'

Lillian, feeling embarrassed and a little silly talking about such things, looked up at the roof of the taxi. 'Well, I know he likes me, but...'

'I'm not saying Sybil White is completely won over yet – she does have reservations about religion and our more modern attitudes to women – but you're going to have to give Andrew some serious thought,' Anna said, 'because you can't lead the poor boy on if you have no interest in him.'

Lillian looked at her. 'I do like him,' she said, 'but there is plenty of time to see how things work out.'

Chapter Thirty-Nine

When they arrived back in Liverpool on Tuesday, a letter was waiting for Lillian from Bon Marché, inviting her for an interview the following day.

'Tomorrow morning at eleven o'clock!' she exclaimed to Anna. 'What am I going to do? I haven't had time to think about it. Why didn't they give me more notice?'

Anna picked up the envelope. 'It was sent last week,' she said, 'and must have arrived in the afternoon post the day we left. You should be pleased, it's really good news. Well done on getting an interview.' She smiled encouragingly. 'It's actually perfect timing because all the information you gathered in London will still be fresh in your mind.'

That night Lillian went through her wardrobe, and with Anna's help, decided on the clothes she would wear the next day: a fine grey skirt, with a long black and grey chiffon blouse with a black bow at the neck. In her plain black coat and hat with her new colourful French scarf, she thought she looked both stylish and yet serious. Then she spent the rest of the evening going through her notes on window displays and current fashions in the London stores.

She rose early in the morning to bathe and arrange her hair in a neat, fashionable style, drawn back from her face with the curls at the back. When she appeared in their private sitting room for breakfast, Anna viewed her with great pride.

'You look so beautiful... and so grown-up Lillian,' she said. 'I don't know what to say.'

Lillian grinned at her. ' "Good luck" would help!'

It was a dry morning, but the sky was heavy with cloud. She pondered over whether to take her bicycle, but decided she would walk, and not risk getting oil on her coat or tearing her stockings. Anna also suggested she take her umbrella along as her hair would be ruined if it started to rain.

When she arrived at Bon Marché, Lillian was shown upstairs to the offices and then taken by the secretary down to the board-room where a very smart woman with short, vivid red hair and two men – one middle-aged and one younger – were waiting for her. Lillian took a deep breath and went in, remembering Miss Churchill's advice about always smiling, and trying to look much more confident than she felt.

At first Lillian felt her answers to the questions were rather stilted. Why, the red-haired lady wanted to know, did she want to work in their particular store, and what experience did she have to bring to the post? Lillian explained that she felt they were the most individual and adventurous of the department stores with their unique French style, and that she had also been impressed by their support for the arts in Liverpool with the store's gallery, which regularly held art exhibitions and lectures on fashion.

She was then asked by one of the men where her particular interests lay, and she explained about having an interest in all areas of fashion and dressmaking. All three made notes and each of them asked her a few more questions, but Lillian felt that there was a flatness about their response, as though she had disappointed them.

She got the sense that the interview was coming to a close, and with a sense of panic she thought back to an article Andrew had sent her about making an impression at interviews. Images of the trip to Selfridge's flew into her mind, and she decided she had nothing to lose.

'I am interested in all areas of fashion,' she started again, 'but what I feel really passionate about are the window displays. I would love to learn how to dress the mannequins, and how to decorate the windows and walls.' She then went on to describe the features she liked about the current Bon Marché displays, to make sure they knew she appreciated their beautiful store. Then, choosing her words carefully, she then talked about her recent visit to Selfridge's in London.

The younger man looked at her and smiled. 'You do know Bon Marché is owned by Selfridge's?'

'Yes,' Lillian said, smiling back at him. 'I read it in a magazine some time ago.' She went on to describe the scarf displays mounted on the individual white wooden frames, as though each one was a work of art.

As she spoke, she noticed each one sitting up straighter and listening intently. Realising she had caught their attention, she reached down to her handbag and picked up her scarf. 'This is one of the actual scarves,' she said, holding it up. 'You can imagine how vividly the colours stand out against the white background.'

Half an hour later, Lillian came out with a beaming smile on her face. At the end of the interview she was asked to sit outside for a few minutes, and then the lady with the red hair came out to invite her back in.

'That scarf is amazing,' she whispered as they walked back in. 'I'm Miss Lynch, the buyer for the fashion department, and I must have a look at the label so we can find the supplier.'

All three shook her hand and said that she had been offered a positon, to start the following Monday, working in the ladies' fashion department. Since she had never been employed before and didn't have work references, all she needed to do in the meantime was to hand in two character references.

As she walked out of the store, Lillian felt the greatest sense of achievement she had ever felt in her life. She hurried along home, desperate to tell Anna her good news, and wary of the darkening sky. If it rained, she decided it might be quicker and more sheltered if she went across Ranelagh Street, then up Wood Street. She had just crossed over when the rain started, so she quickly put her umbrella up and hurried along as it grew heavier. There was a newsagent on the corner and she decided she would treat herself to the new edition of *Vogue* magazine. It advertised the widest selection of fashion brands along with interviews with designers and famous stars, and she reckoned that she would have to start buying it regularly to help keep her up to date in her new world.

She wandered about the shop looking at other magazines for ten or fifteen minutes, the copy of *Vogue* under her arm, whilst keeping an eye on the window in the hope that the rain was dying off. Eventually, a weak sun came out and it seemed to be drying up so she paid for her magazine. She went to the shop door to see it was still drizzling, and was just putting her umbrella back up when a man came around the corner and walked straight into her.

'Oh, I'm so sorry...' he said, 'Are you all right?'

She froze when she saw who it was. 'I'm fine, thank you...'

Paul Larking stepped backwards to look properly at her. 'Lillian? I didn't recognise you...' When she didn't reply, he looked closely at her. 'Are you all right? I didn't hurt you, did I?'

She straightened up to her full height. 'I'm absolutely fine, thank you.'

There was a silence. 'It seems a long time since I saw you last... How are you?'

She felt strained and awkward with him, remembering the last time they had met, and how cold he had been towards her. She had been too friendly with him that night, and she wasn't going to make the same mistake again. 'I'm fine, thank you, Paul,' she said. 'And how are you?' Her voice was deliberately clipped and distant, like Anna's when she was annoyed.

'Good enough, I suppose...'

'And Edie? I hope she is well too?'

'Back at college in Newcastle,' he said.

'Give her my regards when you next see her.' She looked at the sky and then lifted her umbrella again. 'I must get moving before the rain gets heavier.'

She stepped down from the shop and started walking quickly

towards St Luke's Church, from where it was only a quick walk home to Rodney Street.

By the time she reached the house, Lillian had to stop to catch her breath and to recapture the happy feeling she had about the job in Bon Marché. Meeting Paul Larking had unsettled her. He was the first person she had confided in about her past, and the only one who knew how hard it had been adapting to her new life, especially after losing Molly. She felt she had opened herself to him, thinking they would become closer friends and maybe even more, but Paul had made it clear that they were too different, and besides, he had a steady girlfriend. She pushed the feelings of rejection aside, and was determined that meeting him again would not spoil a day of great celebration for her.

She lifted her head and ran up the stairs to the house to tell Anna her good news.

Chapter Forty

On that same Wednesday night, Lillian went to her ballroom dancing classes, eager to tell Irene her news about Bon Marché. Irene was late and by the time she came in Mr Gibb had already paired Lillian off with a partner.

At the break, Irene rushed over to her. 'You're not going to believe it, but I'm going to Ireland on my own on Friday for two whole weeks. My mother has some sort of stomach upset, and she said she can't face the thought of the boat, so I'm going on my own.' She clapped her hands together. 'It will be the first time I've ever travelled by myself, and I'm really looking forward to being completely independent. I can do what I want and talk to whom I want on the boat without my mother chaperoning me, plus it means I can stay out at my grandparents' place all the time, instead of going over to my uncle's house.' She made a little face. 'Plus there's a gorgeous boy who lives just down the road from my grandmother, and several lovely young men I see when they take me out to the yacht club at Dun Laoghaire.'

'Well, I'm glad you're happy about it,' Lillian said, smiling. 'And I'm sure you'll have a great holiday.'

'If it's that good,' Irene laughed, 'I might not come back! How did your trip to London go?'

Lillian told her all about the places they visited and the afternoon out at Andrew's house in Marylebone. Irene quizzed her about the Whytes' house and wanted to know how grand it was, though when she heard about Sybil Whyte's bias against Catholics and women who worked, she called her an uppity old snob. Before Irene got a chance to ask her about her and Andrew, Lillian told her the big news about Bon Marché.

'Oh, how lovely' Irene gasped. 'Dressing windows and doing displays – it sounds amazing! Is your mother okay about it? I thought she seemed rather put out when you were talking about it the night we were out for our birthdays.'

'We talked it out,' Lillian said, 'and she's fine about it. I start on Monday morning.'

That night as she lay in bed, Lillian went over the events of the last few days: the kiss between her and Andrew, the awkwardness between her and Paul Larking, and then the knowledge that – having seen the house in Victoria – she was actually an heiress. And now she was going to start work in a beautiful French-inspired shop.

As she lay in the dark, with all those thoughts turning over in her mind, she fell into a state of semi-sleep, during which she momentarily imagined herself back in the dormitory in Gethsemane House. She floated out of her bed and out of the room she had shared with dozens of girls, down the stairs and along the corridor. She hovered outside a room and then the door opened and she was inside, looking down on the prone figure of her dead little friend.

She woke with a start, struggling to breathe with her heart racing. She sat up and reached out blindly for the lamp, almost knocking it off her bedside cabinet as she did so. Light flooded her bedroom and she held her hands to her eyes for a minute until her eyes had adjusted to it.

She sat there for a while, and then turned to her bedside drawer and lifted out her rosary beads. She bent her head and closed her eyes, silently praying for Molly. For all that her own life had now veered off in a completely new and unimaginable direction, Lillian knew she would never, ever forget the dear little friend who had helped her survive the dire, miserable days in the orphanage.

She finished her prayer, stared around her beautiful bedroom, and then she closed her eyes again. This time she said a prayer of thanks for herself – for the second chance she had been given in life. For all the wonderful things she had – and for all the experiences that poor Molly had never lived to see.

On Saturday morning, just as they were finishing breakfast, Lucy came upstairs with a note which had been hand-delivered for Anna. She gave it to her employer and stood waiting to see if there was a reply.

Anna opened it, and as she read it, a shadow crossed her face. She looked over at Lillian. 'It's from Irene's mother,' she said. 'She wants me to go over to the house to see her.'

'I wonder if she's feeling worse,' Lillian said. 'It was Wednesday night when Irene mentioned she wasn't well, and she can't have improved or she would have gone to Ireland with her yesterday.'

Anna nodded, her face thoughtful. 'She said to go around any time today, so I might go this morning.'

She looked at Lucy. 'Will you please tell the girl that I'll be over to the house within the next half hour.'

When her aunt left the room to get ready, Lillian poured herself another cup of coffee and lifted her *Vogue* magazine and went to sit by the fire. A short while later there was a tap on the door and Mrs Larking came in, closing the door behind her.

'How are you?' she said, smiling over at Lillian.

Lillian put her magazine down. 'I'm fine, thank you, Mrs Larking.'

'And how do you feel about starting work on Monday?'

'Excited and a little bit nervous.'

The cook nodded. 'Paul told me he met you in town the other day. I think it must have been the day you found out about the job in Bon Marché.'

'Yes, that's right. I met him in a newsagent's as I was coming home. It was a terrible day for rain.'

'I was telling him about your job in Bon Marché, and I think he was surprised you hadn't told him, with him working in

Lewis's like. He was asking me if you were okay, he seemed a bit concerned you were so quiet.'

Lillian felt her throat tighten. 'Oh, there was nothing wrong at all,' she said, 'It was a very wet day and I was just rushing home out of the rain. I thought he wouldn't want to stand chatting and get soaked either.'

Mrs Larking nodded. 'I just wondered . . . He hasn't said anything to upset you or anything like that?'

Lillian shook her head. 'No, not at all. He was very kind the time I fainted outside, but since then I haven't seen much of him really. Wednesday was the first time I've seen him in months.'

The cook sighed. 'It's just that he wasn't himself that night he was out at the house just before Christmas – the night he came back for my cough bottle – when you had your friends in for the party. Something made me wonder if you'd had some sort of difference, and then I forgot all about it.'

Lillian didn't know what to make of this, but she could see it had unsettled Paul's mother. 'Honestly, Mrs Larking,' she said smiling now, 'Paul and I have not had any differences, so there's no need to worry. To be honest, we hardly really know each other, so maybe he had something else on his mind that night.'

'That's grand then.' Mrs Larking went over to start clearing the table. 'I believe you visited young Mr Whyte when you were down in London?'

'Yes, we had a nice afternoon tea out at their house.' She looked over smiling. 'The cakes were lovely – but not as light as yours.'

'I'm glad to hear it,' Mrs Larking said, laughing. She put the plates down, then she looked over at Lillian again. 'You've fairly grown up in the time you've been here. You're a proper young lady now, going out to work and stepping out with a nice young man.'

'Oh, it's not like that,' she said, blushing at the suggestions. 'We're just friends really.'

'Well, he must be halfway serious, or I don't think he would have invited you to meet his mam. You're both a good match, and it's lovely for you to have met a nice young man of your own kind.' She smiled. 'And it's the same with our Paul, he's still courting that nice teacher girl, Edie, and they're the same kind as well.'

When she left, Lillian mulled over what Mrs Larking had just said, and wondered what on earth Paul had said to her. She guessed that the night her aunt had invited him in for a drink, he felt uncomfortable when Andrew had arrived early. The class thing still rankled with him, and Lillian thought that if anything had bothered him that night, it was likely to be that. What was confusing her was that down in the kitchen he had been quite clear that he didn't think they should even be friends, and yet now he was asking his mother about her. It just didn't make sense to her.

When lunchtime came, Lillian was debating with herself whether it was a good idea to take a walk down to Bon Marché. She thought she might have a look at the windows, and maybe get to know her way around the store on her own. She heard the front door opening, and then a few minutes' later Anna came in looking very serious.

'Is Mrs Flanagan all right?' Lillian asked. 'Or has she become sicker?'

Anna sat down in the chair opposite Lillian. 'I have something to tell you,' she said, 'but it is totally confidential. You mustn't tell a single person.'

'Of course I won't,' Lillian said. 'What is it?'

Anna's hand fluttered up to her throat. 'Freda is getting married early next Monday morning by special licence, and she has asked me to be a witness at the wedding.'

Lillian opened her mouth in shock, then said, 'To John, the man who drives her car?'

'How did you know?' Anna was completely taken aback. 'Freda thinks that it's a complete secret and that no one knows about their relationship. Did Irene find out and tell you?'

'No,' Lillian said, still startled by the news. 'I saw them the night I was at their house... I saw them kissing.'

Anna sucked in her breath. 'Well, Irene doesn't know a thing about it, and Freda was terrified to tell her before Ireland in case it spoiled it for her.'

'But won't Irene be upset that she's not at her own mother's wedding?'

'Irene doesn't know about Freda and John,' Anna said in a low voice. 'And Freda is convinced she won't be at all happy about it.'

'Well, why doesn't she wait until Irene is back home and then explain it all to her – and then have the wedding after that?'

'Because Freda can't wait...'

'Why?'

'Because,' Anna whispered, 'she has just found out that she is almost five months pregnant.'

Chapter Forty-One

Lillian woke up at quarter to seven on Monday morning. When she remembered about starting work, an anxious feeling started in her stomach. She had learned that doing something was always better than lying worrying, so she got out of bed and went down to the bathroom to start getting ready for the day ahead.

When she was dressed, she went down to the kitchen to let Mrs Larking and Lucy know she was up and about, and to ask if she could have tea and a boiled egg and toast as soon as they were ready. The cook wished her good luck, and said Lucy would bring her breakfast up in ten minutes when they had served the paying guests' breakfasts.

When she came back upstairs Anna was there, dressed, with her hair still wet from her bath. As they ate breakfast, they talked again about Freda's wedding and Anna said she felt awkward about being a witness as it might look to Irene as though she was party to the whole relationship.

'I doubt whether Irene will think about you at all,' Lillian said. 'She will be too shocked coming back to discover that her mother is not only married but expecting a baby in the summer.' Her brow furrowed. 'I thought she was much too old to have a baby.'

Anna raised her eyebrows. 'She's not yet forty, and lots of women have babies at that age.'

'Gosh,' Lillian said. 'Do you ever wish you had had more children?'

Anna shrugged. 'It wasn't meant to be,' she said. 'And I don't think about it now.' She did not explain that the damage – physical and psychological – that had been inflicted on her when she was raped had removed any possibility of that happening.

Lillian finished her tea, leaving half her toast as the butterflies in her stomach were growing stronger. She looked at her watch. 'I'd better get ready now as I want to be good and early to get my uniform sorted, so I'm on the shop floor in plenty of time.'

Just after eight o'clock, Lillian stepped out into the cool morning air and walked briskly down Upper Duke Street towards Liverpool city centre. She had expected it to be quieter at this hour of the morning, but it was surprisingly busy with trams rattling past full of workers going to different parts of the city. She arrived at the staff entrance of Bon Marché at quarter past eight, stopping for a few moments to catch her breath, and then she straightened her back and walked through the doors and into the big new world of work.

Later that evening, Lillian regaled Anna with everything that had happened during her first day, from the minute she put on her smart black uniform with pearls, until the staff doors closed behind her.

'I was really nervous when I was taken to the shop floor,' Lillian said. 'I was told I wouldn't need to go near the till or handle money, so that was a big relief. One of the ladieswear managers, Miss Owens, took me around the floor I'll be working on this week, showing me the different racks of clothes by each designer, and pointing out the labels with the names. Then she took me to the cupboards on the walls and in the middle of the floor where the displays are, and showed me the long drawers where smaller items like gloves, scarves and belts are stocked, as we are not allowed to remove them from the displays to give to customers.

'While I was working, the time flew, but the worst was waiting for something to do, or when a customer asked me something and I didn't know the answer, and I had to ask one of the experienced staff.'

Anna nodded, listening intently. 'And were the staff nice and helpful?'

'Yes, but it's all very strict. We have to help and advise customers, but not in any way push them to buy things. If we are too pushy, they often don't come back.'

'What did you do during your lunch break?' Anna asked.

'One of the younger girls called Aileen invited me to go to a little café a few minutes' walk away from the store, and I really enjoyed that. She's from Bootle, she's very friendly, and she told me all about her family.'

'Oh, I'm delighted you've made a new friend,' Anna said. 'It always helps when you have someone you can talk to.'

'Apart from our breaks, we're not allowed to talk to each other unless it's about work,' Lillian said. 'The manageress walks around all the time, checking.' She pulled a face. 'If she saw me talking to a customer, she always came over to see if they needed any advice from her. As the day went on, I got to know where certain brands were or which colour gloves were in which drawer and that kind of thing, so I felt more relaxed.'

'It all sounds very busy,' Anna said.

'It's better when I am busy,' Lillian said, 'because when I have a definite job, it means I know what I'm doing.'

Each day Lillian got to know more and more about the department, and by the following Monday morning, she felt much more confident walking down to work, knowing she had got through her first week without any major disasters.

Anna was in her bedroom preparing for Freda's wedding. It was only to be attended by her and a friend of John's. It had been strange for Anna as she had to go round to Freda's for an hour one evening to be properly introduced to John, whom she had previously only thought of as a driver and a handyman, and only ever said 'thank you' to. She had to modify her attitude now, to make sure she gave him his proper place. This Anna did unequivocally, as she had been in the exact same position when she married Edward, moving from being a paid member of staff to being a spouse.

Any reservations that Anna had were more to do with his age than status, because John looked more than a few years younger than Freda. But, after talking to him for a while, she discovered that while he was a quiet sort of man, he was friendly and easy to talk to. The eight years' difference between them was hardly noticeable, and they seemed to balance each other. The wedding service at the register office was over very quickly, and then John drove the four of them back to the Adelphi for lunch with champagne.

His friend, Eamonn, a fireman, was a bit of a character, and Anna was grateful he kept things going any time there was a lull in the conversation. When John and Eamonn were deep in conversation about cars, Freda confided in Anna.

'I hope and pray Irene is going to accept this when she comes back from Ireland because there's nothing I can do about it now. I had hoped to wait until she was a bit older and had met someone herself, but unfortunately nature got in the way.' She patted her slightly swollen stomach. 'Who would believe it? David and I had hoped for another baby almost until the week before he died, but there was never any sign of it happening. And now, here I am all these years later expecting again at my age.'

She smiled and shrugged. 'To be honest I'm happy about the baby, and especially happy now I'm married. It wasn't easy having Irene when I was on my own and I couldn't stand the thought of it happening again. And John is an easier sort of man who does anything you ask, and up until now he and Irene have got on great.'

'Well, that's a big help,' Anna said.

'It will be very different,' Freda said anxiously. 'He won't be the handyman any more – he's now Irene's stepfather.'

When Lillian came in from work, Anna filled her in on all the details about the wedding.

'Well, I'm glad they got married and made things official,' Lillian said, then paused. 'Were you and my father happy?'

'Very,' Anna said, a soft look coming into her eyes. 'He was the love of my life, and made up for all the things I went through before I met him.'

She looked at Lillian. 'I have not one regret about being married to your father ... or to Edward, although they were very different sorts of men and different marriages.' She smiled. 'Let's put it this way, I loved Loman in the romantic way that I think Freda loves John, so I can understand them wanting to be together.'

'You're not much older than Freda,' Lillian said. 'Do you think – '

'Never,' Anna said, shaking her head. 'I won't ever get involved with a man again.' She halted. 'I wasn't going to mention it, but since we're being very open ... Oliver Whyte made a romantic overture to me some time ago.'

'Mr Whyte?' Lillian looked appalled. 'Oh my God ... Isn't he far too old to be romantic?'

Anna started to laugh. 'That's what young people always think. I thought the same myself when I was your age.'

'Did he want the same sort of companionship you had with Edward?'

'No,' Anna said, dipping her eyes.

Lillian's hands came up to shield her eyes. 'I can't even bear to think about it ... and I thought he was a lovely old man.'

'He is a lovely man, and I don't want you to think otherwise,' Anna said. 'Just because people get older doesn't mean they can't love anyone. And I'll be very upset if you think differently or any less about him because I told you.'

Lillian sat up straight. 'Okay,' she said, trying not to laugh. 'I'll just blank this conversation out of my mind.'

Anna could see her concealed humour and smiled back. 'You'll learn as you get older yourself, Miss,' she said. 'Life is full of surprises and can catch us all out.'

Chapter Forty-Two

Lillian took her coat from her hook in the staffroom and put it on over her black dress and row of pearls, then she lifted her bag, which held the two library books she wanted to change. She left the store, negotiating her way through the lunchtime shoppers and the city traffic, and was walking up Roe Street when she saw a curiously familiar sight coming towards her. As she passed the scrawny, ragged girl, she recognised her, still pushing the same ancient pram with the two children.

Lillian remembered the shock of seeing the shambolic figure when she first arrived in Liverpool, and thought the poor girl looked no better now than she had all those months ago. Her face and demeanour had poverty stamped all over her. The sight of her brought a lump to Lillian's throat as she hurried across to the library. She had seen lots of poor people since last year, but there was something particularly sad about the poor bedraggled girl.

She stopped at the library door and then whirled around and ran all the way back to where she had seen the girl, but she was nowhere in sight. She stood watching for a few minutes, then she spotted her coming out of a doorway. Lillian ran across the road and just made it to the other side as a speeding car came around the corner.

She got within a few feet of the girl and then came to a sudden halt. What was she to say to this total stranger? She suddenly didn't feel brave enough to approach her. Then an image of Molly came into her mind and propelled her forward. 'I hope you don't mind...' she said.

The girl turned around, then turned back again, checking if there was someone else Lillian might be speaking to. She then came back to face Lillian. 'Are you speaking to *me*?' she said, in a quiet voice.

Lillian stretched her hand out and handed her a two-shilling piece. 'Please get something for yourself and the children...'

The girl looked at her in confusion. 'But why?'

'Because...' Lillian's chest was aching with the running and her anxiety about whether she was doing the right thing – and doing it the right way. 'Because you remind me of my friend – and because it's not fair the way things are for you...'

The girl looked up at Lillian and their eyes met, then the girl's eyes filled up with tears. 'Thank you, Miss,' she said, taking the money, 'you're very kind.'

She put the coin in a corner of the pram and covered it up. Then she stood up straight. 'We weren't always like this; my father lost his job three years ago...'

'I'm sorry,' Lillian said. A sadness filled her, and before the girl could see it, she turned and walked quickly away.

Irene was due back from Ireland the following Sunday morning, and Lillian waited all day expecting to hear something from her. She went to work on Monday and Tuesday and still heard nothing. She guessed that her friend was still coming to terms with the news of her mother's marriage and pregnancy, and hopefully she would be feeling okay by the time their ballroom dancing class came around on Wednesday.

When she came in after work that day, Anna had a sealed letter from Irene waiting for her in the sitting room. 'Freda brought it round this afternoon,' she said in a low voice.

Lillian looked at her. 'What's happening?'

'Irene went back to Ireland this morning. Apparently she went mad when she heard her mother had married John, and that was before the baby was even mentioned.'

'Oh no...'

'When she found out about the baby she went upstairs and locked herself in her room and only came out yesterday evening. She just said she wanted to go back to Ireland to her grand-parents. Freda said she and John hardly slept since Irene came back home, and he has moved out to his parents in Hoylake until they sort things out.'

'But they can't sort it if Irene has gone back to Ireland.'

There was a silence. Lillian opened the letter and read it. It more or less said exactly what Anna had told her, adding that she hated her mother for what she had done and would never forgive her. She had written her grandmother's address at the bottom of the letter and said she would write to Lillian when she felt settled and up to it.

'I'll miss her,' Lillian said. 'She was my first proper friend here, and we had only just started going out to places together. We were planning to go to a dance at the Adelphi over Easter weekend now we can waltz properly without making fools of ourselves. It seems such a waste to have learned the steps, and then have no one to go dancing with.'

'You'll make other friends,' Anna said, 'and you have plenty of time to go to dances.'

Lillian was sure Anna was right, but hearing that Irene had gone away made her feel unsettled. Although the circumstances were totally different, it reminded her of Alice and Molly. She took a deep breath. Life seemed determined to keep taking her friends away from her.

Chapter Forty-Three

By the time her fifth week in Bon Marché came around, Lillian had been moved around to try out most of the ladies' departments such as coats and suits, dresses and knitwear, underwear and nightwear. Recently, she had been working in costume jewellery, and one morning, when she was putting earrings on a stand, Miss Lynch came down looking for her. She was accompanied by another very striking looking lady with straight black hair tied back in a ponytail.

'Lillian,' Miss Lynch said. 'This is Miss Dorothy Cherrington, one of our window-display managers. The window-dressing teams are working on an Easter-themed display downstairs and we thought you might like to help out.'

'Oh, I'd love to!' Lillian said. 'I'll just have to check it's all right with Miss Owens.' She looked around for the department manager.

'It's okay,' Miss Lynch said. 'You go with Miss Cherrington and I'll have a word with Mae Owens. She knows I was planning to bring you down to the windows, so she won't mind.'

Lillian went down in the lift with Miss Cherrington, who told her they were working on three windows today, all with an Easter or early summer feel. One window, she explained, was a picnic theme with fake grass and flowers, picnic baskets filled with crockery, and tartan blankets. Two mannequins would be in the background with bicycles and tennis racquets.

The second window would hold a huge golden urn filled with tall branches, from which would hang foil-covered Easter eggs and delicate glass ornaments. The third window would be decorated like a park with trees, flowers and benches, with mannequins dressed in ladies' pastel-coloured summer suits and dresses, and straw bonnets.

'You will probably just be observing how things are done today,' Miss Cherrington said, 'but you might be asked to help out with some small jobs.'

For the first hour Lillian stood quietly to the side, fascinated to watch how things were constructed, and how the window team worked together. She was delighted when she was shown how to attach special transparent thread to each of the fake Easter eggs to allow them to hang on the branches. After she had finished with the eggs, she was then asked to help stick silk flowers and dried pampas grass onto a background for the picnic scene.

The windows were completed just before lunch, and Lillian was delighted when she was asked to join the team when they went out into the street to see the finished displays.

'It was wonderful,' Lillian told Anna later that evening. 'I just loved it.'

Anna was relieved to see Lillian happy in her work and more relaxed at home in the evenings again, because she could tell that Irene's sudden departure had unsettled her. She hoped that Andrew Whyte's arrival over Easter would help to keep her occupied. She felt that since the families now knew each other better that it would be appropriate for Andrew to come over to the house in the evenings to listen to music on the gramophone or to play draughts or cards. Thankfully, there was no awkwardness between herself and Oliver. He had behaved like the gentleman he was when she turned down his offer of courtship, truthfully explaining that a physical relationship wasn't possible for her due to a medical condition. Although initially disappointed, Oliver now seemed happy enough to have a simple friendship when he needed a partner for an event, or to go on outings when Andrew was visiting.

As the Easter weekend approached, Lillian enjoyed her walks

home from Bon Marché in the April evening sunshine, pleased with all she had learned over the last two months and ready to enjoy a few days' break at home. Her working day was busy from the minute she got into the store until the time she left, but working made her feel complete and fulfilled in a way that studying and sewing at home had not. She still enjoyed them as hobbies, but they were just not enough for her.

She had finished with Miss Churchill in the last few weeks. When the teacher discovered she was working in a department store she had looked shocked. Lillian had actually grown fond of the eccentric teacher, even though she had recently become more erratic. On several occasions, Lillian had turned up at the door and she could tell that Miss Churchill looked surprised and unprepared as though she had forgotten all about the lesson. During her final lesson, Lillian had noticed that she was eating tubes of strong mints, and guessed she was using them to mask the smell of sherry.

Lillian still missed Irene, but she was getting used to the idea of her not being around any more and work helped to stop her dwelling on it. She hoped that things might get easier between Irene and Freda, but so far, there was no sign of any reconciliation. Freda herself was laying low; her baby was due in a few weeks, and she had told Anna that she didn't want to meet people who would ask about Irene or the baby.

Lillian had started to make friends with some of the girls at work; Aileen, in particular. At first she had felt shy in a large group, especially since a few of them had commented curiously on her well-spoken 'posh' accent and the fact she lived in Rodney Street. She felt slightly out of things, but as the weeks went past she began to be accepted as a hard-working and supportive colleague. Gradually they found interests in common such as fashion and dancing, and Lillian got used to them and they had got used to her, and she now felt perfectly comfortable joining them for tea in the staffroom or going to a café at lunchtime.

She always made an excuse, however, if they planned to go to

Lewis's tearoom for lunch as she did not want to risk running into Paul Larking. She had seen him from a distance on several occasions, and each time she had felt awkward, unable to think of anything they might talk about, and had turned and walked in the opposite direction.

Her friends at work had pointed out other young men who had shown admiration for her, including one young manager in the men's department named Max Hunter, and a handsome young Frenchman called Michel, who came to the store regularly with stock from his father's milliners' factory in Paris. Lillian had found both young men nice and friendly, and when Michel invited her to join him for lunch at the Adelphi she had been tempted. After a night's thought she had politely made an excuse as she was afraid it would complicate things at work, and that it wouldn't be fair to Andrew, whom she already had made plans to see when he was in Liverpool.

Andrew had written to say that he would be arriving the Saturday afternoon of Easter weekend and that if she was free, he hoped that they might go to a dance together on Easter Monday at the Adelphi. Lillian was thrilled she had someone else to go to the dance and would discuss it with Anna, and check she was okay about them going on their own. Up until now, they had been accompanied by Anna and Mr Whyte on any outings to the cinema or theatre.

When she got a chance to talk to Anna, Lillian explained that the girls she worked with were all more independent than she was, and were allowed to go to reputable places unchaperoned with their young men. Anna had a word with Andrew's grandfather, and they both agreed that an Easter Ball was a suitable occasion for them to socialise on their own.

Lillian had bought several new outfits from the shop's spring collection, including a lemon and white linen suit with a tiered hem which she intended to wear to Mass on Easter Sunday with her white gloves and a white straw bonnet. With her savings, she had also bought two floral dresses and two cardigans, one white and one red, which she thought would mix well with other outfits. Anna had treated her to a new evening gown for the Easter Ball from George Henry Lee's, which was the most grown-up ensemble she had worn so far.

Lillian had fallen in love with the form-fitting bronze satin gown, with its deep V-neck which enhanced her cleavage, and graceful shawl-style sleeves which gave a glimpse of her shoulders and fell at the back into a train. After listening to the girls talking about the latest hairstyle, Lillian toyed with the idea of having her hair cut to the nape of her neck. It would be more convenient for work, she told Anna, and could be styled into curls or finger-waves. She went as far as going into a hairdresser's to make an appointment, but not only did the lady on the desk look shocked at the thought of cutting her beautiful, thick dark hair, so did the other hairdressers who gathered around Lillian to give their opinion.

She left the salon smiling at all the compliments, and deciding to leave well alone. Instead, she went shopping and treated herself to some new hair clasps and a glamorous hairband with ostrich feathers that matched the colour of her gown.

The Saturday trade in the shop was brisk after being closed the previous day for Good Friday. There was a feeling of expectation and excitement amongst the staff with the sunny, warm weather and the longer, brighter nights. At break-times Lillian had joined in talking about their plans for the weekend and they were all intrigued about her friendship with Andrew. As she did with Irene, Lillian laughed off suggestions of a romance, but when she showed them a photograph he had sent of himself at the races with his father, they had declared him as handsome as a movie star and could not understand her reticence about him.

'Has he kissed you yet?' Aileen asked. She herself had a fiancé and was planning a wedding the following year.

Lillian had hesitated, then shyly admitted that they had indeed kissed. When Aileen pushed for more details, she found herself admitting that she had enjoyed it very much.

'Well, it sounds to me as though you are halfway there,' her friend declared. 'Next thing he will be asking you to marry him.'

Lillian had laughed at the idea, but it had left her thinking. There was no doubt that Andrew was a good catch by any standards, and she wondered whether by keeping him at a distance, she might end up in the future with someone less. He had matured since they first met, and she had been grateful for his support and understanding about her plan to work – plus he was handsome and had a good sense of humour.

This weekend, she decided, during any time she was with him, she would observe her feelings more closely. The ball, she thought, would give her a good opportunity to see how they got on spending a whole evening talking and dancing closely together.

Just after three o'clock Lillian noticed there was a buzz of conversation between the customers, which then spread to the staff. A lady came over to her to ask if she could see a pair of long white gloves, and as Lillian accompanied her to the display stand, the lady said. 'There was a most upsetting accident outside Lewis's department store. A woman was run over by a car. Apparently it came speeding around the corner and ran straight into her. People are saying that they don't know whether she will survive. Apparently she was still unconscious when the ambulance arrived.'

Lillian gasped at the news. 'It's awful,' she said. 'There was another accident only a few days ago, when an elderly man was killed.'

'It's downright disgraceful,' the woman said. 'Something will have to be done about restricting speed. People have gone totally mad about cars, and there are more and more of them on the streets. We're reading about motor accidents in the *Liverpool Echo* every week.'

When she finished work, Lillian walked home carrying an elaborate Easter egg in a decorative basket she had bought for Anna, and three smaller Cadbury's eggs for Lucy and the Larkings. She had pondered about whether she should buy one for Andrew, but decided not to, as she thought it would be embarrassing if he hadn't bought one for her.

When she arrived home, Rose Moran told her that Anna was down in the kitchen talking to Mrs Larking. Lillian went upstairs with the eggs, and when she had taken off her outdoor things she went downstairs to join them.

As she went along the corridor, she could hear her aunt saying, 'It's the most awful news for both families, especially over Easter weekend.'

When Lillian tapped on the kitchen door, they both stopped talking.

'Have you heard the news about the car accident outside Lewis's?' Anna said.

Lillian nodded. 'It's terrible, they were all talking about it in work. Does anyone know how the poor woman is?'

'She's in hospital seriously ill,' Anna said, 'but thankfully Andrew only seems to have a broken arm, and his father escaped with just cuts and bruises.'

Lillian stared at her. 'Andrew?'

'Yes,' Anna said, nodding her head vigorously. 'He was driving the car.' She paused. 'Didn't you know?'

'No, I only heard about the woman...' Lillian's voice was shocked now. 'Is he all right?'

'Oliver came over to tell me on his way to the hospital. He had received a message to say that Andrew was having a plaster cast put on his arm, and he and his father were receiving treatment for the cuts they both suffered. Oliver expects them to be released sometime this evening.'

'That doesn't sound too serious if they are being released,' Lillian said. 'Although he must be very shaken after what has happened.'

'He will have to give a police statement too, no doubt,' Mrs Larking said. 'Especially with the girl being so badly hurt.'

'I thought it was an older woman,' Lillian said.

'She was only a young girl, and she had two children in some kind of an old pram. Michael was down at the cobbler's a while

346

ago, he heard that she just managed to push the pram out of the way in time or all three of them would have been killed.'

Lillian closed her eyes, suddenly feeling sick. It was the girl. It was the poor girl she had given the florin to.

Chapter Forty-Four

Just after nine o'clock that night, Lillian and Anna went across the street to the Whytes to see how Andrew was. Lillian was trembling as they followed the maid along the hallway and down to the drawing room where Andrew, his father and his grandfather were. She didn't know what to expect and she was anxious about what she might say, now that she knew who the girl was.

Oliver Whyte stood up to greet them and quickly introduced them to Andrew's father, George, a surprisingly slight-looking man with a moustache, but handsome in a rakish sort of way. Oliver then asked the maid to bring in drinks.

George guided Anna and Lillian towards the window where Andrew was sitting in a high chair, his plaster cast carefully resting on the tapestry-covered arm. One side of his face was dark red with yellow and blue bruising beginning to appear. The other side had a cut with six stitches, and the hand of the arm which was unbroken had several cuts and scratches.

Anna went straight over to him and put her hand on his good shoulder, offering her sympathies and hopes for a quick recovery. Lillian came behind, a knot in her throat and another in her stomach. She repeated more or less the same words to him that Anna had said, but she didn't move near him or touch him.

'It was awful,' he said, in a low voice. 'It was fine one moment and the next...' He shook his head. 'I can hardly remember...'

Lillian noticed that when he spoke, there was a tiny nerve in his cheek which jumped, indicating how shaken he was. 'Give yourself time...' she said. 'You need to recover.'

'If only the damned police would heed that advice,' Andrew's father suddenly said.

He started pacing up and down in front of the fireplace. 'They turned up at the hospital demanding statements about the accident, acting as though Andrew might be to blame. It's perfectly clear the girl should not have been on the street with that pram thing, when there is speeding traffic around.'

'Now calm down, George,' Oliver Whyte said. 'People were crossing roads long before cars were invented. Pedestrians have as much right to use the road as all the vehicles.'

George made a harrumphing sound. 'People in Liverpool seem to cross the roads with no rhyme or reason. How can a driver be held to blame if someone walks out in front of them?'

Oliver held his hands out. 'I'm not so quick on my feet as I used to be, and there are times when I've just missed being hit by a car.'

There was a silence and then Andrew cleared his throat, and said, 'I just turned the corner and she was there...' He shook his head.

'And you did exactly the right thing – you slammed the brakes on,' his father said, 'but the stupid girl took too long to get out of the way with that rickety old thing she was pushing. People like that shouldn't be allowed out on the streets.'

'Well, I hope she is recovering,' Andrew said. 'I keep getting pictures in my head of her lying on the ground.' His voice faltered. 'The poor girl... I hope it isn't too serious. I would feel awful if anything serious was to happen to her.'

'She'll be fine, and you'll get over it, so don't worry,' his father said. 'The minute that arm is sorted, we'll get you behind the wheel again.'

Lillian's body stiffened. What an awful, uncaring, boor of a man he was. Worse than Andrew's mother. He didn't sound as though he had an ounce of sympathy for the poor girl or his own son.

349

The maid came in with glasses of sherry and went around the group. Lillian was grateful when Mr Whyte started chatting to Anna about the weather and the events which were on over the Easter weekend. Andrew attempted small talk, asking Lillian if Bon Marché had been busy with people buying Easter eggs and bonnets.

Lillian could tell by his strained look and the tremor in his voice that he was trying to put a brave face on things. Underneath, she guessed he was very worried about the accident – both for the girl's situation and for his own future.

'Yes,' she said, 'it was a very good day for the shop, by far the busiest since I started working there.'

'Well, it is the worst possible weekend for me for this accident to happen,' George said to nobody in particular. 'I wasn't keen on coming up here anyway, and I was supposed to catch the train back down to London on Monday morning, but I'll have to stay on until Tuesday now to drive us both back in the car.'

Lillian took a mouthful of her drink, trying not to look at the selfish, arrogant man. She wished she could just get up and walk out, but she didn't want to upset the eldest Mr Whyte.

'I could get the train back home later in the week,' Andrew said in a flat voice. He paused. 'I don't think we can go anyway, until we've seen the police again.'

'I think that might be sorted out now. I've already had a word with a few of the officers,' Andrew's father said. 'and they seemed reasonable chaps when I explained how it happened, and of course I thanked them adequately in the right way.'.

'And what about the girl?' Oliver Whyte asked. 'Surely you can't think of going back to London until you know what's happened to her?'

'Hopefully she'll recover,' George said, 'because it will be one big headache for us if she doesn't pull through.'

Lillian closed her eyes, shocked at his callousness.

Oliver's head jerked up. 'I think you should have more care for the well-being of that poor girl instead of complaining how the accident has inconvenienced you.'

George looked slightly shamefaced as his father's remark. 'Well, of course we're concerned about her well-being...'

Andrew brought his fist up to his mouth, then shook his head. 'I feel like it's all a big nightmare...'

'It's only natural you would feel like that,' Anna said. 'It's the shock of everything...'

'For God's sake, Andrew!' his father said, 'pull yourself together. This is not your fault. The girl bloody well walked out in front of us. And just be grateful that she wasn't a person of any consequence. She didn't look the sort whose family are likely to cause a fuss, whatever happens to her. Once we get you back home to London you'll forget all about it.'

There was a silence, then Anna said, 'I think that's rather uncaring.'

Lillian put her drink down on the table with a shaking hand. She was terrified of saying something she shouldn't, but she was more terrified of staying silent and looking as if she agreed with him.

'That poor girl was a human being, and did not deserve what happened to her.'

Her voice started off hoarse, but grew stronger. 'If she is the person I think she is, then her life seems to be miserable enough without this tragedy happening to her.'

'Absolutely,' Oliver Whyte said. 'Do you know the girl?'

'I just see her sometimes,' Lillian said, 'and it's obvious the poor thing is half-starved and is trying to look after the two young children.' She saw Andrew's father raise his eyebrows in a dismissive gesture. 'Last week I felt so sorry for her I went over and gave her some money.'

'Ha!' George said, 'and I suppose she snatched the hand off you as well?'

'No, she did not,' Lillian stated, with a determination in her voice. 'She started crying, and she told me that the family had not always been poor, and that it happened when her father was made unemployed.'

'There you are!' Mr Whyte said, looking over at his son. 'I'll bet there's no gambling and horse-racing and driving fast cars for their family.'

George strode across the floor. 'I'm going out,' he said, 'and I'll bid you all goodnight.'

When the front door banged, Oliver turned to his two guests. 'My apologies, ladies, I'm afraid feelings are running a bit high with everything that has happened.' He looked over to Andrew. 'Are you all right?'

Andrew nodded, and ran his good hand through his fair hair. 'I just wish this whole mess had never happened. It's ruined everything, and God knows what my mother will have to say when I see her. Hopefully, my father will smooth things over. But he says this will mean the end of trips up to Liverpool for a while. And I think he really means it. I get the feeling he's made some arrangement with the police...'

He looked over at Lillian. 'I'm so sorry I'm going to have to let you down about the Easter Ball.' He lifted the heavy plaster. 'I couldn't go looking like this.'

Lillian felt sorry for him. 'Don't even think about it. It's the least of your worries,' she said. 'Just look after yourself, and get better.'

'When we get this business all sorted,' he said, 'there will be other dances in the summer... maybe down in London.'

Lillian forced a smile. She lifted her glass now and took another sip. She knew now that there would be no future plans for dances for her and Andrew. Although she liked him as a friend, she had always had little doubts about their suitability as a couple. The accident had highlighted the differences between them, between their families and their superior attitudes to other people. This was something Lillian wouldn't find easy to deal with, even if Andrew tried to stand up to his father.

Chapter Forty-Five

Easter Monday was a soft day, neither warm nor cold, neither cloudy nor sunny. Lillian sank down on a stone bench, having leaned her bicycle against a wall. She sat for a while just staring ahead, not thinking of anything, catching her breath. She moved a little, adjusting her cycling skirt until she was comfortable, then sat still again, gazing out over the trees, bushes and flowers in St John's Gardens. It was a place she came to often now, when she wanted to escape from the traffic and the city hustle and bustle.

She sat there, just gazing ahead, watching birds pecking at the grass, people coming and going, and the traffic moving along the perimeter of the gardens. Every so often, all the old thoughts came seeping back into her mind. Thoughts of Molly, gone to heaven, Alice, gone to Canada, Irene, gone to Ireland; and most recently Andrew, gone back to London, hugely relieved that the police were not pressing any charges against him. It all seemed like some strange dance where people were joined together and then each one gradually whirled their way off the floor, leaving Lillian dancing on her own.

But she was lucky. She still had her mother who she knew loved her without reservation, and whom she loved in return. She had a lovely comfortable home. She had a job she looked forward to going to each day. Compared to the other girls back in the orphanage, she was very privileged. And the experiences she had had over the last year had taught her that life carried on regardless, and you had to make the best of things whatever happened.

Sometimes you had to look outwards to other people and other things, and other times you had to look inwards to yourself and find things that distracted you or somehow lifted you up. Lillian had discovered lots of things which helped: reading, sewing, playing the piano, listening to the gramophone, talking to Mrs Larking or Rose Moran. There was always something to lift her up.

Today it was cycling. She had spent an hour cycling through the city, then going down to the docks, stopping to wheel the bike along the edge of the water. Then she had climbed back on and cycled out as far as Bootle. She had walked for a while, looking around, getting to know another new place. Sometime soon, she planned to cycle out to Wavertree, and to find the house she grew up in, to see what memories she had of the place she had lived in with her grandmother, Betty.

Occasionally, it crossed her mind that some fine summer's day, she might even cycle out to Gethsemane House. Just to stand outside it, and see how she felt. She probably wouldn't do it this year, and it might be a long way off. It might be never.

She sat for a while, and then she thought that Anna might be anxious about her being out amidst the bank holiday traffic, where people were coming and going in cars, trams and buses. Like Lillian, they were all looking for something different to do on a special, free day when the shops and libraries were closed.

She looked up at the sky and saw a bright blue patch between the clouds. The weather was softening generally, the days were getting warmer and brighter, and soon it would be summer. The first summer of freedom she would have as an adult. She looked over at the bicycle, and thought of all the places she might go in the light evenings, her half-days off, and on a Sunday. It was all ahead of her.

She stood up now, and as she did, she noticed another cyclist coming towards her, so she moved in to the side of the benches to let them past. The bicycle slowed down and when she glanced

over to see if the cyclist was stopping or passing sh~~...~~ ~~...~~ ~~her~~
heart still.

The bicycle had stopped and the young man had got off and was pushing it straight towards her. 'Lillian...' he said.

She lifted her head. 'Hello, Paul.' There was a pause, during which she thought she did not need this awkwardness today, on top of the situation she had just left behind with Andrew. She did not need Paul Larking pretending to be her friend. She wouldn't waste her time on him again.

She moved towards her bicycle, giving him a distracted smile. 'I'm just heading home now...'

'Don't,' he said, moving a few steps towards her.

She looked at him. 'What do you mean?'

'Don't go... please. I need to talk to you.'

Her brow wrinkled. 'What about?'

He leaned his bicycle beside hers and came to stand next to her. 'Can we sit down Lillian – please?'

'No,' she said, 'we can't. I don't really want to talk to you, Paul. Any time we've talked before, you've made it quite clear that we are very different and have nothing in common.' She looked up at him. 'I can't help who I am and where I live – just as you can't help being who you are.'

'I'm sorry about saying all those things...' He gestured towards the bench. 'Please, Lillian, sit down and listen to what I have to say.'

There was an uncertain note in his voice which she had never heard before. She looked at him, hesitated for another few moments, then moved back to the stone seat. He came to sit beside her.

'I'm not sure where to start,' he said, 'but this problem goes back to the first time I saw you down in the kitchen. The time we were joking about the scones and the cream. Do you remember?'

Of course she remembered.

He sighed. 'My mother knew then.'

'Knew what?'

'She knew the effect you had had on me. She said she could

355

... the way I looked when I was talking about you. When we got back home that night she really went for me, saying that I shouldn't have been so familiar towards you, and that she didn't want me going to the house when you were there.'

'She didn't want you to talk to me at all?' Lillian halted. 'Was it because of my background – the orphanage?'

'It was nothing to do with your background. My mother thinks the world of you. It's me she has the problem with. She could see how we got on really well, too well for her comfort, and she thought I was stepping out of my place, talking to you as though I was your equal.'

He raised his eyebrows and gave an ironic smile. 'All the work and studying I've done to get on in life, and my mother – who tells everyone how proud of me she is – is the one who keeps reminding me of my place.'

Lillian listened carefully now, still not sure what to make of this.

'She was the same the day your friend died, when you fainted. Naturally I was worried about you, and I said I was going to come back later after work to see how you were, but she wasn't happy and told me to keep away from the house.'

'Why did she mind us being friends?' Lillian asked. 'I go down to the kitchen all the time talking to her and your father. Why does she mind you talking to me?'

Paul sat back on the bench now and looked at her. 'Have I got this completely wrong, Lillian?' His hand came up to touch off his forehead. 'Have I been stupid? I thought there was something between us... the night down in the kitchen when you were all dressed up... when I came up to the music room to listen to the gramophone with you. I could really feel something between us.'

'Maybe at the beginning,' she said quietly, 'but then you were... just not very nice to me.'

'I'm so sorry for that, but I knew your aunt would tell my mother first thing in the morning about me having a drink with you, and she would go mad.'

'I'm not sure what this all means...'

He reached and took her hand now, and held it between both of his.

Lillian felt as though a jolt had gone through her. She looked up at him and their eyes met, and a wave of emotion rose inside her, and she wanted to bury her face in his neck and hold onto him. Tears filled her eyes and she dipped her head so he wouldn't see them.

'What it means is that I really care about you, more than I've cared for any other girl.'

'What about Edie?' Lillian suddenly remembered.

'We're finished. She's a nice girl,' he said, 'but she's not you. It wasn't fair stringing her along when I was thinking of you all the time, so I sent her a letter last week to say I thought it was better if we just went our separate ways. She wrote back and said it was all right, that she could tell I wasn't wholehearted about it. She'll meet someone else.'

Lillian bit her lip, hardly able to believe what she was hearing. 'Are you sure?'

'Absolutely,' he said, 'I can't stop thinking about you all the time. You're on my mind from the minute I wake up in the morning, and you're the last thing I think of until I fall asleep at night.'

Her head lifted. 'Really?' she whispered.

'Absolutely. I've never felt anything like it before. If it wasn't so soon, I'd say I'm in love with you. '

Lillian's heart soared now. 'I can hardly believe it...' A tear trickled down her face. 'I've tried hard not to... but I think about you all the time... from the first time we met...' She didn't say that all her recent thoughts had been angry ones.

'Thank God,' he said. 'Thank God...'

He gathered her into his arms and held her close. 'I wasn't going to say anything because of the other chap – Andrew. My mother told me you were going to the fancy ball in the Adelphi with him, and went on about your new dress. It killed me hearing it, as I thought you and him were getting very serious. But then when the accident happened and I heard he'd gone back to London, I decided if I didn't take my chance now, you would soon meet someone else.'

'But I've never thought of anyone else in that way,' she said. 'I sort of tried to be fond of Andrew because I knew how much he liked me, but I kept thinking of you instead. I really thought you didn't like me, and after all I had told you about my past, it made me upset and angry.'

His arms tightened around her. 'I'm so sorry about that, Lillian. I liked you from the minute I saw you. I knew then you were the only girl I wanted.' He shrugged. 'I was worried because you were a bit younger than me, although I've always felt that we were the same age. As time went on my feelings just grew stronger.'

She looked thoughtful, taking in what he had said. 'How did you know where to find me?'

'Do you really want to know?' He rolled his eyes and laughed. 'I've been cycling about the city centre for hours, just looking for you everywhere. Round and round the streets. I knew all your usual places were closed, so I kept coming back here to the gardens hoping you might come out cycling too.'

She laughed too. 'Well, I am glad you found me.'

'I needed to see you on your own, to make sure about your feelings.' He put his hand under her chin now and tilted her head so he could see her eyes. 'If you're sure, we could start courting properly, but first I need to go and see your aunt. It's only right; I'm not going behind her back.' He halted. 'Although I don't know what she'll say.'

Lillian sucked her breath in. 'What about your mother?'

'Whatever happens, happens,' he said. 'I'll deal with it then.'

'When will you see them?'

'Now,' he said. 'We'll go straight to Rodney Street together and then I'll ask to speak to your aunt.'

Lillian made to move.

'But before we go...' He drew her back into his arms, then glanced around to make sure no one was nearby. 'There's something I've wanted to do from the first minute I saw you, and I can't wait another minute...'

He bent his head and kissed her gently on the lips. When he pulled away a short while later, Lillian put her arms around his neck and he moved to kiss her again, longer and deeper. Lillian felt a surge of wanting and desire run through her, and she realised that this was what true passion felt like. The feelings she had had for Andrew had been childish in comparison and hadn't come close to how she felt for Paul.

They heard voices and became aware of children running through the park, and they sat up straight. They sat in silence, their arms wrapped tightly around each other.

'You won't leave me?' she whispered to him. 'Too many people have left me. I need to know that you'll always be there.'

'Always,' he said, 'and whatever happens when I talk to your aunt back at the house, I'll find a way.'

Chapter Forty-Six

They wheeled their bicycles all the way back up Renshaw Street and through the streets towards Rodney Street, deep in conversation as they went along.

Lillian explained what had happened about the car accident and how she vaguely knew the poor girl involved. 'Thankfully, she seems to be making a recovery now. Mr Whyte went down to the hospital to see her, and the doctor told him that they are going to keep her in for a few weeks to build her up.' She sighed. 'She's very thin and undernourished.'

'I recognise the girl too,' Paul said, 'she's been walking the streets with the poor kids in the pram for the last year or two. There are a lot of people in desperate situations, but they seem about the worst. I'm sure she's from the court housing in Clayton Street.'

'The girl who brought me the message about Molly lives there too,' Lillian said. She halted. 'I'm thinking of visiting the girl in hospital, and maybe knitting some jumpers or cardigans for the children.'

'There are a few good charities about which help out families like that,' Paul told her. 'I'm sure St Nicholas has an organisation too. They collect clothes and food from better-off families, and some evenings they open up the church hall and give out bowls of soup. They're always looking for people to help.' He looked at her. 'We could both get involved; at least we would feel we were doing something.'

'That would be wonderful,' Lillian said. 'It would make me feel much better if I could help in some way.'

'I'll find out about it, and I'll let you know.' He grinned at her. 'We would be doing good, and at the same time getting another excuse to be together.'

'There's something else we need to sort out,' she said. 'The way you feel about people from different classes. I'm not sure we agree on that, and I don't want it to cause arguments.'

'We won't argue,' he said. 'I promise. I was just a bit narked about everything before. I knew everyone – including my own mother – would expect you to pick someone like Andrew over me because of his background.'

'Andrew's family were a strange mix,' Lillian told him. 'I knew then that I could never be part of that family, although in fairness, Andrew is more like his grandfather than his parents. I enjoyed his company, but to be honest, I never had the right feelings for him.' She looked shy now. 'I only realised it when I met you. The difference in how I feel when I'm with you... well, it's just incredible. It's like something a girl dreams of...'

'It's a dream come true for me,' he said. He moved his bicycle closer to hers and then leaned over and kissed her again. 'Lillian Taylor, you are the most beautiful, lovely girl and I know I am the luckiest lad to have this happen to me. And it's not just that you're gorgeous, I feel we're similar in so many ways.'

'I think we're really similar too, I've never talked to anyone the way I talk to you.' She suddenly laughed and lightly banged her hands on the handlebars. 'And of course we both have bikes now!'

'The world is our oyster,' he said, laughing along with her. 'And who would have imagined you would be working in a department store just a few streets away from Lewis's.' He shook his head. 'Pity you had to go to our competitors though!'

'I did it deliberately,' Lillian told him. 'Lewis's was the only store I didn't apply to – and it was because of you. I couldn't bear the thought of seeing you every day when we weren't talking.'

'It broke my heart too...' He lifted his eyes to the heavens. 'Thank God we got the chance to sort it all out.'

As they reached the house, they both fell silent. Lillian halted her bicycle. 'We'll go in together. I want you to come in the front door with me this time.'

Paul's brows furrowed. 'I don't want to catch your aunt unawares,' he said, 'and I think it would be starting off on the wrong foot. I want to do things right.'

'I'll come round to the back entrance with you then,' she said. 'I leave my bicycle in the shed in the garden, so that's the way I'm going in too.'

They went around to Pilgrim Street and in through the back. When they got to the door, Lillian went in first. Mr Larking was reading the *Liverpool Echo* in the armchair by the big cooker, and Mrs Larking and Lucy were sitting at the table, relaxing with a cup of tea and a slice of fruit cake. There were various pans steaming on top of the stove, and there was a smell of chicken cooking in the oven. They all turned when the door was tapped and then Lillian came in.

'Did you have a nice trip out, love?' Nan Larking greeted her, a warm smile on her face.

'Lovely,' Lillian said. She gestured behind her. 'Look who I met in the city gardens.' She moved inside and then Paul came behind her.

'Hello,' he said, smiling at them, 'how are you all?'

'Where were you?' his mother demanded.

'I was out for a cycle, and as Lillian said, we bumped into each other in St John's Gardens.'

His father lowered his newspaper. 'Were there many around today?'

'Quite a few out walking, but quieter with the shops being shut.'

Nan looked at Lillian. 'If you want to go on, we'll bring a tea tray up to your sitting room in five minutes.'

Lillian made a little waving gesture with her hands. 'There's no rush, finish your break.'

Nan turned to Paul. 'What about you? Have you time for a cup of tea? There's plenty in the pot.'

He looked over at Lillian, then back to his mother. 'I might have one in a while, after I've spoken to Mrs Ainsley.'

'Mrs Ainsley? What would you need to speak to her? There's nothing wrong, is there?'

'No,' he replied. 'I just want a private word with her.'

There was a silence as Mrs Larking's eyes shifted uneasily from Paul to Lillian. 'I'll send Lucy to get her.'

'It's all right, Mrs Larking,' Lillian said quickly. 'I'll bring Paul up with me now. At this time she's probably upstairs reading the newspaper.'

'She is,' Lucy interrupted. 'I took her tea up not long ago.'

'She usually sees visitors in the library,' Mrs Larking said, a touch of indignation in her tone. 'It's not right to disturb her up in her own quarters.'

'She won't mind,' Lillian said. 'I'm bringing Paul up with me, so there won't be a problem.'

'Please yourself.' Mrs Larking's mouth was set in a straight line, as she watched them going out of the kitchen together.

As they walked along the corridor, Lillian's heart was racing. She had never seen the cook looking so agitated before, and she wondered how she would take the news. 'Will I stay in the sitting room with you?' Lillian asked. 'It might be easier.'

'No, no,' Paul said. 'This is my business. I'm the man, and it has to be done right.'

She reached for his hand and squeezed it. 'Well, I'll show you in at least.'

When they arrived upstairs Lillian tapped on the sitting room door and then went in. Anna was sitting by the fire, relaxing. 'I met Paul when I was out cycling, and we've been talking. He'd like to speak to you, so I brought him up to see you.'

Anna's eyebrows shot up and she moved her newspaper and

got to her feet. 'Why did you bring him upstairs?' she asked in a low voice. 'Is there something wrong?'

'No,' Lillian said, a slight waver in her voice. 'He wants to speak to you privately and I thought this was the best place to do it.' She turned to open the door wider for Paul to come in. 'I'll leave you to talk.'

Chapter Forty-Seven

Lillian sat on the edge of her bed waiting, feeling almost as nervous as the day she had sat waiting for her aunt to arrive in the orphanage. Every so often she looked at her watch and then she walked over to the window, looking down into the street. As she looked over at Mr Whyte's she felt a slight pang about Andrew and hoped he was recovering.

The accident had really shaken him; when they had said goodbye she'd seen a change in him, and she knew he was weighed down by the enormity of what had happened. He didn't have to come back for a court case – everyone said his family had sorted it all out – and he looked like he couldn't wait to put the whole episode behind him. She wondered if he would find the courage to drive again, and she thought it might be best if he didn't, or at least not for some time.

She picked up the child's cardigan she had started knitting the day before and did a few rows, but she could not concentrate. Doing something, however little, for the girl's family made her feel better. She put her knitting down and went over to pick up the book she was reading – *The Mayor of Casterbridge*. Again, she could not keep her mind on it, and tried to read the same page three times before giving up. She paced the room again and then went over to stand by the window.

At one point she thought she heard footsteps and voices, and a door opening and closing. She waited, her heart beating madly, but nothing happened.

Another ten minutes passed before she heard a door opening

again and footsteps coming towards her bedroom and her heart lurched. She put her hand up to her mouth, heard the knock on her door and Anna came in. Her face was almost expressionless, giving Lillian no clue as to how she felt.

'I think it would be best if you come down to the sitting room now, Lillian,' she said in an even tone. 'We all need to have a good talk.'

With her heart in her mouth, Lillian went out into the corridor to walk the few yards to the sitting room. When Anna opened the door, she was taken aback to see Mr and Mrs Larking sitting on the sofa. Neither looked up when she came in, and when she glanced over, Mrs Larking was dabbing her eyes with a handkerchief.

Paul was sitting on a chair by the fire. He caught her eye, then raised his eyebrows and nodded over to his mother.

'Now Lillian, I'm sure you must know we've all been taken by surprise,' Anna said, gesturing over to the Larkings. 'None of us had any idea what was going on. Anyway, I've listened to what Paul had to say, and I've said my piece about the situation. I hope I've been fair and honest.'

'I think so,' Paul said.

Mrs Larking shook her head and made a loud, tutting sound to indicate that he had no business commenting as though he were Mrs Ainsley's equal.

Lillian glanced from Anna to Paul, but could not work out what was happening.

'I thought it was only fair to bring Paul's parents up to inform them as well,' Anna said, 'since we're all connected in this house.' She halted to look over at Lillian. 'I've asked Paul about your relationship and he tells me that you've both had feelings for each other for some time?'

'Yes,' Lillian confirmed. 'We do have feelings for each other... very much.'

'You see!' Mrs Larking suddenly blurted out, shaking her head. 'It's the deceit of it all – none of us knew a thing.'

'But Mam,' Paul said, his voice weary, 'there's been no deceit because until today there was nothing to tell. We only met a few times here in the house, and down in the city. When I mentioned it, you warned me not to even look at Lillian, and to keep away from the house. We've spent the last few months avoiding each other because of it.'

'I told you that because nothing good can come of this.' She gestured with her hanky towards the young couple. 'It's not right – me and your father and Anna all get along fine here together with things just the way they are. This nonsense will change everything. How are we supposed to work here with you courting young Lillian?'

'Nothing will change that, Nan,' Anna said softly.

Nan looked at her employer with tearful eyes, then swung back to Paul. 'What was wrong with Edie? She was a teacher and a nice young lady. She would have suited you fine.'

'Mam, I never cared for Edie the way I care for Lillian. It's completely different... and Lillian feels the same.'

'What does she know? She's only a young girl,' his mother said, jabbing the hanky in Lillian's direction. 'She's plenty of time ahead of her to meet somebody that's right for her.'

'I don't mean to be disrespectful, Mrs Larking,' Lillian said, feeling nervous of speaking out, 'but I believe Paul is right for me.' She looked over at Anna now, her throat tightening. 'I really do. We can talk properly to each other and I trusted him enough to tell him everything about my background, and it helped me to feel much better.'

'Sure, anyone could have kind intentions towards a young girl,' the cook said. 'It's only right and proper.' She thumbed over in her son's direction. 'It's his other intentions that I'm worried about.'

Michael Larking cleared his throat. 'I think you're forgetting, Nan, that you were only fourteen when we took up together, and if I recall, your mother wasn't a bit pleased with it.'

Mrs Larking's eyes grew as wide as saucers. 'Would you listen to him?' she said in a high voice. She jabbed with her hanky again. 'Will you stay quiet! What a thing to say – it was totally different in those days.'

Anna went over to sit on the arm of the sofa beside the cook, and placed a hand on her shoulder. 'I've listened to Paul and everything he has said makes me confident that he has Lillian's best interests at heart.' She looked over at him. 'He's a fine young man. I've known him since he was a child, and I know how decent he is and kind to his parents. He's also very talented and a hard worker, and I admire his ambition. These are all the qualities I would look for, were I to choose someone for her myself.'

Anna looked at Lillian and smiled properly now. A smile that lit up her eyes. 'I know they are only beginning their romance and we don't know what will happen, but in my opinion, they stand as good as chance as any other young couple. And I am more than happy to welcome Paul into this house as Lillian's guest.'

Lillian's heart soared.

'Thank you,' Paul said, 'I really appreciate it.'

Mrs Larking sighed, 'I don't know what to think ...'

'Well,' Anna said, 'Paul and Lillian have my blessing to start courting now she is over sixteen. It might work and it might not, but if they don't give it a try, they will always wonder and maybe regret it forever.'

'But how can it work?' Mrs Larking said, still unconvinced. 'With us down in the kitchen and him coming and going with Lillian?'

'Things will continue the very same way as if Lillian was courting anyone else. If they are going out, Paul will come to collect her and they'll go off together, the same way she would have gone to the ball in the Adelphi tonight with Andrew Whyte.' She shrugged. 'I can't see what difference any of that will make to you and Michael.'

'I agree,' Michael said.

There was a silence now as Mrs Larking folded her hanky and put it into her pocket.

Anna turned to Lillian. 'Will you go downstairs and ask Lucy to bring up a bottle of sherry and five glasses please?'

'Sherry?' Mrs Larking said in a startled voice.

'Yes, unless you prefer a little whiskey or something else. We've all just had tea and it's Easter Monday, so why not?'

Michael clapped his hands and rubbed them together. 'I'll have a drop of whiskey, since you're asking and I'm sure Nan will have the same.'

His wife sighed then motioned with her hands in the air. 'Ah, sure I might as well drink the whole bottle! There's nobody going to listen to me anyway.'

'Ah Mam,' Paul said, coming over to her. He went down on one knee beside her and took her work-worn hands in his. 'Don't be like that. Can't you just wish us well as Mrs Ainsley did?'

She looked at him for a moment, then her face softened. 'I only want what's best for you ... I can't help worrying.'

'Well, this is the best for me,' he said. 'And I'm going to make sure that it all works out.'

'Well then ...' Her voice cracked a little and she gripped his hands tightly and gave them a little shake. Then she looked over at Lillian. 'You know I think the world of you too, and if you're both determined, then there's no more to be said.'

Paul put his arms around her. 'Thanks, Mam.'

A short while later as they sat chatting with their drinks, Anna looked over at Lillian and said, 'While you were out, I got a note from Freda Flanagan to say that Irene is coming home next week. She said she's not sure if it's a holiday or if she's coming home to stay.'

A beaming smile broke out on Lillian's face. 'Oh, that's terrific news. I'll look forward to seeing her.'

'And I've just remembered a bit of news I heard too,' Paul said. 'About your old friend, Mr Guthrie.'

Anna rolled her eyes to the ceiling. 'What? I'm not sure if I want to hear about that imbecile.'

'He came into the store a few weeks ago and opened an

369

account in the tailor's department,' Paul explained, 'and apparently paid a deposit on one of the top-range suits. He bought a bowler hat and shoes as well. He took them off home to make sure they were all fine, and then he was to come back and pay the balance. Apparently he went to George Henry Lee and Blacklers and did the very same thing, and then went on to another two independent tailor's shops in the city.'

'And where, I wonder, is he going to wear them all?' Michael asked.

Nan Larking tutted and shook her head. 'He must have money to burn, buying all them suits.'

'Or won it on a horse,' Anna said, in a cool tone.

'He won nothing,' Paul said. 'It was actually the reverse. It seems he was up to his eyes in debt from his gambling, and owed weeks of rent and various other bills.'

'Oh my goodness!' Anna said.

Paul raised his eyebrows. 'Oh, there's more,' he said, looking amused. 'He thought he would borrow some money from a few of the businesses where he does the accounts. Someone who knows his new landlady said he skipped up north somewhere with five good suits he had only paid a small deposit on.'

'Mr Guthrie? Well I never . . .' his mother said, in a high-pitched, shocked voice.' She thought for a few moments. 'Well, wherever he's gone, at least he'll be well-dressed.'

Everyone laughed, then Anna said, 'It's funny imagining him heading off on the train with a trunkful of stolen suits, but isn't it sad to think that a man of his age would cause such trouble to himself and other people?'

'He's a troubled soul by the sounds of it,' Michael Larking said.

Anna watched as Lillian went over to stand by Paul. She said something, and he bent his head to listen to her, giving her his full attention. At one point, Lillian put her hand on his arm, and he then covered it with his.

As she watched, Anna could see the real closeness between them, and the easy way they were with each other. She could remember feeling like that with Loman – the same smiles, the locked eyes as they talked and the way they found the same things funny. And here it was being played in front of her again. She could not deny Lillian the happiness and pleasure she knew this would bring.

Michael Larking drained the last of his whiskey, and his wife did the same.

'I'd better go and check that chicken isn't burning,' Nan said, 'or that Lucy hasn't fallen asleep.' She looked over at Paul. 'We'll see you later this evening.'

Anna went over to Lillian and Paul. 'I was just thinking, Andrew's grandfather said he had collected the tickets for the Adelphi ball you were to go to tonight. He said if you and I wanted to go we should use them, but I'm not really that interested. It's a pity to see them going to waste. Why don't you and Paul go? You have your lovely new gown.'

Lillian's eyes lit up. 'I'd love to go.' She turned to Paul. 'What do you think?'

He suddenly grinned, thinking about it. 'Going to a dance together would be just great.'

'Oh, I can't wait!' she said excitedly, clasping her hands together. It was like some sort of miracle. How, she wondered, had things turned out like this? A few hours ago her mind was filled with all she had lost, and now she felt her heart was so full it could burst.

Paul looked at his watch. 'I'd better go home now to have a bath and get sorted out.'

'Ah well,' Mrs Larking said, looking over at Anna. 'Isn't it grand to be young?'

Paul said goodbye to his parents, then turned to Anna and shook her hand. 'Thank you again for everything,' he said, 'and I won't let you down.'

She smiled at him. 'I'm counting on it.'

Lillian touched Paul's arm. 'I'll walk you to the door,' she said. When they were walking down the stairs she put her arm through his. 'You know you can't use the front door. You'll have to go through the kitchen and out the back door again, don't you?'

Paul's mind was busy going over everything that had just happened. He could see Lillian was making a point, but he wasn't sure what.

'The bicycle,' she said, smiling. 'You left it at the back door.'

He looked at her and then laughed. 'From now on,' he said, 'we'll go through the same doors together – wherever they lead.'

Acknowledgements

Thanks to all the Orion staff – both past and present – who have worked with me on *A Liverpool Secret*. Their advice and support is much appreciated.

Whilst researching this book in Liverpool city, I found the staff in the library, art galleries, the Philharmonic Dining Rooms, and other places mentioned, always friendly and helpful with information. Thanks to the staff of the Tyrone Guthrie Centre in Monaghan, who make my regular residencies so comfortable, and help provide the peace and solitude which is invaluable.

The theme of friendship which runs through this book made me reflect on the friends I have made since our arrival in Ireland in 1991. They are wonderful people who have enriched our lives in many, different ways and have also been immense supporters of my writing.

From the early days in the Offaly drama group, Mike and I received a warm and lasting welcome from dear friends, Pat and Joe Slamman (our friends in high places indeed, Joe!), along with Margaret and Andy Cunningham and Baisté. The dramatic nights are long gone (and Baisté to Africa!) but the friendship remains.

Shortly afterwards came Patricia Dunne, who I first met through a van window on a rainy November night! Coincidentally, we met again as colleagues in NTDI in Tullamore, enjoying many entertaining tea-breaks with the lovely staff, especially Mary McNamara and Nuala Flanagan.

I was privileged with great colleagues in Daingean National

School, including dear friends and confidantes, Kate Doyle and Brid Dunne.

The Irish Post-Polio Support Group brought a great lady into the heart of our family – Bernie O'Sullivan. A true friend in every way (along with husband, Brian Brady!), and we are often found on the phone at midnight.

I worked on a project recently in the Tyrone Guthrie Centre with the vibrant, talented Anne Scally, and always find our evenings together with lovely ladies Bridget McDonnell and Gemma Dunican both uplifting and enjoyable.

I also appreciate the support of The Offaly Writers' Group – both past and present members – and the members of our long-standing Book Circle.

I have mentioned my dear Stockport friends many times, and it is with great sadness that we had to bid an unexpected farewell last year to the much-loved Neil Singleton, husband of Sandra. He is sorely missed by all.

Thanks to my beloved parents, Teddy and Be-Be O'Neill and the best mother-in-law ever, Mary Hynes. I must also single out my brother-in-law, Kevin Brosnahan, who is always there to cheer me on with every book

I am blessed with my children, Christopher and Clare, and their wonderful partners Kate and Mark. Their love, support, advice and positivity are unstinting.

Finally, my love and endless thanks to my old college boy-friend of 40-odd years, and my *Anam Cara*, Mike Brosnahan.

A heartwarming story of family and friendship, duty and desire

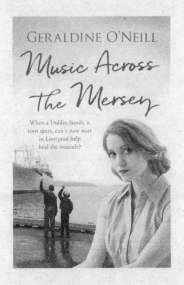

GERALDINE O'NEILL

Music Across The Mersey

When a Dublin family is torn apart, can a new start in Liverpool help heal the wounds?

When a Dublin family is torn apart, can a new start in Liverpool help heal the wounds?

1940s **Dublin.** Handsome widower Johnny Cassidy is out of work, broken-hearted and lost as to how to look after his four children. At his lowest ebb, he's forced to realise that help sometimes comes from the strangest places.

With Johnny's family over the sea in Liverpool, it's his wife's spinster cousin Nora who comes to the rescue and has her life turned upside down by this brood of children.

With Nora around, Ella Cassidy can be a teenager again rather than trying to raise her younger siblings, while older brother, Sean, finds that music might be his salvation. It seems that each member of the Cassidy family cherishes secret dreams, but will they bring them together or tear them apart?